KEEP HER S

Colin Mardell

APS BOOKS
Yorkshire

APS Books,
The Stables Field Lane,
Aberford,
West Yorkshire,
LS25 3AE

APS Books is a subsidiary of the APS Publications imprint

www.andrewsparke.com

First published worldwide by APS Books in 2022

A catalogue record for this book is available from the British Library

One

"That ain't what I signed up for." Delta Force veteran of ten years Drew Parker complained.

"Quit bitching Parker, it's done now." Jake Mitchell the mission leader told him, "Yeah it was TARFU, but shit happens. It weren't nobody's fault. You got six weeks off now to recharge before your reup kicks in."

"I ain't going to reup. Soon as we're back in Bragg I'm gonna withdraw my papers."

"You're kidding. For fucks sake, what you gonna do, you've been in uniform for nearly half your life?"

It was an exaggeration, but almost thirteen years was a long time. "I don't know yet; I'll think of something. I just had enough of being a tool for asshole politicians to achieve their own aims. Our motto is supposed be *To Free The Oppressed*, not *To Protect Politicians' Asses.* People died in that op, innocent people, people who had nothing to do with either side of that argument, and even less to do with the USA."

The detachment of eight men from 'C' Squadron had been sent to Lobaye, a small prefecture of the Central African Republic, their mission to kidnap Andre Mbuti, leader of a small group of rebels claiming independence for the region. The object of the hurriedly arranged mission was to take Mbuti across the border into Cameroon where he was to have been held incommunicado by military contractors until he agreed to give up his struggle for independence.

The team had been told that although there was little or no chance of the rebels achieving their aims, the so far noisy but non-violent struggle was discouraging investment in a new uranium deposit. The US was anxious to secure the rights to develop the resource, if only to deny yet further influence in the area by Russia or China. What they hadn't been told, although had worked out for themselves, was that this was a face-saving exercise for a member of the Senate Energy and Natural Resources Committee who had already given assurances that the rights had been secured.

The last-minute briefing was just that, brief. Mbuti's base was a private compound guarded by six poorly trained and equipped men. They were to arrive in theatre forty-eight hours in advance of the op, and under the cover of darkness recce the area. Then using absolute minimum force, disarm and incapacitate his protection before extraction. It was crucial that no evidence of US involvement be left behind, and that his protection detail be left bound, gagged, and blindfolded for discovery by others the following day.

The mission had been dogged by difficulties from day one. Their arrival at Yaoundé, the Cameroon capital by scheduled flights from Paris via Air France had been delayed by eight hours. The base that had been provided on the outskirts of the city was poorly lit making inspection of the weapons and vehicles difficult and time consuming. The weapons were all pre-used and either Russian manufacture or copies, which although they had all used similar tools before, were not what they would have chosen, and there had been no opportunity to test fire. The anonymous combat uniforms they were given were poorly fitting and uncomfortable, particularly in Drew's case with his massive build.

Journeying through the dense rain forest along poorly constructed and unmaintained roads was an obstacle course for the Land Rover and Toyota pickup, both of which had seen better days. Thankfully they'd had no difficulty crossing the unmanned border but they were over twenty-four hours late arriving in theatre. Despite the delays, base ordered them to complete the mission within the original time frame.

Their recce of the compound took place in the late hours of the evening with the intention of proceeding with the op at midnight. Before they withdrew they satisfied themselves that the compound and the security were largely as described at their briefing.

At midnight Jake gave the go ahead for the first members of the team to go in and subdue the two patrolling perimeter guards. They completed their task quickly and silently before signaling the others to proceed according to plan. Thirty seconds later everything went pear-shaped.

What they had no way of knowing was that a covered truck with twenty new well-armed if only recently trained recruits had been added to the complement of guards. They had been due to arrive at 15:00 that day, but had been delayed by a collapsed bridge. They eventually drove into the compound just as the raid begun.

What followed was a bloodbath resulting in the deaths of nine people including five guards, Mbuti, one of his sons, and two household staff, most of whom were casualties of stray bullets from the reinforcements. By some miracle Mbuti's wife, nine-year-old daughter and baby son went uninjured, and so did eleven guards and staff, but several others received wounds.

Jake and his men did their best to administer first aid to the injured, before making a hurried evacuation. By the time they approached the border there was an alert out for whoever the attackers were, making the return journey a great deal more problematic. The Land Rover and Toyota had to be abandoned ten miles from the Cameroon border and they were forced to fight their way through dense jungle to be picked up by a third vehicle on the other side.

It was thirty hours before they arrived back at their base in Yaoundé, and it was on that journey that the conversation had taken place. Most of Drew's sentiments were echoed by the rest of the team, although he was the only one saying he would hand in his papers. At the time nobody had taken him seriously, but forty-eight hours after returning to Fort Bragg he withdrew his request to re-enlist and handed in his resignation. His commanding officer made a half-hearted attempt to dissuade him, but another forty-eight-hours saw him drive underneath the barrier and head south-east toward Highway 87, and his sister Carolina's home in Wilmington. With outstanding leave he was still a soldier in the US Army for another sixty-three days, but he hoped he had donned that uniform for the last time.

Two

Six months later Drew was getting antsy. Taking up the spare room in Carolina's house and getting under their feet made him feel uncomfortable. He'd stayed there in the past for a week or two at a time, and it had been fun catching up. But taking them out to dinner and his nephew Ben to the movies or sporting events was wearing thin. Drew's brother-in-law Curtiss hadn't said anything but it was clear that the extended stay wasn't something he would want to go on much longer. Curtiss was a great guy but they had nothing in common, Drew was a gym, boxing, MMA, NFL, NBA, and MLB kinda guy, while Curtiss was more golf, gardening, and PBS.

As a kid, Drew had been on the verge of turning bad, real bad, his mother's lifestyle had done little or nothing to keep him under control, and even after being taken in by his grandparents he had continued to be difficult to handle. He was forever getting into fights, and when he did, with his size and physique there would only ever be one winner. Fighting, theft, drunkenness, and smoking weed he'd taken from other kids was routine, and he'd even spent some time in juvie when he was twelve after stealing a car and crashing it into a streetlamp. That was when his grandparents read him the riot act; they told him to shape up or ship out, but when Carolina pitched in and told him she wouldn't plead on his behalf anymore he started to realize that he was wasting an opportunity. Now, In retrospect, he appreciated the efforts they had made on his behalf to help him clean up his act, and develop what people now call a moral compass, but it had been no epiphany. His biggest problem had been his temper, and his violent responses to provocation.

It was only after joining the army that he finally learned to completely control his rages. In his rookie year he got into a fight with four members of his own company in a bar which ended up with all the others in hospital. Witnesses argued that he'd been provoked, and that the others had been the ones to start it, but the Army decided to make an example of him and he was sentenced to three months in Leavenworth. The tough regime was harder than anything he'd had to endure in boot camp but he was tough, and it might have done little to change him except that one day he was marched into the commander's office and told he would spend the final week of his sentence sharing a cell with an inmate on death row.

His new cell mate was Wes Stelling, a twenty-four-year-old private with eighteen months service who had discovered that a fellow platoon member had been sleeping with a girl he had considered his own. He went looking for them and found them in bed. The aftermath left the man so badly beaten that he died from his injuries, and the girl lost the sight in one eye. It was his third conviction for serious violent offences; the prosecution had argued for first degree murder and won. Such was his remorse, he refused to appeal.

The conversations over that week left an indelible impression on Drew. Three weeks after rejoining his platoon he learned of Wes Stelling's execution. After his release he worked hard to find ways to channel his aggression, but only succeeded by becoming introverted and as solitary as it's possible to be as a member of a team.

A month after Drew's conviction, Carolina discovered a video of his fight on YouTube proving conclusively that his actions had been entirely in self-defense. She sent it to Drew's commanding officer, arguing that his conviction was unjust. The CO agreed, but nothing in the US Army happens quickly, and Drew's sentence was complete before the conviction was quashed. Eighteen months later, the CO recommended he apply for the Delta Force selection course.

Despite his rehabilitation there were times when his old traits surfaced. Maltreatment and neglect in his childhood had given him a particular intolerance of injustice or cruelty to children, and when he saw it, it would often provoke a violent response leaving the perpetrator with some kind of injury.

Such was Drew's strength...and his weakness.

Three

After his discharge Drew spent a month earning his close-body protection license, but after finding no employment likely to interest him, he was beginning to consider re-enlistment. Then one Saturday morning he was watching Ben play softball and hitting the ball off the field for the second time when his cell phone rang. It was an unknown number.

"I heard through the grapevine that you're retired Parker. What's that like?"

"Who's this?" His guard went up.

"I guess you'll remember me as Gates, from Gardez."

"Oh yeah, then you'll remember the name of the rookie who joined the op on the second week."

"That would have been Tenderfoot Tony, who'd been serving with your lot for fifteen years or thereabouts, and it was his last op before turning in his papers and opening a gay bar in Manhattan."

"Gates you Limey bastard, how are you?"

"Good thanks. I was wondering if you'd be interested in a little gainful employment."

"As it happens I'm between commitments at the moment, but it would depend on what have you in mind?"

"Don't really want to talk about it on the phone. Can we meet up?"

"Sure, when do you have in mind, and where?"

"How about 16:00 at the KGB bar in Wilmington?"

"Today? Are you serious?"

"Sure, I'm in town, I just got knocked back by one of your former colleagues."

"Okay, if you like. That's on Princess Street isn't it?"

Paul Gates had turned up twice on ops, once when Delta linked up on a combined CIA mission in Iraq, and another in Afghanistan. They had been led to believe he was SAS or MI6.

Drew parked his twelve-year-old Ford pickup nearby and walked around the corner to the bar. It was quiet inside; the lunchtime crowd had dispersed and it was way too early for the real busy part of the day. It looked like he was their only customer when he walked to the bar.

"You eating?" he was asked.

"Maybe later. Just meeting somebody. Can I get a light beer while I wait?"

"What kind?"

"Surprise me, but I want it in a glass."

Halfway through the beer Gates appeared beside him. "You started without me Parker."

"Gates; good to see you. What can I get you?"

"I'll have the same as you. Let's go sit where we can talk."

"I'm guessing you're out of the game too then."

"That's right, got pissed off being expected to do too much with too little for too long, given half the resources, and then getting my ass kicked when it goes tits up. I've been private for about two years.

"Doing what?"

"Security."

"What sort?"

"Mostly short-term stuff for events or transporting high-risk valuables, that sort of thing."

"It sounds kinda tedious."

"And it was, but I just landed a contract to provide close-body protection for a multi-millionaire and his family."

"What standing around in a tux with a bulge under your left-arm while some rich guy and his spoiled family get their rocks off pretending they're important. That don't sound too exciting either."

"Under normal circumstances I'd agree with you, but you might think this a bit different if I told you who it is and why he needs protection."

"I'm listening."

"The guy travels all over, mostly the States and the UK, but elsewhere too. Often by private jet but often by limo as well. He has three homes over here and his wife has property in England."

"So I'm getting that his wife is wealthy in her own right."

"She inherited millions from her father who died last year to add to the enormous, combined wealth she held with her late first husband."

"Tell me what's involved."

"It's a six-month contract providing protection to the husband, wife, and her eleven-year-old daughter. Me and six full-time special ops guys, plus two on standby."

"That's an awful lot of muscle. Why so many?"

"Her fourteen-year-old older daughter was killed in a kidnap attempt three months ago."

"Are you talking about Theo Lemonis?"

"That's right and his wife Lady Annabelle Astley-West."

"An aristocrat; wow, you're moving in rarified circles now then buddy."

"She's not an aristo, the title came with her first husband who was only a knight. Astley-West was chief executive and majority shareholder of Silico Industries, a UK based computer chip company. He was killed about five years ago when his car hit a motorway bridge. She married Lemonis two years later."

"Why is he changing his protection now?"

"He's had a complete review of his personal security and it was concluded that the death of his stepdaughter would have been avoidable if the team had been doing their job; the head of the detail was badly injured in the incident."

"Why you though? No offense but you ain't got history."

"Right place, right time; and I promised him I could put together a team of ex-special forces guys that could cover any potential threat in the time available."

"So who have you got?"

"Guys from the Rangers, Canadian Task Force 2, Airborne, a SEAL, and a guy from the 112th. I had a full complement until I lost a guy last week because he'd picked up a criminal record for selling hash. That's why I'm here, I was in Bragg and I heard a whisper you might be available. What do you think?"

"That's a pretty mixed bag."

"Yeah, well it's been a bit of a rush getting it together."

"What does it pay, when would I start, and where would I be based?"

"If you're interested we would need you to start almost immediately. Initially you'd be based at their place in Santa Monica, and the pay would start at twelve grand a month plus expenses."

"What about weapons?"

"Your choice, but they would be provided for you."

"Clothes?"

"On expenses, but you'd be expected to wear whatever's appropriate for the occasion."

"Don't I have to go through some sort of vetting?"

"You've already been vetted. Nobody made it to the short list without being vetted beforehand. To be honest you were the first guy I was going to call on, but I didn't think you'd be interested. Everybody used to say if you didn't get killed on an op you'd be the first geriatric in Delta."

"Very funny."

"So, what do you think?"

"Tell me about the principals."

"As you know Lemonis was born in Greece - his family made their money in shipping. He was the second son, twenty-one when he inherited the lot after his parents, older brother and sister died when the family cabin cruiser sank after hitting a rock off the coast of Italy. He began investing in tech stocks, and among his major investments was NorArm. He's now their biggest shareholder, but doesn't hold a controlling interest. The company is currently developing controls systems for unmanned tanks, and it's rumored that they want to move up into the military hardware business."

"What about the wife?"

"I gather she went to pieces when her first husband died. Theodore was a close family friend who helped her get through it. They married two years later and they've been happy. She's still a majority shareholder in Silico, her first husband's company that's based in the UK, but she no longer takes part in the day to day running of the business. She refuses to sell, not even part of her holdings, in spite of many lucrative offers. She maintains it's her husband's legacy. Nowadays she seems happy to follow Theo around and play the dutiful wife."

"What do you know about the hijack?"

"The head security guy was Rupert Loughty. He was in The Regiment like me; we never served together but he had a great reputation. The family were staying at their home in Washington State and Loughty had been on leave visiting his parents in Northern Ireland; the family had nothing planned, but there was a late decision to fly to England. As they were about to leave for the airport Theo took a call from his plant near the city - there was some sort of emergency, and he told Anna to take the kids and he would follow on the next day.

"Their car was ten minutes out from their home when they were hijacked. What the bad guys hadn't banked on was Loughty deciding to cut short his stay in Ulster. He was on his way back to their Stillwater spread from Tacoma airport and passed a car parked up somewhere he thought was slightly suspicious. So, when he saw the family limo pass him going in the opposite direction with another car following closely behind, he threw a U-turn and caught them up just as the hijack was happening. There was a lot of fire exchanged, the limo driver was killed, so were two of the hijackers. Loughty took a hit, but managed to keep firing until they drove off, taking the oldest daughter Isolde, but abandoning Annabelle and Cassandra."

"What happened to Isolde?"

"The cops didn't seem to have a clue so Lemonis hired a private firm of investigators who located her within a few days but the rescue attempt was too late; the hijackers had killed her minutes before the hit. There was a shootout and the hijackers were all killed."

"How did she die?"

"Strangled, but the coroner said she'd been raped multiple times."

"The rescue sounds like a fuck up. Who were the company?"

"A company based in Toronto."

"Surely not IBIS?"

"No, it would have been better if it were. It was a small firm called Rescue and Crisis Management."

"None of that sounds right to me."

"Me neither. Lemonis' team are convinced there was a leak from somewhere in the house staff so he's had a complete clear out of domestic and security staff, hence my involvement."

"What's the accommodation?"

"We'll find you an apartment, but a motel in the first instance."

"What about transport?"

"What are you driving at the moment?"

"F150 circa 2005 - had it since I joined the army."

"Might be a good time to off-load it. There isn't time for you to drive it to California. You can use one of the family's Lincoln Navigators.

"Okay, you're on. When do I start?"

"If you can get to Santa Monica by Monday p.m. you can meet with Lemonis and his Personal Assistant or Fixer, Manos Stamelis, they call him the *Grim Reaper*."

"How is he still there if they've had a complete clear out?"

"He's been with Lemonis since Greece. After selling off all the remaining business interests over there he now has US citizenship; so does Stamelis. Lemonis trusts him implicitly"

Four

Santa Monica two months earlier.

"How are you today Anna my darling?"

"How do you think I am Theo? I've lost my beautiful daughter to a gang of murdering rapists, and we still have no idea how they knew we'd be there at that time. What's worse is the police have no leads."

"Manos thinks it's possible it was random; the dead guys were all members of a Seattle street gang, Point Side."

"That's not what Sergeant McCluskey thinks. He says it was too far off their patch, too well executed, and not their M.O. He thinks they may have been paid to do it. If it hadn't been for Rupert happening to be there, Cassie and I would be dead too, and you as well, were it not for that system shutdown at your plant."

"I think I agree and to be on the safe side I've told Manos to bring in a completely new security team of professional close protection bodyguards. And I'm changing all the domestic staff in all our US homes, not just at Stillwater, I don't want us to leave California until that's complete."

"Okay. Who's recruiting the security team?"

"Manos has brought in a consultant with years of experience working with the best in the business."

"What's his name?"

"Paul Gates, ex-SAS."

"Wasn't Rupert in the SAS?"

"Yes he was, Manos tells me they served together, apparently it was him that recommended Gates."

"How is Rupert, do you know?"

"No too bad I think. He's out of hospital, but after that punctured lung he's unlikely to work in the security industry in a hands-on role again."

"I feel guilty for not contacting him, but I've been so mixed up since it happened. I must visit him."

"He's back in the UK now."

"Did you make sure he was adequately compensated?"

"Of course my darling. Is Cassie okay?"

"She's very quiet most of the time and keeps asking to move back to Pangbourne, she doesn't believe we're safe here."

"That's understandable I suppose, but it would be totally impracticable for me to move to the UK as things stand. You could consider boarding school."

"I can't send her away, especially now. She would never forgive me," Anna told him. "I'll spend some time with her there when the new security team are in place and see how it goes."

"Maybe that will help. I need to go to the office today; I hope you don't mind me leaving you."

"No you go ahead, somebody in the family has to keep functioning normally. Will you be back for dinner?"

"I doubt it. You go ahead; I'll get something sent to the office. I love you."

"I love you too."

Anna turned back to her computer where she had been dealing with work and personal correspondence. Although she no longer held an executive post at Silico, as majority shareholder there was still a steady stream of mail to deal with. Cassie was with her tutor, Judith.

Judith Anstruther had been with Anna and her children since Cassie was four years old, her presence in the days after the kidnapping had been one of the main influences that helped Anna hold it together. Theo had made all the right noises but he never quite managed to convince her that he felt her daughter's loss as much as she did herself.

She heard the roar of Theo's Audi R8 as it shot away along the drive with a Navigator in pursuit and Pavel at the wheel. Pavel was one of the last two of the security team from before the events of the previous month. Anna didn't like the Russian bodyguard; she didn't like the way he looked at her, always with a patronizing smirk. She didn't trust him even though he'd done nothing that she could accuse him of. She thought for a minute before coming to a decision, then lifted her phone and selected a number from her list of 'favorites'.

"Percy." Percy Belton was her own equivalent of Manos; he managed her affairs in the UK, he'd acted in a similar capacity for her father and her first husband.

"Lady Annabelle, what can I do for you?"

Sighing, she replied, "For the umpteenth time will you call me Anna."

"I'll try to remember."

"I doubt you've forgotten a single thing in your life. Anyway, Theo's decided to hire a new security team and he's brought in a security consultant to recruit them. I wonder if you can get someone to give him a thorough screening for me. Also if he comes up clean, which I'm sure he will, I'd like you to do the same to anyone he chooses for the team. For the time being though, can we keep this between ourselves. I don't want Theo to think I don't trust him."

"No problem, I'll get on to that straight away. What's the guy's name?"

"Paul Gates. Manos says he's ex-SAS and was recommended by Rupert, I gather they served together. Oh, and can you get me a contact number for Rupert. I need to thank him properly for everything. Theo says he's back in the UK."

"I'll get back to you as soon as possible."

Two hours later Cassie came running into the room, "Mummy, Judith says I've passed all my 6th Grade SATs above average!"

"But you're only in Grade 5."

"I know, but Judith thought I'd been doing so well she got me to sit them early."

"She didn't tell me she was going to do that. You're such a clever girl, I'm really proud of you."

"Can I ask you a favor, Mummy?"

"Of course sweetheart, what is it?"

"I want to take self-defense classes."

"You're a bit young for that yet Cassie. Can't we leave it for a while?"

"After what happened to Izzy I want to know how to defend myself."

"I'm not sure it would have helped your sister though Sweetie."

"We don't know that do we?" Cassie protested.

"Theo's going to hire a whole new security team, professional bodyguards, not just men with guns who can drive fast."

"Does that mean he's going to get rid of Pavel?"

"I don't know. He may just transfer him to other duties."

"I don't like him."

"Why do you say that?"

Looking down she quietly said, "I think it was him that told those men where we were when we were hijacked."

"Really why?" Anna was shocked at her daughter's claim.

"I heard him say something on the phone several days after."

"Tell me."

"He said something like he was sorry, but it wasn't his fault because he had no way of knowing that it would happen but not to worry, whoever he was talking to was going to get paid anyway. Then he told them not to bother trying again. He was making other arrangements."

"He could have been talking about anything."

"I suppose, but as soon as he saw me he stopped talking and gave me one those creepy smiles."

"I'm sure it was nothing darling, he's been with Theo almost as long as Manos."

Over the next few hours Anna thought about what Cassie had said. She didn't seriously think that Pavel was the culprit, even if there was one, but she decided to keep an extra eye out whenever he was around.

Theo hurried through the door at ten o'clock and gave her a fleeting kiss on the cheek, "I'm flying up to Seattle first thing tomorrow.".

"Just you darling?"

"No Manos is going with me. Pavel will drive us to the airport then he'll come back. So it will be just you, Cassie, Judith, the domestic staff, Pavel and Mark."

"Okay, we'll cope, I'm sure. How long will you be away?"

"Could be until Monday, will that be alright?"

"We'll be fine thanks. I'll miss you."

"Me too. Just make sure you stick to the security rules, okay?"

"Okay, I'll be good."

"How are the new domestics working out?"

"Fine, very good in fact. I was sorry to see Selena go, but the new guy Jules is just as good; he makes the best tacos I've ever tasted."

"That's good."

They were just finishing breakfast the following day when her cellphone buzzed with an incoming text message from an unknown number saying. *Please check your online account to authorize payment of $9.99 to AT&T, failure to do so may result in withdrawal of services.* To most people this would have been an obvious phishing scam, but to Anna it was a signal to call Percy using a different cellphone.

Normally she would have used the burner that she had kept for covert messaging between her and her PA, but that phone had gone missing in the hijack. So she went to the room originally intended as a family room but now doubled as a schoolroom.

Anna and Percy introduced this secret line of communication after Percy suspected that Manos was monitoring Silico boardroom activity.

"It's about time we went to the hairdresser darling. What do you think?" she said to Cassie.

"Is it safe?"

"We'll get Mark to drive us, okay?"

"Okay," she replied less than enthusiastically.

"What about you Judith, do you fancy a run out? I think you and Cassie both deserve a break after those fantastic scores in her SATs."

"That would be lovely," The tutor replied, "I don't need to visit the hairdresser though."

"I haven't made an appointment, but I'm sure they'll fit at least one of us in if I ask nicely. Let me go and find Mark."

"Mummy, can I have a bob this time?"

"And cut all those lovely locks. Are you sure?"

"Yes, I want to look like Maisie Williams from Game of Thrones."

"Okay if that's what you want. I didn't know you watched that."

"I only just started, it's awesome."

Unsurprisingly, she found Mark in the kitchen chatting to Jules. She was sure they were gay. Not that she cared.

"Hi Mark. Cassie, Judith, and I want to take a run out, would you drive us please?"

"Sure Mrs. West, I'll just let Pavel know."

"Don't bother him. I'm sure he's busy."

"He said to keep him informed where you are at all times."

"Really, well we won't trouble him this once. We'll just hop in one of the cars and shoot off."

Cassie and Judith joined them and they all followed Mark to the garage.

While they waited for the bodyguard to pull the car forward, Anna slipped Judith $500. "Can you do me a favor while we're in the hairdresser?"

"Sure, what do you want?"

"Get me a good prepay cellphone. If they need a name would you mind giving them yours?"

"No problem."

As they drove out the gate, Mark's cellphone rang. "Mrs. West wanted to go to the hairdresser....She said not to bother you...Of course I'll keep an eye on her. I'm not a bloody amateur."

The hairdressing salon agreed to do Cassie's bob but didn't have time to do Anna too. "Don't worry I'll sit and wait for my daughter. You're very kind to fit her in at such short notice."

Judith returned with the phone after about an hour. "It's in my name, with my apartment address. I used the change to put credit on the phone."

"Thanks Judith. This is just between us you understand."

"Of course, it's my phone and you're just looking after it for me after I left it somewhere, aren't you? I'm going to do some shopping of my own now if that's okay, I'll see you both tomorrow."

Anna didn't know what Judith really thought about the transaction and she wasn't going to ask, but the two women had known one another far too long not to trust each other. She asked the hairdresser if there were somewhere she could go to make a private call and was offered the use of the office.

She copied the number that Percy had used to text her into the new phone and saved it as *Mother* before sending a message. *I settled that bill you spoke of.*

A few minutes later the phone in her hand buzzed.

"Percy, thanks for getting back to me so quickly, and I'm sorry it's taken so long to contact you but the old burner got lost in the hijack and I had to find a reason to get out of the house to get another one. What have you got?"

"I'll let you be the judge of what it all means, but it's interesting."

"Go ahead."

"First Paul Gates is his real name, but he wasn't in the SAS. He was an analyst with MI6 so he didn't serve with Rupert but could well have been on SAS ops. I called Rupert and he says they never even met. In fact Gates didn't join MI6 until a year after Rupert left the service."

"That's interesting. I wonder who's lying to whom."

"Gates is a new boy on the block as far as security consultancy is concerned. In fact this looks his first serious contract."

"What about his service record?"

"As far as Rupert was able to find out in the time available, he had nothing bad on his record, but he only did five and a half years in SIS, and he left under something of a cloud. Rupert thinks it can't have been anything too serious or he'd have gone to prison. He's going to try and find out more."

"Thanks Percy. How is Rupert?"

"All things considered not too bad I suppose, but he's out of the game."

"Is he happy with his compensation package?"

"He says he hadn't received anything yet, so I authorized an immediate payment of a million pounds. I hope that was okay."

"Fine, but next time I'm in the UK I'm going to go and see him."

"You might have to wait for a while. He's gone into hiding. Somebody had another go at killing him a few days ago."

"For God's sake what was all that about?"

"He doesn't know, but he said he wouldn't rule out it having something to do with the hijack."

"What?!"

"If he's right, it means that what happened, definitely wasn't a random attack. It might mean they'll try again. I don't understand why though, or what they hope to achieve. Killing a hostage before you've asked for ransom makes no sense. Which is why I thought you needed this information as soon as possible."

"This new team that Theo is recruiting - I need you to vet and double vet every one of them. I don't care what it costs."

"No problem; anything else?"

"I don't think so…no wait. Percy, I want somebody on that team whose working for me and nobody else. Whoever you find I need him to be the very best at what he does and to be in no doubt that it's me he's working for and me alone.

Five

After his meeting with Gates, Drew's drive back to his sister's home was quick, but when he got there he found a strange car on the driveway, and when he got inside he found Carolina and Curtiss, drinking coffee with Jake Mitchell and his nephew Ben was with them.

"Jake. What the hell…?"

"Your pal's been telling us tales of some of your adventures together." Carolina said with a smile.

"Uncle Drew, is it true you saved a whole coach full of schoolgirls in Nigeria by yourself?"

"Not entirely on my own, Jake and a couple of other guys helped out a bit."

"What about abseiling onto the conning tower of a French nuclear sub in a force eight gale to loosen the hatch so that the crew could get out?"

"Yeah, I guess that happened, but the wind was only force six. It wasn't a big deal; we train for stuff like that all the time."

"I've invited Jake to stay for dinner,' his sister said.

"That's great Lina, thanks."

"So what brings you to Wilmington buddy?"

"I come bearing tidings, I'll tell you about it after dinner."

"Are you gonna tell us any more stories about being a soldier?" Ben asked enthusiastically.

"We'd really like to Ben, but most of our ops are classified and we're not allowed to talk about them."

Later in the backyard.

"It's great to see you Jake, but what the hell are you doing here?" Drew said handing his former teammate a beer.

"I hear you've got a job offer."

"What the fuck, I only heard myself five hours ago."

"I probably found out about the same time as you did then."

"What the fuck is going on."

"I got called into the Colonel's office first thing this morning."

"I hope they ain't gonna ask me to go back in."

"Don't worry you're probably safe unless Putin kicks off; no he says he's been put in a position by a former friend of the squadron, and he hope's you can help. You remember Gates the Limey from Gardez?"

Drew nodded, but didn't say anything, "He's been trawling around among former special ops guys trying to put together a close-protection team for Theo Lemonis and his family after that assassination attempt or kidnap or whatever the fuck it was. There's suspicion that the Gates' job ain't all it seems. The guy calling in the favor is Rupert Loughty."

"I remember Loughty; had a great rep. He was on my first op in Iraq."

"Loughty says he's got reason to suspect that Gates has gone rogue, but there's no proof and could be wrong. If he's right his team could be used as cover for another assassination or kidnap attempt on Lemonis and his family. He thinks that one or more of the team might end up being fall guys when it happens."

"So, they want me to be the inside man. I don't want to be the guy that ends up in the electric chair when it all goes tits up though Jake. Who're the bad actors here?"

"At the moment, the suspicion is that it's someone to try to engineer a merger between Silico, the wife's company and NorArm, the husband's. They're both operating in similar areas of military IT systems. The wife has rejected all offers - nobody knows if there have been discussions between the husband and wife."

"Kidnap and murder – that's a bit extreme to achieve a company merger. Who benefits, and what are the motives?"

"Motives include greed, and either industrial or foreign espionage. At the moment the suspects include Lemonis, his sidekick Manos Stamelis, and/or a foreign power; most likely candidate among those would be Ivan."

"Russia, hmm. What about Lemonis, is he short of money?"

"Whoever it is, your proposed employer is coming to this late in the game so at the moment they don't know."

"Great who will I report to?"

"I'm told the principal mover is someone close to the family and they will make themselves known to you once you're in post by asking you about your time in the SEALs. Should you decide to accept the job that is."

"It's a bit late now I've already taken it."

"Well whoever that turns out to be will give you your contact details for intel. Make no mistake though, it's them you're working for not Gates. The list of candidates was doctored so that to get the number he needs to start the contract Gates had to include you."

"Okay, I won't ask how for the moment, but who else knows?"

"As of this moment, me, you, the Colonel, Loughty, and your contact."

"This is beginning to look a whole lot too much like spook work for my liking - but what the hell, it's better than standing on nightclub doors dealing with drunks."

"Good luck pal. This is purely private enterprise stuff so I doubt I'll have any more to do with it. Make sure you watch your six.

They shook hands and Jake made his way back to his car via the side gate.

Once inside Drew booked a 6 a.m. flight to LAX the following day and told the family he'd be leaving first thing. "Can you sell the Ford for me Lina, just get what you can for it and put it in Ben's college fund."

"Are you sure. You might need it when this job is over? How long you expecting to be away?"

"The initial contract is six months but it pays well and could go on or lead to other things. The car's probably only worth about six or seven grand, and I'll want to upgrade when I next need my own wheels."

"It's a lotta money Drew."

"I've missed far too many of his birthdays and Christmases; call it catch up. Say goodbye to him for me will you. I've ordered a cab for four-thirty, don't bother to get up, I'll let myself out."

"Is this gonna be dangerous?"

"I doubt it. I'll try to stay in touch, but don't bother contacting me unless it's an emergency."

"No change then eh bro?"

He kissed her cheek, shook hands with Curtiss and went to bed.

Six

It was an eight-hour flight to Los Angeles, so having loaded up with a big breakfast at the airport, he used most of the journey loading up on shuteye; eat and sleep *what you can when you can because you can never be sure when you'll get your next opportunity* is what had been drummed into him in army boot camp.

The cab dropped him outside the Lemonis home just before 3 p.m. He rang the bell on the gate and a man's voice asked, "Hello, can I help you?"

"Drew Parker. I'm expected."

There was a short pause and a male voice with an Eastern European accent said, "Come in walk up drive towards house and I meet you."

The electric gate opened enough to allow him through and closed behind him. Walking up the short drive he looked up at the house. The white, stucco rendered property was a sizeable residential building and although not as big as some of its neighbors, would still be valued in excess of $20 million if only because of its location. A stockily built man, about six-foot tall, with a shaven head and dark stubble met him outside the garages at the side of the house.

"I am Pavel Volkov. At present I head of security for Lemonis family until your new team take over tomorrow. Are you armed?" he asked.

"Other than a knife in my bag, no."

"Put arms out," Drew did as he'd been asked and waited impassively while Volkov professionally frisked him. "Follow me."

He was led into a room that separated the house from the three-car garage. It was clearly being used as the security room. There were about ten CCTV screens showing the grounds and parts of the house. Another man was sitting at the desk teaching a third how to operate the security system.

"Put bag on desk and empty out." Volkov demanded.

Drew unpacked the bag without speaking and watched the Russian deliberately make a mess of every piece of clothing that had been meticulously folded to ensure it fitted into the limited space.

"You looking for something in particular?" Drew asked.

"Making sure you not carrying unauthorized communication devices."

"Such as?"

"Phones, radios, listening bugs. Give me phone."

"No, you don't need it and I do. You gonna fold that up and repack it?"

"No."

"I thought not."

"You being smart with me?"

"No, I wouldn't want to overtax you; wouldn't be polite."

"You want lose job before you even start?"

"If we're gonna be working together, you need to start treating me with some respect. If you can't manage that, then I'm easy. But as I understand it you won't be head security honcho from tomorrow, so I guess the question is moot."

"Get through there into garage and join others."

"Just as soon as I've repacked my bag I'll be happy to oblige."

Volkov turned and headed to the door.

"Just a second, you forgot something," Drew said, holding out a little black object about the size of a small thumb drive. "If you want to know where I am just call me, and if you want to know what I'm talking about just ask and if it's any of your business I'll tell you; if it isn't I'll tell you to fuck off."

The two guys working on the security system had stopped what they were doing to watch the exchange.

"I was just testing to see how alert you are; we need the best people for this job."

"I wouldn't be here if I wasn't one of the best, and I'm clearly better than you, because I saw that gadget the moment you took it out of your pocket."

Volkov stormed out of the room. A few moments later Gates came in. "Parker, just in time; come through and join the rest of us."

"I'll be right there, just as soon as I've put my worldly possessions back in my bag. Ivan decided to pretend he was a boot camp sergeant major and turf them out all over the floor."

Gates clearly wasn't happy being asked to wait but didn't say anything and left the room.

"You ain't great at making new friends, buddy," One of the guys sitting at the security system controls said with a Scots accent. "I'm Mac."

"Parker. Good to meet you. I'm not good at being treated like an asshole by an amateur either. You one of the new team too?"

"Aye, looks like I've been voted tech expert."

They shook hands, and Drew quickly and efficiently repacked his bag before going through to the garage where Gates was leaning against a workbench talking to four other guys.

"Drew let me introduce the rest of the team; Gaston aka *Frenchie*, Eli, aka *The Priest*, Mickey aka *Mouse*, Atticus aka *Mockingbird*, and Mac you've already met. Boys this is Drew, aka …?"

"Parker; never acquired a handle. Not one I'll answer to anyway."

"Okay guys from 07:00 hours tomorrow we take over the reins handling the security for the Lemonis family which consists of Theodore Lemonis head of the household, Annabelle Astley-West lady of the house, and Cassandra Astley-West, Mrs. West's eleven-year-old daughter by her previous marriage. To us they are Mr. Lemonis, Mrs. West, and Cassie.

"The family have three homes in the USA, this one, another in Stillwater just outside Seattle, and an apartment in New York as well as property in Greece. There's also another home near Reading, England, which was Mrs. West's family home during her first marriage. Predominantly the family base themselves in Seattle, but since the recent hijacking they've decided to base themselves here for the time being. The New York apartment is rarely used and often when it is, it's usually by Mr. Lemonis on his own."

"This lot must have some serious money," Mickey observed.

"Not that it's relevant, but that's true. Mr. Lemonis is the biggest shareholder and Chief Executive of NorArm a big player in military software. Mrs. West comes from a wealthy family and co-founded Silico Industries with her first husband Henry, Chief Exec until he was killed in a road accident leaving his entire estate to his wife. Two years ago her own father died leaving a big chunk of his estate including his own holdings in Silico to her as well. So I think you can safely say the family are extremely wealthy.

"After the recent hijack resulting in their eldest daughter's kidnap, rape and murder, they understandably felt it necessary to beef up their security measures and they asked me to pull together a team of the best in the business and here you are. There are seven of us and we'll be providing active security twenty-four seven for the next six months, two at a time on duty whenever they're at home, one manning the control center here. When the family are away travelling, I'll supplement the team with two additional team members. Any questions so far."

"Where are we going to be staying?" Mockingbird wanted to know.

"For the next three weeks you'll be in a motel. We'll cab you there later. After that you can make your own arrangements if you wish."

"What about transport?"

"For the time being, while you're on duty you'll be using the family's vehicles. You'll need to make your own arrangements for your down time I'm afraid Frenchie."

"Worried the chicks won't be impressed when you take 'em out on a bus then Gaston?" One of the others asked.

"You haven't said anything yet Eli, nor you Parker."

"Parker's probably wondering about weapons, same as me."

"No, I was wondering if Ivan the Useless tried to take your phones or put bugs in your baggage as well."

Mouse exploded, "What's that?!"

"I'm not sure whether it was a tracker or a listening device but I caught him trying to hide it in my passport wallet when he searched it."

"He searched your bag. What the fuck!"

"So I'm guessing he didn't search everyone's then." There was a universal denial. "You wanna tell me what's going on Gates?"

"I don't know Parker; I'll find out for you and let you know."

"When you do, let them know that the next time I find anyone messing with my kit, I'll fuck them up. I assume everyone on this team's been deep vetted. If that's so there should be no reason not to trust us. If that's not the case then how the fuck are we supposed to keep this family alive if we can't trust each other to watch our six?"

It sounded like the consensus of opinion agreed with what he said.

"Look Parker I don't know what happened, but it had nothing to do with me. I'll get to the bottom of it, but Pavel won't have anything to do with security after today. He'll be around but completely out of our hair. As for weapons, you'll be given your guns tomorrow. Glock 22s with 17 round clips and one spare, with Kydex waistband holsters. Unless anyone has a particular requirement, that's it. The dress code is smart casual except if the principals have a formal engagement.

"Food will be provided by the kitchen staff while you're on duty."

"When do we get to meet the family?" Priest wanted to know.

"I'll introduce you to the family tomorrow morning, but I'll walk you around the property now if you're ready. The family are visiting friends and are expected back in two hours."

"Who's providing security while they're out today?" Drew asked, "If they're unhappy with their existing security arrangements I mean."

"They have two members of the temporary security team with them I think."

"Have the family been told how intrusive full-on close protection routine can be." Drew asked, "as opposed to the bunch of amateurs that've been running the show lately."

Pavel was standing behind Gates. "I was doing job while you were in kindergarten asshole."

"Then you should have picked up the basics by now. If you had doubts about my suitability for the job I should never been allowed to walk through the gate. Then you let me walk up the drive unaccompanied. I could have hidden any sort of weapon between there and here, and the camera positions wouldn't have allowed anybody to see what I did. When you frisked me you were alone; I could have put you down at least three times. Then you pulled that stunt with the listening device, which you still haven't explained. Worst of all you let the family go out on the day when they are probably most at risk since their hijack, accompanied only by two temporary staff. You should have been glued to their side. You want me to go on?"

"Okay Parker, I think we've got the message. Pavel can you help us do our survey now please."

The furnishing of the luxury accommodation was curiously understated, considering the wealth of the family but it had everything you would expect to find inside a home in that zip code.

Back in the garage Pavel left them to their devices and Mac joined them.

"Everybody happy?" Gates asked. When nobody replied, he told them the cabs would shortly be there to take them to the motel.

Gates, climbed in the first with Mickey and Eli, Frenchie and Mockingbird in the second, then Mac and Drew in the last one. The three cabs moved off in convoy and fifteen minutes later pulled into the parking lot of a motel. Everybody climbed out of their respective cabs except Drew.

"What's up Parker, you quitting already?" Mickey asked.

"Nope I'm just not staying here. I've a room elsewhere."

Gates pushed his head in the door, "We not good enough for you, Parker?"

"You're just fine. I just ain't staying here is all. That's okay ain't it?"

"I guess. Just this place is paid for."

"Yeah but it ain't secure."

"What do you mean?"

"I shouldn't have to explain, but since you ask. If someone wants to get at the Lemonis family they could come here and wipe out half the security detail in one hit. I'll see you tomorrow, 07:00, okay."

"Yeah."

"Sleep well. You want to drive on buddy?"

When the cab was underway he told the driver to drop him at a diner somewhere near the interchange of I-10 and I-405. After loading up with protein and carbs he asked directions to his hotel. It was two miles but he needed to stretch his muscles so he walked and checked into his prebooked room at about 7 p.m.

After showering he lay down on the enormous bed in his underwear thinking about what he'd learned. He was about to turn the light out to go to sleep when his cellphone rang. "What can I do for you Gates?"

"What's up with you Parker? Are you gonna give me trouble?"

"I don't know Gates, a.m. I?"

"What do you mean?"

"I can take it when I get fucked about, it's not called SNAFU in the military for nothing. But this time we're being paid for one simple task, protecting the lives of three people, including an eleven-year-old girl, and nobody seems to be taking it seriously."

"If you ain't happy you can take a hike Parker."

"Yeah, and how does that help that little girl? I'll see you in the morning; and keep that asshole Volkov out of my way."

He ended the call before Gates had the chance to reply.

Seven

At 05:30 the following morning he was at the gate of the Lemonis property pressing the bell.

"Yes?" A sleepy voice answered.

"New security detail reporting for duty."

"You're too early. Come back in an hour."

"Okay."

Drew turned away and walked half a block back down the street, climbed over a wall into a neighbor's yard and made his way back towards the Lemonis property activating a PIR security lamp on the back of one house. It was early April and still nearly an hour before sunrise.

Taking care to avoid the areas that he'd spotted were covered by CCTV cameras, he quickly scaled the final wall into their yard dropping behind a mature shrub. Light from streetlamps gave him enough visibility to see what he was doing, enabling him to quickly dodge from one obscuring object to another, and staying in sight for only seconds at a time. As he skirted the pool he picked up a kiddie's dive stick.

Finally he was pressing his back against the security office wall. The rear door was closed but when he quietly turned the handle he found it unlocked. The door slowly opened, thankfully without a squeak, revealing a man sitting at the desk engrossed in a book of Sudoku puzzles. A quick scan of the room revealed that the man was alone so Drew noiselessly crept across the room, pressed the dive stick to the man's head and ordered him not to move or make a sound.

"Okay, okay,' he said, lifting his hands in the air.

"Where's your gun?"

"I'm not armed."

"Seriously?!"

"No, I promise; I don't own a gun; I've never owned one. I'm just the night guy."

"What are you supposed to do if you see anything or anybody gets in?"

"Press the button under the desk and call 911."

"Who else is on duty tonight?"

"Just Pavel and Mark."

"Where are they?"

"I expect Pavel's in his room, I don't know about Mark. I haven't seen him since our break at two."

"What happens when you press the button?"

"I think it alerts Pavel."

"Doesn't it sound an alarm?"

"I don't know, I've never done it. I've only been here two months."

"Is there a procedure to protect the family?"

"Probably but I don't know what it is, Pavel probably knows."

"Okay, what's your name, how old are you, and what did you do before you got this job?"

"My name is Oliver Bailey, I'm twenty-two, and I'm a post-grad student at UCLA studying for my masters in fine art history. I just do this part-time."

"Okay Ollie, push your chair away from the desk, turn it to face me, and put your hands down."

His jaw fell open when he saw the dive stick in Drew's hand. "Haven't you got a gun either?"

"Didn't need one did I, but be honest with yourself, would it have made much difference if you'd known that?"

The young guy looked at the six-foot five-inch hulk in front of him, "No, I guess not,' he dejectedly replied.

Drew nodded at the screens, "Is this footage all being recorded?"

"Yes," he looked at the control panel, "Oh hell no, it's been turned off. It was on before I went on my break."

"Start the recording again now would you."

Bailey pressed a button and a red light appeared on the panel.

"Okay Ollie, grab your coat if you've got one - consider yourself relieved."

"You mean you're sending me home?"

"You can stay if you really want to, but you might prefer to be somewhere else at seven o'clock, it could be embarrassing."

The disconsolate youngster grabbed his coat from a hook on the wall, picked up a small rucksack, and his book of Sudoku.

"Which button opens the gate?"

Oliver pointed and headed out the door. Drew watched him walk down the drive, opened the gate for him when he reappeared, then closed it again before making a silent circuit of the property.

In the garage he found an armed man asleep in the driving seat of an SUV. He opened the door, took the man's gun from the holster at his belt and prodded him with it. There was no reaction at first, so Drew prodded him again, a lot harder the second time. The man groggily awoke.

"Wha... who..." He saw Drew and fumbled for his empty holster.

Drew stepped back and flicked the nozzle of the gun. "This what you're looking for?"

"Who're you?"

"Maybe your savior. Are you Mark?"

"Yeah, who are you?"

"The names Parker, I'm here to relieve you. Drop off did you?"

"What time is it?"

"About Zero five-forty."

"Jesus. You gonna let me get out?"

"Sure, easy does it though. Getting shot with your own gun can be a bit of a career killer for a security professional."

Mark stepped down and staggered.

"You okay?"

"I must've been drugged; I can't see straight and I'm dizzy."

"I kinda guessed that. Go and sit on the floor over there. I'll give you your gun back when you feel better. I'll be at the control panel."

In the security office Drew watched the monitors for any sign of activity, after five minutes of no movement he saw a man stagger into view on the second-floor landing. He hit the alarm button, the lights came on throughout the building and grounds and a high-pitched pulsating siren began to wail. Milliseconds later a shot sounded somewhere and the intruder fell forward.

Drew was on his feet, into the house, and halfway up the stairs when a second shot sounded. He found Pavel standing over the intruder pointing his gun.

"Put the gun down Volkov, he's probably already dead." He pulled his phone from his pocket and dialed 911. "Police. Armed house invasion. Shots fired, man down.' He gave the address.

"What the hell are you doing here?"

"I work here."

"Not for another hour you don't."

"Aren't you going to tell the family they're safe?"

Volkov sneered, stepped over the body, and knocked on a bedroom door. "It's me Pavel, Mrs. West, you safe now."

A small voice came from a door across the hall, "Mummy."

Anna West's wan face appeared as she cautiously opened the door. As soon as she saw Pavel she snatched the door the whole way open and dashed across to her daughter's room. "It's okay darling, we're safe now.

"Wha-what happened Mummy?"

"I don't know sweetie we'll find out in a minute."

"You should probably take your daughter and wait downstairs until the police get here, Mrs. West," Drew told her from the door.

"Who are you?" the woman asked, disheveled from sleep.

"Drew Parker ma'am, one of the new security team."

She looked the enormous man up and down. Everything about him was intimidating. Parker's six-foot five inch frame bulged with muscle, from his broad shoulders, enormous biceps and tree trunk thighs. His tanned face scarred along one side of his jaw, his pock-marked skin, and his close-cropped hair, together with his dispassionate expression completed a truly menacing appearance.

"Tell me what happened, Pavel?"

"I caught sight of someone coming upstairs and followed him. When he approached your bedroom door I called for him to stop. He didn't so I shot him."

"Who is it?"

"I not know yet."

"He's wearing kitchen-wear, ma'am," Drew informed her.

"Please tell me it's not Jules."

"Volkov?" Drew asked.

"I think it Jules, Mrs. West."

Her response was halted by the sound of police sirens.

"You better let them in Pavel," Anna told him.

"But…"

"Quickly, I don't want them breaking the gate down to get in. Should we go downstairs now do you think?"

Drew said, "They're here now ma'am, I should wait in your daughter's room until they come up here."

"Is he armed?"

"I don't think so ma'am but I haven't checked because there's little doubt he's dead."

Two police patrol officers came up the stairs with their guns drawn, "Drop your weapon, get on the floor with your hands behind you."

Drew complied with the instruction and passively lay as he was cuffed.

"Make sure that the security tape is preserved,' he told them, "I've reason to suspect it may get tampered with."

The cop radioed a colleague to secure the control room.

Eight

The next four hours were frantic. First they covered Cassie's head and escorted her past the body and down the stairs with her mother, both of them in tears. Mark had been adjudged unfit to answer questions and was taken to hospital, escorted by a cop. Drew gave a preliminarily interview in the garage. Meanwhile Gates was outside the gate kicking up dust with rest of the team and wasn't being allowed in. Pavel had been taken to the cop shop for questioning.

Later, detectives interviewed Drew again at length and he answered the questions entirely truthfully, without offering any explanations or opinions as to why things might have happened that way. They reviewed the tape and verified events with Mark, who the hospital confirmed had been drugged with Rohypnol. Bailey was located in a lecture on UCLA campus, interviewed, and his account verified Drew's, and tallied with the physical and video evidence. Lemonis hadn't yet returned from Seattle where he'd been overnight.

The rest of the new crew were finally allowed into the grounds, but it wasn't until Gates walked inside the control room that he realized Drew had been involved.

"What the hell were you doing here?"

"Your job."

"What the fuck are you talking about. We weren't supposed to take over until oh-seven-hundred."

"That's the sort of talk I'd expect from a parking attendant. I showed you yesterday what a bunch of incompetent jerkoffs Volkov and his crew were; that was something you should have been able to see for yourself. Anybody with bad intent could have walked in here overnight and done whatever they wanted, just like I did this morning. You should have insisted on taking over then and there, and because you didn't an innocent unarmed man ended up dead. That's on you."

"Fuck you, you're fired…"

"No he isn't," Anna said from the door, "but if you don't get your act together you will be."

"I'm sorry ma'am but Parker exceeded his authority. He can't continue."

"Did I just hear you contradict me?"

"No ma'am."

"Good. I'll remind you who's paying for your services. I've seen the service records of everyone in your team, and as I see it, you are all equally qualified to lead the team."

"Okay, ma'am, you're the boss."

"That's right, I am. My daughter is with her tutor in the school room, trying to recover. I'd be grateful if you could try not to be too intrusive when you do your patrols."

"Patrols?"

"I'm not sure how else you propose to ensure our safety, I hope it isn't by sitting in the control room and watching monitors like the last lot."

"No, ma'am."

"Good. Once you've got yourself settled in I want to meet each of you, one at a time. My husband will be back within the next hour or two but I don't want to wait for him. I'll start with Mr. Parker."

Gates' pep talk to the new security crew that followed didn't resemble anything he'd mapped out in his mind when he left the motel. When he finished he asked if anybody had anything to add. There were a couple of relevant questions and observations from the five other team members and then silence.

"What about you Parker, you seemed to have a lot to say earlier?"

"Since you ask, yes. I have no idea of the motive but it's obvious that somebody is out to fuck this family up. First the hijacking three months ago. I don't care what anybody else is telling them, but there's no way on this planet it wasn't a set up involving somebody inside the household. My understanding is the all the domestic staff have been changed, and now all the security team. The only person that's still here is Volkov so it would be my guess that he's somehow involved. You need to have him kept away from the family at the very least, I don't care how long he's been with them."

"That's a decision that can only be taken by Mr. Lemonis."

"Maybe, but if this goes tits up next time they might not be saved by the chance arrival of a conscientious close protection officer. The family are at risk, so are the rest of the staff, and so are we. So I suggest we treat this as a serious job and work together to find out which asshole is responsible, and not just sit around waiting for something to happen."

There were nods all round.

"That's right," Gates said, as if it had been his idea all along, "Mac if you can go back to the control desk this morning; Frenchie, Mockingbird on patrol as lady muck calls it; Mickey, Priest you can hang around until everybody has had their chat with Mrs. West, and Parker you go and have yours now."

Drew knocked on the lounge door and waited to be invited in. Expecting to hear her call, *Enter*, he was surprised when she opened the door herself and asked him to take a seat. Having recovered from the shock of a staff member shot to death outside her bedroom door, she had dressed and brushed her dark-blond hair. Even with very little make up, the woman, in her thirties, was extremely attractive.

"Good morning, Mr. Parker, I won't bore you with a lot of talk about your time in the SEALs, let's get down to business. Thank you for your intervention earlier by the way. I'm sure there is much more to what went on this morning than I've been told by Pavel. Please tell me your side of things; what you know, and what you suspect."

"Morning ma'am. My initial thoughts were as soon as I rolled up here yesterday that the security team that had been looking after you since the hijacking were very poor amateurs, criminally negligent, or possibly deliberately operating with malign intent. From everything I've been told, given the nature of the hijack, it would be difficult to conclude anything other than that the hijackers were acting on inside information. With that in mind, as your head of security, I would have expected Volkov to respond with a root and branch overhaul of every aspect of your protection. That clearly hadn't been the case."

"Explain."

"Changing your domestic staffing arrangements was a good idea as far as it went, but if it resulted in the recruitment of somebody who allegedly had malicious intent or could be easily turned then the process was flawed from the start. The guy operating the security system last night was a college kid who had been given no training nor any instruction what to do in an emergency. The security cameras are inappropriately positioned allowing me to easily enter the property without detection even though I had almost no advance knowledge of your system. Coupled with the absence of any motion detection to alert anybody of an unwanted presence in the grounds, I was able to gain access to the control room and take it over armed with nothing more than a child's dive stick, and without physical force."

"Why did you do that?"

"If you'll forgive me for saying so, ma'am, but your family is powerful and massively wealthy. Whoever was behind the hijacking, and probably the events of earlier this morning, will almost certainly be motivated by one of three things - money, industrial competition, or foreign espionage, money being the favorite in my opinion. It seems to me that Volkov should have been aware of that and taken much stricter control of your safety, particularly as an insider from the hijack hasn't been identified."

"Espionage, industrial competition, what do you mean?"

"It's my understanding that both yours and your husband's companies are involved in military technology. I don't know the details but I guess that there is potential for conflict there."

"Are you suggesting that my husband could be behind these things?"

"I'm not suggesting anything. You asked me to give my opinion on possibilities and that's what I'm doing. I'm guessing that your husband isn't the only person with money in NorArm, and I don't know enough about either of your companies or their products to comment further. I'm not a private investigator, I'm a protection officer looking after your personal safety."

"For someone who isn't a PI you're not doing bad so far but go on."

"If money was the motive for what happened, I doubt you've become significantly poorer since the hijack so for whoever was behind this, their motivations haven't evaporated, and on that basis nor have they for any of the other motives. Your protection needs to be the best you can get."

"Go back to explaining why you were here this morning, an hour and a half ahead of when you were required."

"My observations from yesterday were enough to convince me that security was poor. I wanted to discover how poor, and who might be responsible, in case whoever it was might still be involved once we'd taken over."

"Couldn't you have trusted Mr. Gates to have that under control?"

"Gates and I have crossed paths a couple of times in the past but we've never worked closely together. I've been in special forces for over ten years and I'm still alive, and I didn't get to stay that way by taking things for granted."

"What about your teammates?"

"I've heard of a couple of them once or twice, and I don't know anything bad about any of them."

"None of that suggests that you trust them completely."

"It is what it is ma'am, but I note that up to this point none of us have been given a weapon, and the first thing Volkov did when I arrived yesterday was attempt to put a listening device or tracker in my belongings and confiscate my phone, but apparently none of the others."

"What do you think happened this morning?"

"Somebody deliberately placed a totally unsuitable kid in charge of the security system then turned off the recorder while he wasn't looking. Then whoever it was, drugged the only armed guard on duty, and compelled the cook, who wasn't supposed to be on the premises at that time of day to go to the second floor and to make it appear as if he had malicious intent. Not necessarily to actually cause harm but perhaps to throw suspicion away from themselves."

"Pavel you mean?"

"That would be my guess. I saw it happen from the control room; the cook was pushed into the view of the camera by someone out of the camera's eye. At the same moment as I sounded the alarm someone shot him in the back. As Volkov was the only person up there with a gun and I'm assuming he hasn't denied it, that person was him. The cook who I believe you said was called Jules, wasn't armed and he was incapable of further resistance after the first shot even if he'd still been alive, so there was absolutely no need for the second shot in the back of his head."

"If you were heading this team what would your actions be now?"

"Until whoever has been responsible for the hijacking is identified, my first action would be to remove any responsibility for security from Volkov. Better still get rid of him altogether. Second, increase the security team to nine, three on duty at all times, one inside and two outside; three to travel with you when using commercial transport two at other times. Introduce an electronic log of all comings and goings from the property. Develop emergency response procedures and ensure that everybody including the family is fully conversant with them. Employ fully trained security system operators in addition to protection guards. The on-duty security team to have constant contact via headset radios, and the security system here and your other homes should be evaluated and where necessary upgraded. Lastly, I would recommend a personal close-body protection officer just for you and your daughter, preferably female. But there's something else that puzzles me. Why hasn't Mr. Lemonis arranged security for himself?'

"Why the personal bodyguard for me?"

"May I speak plainly ma'am?"

"Go ahead."

"I draw no conclusions, but I can't ignore the fact that your husband wasn't present when either of these incidents occurred, so it appears that either you, or you and your children could be the prime targets."

"You don't pull any punches do you?"

"Would you prefer if I iced it up all pretty like?"

"No that was exactly what I wanted." She handed him a cellphone, "Take this, so we can communicate without others knowing. The number of my second phone is programmed in as Kathy. Your contact for information and/or supplies is in there as 'Smithy'; he's available 24/7. Text before you call. We'll do likewise. Would you ask Gates to send in the next team member?"

Drew rejoined the team in the garage where they were discussing the detail. There was nobody in the control room.

"Okay Mickey, you're up next."

"No headset radios then Gates?" Drew asked.

"Yeah, they're on their way. They'll be here in a day or two."

"Are we supposed to wrestle hitmen to the floor, and ask them nicely to desist, or are you planning on giving us weapons sometime soon?"

"I thought I'd wait until everybody has met the family; they might be uncomfortable around armed men."

"I'm going to pretend I didn't hear that; do you think they're expecting us to go weapons free or use feather dusters?"

"Yeah okay, okay. Your guns are in the bag on the bench. They've got your names on; help yourselves."

"You were in there a long time Parker." Gates remarked a few minutes later

"She wanted to talk about this morning," Drew replied, examining his allocated handgun.

"You can take the rest of the day off. We'll see you back here at seven. You can take the night shift."

"Okay, who with?"

"What do you mean who with?"

"As in who else will be providing protection?"

"Just you. You seem to prefer to work better on your own. Volkov will continue to provide the extra night cover."

"I'm guessing he'll be asleep then."

"Yeah, seemed to work okay last night."

"You're kidding right?"

"No. If you're not happy, I'm sure I can get someone else if you think you can't cope."

He didn't respond. Two hours later, Drew was in the control room adjusting the zoom on some of the cameras.

"What the Hell are you doing?" Gates shouted from the door.

"Trying to get the cameras to cover more of the property. What are you doing?"

"I didn't ask you to do that."

"Who did you ask?"

"Nobody." Gates was clearly agitated.

"Why not?"

"I don't answer to you."

"Who do you answer to, because I'm beginning to wonder?"

"Listen asshole, it wasn't my idea to pick you for this job, and if I'd had my way you wouldn't have been allowed anywhere near it, but that doesn't mean I can't get rid of you."

"I seem to remember you telling me something completely different when you asked me take the job."

"I told you to go home hours ago. So piss off and don't be late for your detail later. Mrs. West and Mr. Lemonis asked for my opinion of you. I told them I thought you weren't a team player and you could cause trouble, so one word from me and you'll have the skids under you."

"For accuracy, you didn't tell me to go home; you said I could take the rest of the day off. I decided that as you were going to put me on detail by myself tonight I'd do my best to prevent anybody getting the drop on me the same way I did this morning, seeing as you were too busy."

"You're not on detail by yourself. I told you, Pavel will be your backup."

"You also told me he would be asleep, leaving me to stare at security monitors all night on my own."

"How did you get in unnoticed?"

"It's taken you the whole day to ask me my version of events. Why is that?"

"Because…" His phone buzzed. "Yes sir. He is…I'll send him up right away. Looks like your attitude might have upset the family. They want to see you." A smug expression spread across his face.

"I guess we'll have to continue this fascinating conversation another time then."

He knocked on the living room door and a man's voice called for him to enter. He pushed the door and found Lemonis in the room with his wife.

"Mr. Parker?" The classically Greek looking man asked.

"Yes Sir."

"You've presented me with something of a problem."

"I'm sorry to hear that sir. How did that happen?"

"In less than twenty-four hours you've gone from the hero of the day, to troublemaker and I'm not sure what to do about it."

"You've lost me sir."

"First thing this morning your intervention helped prevent an attempt on my wife's life from succeeding, earning my eternal gratitude. Now I'm being told by Mr. Gates that you are a disruptive influence and he's advising me to dismiss you."

"To be fair, nothing I did this morning prevented an attempt on Mrs. West's life by your cook. He wasn't there to do anybody any harm and I doubt he would have been capable even had he wanted to. He was about five-feet one-inch tall couldn't have weighed more than a hundred and fifty pounds. He wasn't armed, and clearly wasn't there voluntarily."

"I don't understand."

"When I first observed Jules appear outside the bedroom door he was thrust in front of the camera by someone with a gun. I couldn't see who was holding the gun, but at the exact moment I pressed the alarm button Volkov shot him in the back. I don't know if there was any sort of challenge because there's no sound on the recording but I rushed to the stairs and between the first shot and when I was halfway up the stairs there was a pause of maybe twenty seconds before Pavel shot him a second time in the back of the head."

"It's a pity that there's no recording to verify that."

"I understood that the police saw the recording."

"I looked earlier and couldn't find anything. They must have somehow erased it when they messed with the system. That's a pity."

"I'm sure if you ask, they'll let you have a copy."

"I did ask, they told me that, as it's evidence in a suspicious death that wouldn't be allowed."

"That's a pity sir. As for me being disruptive, I'm not sure what Gates is saying, but if he means doing everything I can to ensure your safety by trying to eliminate the gaps in your security arrangements, I'm sorry if that inconveniences him. None of the rest of the team have complained."

"Gaps? What do you mean?"

"For example, the poorly positioned cameras covering your yard."

"Poorly positioned, I didn't realize that?"

"It was one of the things that enabled me to gain undetected access to the property this morning."

"I'm sure he had that in hand."

"Could be, sir. Perhaps that's why he reprimanded me for doing it just now, before you called me up here."

"There you go then."

"I wanted to be sure it was the best it could be, for my own peace of mind, as I'll be on duty on my own tonight."

"On your own?" Mrs. West spoke for the first time.

"Yes, ma'am."

Lemonis jumped in, "What about Pavel?"

"With respect sir, he's about as useful as a chocolate coffeepot."

"What do you mean?"

"Isn't he the one who's been in charge for the last three months and supervised the camera placement in the first place. If not he's had plenty of time to correct them? He's definitely the one who arranged for an untrained college kid to be in charge of the system, without instructions on what to do in an emergency. As a consequence of that the single qualified guard was disabled with drugs and a guy who was not supposed to be on the property was either granted admission or allowed to stay overnight. Whatever, it resulted in a shooting incident yards from your wife and child's bedroom doors. I'm sure Volkov is good at some things sir, but close-body protection isn't one of them. However, if you're not happy with my services, I'll leave you in Volkov's hands."

"You're not going anywhere." Mrs. West intervened. "Theo, I don't want Pavel anywhere near me or Cassie. If you want to find work for him somewhere else in your organization, that's your decision, but from now on, not in the same house as me. I don't trust him. Thank you Parker."

Drew returned to the control room, where Mac was demonstrating the sophisticated controls to Gates.

"I'm going to take my break now Gates. I'll take the Navigator that's nearest the gate, thanks," he said taking a key fob from a hook on the wall.

"You can't just take a car whenever you want to."

"You told me it was part of the deal, and as nobody's using the cars it seems a waste not to. I'll see you later."

He drove to the diner he'd used the previous day and sent a text to his contact to expect a call from him in the next hour.

After a loading up with carbs and protein he returned to his hotel room and made the call.

"Mr. Parker, how's it been?" The English voice answered.

"Not brilliant,' he replied and recounted the events of the previous 24 hours.

"What's your assessment?"

"Lemonis is either the dumbest and most gullible guy on the planet, or he has a hand in what's going on. I'm going with the second. He wouldn't be in charge of a corporation that size if he were stupid. As to what his motives are, I've no idea."

"I'm inclined to agree, although I'm supposing it's his sidekick Manos Stamelis that's the prime mover. What next?"

"I can see that Mrs. West has strong feelings for her husband. it might be a big ask to convince her that he's involved at the moment. I'd suggest you do whatever you can to keep me in post until the Lemonis accomplices do something to expose themselves. I'm as certain as I can be that Volkov is involved, and I reserve judgement on Gates. Too soon to say about any of the others."

"What about Stamelis?"

"I haven't met him yet. Can you do a couple of things for me?"

"What do you need?"

"Find out if the police still have a copy of the security tape from this morning. Lemonis is claiming that it's been deleted from their system and the cops won't release it because it's evidence. If they have, try and get a copy. I don't know if that's possible."

"That shouldn't be too difficult. I think Mrs. West has enough swing to get that. What's the other thing?"

"I need a couple of guns. A Glock G22 with two 17 round magazines, and a Glock G43 with ankle holster, and ammo."

"I thought Gates was providing arms."

"He did but mine may have been tampered with."

"I think that would pretty much confirm his involvement don't you?"

"That's right. What I can't be sure of is who picked him for the job, it could have been Stamelis, in which case it's possible that Lemonis doesn't know what's going on. And I have no idea what the end game is supposed to be."

"If you had to speculate about that, what would your guess be?"

"Mrs. West asked that. I told her, money, industrial competition, or foreign espionage: with money as the hot favorite. I don't know about the state of Lemonis' finances but adding Mrs. West's to the pot wouldn't hurt him any. Having said that I don't know if merging the two corporations would bring significant benefits, nor do I know if there's any classified military involvement that might be influencing anyone."

"That could be an issue. I won't elaborate."

"Who exactly am I working for here?"

"Mr. Lemonis engaged Gates to provide the security detail, but Mrs. West insisted on paying for it and demanded final say so on who was included after vetting by her own company security section. There's no question, you're working for her; your first responsibility is her and her daughter's safety; everything else is secondary as far as she's concerned. I'll arrange for those items to be delivered to you by Fed Ex as soon as possible. Take care, I don't think these people are finished yet."

After a shower, he stripped the Glock to its component parts and immediately found what he was looking for. It was a new gun and it would normally be expected to be in factory condition, but as soon as he picked it up he spotted a minute tell-tale scratch on the slide cover plate. That sort of thing that happens when a gun is clumsily dis-assembled. He took the gun apart and looked at the spacer sleeve that controlled the distance the firing pin moved; to any professional it would be obvious it wasn't original - the color was wrong. The tubular sleeve was either from a different model or a replica and the cut out was shorter so the pin wouldn't travel far enough to hit the bullet primer. When the trigger was pulled the gun simply wouldn't fire.

He reassembled the weapon put it back in its holster and grabbed a couple of hours sleep.

At 18:45 hours he was pressing the button on the gate of the Lemonis residence.

"Can I help you?" A strange voice asked.

"Drew Parker, night security."

"Wait there." There was a long pause then. "I'm told that you've been relieved of your duties. Go back to your hotel and someone will contact you about severance."

"Okay." He got back in the Navigator, drove around the block, and texted Mrs. West. *'Just been told I've been fired.'*

Ten minutes passed and his phone buzzed. "What happened?" she asked.

Drew explained and she told him to leave it ten minutes and try again.

When he pressed the gate bell the same voice asked, "Can I help you?"

"Drew Parker, night security."

"I told you, you've been relieved of your duties."

"Okay." He left the car by the curb and retraced his steps from earlier in the day. A Latino gardener looked at him with astonishment when he dropped over the wall close to where he was tending a flower bed. "Excuse me,' he said with a friendly smile, before nimbly climbing the final wall into the Lemonis' yard.

It was dusk, there was a lot of cloud and visibility was poor. Using almost the same care as he had before, he came up against the control room wall. Taking out the contact phone he texted, *Just had to make a covert entry into the property because they denied me access again. I'm going to attempt to get to the day room without detection.*

She responded immediately, *OK.*

The outside door to the control room was closed. He put his ear to it and heard laughter and then Gates said, "If he tries again just keeping repeating until I tell you to stop. I'll her ladyship and say that he was a no show for duty and I had to fire him."

The other guy laughed.

At the front of the garage one of the parking bay doors was fully open. He glanced inside and could see Gates talking to the man at the desk with his back to him. Silently he crossed the floor and opened the door into the kitchen and laundry room area. A man in kitchen clothes was preparing a meal.

"Hi," he said. "I'm Drew, night security."

"Oh hi I'm Alejandro, the new cook."

"Nice to meet you. I'll see you later, Mrs. West wants to see me."

Casually he walked across the hallway to the dayroom door and knocked.

"Come in."

"Good evening, ma'am."

"Parker, good to see you again."

"Mr. Lemonis not with you tonight?"

"No he's gone into the office for an hour or two. Tell me what's been happening?" He explained the sequence of events. "Let's ask Mr. Gates what he thinks." She picked up her cell and called him. "Mr. Gates, could you spare me a minute."

A minute or two later, he knocked and entered. As soon as he saw Drew, his surprise and annoyance were clear, but he quickly recovered. "Parker, you're late for duty,"

"Mr. Gates perhaps if the rest of your staff didn't willfully obstruct Mr. Parker from doing his work he wouldn't have been late. But to put you at ease it is unlikely to be a problem for you in the future. As of this moment, Mr. Parker no longer works for you." A grin began to spread across Gates' face. "That's because as of now he works exclusively as personal bodyguard for me and my daughter. He will be taking over Pavel's room so you can tell him, he'll need to make other arrangements."

"But…"

"I don't know what you think you were employed for Mr. Gates but it's obvious to me that you're not very good at it. Mr. Parker again entered the property and gained access to the living quarters without detection using precisely the same method he did earlier today. You've spent the first day on the job engaging in petty squabbles rather than concentrating on your prime function. If I have my way you will find yourself unemployed again, but I'll await Mr. Lemonis' opinion on that. In the meantime, you are instructed to put aside any personal difficulties you and Mr. Parker have. You are to work together to make the security surrounding my family as tight as it can be, is that clear?"

"But…"

"I said, is that clear?"

"Yes, ma'am."

"Good and for future reference, I don't use my title so it won't be necessary to refer to me as *her ladyship* or *lady muck*. I may be a mere woman but I have ears and a brain and I expect loyalty and respect from those around me. That will be all."

"Yes ma'am."

"And you, Parker."

"Yes, ma'am, thank you."

They left the room together.

"Well you got your wish, Parker."

"I didn't have a wish; only to do the job I was being paid to do. It was looking like you had other plans, or perhaps you had different instructions. Anyway, are you going to tell the new guy in the control room that I now have a job here and I'm outside your line of command, then we can get on with drawing up some security plans that might actually work."

Between them they compiled a long to do list. Some of the items were simple procedural things such as arranging a duty roster with three people on duty day and night; other arrangements would need to be made for travelling and for when Mr. Lemonis travelled alone. Other issues were more substantial and would require Lemonis to invest significant sums of money such as the upgrade of the security alarm, the installation of motion sensors, and good headset radios for security staff to communicate.

To Drew it was obvious that Gates was pissed off because he was going to have to recruit more people and include himself in the roster.

The new guy on the desk was called Sam and was one of the three people Gates had employed on a short-term contract. He came recommended by the company that maintained the alarm system; they had yet to be fully vetted.

Gates said, "Volkov will be out to get you now. He might not be working here any longer, but he hasn't been sacked so you're bound to cross paths with him again. I expect Lemonis will use him as a driver."

"I'll try to bear the disappointment of not being on his Christmas card list. The man's an incompetent asshole."

"He's not a fool."

"Did you know him before then?"

"No but it was him that approached me to take the contract."

His contact phone vibrated in his pocket.

"So who are tonight's detail?"

"Sam, with Mockingbird and Priest."

"Where are they right now?"

"Mockingbird is outside. Your fucking around meant changing the roster. Priest will be here soon. He's pissed off at you for being fucked around. He was planning on visiting his parents in LA."

"He's a big boy; he'll get over it. You staying until he gets here?"

"Yes."

"I'll shoot off in a while and collect my gear from my hotel."

By the time he went outside to speak to Mockingbird it was completely dark. He stood in the shadow of the house waiting for the other man to find him, while he waited he check the message on his phone, *Your package has been delivered to Fed Ex Wilshire Blvd under your name.*

That was quick, he thought, *They must have someone else in the area.*

"I could have killed you and you'd never known I was close," a voice said.

"Evening Atticus. I saw you move behind that shrub about five minutes ago."

"What the fuck's going on. Gates says you ain't part of the team any longer."

"That's right. I've been transferred to Mrs. West as her personal guard dog. We're still on the same side but the lady wanted a more personal service."

"You getting a pay rise?"

"I shouldn't think so; we haven't discussed money. Gates and I were rubbing each other up the wrong way and I guess she thought it wasn't helping. She was probably right."

A car slowed as it passed, and Atticus looked. "I've not really worked with him before. You?"

"Not in so many words. He appeared on the scene on a couple of ops during the last few years that's all. What about you?"

"The same. The last time was just over two years ago on an op in Columbia. It all went pear-shaped and we lost a guy. That's when I quit, I think Gates quit at the same time. He had a nickname back then. They called him *Super* - short for superficial; wouldn't cover all the bases."

"I'm a bit of a prowler, so try not to put a bullet in me."

Back inside he told Sam he was going to be taking the Navigator that was still parked in the street but he'd be back inside the hour.

He signed for the heavy package at Fed Ex a few minutes before they closed for the night, then took it back to his hotel. After unpacking the contents he stripped the two guns, loaded the magazines, strapped the ankle holster to his left leg and then packed his bag before checking out.

Halfway back to the Lemonis property he stopped at a dumpster and dropped the gun packaging inside.

As he hung the key fob for the car back on the hook, Sam was playing some kind of game on his phone. "Can I see the log," he asked.

"Log?"

"Weren't you told to keep a log of all comings and goings from the property?"

"Yeah, but they never provided me with a book to record it in."

"What's that thing in front of you?"

"A computer."

"I might have got it wrong, but I thought there were things like word processors and spreadsheets on computers."

"Oh yeah, great idea."

"So since you came on duty, who's come onto the property, and whose left. Can you remember?"

"I was told you don't work for Mr. Gates anymore."

"That's true. Do you like it here?"

"It's okay I guess."

"They paying you well?"

"Yeah, double time."

"Why do you think you're here?"

"To watch the security system because you got fired."

"Why do you think any of us are here?"

"To watch the property in case anything happens."

"And why do they think something is going to happen do you think."

"I heard that they were caught up in some kind of carjacking a few months ago. Seems a bit OTT all this, if you ask me."

Seeing red, Drew grabbed by the guy by the scruff of the neck and lifted him from his chair and pulled their faces together.

"Nobody is asking you though are they? That *some kind of carjacking* you were talking about resulted in the kidnap, rape and murder of the family's eldest daughter. This morning one of the employees here was shot dead. The people who own this place are prime targets for some bad actors as yet unidentified. So you need to start taking this fucking job seriously, and if I catch you not taking it seriously again I'll shove your teeth so far down your throat you'll have to chew your food as it comes out your ass."

"Okay, okay."

Drew pushed him back in his chair, "And as for my status here, I wasn't fired. I resigned when Mrs. West appointed me her personal bodyguard, so if you have any more ideas about withholding security information from me you'll be out the door and you'll never work for a security company again. You got it?"

"Yeah, sorry."

"Right let's start again. Who's come onto the property, and whose left since you came on duty?"

"Mr. Priest arrived and Mr. Gates went home. Then Mr. Lemonis came home with another man. I don't know his name."

"You've forgotten a few things. There were the two times I pressed the gate bell and you sent me away. Then when I made the unauthorized entry, and then later I left to collect my things and returned just now. These are all things that need to be logged. It doesn't matter how trivial they seem."

"I got it."

"Good, put your phone in your pocket and don't take it out until you go home. You don't carry a gun but you're as important a member of the team as all the rest of us. You do that well and you and I'll be good buddies."

Drew put his bag in what had been Volkov's room. It occurred to him that Gates had probably been assuming he would take it over. Another reason for him to be pissed off.

The housekeeper had clearly been in to tidy and remake the bed so Drew just unpacked his few belongings. He was considering going to the kitchen for something to eat when his regular phone sounded.

"Hello."

"Mr. Parker, this is Theo Lemonis. Could you join me in the study?"

"Be right with you, sir."

The study door was open but he knocked anyway. Lemonis was at the desk and a man he assumed was Manos Stamelis was standing at his side.

"Come in Parker. You seem to have impressed my wife."

He didn't reply.

"In fact in less than twenty-four hours you've turned my whole household upside down. What do you have to say?"

"I have no wish to change the way you and your family live, sir. In fact quite the reverse. I see my job as making sure you're all able to carry on your day to day lives with little or no change but comfortable in the knowledge that everything is being done to secure your safety."

"Do you think you may have overstepped your remit?"

"I hope not, sir. There are considerable gaps in your security, that could easily result in placing yourself and your family at risk. It would be negligent to allow them to go unaddressed."

"I agree and I'm grateful for your diligence. Mrs. West has asked that you be attached to her as her personal bodyguard. I think that's a good idea. I have taken your advice and transferred Pavel to other duties, one of which will be as my driver, and also to take on a similar role as yourself for me personally. I ask you to liaise with him in the same way you will need to with Mr. Gates to ensure that all your actions are coordinated."

"No problem, sir."

"That will be all Parker, thank you. I hope you enjoy your new position. You'll need to discuss your terms of employment with her, sir."

He went to the kitchen and as he was making himself a sandwich, Priest joined him.

"Movin' up then Parker."

"Not really. I didn't ask to change. In fact if Gates had carried on behaving like a complete cunt I'd have quit. As it is, this gives me a chance to actually do the job I thought I was employed to do in the first place. I don't know what he thinks his job is but it don't seem like it's protecting the family."

"Yeah, I agree. He's bloody useless. If this were a high-risk job, I'd have taken a hike by now."

"In my view it is a high-risk job and at the moment it ain't clear who's on whose side, so watch your six."

"What do you mean?"

"Ask yourself, why Gates? He has no history of taking on contracts like this. If you were head of a family with a combined wealth of over a billion dollars, and you were worried about your safety would you hire a newcomer to the scene?"

"Lemonis just got the wind up after a couple of gangbangers tried to make a name for themselves."

"How much do you know about that hijacking?"

"Just that, what Gates told me when he asked me to be a part of this."

"Then you're poorly informed. The only reason that Mrs. West and Cassie survived was because the head of Lemonis' security, returned from leave three days earlier than expected and happened upon the scene."

"Maybe he was in on it."

"We're talking about Rupert Loughty here. He was an SAS legend, and he took a bullet in the lung in the process so I don't think so. How many of us have worked together before, as part of the same team I mean? From what I can see, none of us."

"Yeah there is that. So, do you think Gates is crooked then?"

"I haven't worked out if he's a player or he's being played yet but for now I'm not taking any chances."

"You seem to have had him in your sights since day one."

"I did some research before I arrived, so I had some idea what I ought to expect. Instead of that I was greeted by a tsunami of bullshit from Volkov - he tried to bug my gear and take my phone, but not the rest of you from what I gather. Then our initial briefing was held in the garage like a boy scout group preparing for a nature ramble - no information, no detail, no radios, and our armory wasn't issued until after we were in post. So I decided to test the water. Turns out I was almost right, only it was worse than even I thought it might be. There's a scared woman and her little girl up there, and I ain't walking away unless I'm forced to."

"What do you reckon went on when the cook got shot?"

"I've got my own ideas, but as cook, drugging the guard could easily be blamed on him. Unarmed, untrained, and with the physique of an anorexic stick insect there was no way he was going to kill anyone."

"Perhaps it was just a case of Volkov being over cautious and panicking when he saw the cook somewhere he thought he shouldn't be."

"Maybe."

Drew left Priest to ponder that thought and went to his room to grab a few hours' sleep. He slept with the new G43 under his pillow, the faulty one still in its holster on the chair with his pants.

Nine

At 3 a.m. he was woken by the door slowly opening. He heard feet slide across the carpet and smelled a faint wisp of body soap.

"Whoever you are, you better make yourself known pretty quick. I have a gun in my hand."

"Please don't shoot me, Mr. Parker. It's me, Cassie, I just want to ask you something."

He switched the bedside light on and the young girl was standing just inside the door wearing a cotton pajama suit with short pants.

"What's up, miss?"

"I'm scared."

"Have a seat on the chair just there, I'll move my stuff. Tell me what's worrying you. Have you heard a noise or something?"

"I'm not scared of things right this minute, Mr. Parker; but I'm scared that people are trying to kill us."

"Just call me Drew, but maybe it would be better to go to your mom if you're scared."

"I've talked to Mummy about it, but I don't think she believes me."

"Tell me what in particular is frightening you. Is it just because of what happened to your sister?"

"Not just that, but I heard Pavel talking on the phone and it sounded like he planned that attack and is planning another one."

"I guess that's why me and the rest of the guys are here."

"I know but I don't trust the other men."

"Why not?"

"I heard what you told Mummy. I was supposed to be in lessons with Judith but she was on the phone. Then I heard what you told Theo and Mummy."

"You sure do overhear a lot of things."

"I listen. Mummy's always saying I shouldn't be nosey, but since Izzy was taken I've been doing it more. I think something's going on."

"What do you think is happening?"

"I think Theo wants us dead."

"What makes you say that?"

"The day before the hijack happened, I heard him and Pavel talking about *Point Side.* That was the name of the gang that the hijackers belonged to wasn't it?"

"That's right but there are many contexts that those words could be used. Why would Theo want you dead do you think?"

"I don't know; maybe he wants Mummy's money."

"He's very wealthy already though isn't he?"

"Yes, but not as much as Mummy."

"Well I'm not going to tell you that you should always listen to other people's private conversations but if you hear something that worries you about your safety, you can always talk to me about it. Probably not a good idea to come to me in my bedroom when neither of us are fully dressed though unless it's really urgent; people might get the wrong idea. Why do you trust me though Cassie? We've barely spoken, and you don't know me anymore than any of the others."

"Because the things you say make sense, Mummy trusts you, and you've got kind eyes."

"People's eyes aren't a very reliable guide to their trustworthiness."

"Judith says that the eyes are windows to the soul, I believe that. Pavel's eyes are creepy, Mr. Gates won't look you in the eyes properly, Manos eyes are dead, and Theo's are cold, but yours are warm. You put on a detached face a lot of the time, but I can see when you're angry and when you care."

"I'm flattered, but if it helps, you may think your mom's been dismissing your concerns, but I can assure you she's considered all the things you've told me about, and they would be part of the reason why she's asked me to be personal bodyguard to you both. I think she's a pretty smart cookie, and she won't take anything for granted. Your safety is right at the top of her concerns, and I promise it's right at the top of mine too."

"Thank you Drew, can I give you a hug?"

"Maybe when we're both dressed eh? Just let me slip my clothes on and I'll walk with you back to your room; you need to get some sleep."

"I'm sorry I woke you."

"Don't be, it's what I'm paid for."

After wishing her a good night, he went to the control room.

"Hi, Mr. Parker." Sam greeted him guardedly.

"Sam. How's it going?"

"Nothing happening."

"Let's see the log."

He turned the monitor toward him. The most recent entries showed Cassie leaving her room, appearing at the bottom of the stairs, proceeding to Drew's room and going inside, followed by their exit and returning to her room a few minutes later."

"Do you want me to delete those last entries?"

"Absolutely not. The whole purpose of the log is an accurate recording of events on the property. It happened therefore it goes in the log. If for some reason you make a mistake make a separate sub-entry to correct it and say why. Nothing gets deleted. It must tally with the camera recording and it's for everybody's protection. I see you recorded the movements of the other two guys; that's good. It might be a good idea to record activity outside the property, what you can see or hear. You might not be able to read license plates but you can make a note of make, model, and color of vehicles, pedestrians, dog walkers, that sort of thing. That's great, keep it up - try to keep the times accurate."

Mockingbird was in the kitchen when he passed through on the way to his room. They nodded to each other and went on with what they were doing. Drew managed another hour or so of sleep before the alarm on his phone buzzed at 05:15. He dressed and noted that whilst he was in the shower he'd had a message from his contact.

The message included a link to a private YouTube channel. He tapped the link and it was a montage of videos showing the various security camera videos of the events of the previous morning. It was difficult to see the detail on the small screen but he thought he could see the hand shoving Jules into the picture.

In the control room Sam looked up as he entered.

"All quiet?" Drew asked.

"Yes, it's surprising how many vehicles go up and down the street overnight in a quiet wealthy neighborhood like this. Look."

Drew looked over his shoulder and he could see that number of entries had increased since he'd looked earlier. "That's great Sam. It will be difficult to keep that up during daylight hours but if we can keep a good idea of what's happening it is easier than reviewing a tape in real time. Who's taking over from you at seven?"

"Raoul, I think. If not it'll be Matt."

"Make sure you bring him up to speed with what's expected of him when you hand over. I'm going to try to get some software that's designed for this purpose in the next day or two. In the meantime continue with the spreadsheet."

Both Eli and Atticus said they were looking forward to being spelled by Gates and Mouse at seven, but they were professionals and this was easy money as far as they were concerned. He returned to his room and texted his contact. *Thanks for the vids. Need small listening/tracking device detector asap. Same delivery arrangements as before if poss.*

Ten

Alejandro the new cook arrived at 06:30. He'd been given instructions to feed the off-going security crew before preparing breakfast for the family and any guests, but Drew was too busy to eat.

The handover at seven went almost without a hitch, Gates grunted his approval at the security log that Drew had instituted. Otherwise their exchange was largely monosyllabic. The only unexpected event was that the guy from the alarm company to man the control room was not Raoul or Matt but a guy called Otis. He was about the same height and weight as Drew, but that was where the similarity ended. The new guy was black and his bulk wasn't muscle; it was mostly fat.

"What happened to Raoul and Matt?" Drew asked.

"Raoul quit, and as Matt had already made arrangements for today, it'll probably be Sam again tonight."

"Are you permanent now?"

"Yeah."

"Did Sam give you the rundown on how things are done?"

"Yeah."

"You need to pay attention with what's happening. Mr. Gates and I will be checking up from time to time throughout the day."

"Okay, 'boss',' he replied with something akin to a sneer.

Drew took out his contact phone and sent another text. *The day shift guy from the alarm company who was supposed to be manning the desk today, quit without notice. His name is Raoul. Can you get me his full name and address., I'd like to pay him a welfare visit.*

The reply came within minutes. *Will do. Your scanner should be delivered by midday.*

Mouse was patrolling the grounds in the light rain that had begun in last hour when he caught up with him. "Okay Mickey?"

"Sure, this has got to be the easiest money I ever earned. Boring though."

"Got to be better than being hunkered down in an African rainforest in the pissing rain getting bitten by snakes and insects."

"You got that right. Were you involved in that Central African Republic op?"

"No, what op was that?"

"It all went belly up; the target and a load of civvies got killed."

"That wasn't us was it? I saw that on the news; thought it was a private job."

"Nah, the scuttlebutt is that it was Delta."

"I wouldn't take too much notice of that. It's exactly what the privates would say if they're trying to crawl out from under."

"Okay, if you say so."

The conversation made Drew uncomfortable. The special forces creed was that you didn't discuss an op with anybody that hadn't actually been on it themselves. Mouse was the one member of the team he'd never crossed paths with or heard mention of before. He was alleged to have been in the Army Rangers, and fully vetted, but now he was having doubts. He pulled out his contact phone and was about to send another text when an incoming one made it vibrate in his hands.

Raoul Fernandez, 11670 San Vicente Blvd, West LA, CA 90049.

He rapidly typed his reply. *Thanks, that's great. Can you check the vetting of team member 'Mickey' (Mouse) and send me a pic? I have doubts about him.*

Five minutes later, the phone vibrated again. *Michael 'Mickey Mouse' Maus was exhaustively vetted along with the other team members. Photo attached.*

He immediately responded. *That is not the guy that's here. I'll try and get a pic for you to attempt to ID him.*

After the family had breakfasted, Volkov arrived to pick up Lemonis, giving Drew the death stare to which he responded with a friendly smile. A few minutes later Mrs. West asked him to drive them to a mall and plan to be out for several hours. He took the key fob for one of the Navigators and checked it over for bugs. There was nothing obvious so he drove it to the front of the house. Mother and daughter joined him shortly and he opened the back door for them. Cassie smiled at him and climbed in but Anna opened the front passenger door and sat beside him up front.

"How are you today, Mr. Parker?" she asked as he drove through the gate that Otis opened for them.

"I'm very well thank you, ma'am."

"Is the room comfortable?"

"It's fine, ma'am, but would you mind if we didn't talk too much? I like to concentrate on my driving."

"Oh, of course. I didn't think."

He turned his head towards her and put a finger to his lips. Her mouth and eyes opened wide.

"Did you hear that Cassie?"

"Yes Mummy."

"Which mall would you prefer, ma'am?"

"I think Santa Monica Place will be best."

They drove in silence the short distance to the mall. He parked and went to open her door, but she had already stepped onto the tarmac.

"You don't have to do that for me Drew. You're our bodyguard not chauffeur. Let's go somewhere we can talk without being uninterrupted or overheard. There are seats outside, and the rain's stopped, so they should be dry by now."

He silently followed, his eyes ceaselessly scanning the people around them.

She found an oval seater in the central open area and sat down.

"Sit down Drew we need to chat."

"If it's okay, ma'am, it would be better if I stand. If I sit it means I only get a 180 view, and in an open space that's not good."

"Is there somewhere better you can suggest?"

"Maybe a coffee shop or café, where I can sit with my back to a wall and see the door."

"I know exactly the place. Let's go to Gelato Heaven. What do you think Cassie?"

"Yay! Ice cream on a weekday."

Drew couldn't help but smile. The child's naivete made her seem younger than her years.

The ice cream parlor and coffee shop was perfect for his purposes. She ordered a cone for Cassie and coffees for them both.

"I'll take mine big, strong, and black, I don't care what fancy name you give it," he told the server after Mrs. West specified a cortado.

"Right," she began, "are our cars bugged?"

"At the moment, I can't be sure, but to be on the safe side I suggest we behave as if they are. I've ordered a scanner so I can check."

"Cassie confessed to her midnight liaison with you, and she told me what you said. I'm grateful for the sensitive way you dealt with it. I understand her concerns and I haven't dismissed them, but the personal consequences if I get it wrong would be huge. That's part of the reason you're here. I'm happy for her to talk to you about things, but I'd prefer if I was kept in the loop."

"I understand, ma'am, and I agree."

"So any developments since we spoke yesterday?"

"Yes, a couple. Two in particular that concern me. One of the team is not who he's supposed to be."

"Which one is that?"

"Michael Maus. *Mouse.*"

"How do you mean?"

"Your contact sent me a mug shot and it doesn't match. Have you got a copy of the photo you were sent?"

"Sure, hold on." She tapped and swiped at her phone for a while. "Here." She handed him her phone.

"That's not the photo your contact sent me."

"So the résumés I've been given have been tampered with."

"Well, that one at least. Ask him to retransmit them to you."

"Okay what's the other thing troubling you?"

"The guy they sent to operate the control room today was changed at the last minute. I need to check that out."

"What on earth is going on Drew?"

"I don't know yet, ma'am, but I'm concerned that Santa Monica might not be the best place for you to be."

"You might be right; but can we give it a day or two before we up sticks and move though?"

"It's your decision, but I'll stay on the case. Let me know if and when you're ready and give me as much notice as possible. Also, don't tell anybody who doesn't need to know."

"I gather Cassie told you about her suspicion that Theo wants me dead."

"Yes ma'am."

"You're not commenting."

"At the moment, from where I stand, I see a lot of information that would lead me to suspect your husband, but that may just mean that it's what whoever is responsible wants people to think."

"I don't understand why he would want to do it though. We've been so happy, or I thought so, anyway. We have an unconventional relationship, but he was the only reason I got through the loss of my first husband and retained my sanity."

"Why can't we go back to England?" Cassie asked.

"We shouldn't abandon Theo until we're sure darling. It wouldn't be right. Drew will keep us safe; won't you Drew?"

"I'll do everything in my power, ma'am."

"Okay then sweetheart, let's go shopping. We need to buy Drew something suitable to wear if we have to take him places that need a suit."

"With respect, ma'am, I can buy my own clothes."

"I know that Drew, but if we need to travel to England, you can't fly first or business class in combat pants and a camouflage jacket. You'd stick out like a sore thumb."

"I guess so, but I have trouble finding clothes to fit."

"That's why we're going to a tailor. We'll go to Theo's. He'll know exactly what you need. Then we can get some lunch. That's okay, isn't it?."

"Yes, ma'am."

"Can I get some new sneakers, Mummy. These ones are getting tight."

"We'll do that first."

Choosing footwear for an eleven-year-old girl was outside Drew's world of experience and took longer than he could have imagined. He waited patiently, maintaining constant surveillance while Cassie tried on endless styles, eventually choosing two pairs.

"Where is this tailor, ma'am?"

"Santa Monica Boulevard, about two or three miles away."

"Would you mind if I picked up a package at Fed Ex before we went?"

"No problem. Birthday present from your girlfriend?" she teased.

"No, ma'am."

The shift from military to civilian life was going to be more difficult than he thought. In the army you know where you stand, you either did what you were told or told other people what to do, and when people you worked for spoke, you knew how to take it. He had been led to believe that Mrs. West was a timid spoiled widow needing reassurance and protection after an attempt on her and her family's lives, but there was clearly more to her than that. Anna West had an undefinable presence, a sharp intellect, and an unexpected confidence, albeit undermined by her current situation. She also had a wry sense of humor.

He collected his parcel and as soon as he was back in the car he ripped the packaging open, switched the scanning device on and waved it around. The device, which was no bigger than a pocket Maglite, immediately began to beep. He immediately turned it off again.

Anna looked at him with concern, but he shook his head reassuringly. Once they were out of the car outside the tailor's shop he silently indicated that he wanted to examine her purse. She handed it over and he waved the gadget over it and loud rapid beeps began and increased the closer it got to it.

"It's just a tracker like the one Volkov tried to put in my passport. It's not a listening device like the one in the car."

"Jesus Parker, these people are terrifying me. Take it out."

"I'd prefer to leave it in place for the moment, ma'am. If we remove it they'll know we're on to them. We can use it to misdirect them when the time is right. We can't avoid the car being tracked because there's a tracker built in, but we can control what we talk about while we're inside it. There will be bugs in the other cars as well I expect, so whoever is behind this has got someone somewhere monitoring all this. It takes money to do that."

"Mummy this is really scary."

"Miss Cassie, it would be much more dangerous if we didn't know it was happening. At the moment, they don't know we know. If we keep it like that, when the time comes we can use that information to give them the slip."

"You're very clever."

"I've been trained to do this. It's my job."

Drew had never been so embarrassed when he stood in the tailor's fitting room while his employer and her daughter supervised him being measured and trying on different jackets.

"Do you prefer to wear your gun as a sidearm sir, or use a shoulder holster?"

"I'd like the option to do either, if that's possible."

"Very good, sir. When would you require your suit, sir?"

"He needs two, one for daywear and something for more formal occasions," Anna interrupted, "I'll leave it to you to decide on the fabrics. And I'm sorry, but it's a bit of an emergency. Is there any way to have them ready by tomorrow? I'll pay whatever is necessary."

"I'm sure that can be arranged. There will be a 20% surcharge I'm afraid, and will mean there won't be an opportunity for a late fitting."

"No problem. If you could text me when they're ready. Can I settle up with you now?"

"Where to now ma'am?" Drew asked as they left the tailors.

"There's a nice little Italian place on Wilshire, I booked a table while you were choosing your suit."

When they pulled up outside the restaurant it turned out to be upmarket dining rather than the modest *nice little place* he'd led to expect. As Cassie stepped onto the sidewalk, Drew whispered to her, "Can you bring the bag with the sneakers with you please, miss."

Cassie looked puzzled but did as he asked.

The greeter met Anna like a long-lost friend. "Mrs. West, how lovely to see you again. It's been far too long."

"Thank you, Tony. Were you able to find us a table as I described?"

"It was no problem. One or two of our other distinguished guests have similar requirements."

They took their seats, Drew with his back to the wall and facing the door.

They took the menus that Tony handed them.

"San Pellegrino Orange for me and Cassie please Tony."

"And the same for me, thanks," Drew added.

As they looked through the menu, Anna asked, "What's the shoe bag business all about?"

"We're being followed, and I don't want him or whoever is tracking the little device in your purse to know where we're going next, so we're going to temporarily leave the bug here in Cassie's shoe bag, then come back for it."

"How do you know we're being followed?"

"I spotted him when we sat down on that seater thing at the mall. He's turned up everywhere we've been since. He's not very good at what he's doing, and as far as I can tell he's on his own. When we leave here I'm going to take a roundabout route and lose him."

"Won't they be able to find us with the vehicle tracker?"

"The standard fit trackers don't allow you to follow a car, only locate it where it is at a specific moment and logging on to the system takes time. I'm hoping by the time they realize we're off their radar, we'll have picked up the shoe bag and be on our way home."

"Okay."

"As you know, this is my first assignment as a CPO, but having me eat with you isn't what I've been trained to expect ma'am."

"This is my first experience of using a bodyguard and this is the way I'd prefer it to be. I don't want a trained monkey on a lead. I want someone by my side looking out for things I'm not qualified to spot or respond to. I want someone with whom I can build a relationship based on mutual trust and respect, so unless it's going to cause you undue difficulties, can we carry on like this?"

"Of course, ma'am."

"Okay, what are you going to eat?"

"I don't know what half these things are. Bruschetta is bread isn't it?"

"That's right."

"I'll have two of them then if that's okay."

"Fine, what are you going to have after?"

"I've had spaghetti carbonara before. I like that."

"Okay, what about you, Cassie?"

"Can I have prosciutto with melon, Mummy, with the chicken ravioli to follow, please."

"That's a good choice sweetheart, I'll have the same."

When the waiter brought the drinks, Anna told him their orders.

"Can I get a couple of steak sandwiches, on the side with that spaghetti, hold the potato salad and coleslaw?"

Cassie's eyes opened wide. "Are you going to eat two steak sandwiches as well as spaghetti?"

"In the army they teach you to eat and sleep when you can because you never know when you'll be able to next, and I skipped breakfast this morning. Things seem to be happening at a pace around here at the moment. I need to keep myself fueled up. I don't eat dessert."

"Did you learn to do all this bodyguard stuff in the army?" The young girl asked.

"A lot of it, but after I left a did some special training. Most of it is common sense if you treat every day like somebody is out to get you, even if they aren't."

"I thought that soldiers just fired guns or drove tanks."

"There are lots of things soldiers do these days as well as that. Some fly helicopters, some operate drones and missile controls, there are doctors, nurses, cooks, radar operators, weather forecasters, engineers and intelligence specialists, as well as the tank drivers…the list goes on - but all of them have to know how to use their basic weapons and how to fight. The army does other things too. It provides help to poor countries, if there's a famine or disaster. The same in this country."

"Wow, I didn't know any of that. What did you do?"

"I was a bit of an oddball; I did a bit of everything."

"Why did you leave?"

"I decided it was time I got to spend time with people, ones whose job isn't just to hurt other people."

"Do you like being a bodyguard?"

"Well you and your family are the first bodies I've got to guard, and I like that, so I'm optimistic."

"Are you going to leave us then when the bad people have been caught?"

"I'll stay as long as I'm needed."

"Have you got a girlfriend?"

"Cassie, that's a bit personal," Anna said. "Sorry."

"It's okay, ma'am. No, not at the moment."

"Where do you come from?" Anna asked.

"Bridgeville Delaware originally. Me and my sister were mostly raised in North Carolina by my grandparents after our pop ran off and our mom died."

"That's really sad," Cassie said.

"I guess, but I was too young to remember. Our grandparents have both passed now. My sister Carolina lives in Wilmington with her husband and their son."

"How old is she?"

"Three years older than me; thirty-six."

"Have you got lots of friends from the army?" Cassie asked after their entrees arrived.

"Not really, it wasn't the kind of unit where you did a lot of socializing. Most of the guys and girls only stayed four or five years tops, but as I said I'm an oddball, and I was in the unit for ten years."

"You must have enjoyed it," Anna remarked.

"A lot of the time yeah, and I guess I was good at it. That makes it easier."

"I'll be your friend, Drew." Cassie assured him.

"That's nice, Miss Cassie. Thank you."

She smiled.

"I need to use the washroom, Mummy."

"You know where it is. Will you be okay on your own? Would that be alright do you think, Drew?"

"I've kept an eye out since we've been in here. She should be okay, there's nobody in there at the moment."

"I don't know what you've done to my daughter, Mr. Parker, but that's the longest conversation I've heard her have since the hijack."

"She's a nice kid."

"Yes she is, isn't she? How do you go about losing our tail? I'd rather not get involved in a high-speed car chase."

"That won't be necessary this morning. I'll tell you what I want you to do when Cassie gets back."

"Do?"

"Nothing complicated or dangerous, just enough so that we're all singing from the same hymn sheet when the time comes."

Cassie returned to the table.

"Do you want dessert sweetie?"

"No thank you, Mummy. What are we doing now?"

"No dessert. Lord it's a miracle."

"Drew doesn't eat dessert and anyway I had ice cream earlier."

"Parenting by example from an army vet; who knew?"

Drew was feeling awkward with the personal conversation so changed the subject. "If you decide you want to relocate in a hurry, you should make sure you have plenty of cash, because you may need to disguise your destination, at least temporarily."

"I have $10,000 I can put my hands on at short notice."

"That should be enough, but I have another suggestion for your long-term security. It's a bit radical so I'll understand if you think it's too much."

"What is it?"

"Having yourselves chipped."

"You mean like a dog or cat?"

"Kinda. Slightly different, you can't trace an animal by its chip, but the ones I'm suggesting would allow either of you to be located anywhere in the world. The technology has been around for quite a while now and it's perfectly safe."

"Who could trace us though?"

"Only those with the right software and authority granted by you."

"Who would do it?"

"You would need someone you have complete trust in to arrange it. I doubt it can be arranged overnight."

"I'll get my PA to look into it. Where do they put it?"

"I think there are different options, wrist is common, but back of the neck or butt cheeks have been used I think."

Cassie giggled.

"When we're in the car I'm going to take a long route to our next stop, and when we're in an appropriate place I'm going stop suddenly, get out and speak to the fellow and discourage him from taking any further interest in our activities today."

"How will we know when you're going to stop?"

"I'll say, *I'm glad it's stopped raining.* Then ten seconds later I'll brake hard, so make sure your seatbelts are tight and brace yourselves. First though ma'am, hand me your purses."

Anna handed it over, and in seconds he located the bug in the lining, Cassie's didn't have one. He put the small device inside one of Cassie's new shoes.

Signaling the waiter that she wanted to settle up. She handed over her card and said, "Would you do me a small favor? It's a silly little thing but it will be a great help."

"Of course madam, whatever you want."

"If you could look after my daughter's new shoes, for a little while and we'll collect them in an hour or two."

"Absolutely no problem madam. I'll leave them behind the greeter's stand."

"Thank you so much."

"Where are we going?" Anna asked before they got in the car.

"I'm going to visit the guy from the alarm company who was supposed to operate the system today but didn't turn up."

They got in the car and Drew took the follower on a merry little trip, signaling late whenever he turned, encouraging him to close up, when they reached an open stretch of road where there was little traffic and few people, he said, "I'm glad it's stopped raining."

Then he accelerated slightly before braked so harshly that the guy behind him locked wheels to avoid rear-ending them. Drew leapt out of the car went straight to the other guy's door, whipped it open, and grabbed him by the scruff of his neck. He didn't wait for the man to speak. He just hit him hard on the nose.

"Who are you and what do you want?"

"You broke my nose you asshole."

"Shut up and answer my question or I'll break a few more bones."

"Fuck off."

Drew spotted his right-hand reach for his pocket, so he pulled him out of the vehicle viciously twisted his arm behind his back, dislocating his shoulder joint and tearing his rotator cuff muscles and causing him to scream in agony. The gun he'd been reaching for clattered to the ground. Dragging him back to his feet and holding him against the car with one hand, Drew quickly frisked him and found his cellphone and wallet, read his ID and then put both items in his own pocket. He waited until the man recovered sufficiently and said, "So Eric Johannsen, you gonna answer my questions now, or do I have to fuck you up a bit more?"

"Okay, okay. The guy told me to follow you wherever you went and report back to him."

"Me or the lady?"

"He said you."

"What guy?"

"Said his name was Steve."

"What'd he look like?"

"Skinny guy with a scar down the side of his nose."

"His number in your phone?"

"Yeah the last one dialed."

"Where'd you meet him?"

"In a bar in West LA."

"He pay you?"

"Gave me a hundred bucks. Said he'd give me another hundred if I did it right."

Drew let him go, reached in his own pocket and took out two hundred-dollar bills. "Take this. If I ever see your ugly face again, what just happened will seem like an affectionate kiss. Are we clear?"

"I got it."

"This your car?"

"Yeah."

"Okay I'll leave the keys then."

Taking the guy's phone out, Drew memorized the last number and then dialed 911. "Fire department medic. A guy here's been beat up pretty bad, got a broken nose and a busted arm, looks of things. Old Ranch Road LA." Then hung up before he could be asked any questions.

"I'm not expecting you to remember anything about who I am, my car, or why you were here. Do we understand each other?"

"Yeah, I got it."

"That's good because I have your name and address, Eric, and I have a very good memory."

He picked up the gun with his handkerchief, pushed it into a nearby storm drain along with the guy's phone, and climbed back in their car.

"Sorry about that."

Anna was about to speak but he put his finger to his lips, and headed to Raoul's address, hoping he'd be at home.

Eleven

Leaving his charges in the car, Drew crossed the street to Raoul's apartment. It was a scruffy little place above a neighborhood drug store, he walked up the steps and knocked. There was no reply so he knocked again.

"Raoul, I'm Mrs. Lemonis' personal protection officer. You didn't turn up for work today. I'd like to know why."

"Go away. I not talkin' to anybody about it."

"Just tell me if someone paid you not to turn up."

"I not sayin' anythin' to anybody."

"What if I shove a couple of hundred bucks under the door? I've got Mrs. Lemonis and her daughter in the car. Would you prefer if they were here. She's frightened for her safety. We ain't going to mention anything you say."

"If they come up here, I'll talk."

"Okay," he went downstairs and asked if they would help persuade Raoul to talk, and Anna agreed.

"Who was the man in the car though?" she asked.

"Somebody paid by Gates to follow me."

The three of them gathered outside Raoul's door, and he eventually agreed to open it.

The man had been savagely beaten. One eye was completely closed, and there was a long line of stitches down one side of his face. One arm was in plaster from above the elbow to the wrist, and the other hand was wrapped in thick bandages.

"Oh my God, you poor man. Who did this to you?" Anna asked.

"I don't know their names; one was an enormous black man about his size and the other one was white, a bit taller than you Senora, and he had scar on the side of his nose."

"Did they say why?"

"The white man asked me not to turn up. I tell him in the security industry we only take orders from boss. Then he offer me hundred bucks not to turn in for work today. I tell him fuck off, and they beat me up real bad. Black guy cut two of my fingers off and say if I tell police or anybody else he come back and cut off rest."

"We won't tell them we've been here, but both of them will be too busy to worry about anything you might or not say after the next day or two, so if you want to tell the police go ahead. The black guy is called Otis something, and the other's name is Gates."

"I not say anything to anybody ever."

"I'm so sorry for what you've suffered just for trying to do your job," Anna told him.

"It not your fault, Senora. You not send them?"

"No, but they came because they're plotting something against me." She place a handful of banknotes on his coffee table and they left.

Outside, Drew turned to Cassie, "Do you have a cellphone that can take photos?"

"Yes."

"Sometime after we get back can you take a photo of the guy that calls himself Mickey? If you manage to do that, next time you're near me, Bluetooth it to my phone. You've got the number, I take it."

"I can do that."

"These bastards, whoever they are, are evil. I've got to get us away from here," Anna said, before they got back in the car."

"I think you're right, but I don't want them to know about our travel arrangements. I'll jot some instructions on a piece of paper and slip it to you when we're not under observation."

They drove home in silence, stopping on the way to pick up Cassie's shoes.

Back at the Lemonis home a subdued Anna and Cassie returned to the family room.

The first thing Drew did was check the log. There was nothing in it.

"Are you trying to tell me that nothing happened here the whole day?" he said to Otis.

"It's been a quiet day."

"You haven't made a single entry; you haven't even recorded when we went out or returned."

"Nothing happened. Didn't seem a lotta point."

"What do you think you're here for?"

"In case anything happens or goes wrong."

"Incorrect. You have only one function here and that is to watch and record anything and everything that happens here, and if something happens that even resembles an emergency you are to sound the alarm. Nothing else. You are not qualified, capable, or authorized to do anything else. Is that clear?"

"Don't get your panties in a twist soldier boy, you ain't my boss."

Drew picked up a piece of paper from the desk with the alarm company's contact details and punched the number into the phone and put it on speaker: *Hollywood and LA Security Systems.*

"My name is Drew Parker. I'm lead personal protection officer at the Lemonis residence, I need to speak to the day supervisor as a matter of urgency."

"Certainly, sir, hold the line."

"Ain't no need to do that. I'll record your fucking movements if it keeps you happy."

Drew ignored him and stepped out of the room.

"Alan Anka, Branch Manager speaking, can I help you?"

"Good Afternoon Mr. Anka, I'm sorry to have to report that we have a problem with one of your employees."

"I'm sorry to hear that Mr. Parker, who's the employee, and what's the problem?"

"The guy's name is Otis something, he's neglected his duties all day and he's insolent."

"We don't have an employee called Otis, are you sure you're calling the right number?"

"He turned up here today claiming to be a stand in for Raoul."

"I don't know who he is but he doesn't work for us. Call the police and I'll be right over. I'll be there in thirty minutes."

"I'll do that." He dialed 911 and reported an armed intrusion at the Lemonis address.

Walking back to the control room Drew pulled the gun from the holster at his waist, "Stand over there."

"Fuck off whitey and put that gun away or I'll take it off you and shove it up your skinny white ass. I'm leaving now anyway."

"No you aren't. You're an unauthorized intruder. If you try to leave I'll put a bullet in you."

The imposter's hand shot out and grabbed the barrel of the gun, but to his surprise Drew just released his grip on it. A wide grin spread across Otis' face as he turned the gun on Drew, "Not such a smart ass anymore then soldier boy, eh?"

"You think?"

"This says that you ain't."

"Put a bullet in him Otis." Gates said coming from behind Drew having not seen the first part of the encounter.

Drew put his hand behind him to pull the other gun tucked into his belt under his jacket.

Otis grinned and pulled the trigger resulting only in a click, he pumped another round into the chamber and the same thing happened. Before he could repeat the exercise Drew took two steps across the room and pistol whipped the thug, dropping him senseless to the floor.

"I guess you thought it would be my gun to misfire then Gates eh. I wonder why that is."

"I'll put you six feet under before this is over, Parker, you fucking smart-ass piece of shit. You got no team loyalty."

"I'm sorry, I thought our loyalty was supposed to be the people paying our wages. Do you have other ideas?"

"The Lemonis family are paying but they're not who's pulling the strings."

"Oh really. Who is then. I'm curious."

The sound of police sirens interrupted them.

"Did you call the cops, you stupid asshole."

Mickey rushed to the control room door. "There's two cop cars coming down the road..." Then seeing the unconscious crook on the floor; "What the hell's happened here?"

Drew pressed the button to open the gate and the patrol cars screeched to a halt on the driveway spilling their occupants, all with drawn weapons.

"That's what I'd like to know Mickey."

The cops spread out around the property. One appeared behind Mickey. "Get round the side of the garage Benny. Call for back up and get an ambulance."

"Arrest this guy Officer," Gates shouted. "He attacked this man without any provocation."

"Shut the fuck up," the cop demanded, his gun covering the three of them. Mickey had stepped away and was holding his hands out to indicate he presented no threat. "All of you lay your weapons on the floor and step out here without touching a fucking thing."

The cops were a professional team, who worked with each other day in and day out. They efficiently took complete control of the situation and calmed things down.

Drew led the way by laying his on the ground, stepping over Otis while holding his hands to the sides in a similar manner to Mickey. Gates followed suit.

"Officer there's woman and child inside, probably scared out of their wits, and without a clue as to what's going on. Also I should tell you that I have another gun strapped to my ankle."

"Okay buddy, very, very slowly and carefully bend down, remove the holster and kick it over here. Are they the only people inside?"

"As far as I know. I haven't had time to check, although there could be domestic staff here too," Drew told him.

"What about you two, you got any idea?" They both confirmed that it was only Anna and Cassie.

"Benny go and let the lady know that it's all under control,' he said as another car pulled into the drive.

Within fifteen minutes there were two more patrol cars, an ambulance and two detectives, one of whom was Sergeant Perez from the previous day."

They listened to everybody except Otis. He'd been taken to hospital under police guard. During the process Lemonis and Pavel had returned, their arrival following hot on the heels of Alan Anka, who looked on in horror.

Theo immediately tried to intervene and direct operations but the lead detective merely listened politely and then asked, "Mr. Lemonis, you live here right?"

"Yes, of course."

"And I guess you're anxious to find out exactly went on."

"That's right."

"Then I suggest you go comfort your wife and child and leave us to do our job."

"I want to hear exactly what happened."

"And so you will, when me and my colleagues have determined what that was."

"No, I insist on staying and finding out for myself."

"Once again Mr. Lemonis please go…"

"Do you realize who you're talking to?"

"I know exactly who I'm talking to. Now if you don't leave us to get on with our jobs, I'll book you for obstruction and put you in one of these patrol cars in cuffs. Have you got it now?"

"You'll be hearing from my lawyer."

"I'm breathless in anticipation."

Theo disappeared into the house.

"Right you so-called security professionals, I've got three conflicting accounts of what went on here, and we've got a man in hospital, possibly with serious head injuries. Any of you got anything to add to your stories that might stop me hauling all of you down to the station and locking you in a cell until somebody tells me the truth?"

"If it helps Sergeant, the whole incident is probably on film and tape, including my call to Mr. Anka over there."

"He's lying, detective, playing for time."

"What's your name again?"

"Gates."

"I met you here the other morning, didn't I? You were being an obstructive asshole then too, so why don't you shut the fuck up and we'll find out if Parker is lying or not. Then we'll all know, won't we? Show me this film then, Parker.

Drew led him back into the control room and opened the webcam software on the computer that he'd installed. After winding the recording back to about the time, he and the family had returned, he pressed play.

The webcam angle wasn't the best it could have been, but it was good enough to capture most of the activity including sound. It was more than adequate to corroborate Drew's account of things.

"Well Mr. Gates it turns out Mr. Parker wasn't lying after all. Cuff him, Baldwin."

Completely unexpectedly Gates made a break for it and was over the wall into the property at the back of the Lemonis' before anybody could stop him.

"Fuck. Get after him you two,' the detective shouted superfluously after the two patrol officers who were already on the move. "Baldwin, cuff this other guy. What's your name again? Maus did you say? What you said was a pile of horseshit as well."

Mickey quietly allowed the cop to put the cuffs on him and put him in the back of a patrol car.

The detective turned to Drew, "Did you say you've got a voice recording of that as well?"

"Yes on my phone. I haven't listened to it yet, but it should be okay." He pulled out his phone and played it from the start and it was soon obvious that it was identical to the video. Can you email me that recording and the video?"

"Sure, give me the address."

The detective handed him a card. It took a few minutes to gather the two files and attach them to emails, but the detective nodded when his phone pinged notifying him of their arrival.

"What's going on here, Parker?" The cop asked, "There's altogether too many fatal or life-threatening incidents around this family and I don't accept it's a coincidence. In this neck of the woods there are more self-entitled millionaire assholes than you can shake a stick at and they don't impress me anymore, but that don't mean I'm happy to see them dead."

Drew spent the next twenty minutes giving Perez a full account of events, omitting the bugging, the business of the tail, his visit to Fernandez, and his suspicions about Lemonis and Mickey Maus.

"At the moment, I'm not entirely sure who's behind it or what the motive is but in my opinion, there's a concerted effort to endanger the family; whether it's the whole family or the just the wife and child I don't know. I've had my suspicions about Gates from the first day, and I'm certain Volkov is crooked, but Lemonis is supporting him at the moment. Fortunately Mrs. West insisted that she doesn't want him anywhere near her and he's been moved to other duties."

"You sure were one lucky son of a bitch when that gun misfired, but I don't understand why you took the chance that it wouldn't fire the next time, you could easily and justifiably put a round or two in him.

"I knew it wouldn't fire. That was the gun that Gates provided me with when we started the op. It had been messed with. That's why I was carrying another gun. I didn't kill him because there's no point killing people just for the sake of it. As it was he went down harder than I intended."

"I think so. He's still unconscious. We've identified him as Otis Williams, aka *The Crush*. He's a gangbanger from South LA. So, you dismantled the slide of a new gun. That's damned thorough. You always do that?"

"I'm still alive ain't I? Can I pick up my own weapons now?"

"Go ahead. We'll hang on to the one Williams was holding. By the way, what was that Gates said about the Lemonis family not pulling the strings?"

"That was a surprise to me too, and I've no idea what it means. Mrs. West is paying for the security team, and believes she's in charge. Obviously Gates thought differently or perhaps he's being paid by someone else as well."

"You're a lot cooler than I'd have been in this situation. Where did you do your close-protection training? Your methods don't look commercial."

"Special Service Academy, Maryland."

"Is that what you did before. I saw that your license was new."

"No, nearly thirteen years army. Someone who owed me a favor got me in there."

"Right, stay here while I talk to the family."

He was gone for about five minutes before Lemonis summoned Drew to join them. When he did Alan Anka was already there.

"I asked Detective Perez to include you in the conversation, Parker. It will save going over things more than once. Is that okay?"

"Sure, good idea, Mr. Lemonis."

"So this Otis guy, if that's his real name, was working with Gates by the looks of things. Where is Raoul Fernandez then, if Otis took his place?" Lemonis asked.

"I don't know." Anka replied.

Perez stepped in. "I've sent a car to his home to find out.".

Drew's phone vibrated. He quickly glanced at it to see a request to accept a file from Cassie via Bluetooth. He accepted it, looked up and winked at the young girl, who gleamed with pride at have completed her undercover assignment.

One of the patrol officers entered and whispered something to Perez.

"Mr. Lemonis, there's a Mr. Stamelis outside; says he's your PA. Is that right."

"That's right Sergeant. Could you allow him in. He'll be invaluable in helping to sort this out. What's happening with Gates?"

"They're still searching the area, but it's looking like he got away."

"For God's sake Perez, can't you people do anything right? He could be dangerous."

"To answer your question, Mr. Lemonis, we weren't the ones who hired a team of random security people, half of whom seem to be acting against you. We had no reason to suspect that your head security guy was anything other than that. Do you want to explain who was responsible for that? Don't get me wrong though, you can hire anyone you want to protect you; just don't get too surprised if you wake up dead one morning."

Lemonis was obviously furious at being so humiliatingly put down in front of his family and Drew, but there was little in anything Perez had said for him to argue with.

"Ah Manos, thank God you're here," Lemonis greeted his dour PA, "Sergeant Perez was just asking how our security team were selected."

"I acted on advice from our previous head of security, Rupert Loughty. He advised that Paul Gates was the best man for the job, so I asked him to establish a team and make certain they'd been fully vetted. I thought I was acting in the most prudent way. Of course I regret if my actions put the family in danger in any way at all. Mr. Loughty had been excellent in his post, and I'm surprised that his advice on this occasion fell short. We must be thankful that it didn't result in a tragic outcome."

"I'm sure Mr. Lemonis and his family are grateful for that even if they have been unnecessarily put in harm's way. I don't know what charges if any we'll be able to bring against Otis Williams," Perez said, looking at his phone, "but I've just received a message to say that Raoul Fernandez, who was to have been your on-site alarm system operator today, has just been found with his throat cut. If this is in anyway connected to the events here then, I doubt this will be the last you hear of this, and the non-tragic outcome you spoke of would clearly not be the case."

Cassie was very obviously distressed by the latest news and went to her mom for comfort.

"There's one thing you can be grateful for, and that's that you managed to recruit at least one person who knows what he's doing; Mr. Parker here. Although whether it was by luck or judgement remains to be seen. If Fernandez's murder is suspected to be by Gates or someone else connected to this place you can expect a visit from SMPD Robbery/Homicide detectives. I'll leave you to it now."

As he turned to leave the room, Drew said, "Sergeant, there's something else you should know."

"What is it?"

"Earlier today, I visited Fernandez to try to find out why he was a no show this morning. He had been severely beaten up and had two fingers cut off. At first he wouldn't talk about it, but after a lot of buttering up I managed to convince him to tell me what happened. He told me that two people who matched the descriptions of Gates and Williams had tried to bribe him to stay away. When he refused, they beat him up so badly he was terrified for his life. He made me promise not to say anything to anybody. I agreed but there's no point in holding my silence now."

"You got anybody can support that?"

"Yes Sergeant, me."

"What! You took my wife into a criminal's apartment?"

"He wasn't a criminal, there was nothing to suggest he was, and he needed to be convinced to talk. Given the circumstances, the information I had, and the sheer volume of suspicious things that have been happening, I assessed the risk as negligible and the benefits as potentially important. That turned out to be right; it enabled me to identify Williams and Gates as bad actors."

"Tell me what happened Mrs. West."

"We had been out and on the way back Mr. Parker asked if we could stop at Mr. Fernandez's house and explained the reason why. Cassandra and I waited in the car while Mr. Parker went inside. A short while later, Mr. Parker returned and explained that Mr. Fernandez needed to be persuaded, and I offered to speak to him. In the end he reluctantly agreed to speak to us, but when we went inside we were horrified to see the extent of his injuries and understood why he was so concerned that Gates and Williams might return, justifiably it seems."

"Okay, I'll accept that for now, my colleagues in RHD may have a different view, but I want you both to come to the station in the morning to make a statement."

"That's fine Sergeant, we'll be there."

"Will you see me out, Mr. Parker?"

When they reached the cop's car, Perez turned to him. "Listen to me Parker, you may be a shit hot bodyguard, but you ain't a detective. It ain't your job to be investigating crimes. A lot of cops would have you in cuffs by now for interfering with a police investigation, but I've seen your sheet, and my gut feeling tells me you're straight up and my gut is rarely wrong. However if I find out that you're fucking me around you're gonna find yourself in a tsunami of shit, you understand?"

"I've got it, Sergeant."

"You need to watch out for yourself and that family. Something ain't right here. I just don't know what it is."

"My thoughts exactly."

The cop drove away, and Drew gathered his thoughts. Guarding Mrs. West and Cassie on his own while there were so many unanswered questions was risky to say the least. He was left with only Frenchie,

Mockingbird, Priest and Mac and as of now the guy that had recruited them was on the run. Having sent Cassie's photo of Mickey to his contact he had to wait for them to learn more about him, if he could.

He turned away to see Alan Anka talking to one of the two remaining patrolmen. He went over to speak to him. "Mr. Anka?" he offered his hand. "Drew Parker. Sorry we haven't had time to speak. I've just been told about your Mr. Fernandez. I'm sorry for your loss."

"Mr. Parker, I'm devastated. Raoul was one of our most trusted employees. Manning a security desk isn't a service we normally provide, but when Mr. Gates phoned and asked us to help out, I agreed to try and find volunteers because the Lemonis family have been good clients. I'm afraid it won't be able to carry on after this. We'll continue to service our normal maintenance contract of course."

"I completely understand, Mr. Anka. Once again I'd like to express my regrets, but I should tell you that at the moment Gates is a person of interest in his murder."

"Oh God, this is awful, and I could lose my job over this. I need to speak to my manager."

Drew left him alone and rejoined the family in the day room. He knocked on the open door and Lemonis summoned him in with a wave of his hand.

"It looks like your intervention might have averted yet another unfortunate event, so thank you."

"It's my job, sir."

"I can't say I approve of taking my wife and daughter on an investigative jaunt though."

"I didn't feel I had any other choice. There've been far too many suspicious activities and I wasn't sure who I could trust. In fact I'm still not. All the team members were recruited by Gates, and he told me himself that he only came to me because others weren't available. I have thoughts about that, but I'm making my own enquiries about the others, and hope to get the results in the near future."

"Very good, Parker. I'm grateful. If there is any cost to you then Manos will see that you are fully reimbursed."

"That leads me to the other question. Until now everyone except me has been employed via Gates. Now he's out of the picture, presuming they want to stay, they'll need to know who they're working for, how much they're being paid, and what their duties are."

"Perhaps you would be willing to take them on."

"Mr. Lemonis, this is my first job since leaving the army. I'm not ready to be an employer. I may never be, but I'm happy to lead the security detail. That's what I'm trained for."

"Manos could you arrange to take the others on, those that Mr. Parker has given his seal of approval to that is?" Drew noted the slight hint of sarcasm in his voice.

"No problem, sir. Let me know as soon as you've spoken to whoever you need to then Parker, and to them of course."

"Thanks, Manos."

He was clearly unhappy about being addressed by his first name, but Drew couldn't give a shit.

Anna called him over, "We haven't had time to talk about your conditions of employment yet, Parker. Perhaps we could go to the lounge and talk right now. Before you get involved in anything else that is."

"I guess I could spare a minute while the cops are still here, but there's no hurry as far as I'm concerned, I'm happy to continue on the same terms as before."

"Nevertheless, let's get it out of the way."

She led the way to the living room with Cassie and Drew following behind and closed the door when they were all inside. He tapped her on the shoulder, held a finger to his lips, and began to sweep the room with his bug detector. It came up clean.

"I don't want to discuss your terms of employment Drew; I just want to get the hell out of here and I want to know how best to go about it."

"I haven't had time to make the list I spoke of but it's straightforward. You need to get your PA in England to book you four tickets from LAX to Tacoma for as early as possible the day after tomorrow, that's one each for you, Cassie, Judith, and me. You also need him to book three tickets from LAX to Heathrow or Gatwick at roughly the same time or very shortly after if possible, for just you, Miss Cassie and me.

"Judith won't fly to the UK. She'll be carrying the tracker from your bag. If she's willing she can follow when you're ready. That morning we'll take a cab to the airport and fly to our various destinations. The Brits have very strict gun control laws, and of course I won't be able to carry weapons to fly, but I will need a UK work visa and close-body protection license. If your guy can arrange that, it would be great."

"While we're about it, what about your pay and conditions?"

"I guess your guy knows what I was being paid before. If you just copy that it will be fine."

"I was thinking of a substantial raise."

"I'm already getting double what I did in the army. I'm okay with that."

"To use a British expression, that's bollocks. In your job you need to have a nest egg in case the worst happens. As of today you are on thirty thousand a month plus pension and healthcare, and I don't want an argument."

"Mummy! That's a really naughty word."

"I know, sweetie, I'm sorry. I'll try not to say it again."

"What's it mean anyway?"

"It's a boy cow that can't make babies, but that's a conversation for another day."

Drew smiled. "Nice recovery ma'am. Will that be all?"

"Of course, thank you."

"It doesn't mean that at all, does it?" Cassie was saying as Drew walked out the door.

On his way to the control room he received a text from his contact saying to expect a call in five. When it came, the information it provided couldn't have been more unexpected.

"F.B.I.! You're kidding me. Why, how?"

"They're not saying much, but they're keeping an eye on Lemonis and his buddy Stamelis. I suspect they think there's Russian involvement. If I was asked to make a wild guess it would be that Anna is seen as an obstacle to a merger between NorArm and Silico. If I'm right they couldn't be confident of achieving their aims without getting rid of Cassandra at the same time. As of now she is Anna's sole heir of note."

"Are you saying that Anna and Cassie are both being targeted by Theo?"

"At present I can't be certain that Theo is involved, or if he is, to what extent. I think it's possible the Russians may have some sort of hold over him."

"Why is it so important for them to get their hands on Silico?"

"I can't go into that but rest assured, what Silico has to offer is quite revolutionary."

"What can you tell me about the rest of the team?"

Well from Anna's verification, they are all who they say they are at least, but I can't comment on their loyalty.

"Great. Thanks for that, I think."

"Good luck, we're relying on you."

What the fuck? he thought after ending the call. *I didn't sign up to be a spook, I'm supposed to be a bodyguard. Well fuck 'em, I'll just concentrate on protecting Mrs. West and Cassie, nothing's going to happen to them on my watch if I can help it.*

The sense of right and wrong developed from the seeds sown by his grandparents, together with his strong bullshit filter, and the low asshole tolerance threshold he'd developed in Delta had kicked in.

He called the other four team members and without going into details asked them to immediately come to the house for an urgent meeting because Gates was now out of the picture.

The last of the cops were leaving when Frenchie, Priest, Mac, and Mockingbird arrived in a cab. He gathered in the garage and to their astonishment and outrage explained the events of earlier in the day.

"What the fuck, Parker?" Mac demanded, "Are you saying we've been working for a rat the whole time we've been here?"

"That's what it looks like."

"I don't believe it, Gates was always a weird bastard, but I can't believe he'd do something like that," Priest said.

"Why though?" Frenchie demanded.

"Money I expect," Drew told them. "It's usually money. I've never had a beef with him. I hardly knew him before he contacted me for this job. We ran into each other on a couple of ops in the past that's all."

"What did he hope to achieve?" Mockingbird asked.

"The family's theory is that there's someone, they don't know who, out to kill some or all of them. The motive is unclear, but it's linked to the hijack a few months ago."

"Where's Mickey?"

"He got cuffed and taken to the cop house…"

"That's it. This is bullshit. There's no way Mickey is bent," Priest insisted.

"Did you serve with Gates?"

"Gates? Yeah once in 'Stan, and again on Operation Black Swan. He's good people."

"Maybe if you let me…"

"Fuck you…"

"As I was trying to say if you'll stop shootin' your mouth off for two seconds Priest, the cops cleared Mouse and are letting him go. He'll be back in a minute."

"Okay, I guess that's alright then. I still don't believe that shit about Gates."

"If I show you the video, would that help?"

"There's a video?"

"It's on the computer in the control room.' He led them into the small room and played the film.

"The douchebag told that asshole to kill you." Mockingbird couldn't believe it. "Lucky your gun misfired though.

"It wasn't luck. It had been rigged not to fire."

"What're you talking about?"

"Remember the day Gates told us to pick our weapons from the bag, and how they were all in the hold-all marked with our names? That was the gun he had marked up for me. It had the wrong spacer sleeve - it wouldn't ever fire."

"And you discovered that?" Frenchie asked.

"I spotted that the slider cap had been messed with. I thought that was odd so I completely stripped it down and found the slider sleeve had been changed. I suggest you all do the same thing if you haven't already."

"I already did mine," Mockingbird confirmed. "It was okay."

"Me too," Mac added.

"You happy now then Priest?"

"I guess."

"Have you checked your weapon?"

"I did a field strip; seemed okay."

"Give it here. I'll show you what made me suspicious."

He tentatively handed it over. Drew took it. "Thanks Eli. Now you can fuck off, and if I see you again, it better be the back of your head walking away."

"What..."

"Now what the fuck is going on, Parker?" Frenchie asked.

"This piece of shit is out of shape too. Gates wasn't on Operation Black Swan. It was exclusively a Delta op, so neither were you, Priest. The SAS wouldn't have been anywhere near it. What's more nobody that was on it would ever mention it again. That's right, isn't it, Priest? Like you would know?"

"You smart ass, Parker. I'll fuck you up next time I see you."

"If you say so, but my generosity of spirit only lasts so long, so you'd better be gone from here soon or I'll get the cops to collect you. I'll open the gate."

Mac hadn't said a lot up to then. "What the fuck is happening, Parker? This was supposed to be a straightforward bodyguard job with good pay. Now it turns out we're neck deep in some kind of conspiracy."

"I'm hoping that's the last of it now, but either way we'll have to manage with just us, and Mickey - that's if he doesn't throw his toys out of the buggy, for getting arrested."

"How did they hope to get away with it?"

"My guess would be that at a time of their choosing they'd make their move and pin the blame on one or more of us, after the stunt with my gun, I think I was the patsy they had lined up.

"In the meantime, your six months contract will transfer to Mr. Lemonis. Stamelis will be in touch about that. I'll be nominal team leader, although I'll be employed by Mrs. Lemonis and will travel with her when necessary. Mockingbird, if that happens I'd like for you to take over as leader. Any questions?"

Nobody spoke.

"Right then you ugly bastards, onwards and upwards. Mac can you and Frenchie take tonight's shift as originally planned. I'll spell each one of you for half an hour between three and four."

Mickey returned about eight p.m. and knocked on Drew's door. "Those cops, what a bunch of assholes. What the fuck made them think I was hooked up with Gates?"

"I don't know Mickey. Maybe it was because what you told them at first was, how did Perez put it, *a pile of horseshit*? Why the fuck didn't you just say it like it was?"

"I didn't know what was happening did I? I was just trying to run interference against whoever it was that was acting in bad faith."

"Let's go outside where we can talk and be sure of not being overheard." He led the way and stopped by the cabana. "You can cut the crap now Mickey, I know you're a fed."

"What…How did you know that, did the cops tell…?"

"Never mind how I know, I just do. I don't know why you're here, although I think I could make a pretty good guess, but we're on the same side and we need to be working together. My only job is to keep to Mrs. West and her kid safe, and one way or another that's gotta be in your interests too. I just need you to understand that if you get in my way or in any way put their lives at risk then I'll walk right through you, and I don't give a fuck who you're working for."

"Jesus, Parker; okay I got it. Keeping her alive is part of my remit, but I also need to find out who's orchestrating this. There's a chance it could be Lemonis himself, motivated by greed. On the other hand he could know nothing and it could all be Stamelis. We're pretty sure he has a strong influence over his boss. If Lemonis were to be widowed then Manos would likely be persuading him to do whatever is in the interests of whoever he's really working for."

"Who's he working for?"

"There's the thing, he's working for the Russians."

"Why not just pick him up?"

"Because the stuff he's been leaking so far is low-grade control software that we're not concerned about, until we've determined if Lemonis is involved."

"I don't understand why they're so anxious to kill off Mrs. West though?"

"Earlier this year, Lemonis and his wife changed their wills to be reciprocal, so that they each leave the other the majority of their estate. Anna would get practically everything, or Theo would get her entire holding in Silico, and Cassandra would get everything else. It's not like for like because the value of her Silico holdings outweigh his entire estate by two or three times…"

"So why now?"

"Because Silico has just produced a groundbreaking new type of chip specifically designed for military use, if it were used with the most recent tank and drone software that NorArm are producing it would revolutionize battlefield warfare. If the companies were merged there could be little to prevent it falling into the wrong hands. The US and UK governments need to stop that happening."

"Okay I think I've got it now, but I can't get involved in any of that. My priority will stay with my two principals."

"That's okay, but don't blow my cover or us Feebies will hang you out to dry."

"Are you working alone?"

"I'm a Fed. What do you think?"

Twelve

His cellphone hadn't vibrated to wake him so he knew it was before 2 a.m. when he heard the door push over the book he'd leaned against it. His hand went to the gun under his pillow.

"It's me," he heard Anna's voice say.

He switched his bedside light on. "Come in, ma'am."

"I couldn't sleep. I'm so scared about what's going on," Anna was there with a bathrobe over her nightwear."

"Won't Mr. Lemonis be unhappy about you being in my room in the middle of the night?"

"Theo's not here. He went out about midnight. He never goes out that late, and when I asked him where he was going, he was very evasive."

"I'm hoping we've winkled out all the bad apples now. You should be safe inside the grounds,' he said, not entirely convinced it was true.

"I'm not so worried about when we're at home - more about when we're out and about."

"We've got to go to the police station in the morning, the airport tomorrow. Then that's it, we'll be out of the country."

"I know, but that won't mean we're entirely safe, will it?"

"Possibly not until we're certain who's behind it all, but I've been playing catch up since I started here. Shifting base to the UK will give me a chance to start afresh with an entirely new team if necessary. This house isn't best suited to providing close protection."

"You don't know what my home in England is like yet."

"I've a pretty good idea."

"How?"

"I looked on the internet. It's beautiful. I can't think why you want to live here when you have a home like that."

"I'm married to Theo."

"I know."

"What does that mean?"

"Nothing, ma'am."

"Come on, you can speak freely."

"You may not like what I say."

"I don't care; say it anyway."

"I may be completely off base here, so tell me if I am. I know it's not my place to say it. Where did Theo live before you were married?"

"In Chobham, about five miles from my husband and I."

"What made you move to the US?"

"Theo said he needed to spend more time at his factories over here, and to be honest I was so utterly broken after Henry died, I didn't put up much of a fight. I'd already handed executive control of Silico to a management team I have complete faith in. Judith was happy to come with us, and Izzy was so excited at the prospect at living on a ranch in Washington State she couldn't wait."

"Are you happy?"

"I suppose so. My marriage isn't a fairy tale romance like it was with Henry, but he was so supportive after Henry died we sort of fell into it. I suppose you're alluding to the fact that we don't sleep together."

"It's not my business, but you're a beautiful woman. I'd imagine most men would find it difficult not to sleep with you at every given opportunity."

"Thank you, but Theo is gay."

"I didn't see that coming."

"It's something that he's fanatical about concealing. I know about it, so does Manos, and maybe Pavel. Izzy said she guessed he couldn't be straight if he didn't want to sleep with me, but I don't think she told Cassie."

"Would that be why he didn't sack Volkov I wonder."

"I hadn't thought of that, but maybe."

"I miss the intimate side of my marriage. Henry was such a passionate lover but sex isn't the most important thing."

"Is he in a relationship?"

"He has a lover, who has an apartment here and another in Seattle. I don't know who it is, and I don't ask."

"I didn't know Theo was gay, Mummy," Cassie said from the doorway.

"Have you been eavesdropping again, sweetie? You're not supposed to do that are you?"

"I didn't mean to, but I went to get into bed with you and you weren't there. I didn't want to interrupt you talking."

"Drew was telling me how he'll keep us safe in England, and we just got talking."

"I agree with Drew, you're beautiful and you should be able to have sex if you want."

"Yes, well, that is definitely a conversation for another day. We'll let him get some sleep."

"I suggest we leave here about 09:45 tomorrow, ma'am."

"I've made the arrangements you suggested."

"That's good, ma'am. Sleep well."

Once they'd gone, he dressed and went to speak to the on-duty team members. Frenchie was in the control room while Mac was patrolling the grounds.

"Anything happening Gaston?"

"Not really. A couple of cars in the street, but nothing suspicious, the cops have driven by twice. I logged your visitors just now, was that okay?"

"Absolutely, that's what the log's for. They're just a couple of people scared shitless that someone is trying to kill them; who's to blame them? Get yourself something to eat and drink, I'll take over here."

He read the log, and unsurprisingly everything was exactly as he would have expected from a professional security guy at the top of his game; concise entries giving all the relevant information.

As he watched the screen, another cop car drove slowly past the house. That was good news. Perez hadn't said he was going to arrange it, but it was a welcome addition to his arsenal.

Frenchie returned with a cup and a sandwich. "This is the weirdest situation I've ever heard of, Parker. A single incident where the protection team was involved would be unusual but a whole series of them? This is queer stuff."

"Tell me about it. It can't go on. If anything else happens, I'll have to insist we change location."

"Where to?"

"Seattle I expect."

"Would we move with you?"

"I expect so. You okay if I spell Mac now?"

"Sure go ahead."

He found Mac checking the perimeter wall where he'd climbed over from the neighbor's yard days earlier. Mac made similar remarks to Frenchie, but added something else, something that had crossed his own mind.

"Don't you think this whole thing is amateur? If it had been professionals like us doing something like this it would have been done and dusted in a single operation and we'd have been on a plane out of here within the hour. Even if the first op went belly up, we'd have just regrouped and finished the job a week or two later. They're clearly not bothered that people won't believe it's an opportunist thing. I think they're laying down chaff to confuse an investigation."

"Those are my thoughts precisely, but their acts are so badly planned and executed there has to be an amateur managing it. Is that just Gates I wonder? Anyway, time you took your break I'll hang around out here."

"This is a bit like a normal op, except with better conditions where you get to go back to camp for a break, get worse armory, and a dumb adversary is a team member."

Drew laughed. Half an hour later he was back in bed after setting his alarm for 06:30.

Thirteen

When Drew checked the log in the morning he noted that the second half of the night had been similarly uneventful. Mockingbird, and Mickey had already arrived.

Lemonis hadn't returned.

After thanking Frenchie and Mac he went to brief the new shift.

"Mockingbird, you'll be on your own for part of the morning because Mrs. West and I have got to go to the police station this morning. Cassie will probably come along for the ride. We'll take the black Lincoln, and Mickey I want you to follow behind at a discrete distance in the white one."

When they were on their own he added to Mickey, "In case you didn't know, the cars are bugged, although I have no idea who's listening in."

"Okay. I see that Lemonis hasn't come back then. Probably at his little love shack down by Venice Beach."

"Who is he, do you know?"

"Who?"

"Lemonis' toy boy."

"It ain't a guy. She calls herself Ariana Georgiou. He's been fucking her since they were teenagers. What made you think he was gay."

"I was told he was."

"We have no evidence of that, none at all. She's absolutely stunning and she's got two kids by him; girls, four and two years old."

"So are you telling me that he married Anna at around the same time he was having a baby with this other woman? What an absolute piece of shit."

"You haven't heard the best bit."

"What's that?"

"She's Stamelis' daughter."

"Jeezus!"

"There's got to be something of that in the motive behind all this," Mickey suggested.

"Thanks for telling me that. It might be useful."

The next thing he did was send a text to his contact.

Don't know how relevant this is. Just discovered Lemonis has a long-term relationship with daughter of Manos Stamelis. Allegedly they were childhood friends.

They have two daughters two and four and she has a home at Venice Beach. Calls herself Ariana Georgiou. Don't believe Mrs. West knows. She seems to think he's gay.'

He went to the kitchen, where Alejandro had prepared breakfast for him and the off going shift. He was halfway through eating it when the contact phone vibrated with an incoming text. *Expect call in 5.*

He put the last forkful of flat sausage in his mouth, picked up his coffee cup and went into the yard. The phone vibrated again almost right away.

"Where the hell do you find that out?!"

"A reliable source I think, but maybe you should check it out."

"Too right I will. Don't tell Anna for Christ's sake, it'll destroy her."

"I wasn't planning to. It's not my place. She'll need to know at some time surely."

"Of course she will, and I'll decide when. The plans are in place for tomorrow. Anna will handle the online check-ins and print the tickets. Your visa is in place and your license will go active tomorrow morning, so by the time you land you'll be good to go. I'll text you a number, just in case there're any issues at Passport Control. I'm not expecting any. Hand luggage only if possible. There'll be a car waiting, Anna will know the driver. Is there anything else you need?"

"I don't think so."

He ended the call and inspected the perimeter for evidence of any further intrusions. There were none. Giving the cars a thorough check he confirmed that the listening devices were still in place but there was nothing else to indicate they'd been interfered with.

Leaving it to the last minute he knocked on the day room door to collect Anna and Cassie.

"Are you ready, ma'am?"

"Yes of course," Anna replied, "We're both very tired though because a certain little girl wanted to learn a bit more about making babies."

"Muuummmy!"

"Don't worry, Miss Cassie. I don't know either. You can explain it to me when your mom's not around."

She giggled.

"Come on let's get this over. Are you coming too, Cassie?"

"I've never been in a police station."

"Probably not a destination that needs to be high on your bucket list, I've been in too many. Fire stations are much more exciting."

In the car, as would be usual for a bodyguard in these circumstances, Drew checked to ensure his passengers were tightly belted up before driving off. The journey to the station took only fifteen minutes, staying alert to everything around him. Mickey stayed on station two or three cars behind the whole way.

Sergeant Perez interviewed them separately while Cassie waited outside with whoever wasn't in the room."

"Are we free to go now, Sergeant?"

"Yes of course. Neither of you are suspected of a crime."

On the way out Cassie said, "You were right, Drew; police stations are boring."

"Let's get back now,' he said before they got into the car.

"We can't go back yet; we have to collect the suits." Cassie told him.

"Cassie's right, you'll need a suit for the flight."

"Okay, but let's be quick, and I'm not leaving you alone in the car while I go inside."

Even though they were early, the suits were ready, but Anna insisted he try at least one of them on. Standing in front them while they gave their verdict made him feel ridiculous.

"I think he looks very handsome in that one, don't you, Cassie?"

She giggled, "Yes, he looks like Jason Momoa but with a proper haircut."

"I'm still here you know."

"Sorry, but us girls haven't had a lot of fun lately."

"I need to get out of this monkey suit. We have to get going. There's no way I'm trying the other one on."

Back in the car Drew reminded the girls to keep their seat belts on tight, checked to see that Mickey was in position, and pulled away. Coincidentally, their route took them along Old Ranch Road, where he'd stopped the car tailing them from the restaurant. The realization momentarily distracted him, and he didn't immediately notice two pickup trucks pull out of a side turning between their car and Mickey's.

The lead vehicle suddenly accelerated, overtook, turned sharply in front of them, and stopped. The driver's arm appeared through his open window a gun in its hand, fired, shattering their windscreen.

Acting instinctively, Drew braked hard, throwing the wheel into a violent turn and shouting, "Hold tight, stay low, keep the doors locked!"

The car skidded round, its tail clipping the rear of the pickup. As he completed his turn he accelerated and began to gather speed again the second pickup turned across the road in front to block his path. He flipped the car into reverse and floored the gas pedal, smoke belching from the tires as the wheels spun, and the car quickly gathered pace in the opposite direction. "Brace for impact," he shouted.

Seconds later the back of their car smashed into the first vehicle's tailgate just as its ski-masked driver was attempting to climb out and bring his handgun to bear on them. The impact airbags inflated sent the man flying and he lost the grip on his gun which skidded harmlessly away.

Drew anticipated the explosive inflation of their airbags and as they deflated he flipped the car back into drive, spurred on by the familiar thump of two bullets hitting the front of the car. Then the engine lost power. "Stay down…call 911…Old Ranch Road!"

He leapt out, gun in his hand, firing at the driver of the second pickup. His first shots missed, harmlessly hitting the side of the pickup as its driver turned and loosed off several shots in the opposite direction, presumably at Mickey. He spun back toward Drew who took two carefully aimed shots of his own, bringing the gunman to the floor. He didn't move again.

Drew didn't expect him to.

Quickly spinning on the balls of his feet Drew was in time to see the driver of the first pick-up limping away in amongst the dense trees and brush at the side of the road.

"Are you both okay?" he shouted.

"We're fine," Anna called back. "What's happening?"

"I think it's safe now but stay down until the cops get here. The car isn't going anywhere."

Drew was still trying to get Mickey on his cellphone when the first patrol car arrived two minutes later. He laid his gun on the floor and held his hands up.

"Step away from the vehicle, get on the floor face down, and put your hands behind your head with your fingers interlocked," the cop yelled at him.

Drew carefully complied.

Three more LAPD patrol cars were quick to arrive. "Looks like we got two DBs over there." The second cop said kneeling on Drew as he cuffed him.

"I need to make you aware officer, I have a second gun in an ankle holster but no other weapons. I'm a close-protection officer to the woman and child in the car behind me."

Anna and Cassie were ferried to the police station, but a different one to earlier. It was three quarters of an hour before they let Drew off the floor and uncuffed him and only then after an intervention by phone from Sergeant Perez. They drove him to the station and put him in a room where two LAPD detectives attempted to question him."

"So who are these people? What was that all about?" one of the detectives asked.

"No disrespect, but I need to speak to someone more senior.

"Just because you're bodyguard to wealthy people, don't grant you special privileges. They're two cents a pound around here."

"There are things happening here that are above your pay grade detective, and there's some urgency that they're acknowledged."

Eventually, a Sergeant Salah came into the interview room.

"I need to speak to you alone, Sergeant or with your lieutenant."

"Why?"

"As I've told your colleagues, there things at play that neither of us may ever be allowed to know in full. I'll tell you who I believe the two bad guys were as soon as we're alone, and I've been assured we're not being recorded."

Salah ushered the other two out of the room telling them to turn off the mikes.

"Right then, Parker, what the fuck's going on and don't take long to get to the point."

"The first thing you need to know is about the guy from the second Lincoln. I know him as Michael 'Mickey' Maus and I believe him to be an F.B.I. special agent who's been working undercover in the Lemonis household. I'm sure the feds would be grateful if that didn't become general knowledge; he's involved in a highly sensitive operation."

Salah cursed.

"Other than that I can give you a full account of the incident with or without a tape, most of which will be verifiable from the footage on the dashcams of the Lincolns. I believe the dead hijacker was Otis Williams can you confirm that?"

"That's right, who's the other guy, the one that got away?"

"From his size and stature, I believe him to be a guy who goes by the name, Paul Gates. Detective Perez will confirm he's a bad actor who infiltrated the Lemonis' security detail and escaped custody yesterday."

Salah stormed out of the room and sent the other two back in to take his statement, returning twenty minutes later. "Okay, Parker, you can go but don't leave California."

"That might be a problem, Sergeant. I'll be recommending that Mrs. West relocate out of state as soon as possible and I'll be escorting her."

"Not anymore you're not."

"I'm not suspected of a crime, the whole incident is on video for you to verify my account, as well as those of Mrs. West and her daughter. If you ever catch Gates I'll return to appear as a witness at his trial, but he's a former member of UK special forces and I doubt that Gates is his real name. I'll wait while you clarify that if you need to."

The cops left the room; one returned ten minutes later with his guns and confirmed that he was free to leave without restriction.

"Thank you, officers. I'm grateful for your professional handling of the incident. Where are Mrs. West and Cassandra?"

"They're in our public waiting room. We offered to take them home before, but Mrs. West refused to leave without you. I'll get a patrol car to run you home now."

As soon as he entered the room, Cassie rushed to him and wrapped her arms around his waist. "You saved us, again. Thank you. I love you."

"Cassie, I've only been doing my job, the job I've been trained to do. I appreciate your gratitude I really do, but I'm just your mom's employee, and you wouldn't offer your love to a plumber who fixes your bathroom."

"I know but I love you anyway."

Anna was strangely silent as she watched the interaction. Drew looked at her and saw the clear response to trauma written on her face. It was something he'd seen on survivors' faces many, many times.

She handed him the cardboard carrying case containing his new suits, and he accepted it without speaking.

The ride back to the Lemonis home was quiet. As they reached the street they could see two TV vans and a cop car parked outside. The electronic gates opened as the patrol car approached, and they drove straight in.

Drew had called ahead.

"What the hell's going on, Parker?" Atticus asked as he climbed from the passenger seat. The cops won't tell me shit, but the TV assholes say there was another hijack."

"There was an attempted hijack. That's right; it was Gates and Williams."

"For fucks sake, where's Mickey?"

"Mickey didn't make it. I'll talk you through it in a minute. Let me get these two inside. Is Lemonis here?"

"Not yet. I haven't heard anything from either him or Pavel the whole day."

He opened the car's back door for Anna who stepped out and waited for Cassie to shuffle across the seat and join her. They led the way up the steps to the front door and went straight through to the dayroom.

"Come in and close the door please, Drew. I don't have words to thank you, I'm sorry. People like Mickey, Rupert, and you are so courageous and selfless you make me feel inadequate."

"We can only do what we do because there's a little something inside us that switches off and allows us to make cold calculated decisions. There are horrible people in the world, so I guess it's kinda handy there are people like us who can do what we do. I know dozens of people who do this work for wealthy, famous, and powerful people some of whom aren't very nice; some are even bad guys. I regard myself as fortunate to be working with you and Miss Cassie for my first job."

Anna's knees gave way then and she staggered. Drew was close enough to prevent her falling and he helped her to the nearby sofa.

"Mummy, are you okay?" Cassie called.

"She'll be fine, Cassie. Will you ask someone to make her a strong black coffee with three spoons of sugar?"

The young girl rushed off, happy to be asked to contribute.

"You're in shock, ma'am, just sit still and wait for the coffee,' he said.

"Fuck the coffee. Get me a large Jack Daniels. The bottle's over there."

He was quickly back with the glass.

"Where's Theo? I tried calling him but his cellphone was turned off. I left a message, and I've sent texts but he hasn't replied. I've even left messages with Pavel and Manos. Do you think something's happened to him too?"

Drew had already sent a message to his contact so he left the room and called. The man picked up instantly.

"If you weren't already aware there's been another hijack attempt. Mrs. West and Cassandra are unharmed, and we're back at the house. Maus was killed. I got one of the hijackers with a couple of rounds. He's dead. It was Otis Williams the gangbanger from yesterday. The second one escaped with what appeared to be minor injuries from the collision, I'm pretty certain it was Gates."

"For God's sake Parker, this is getting out of control, the sooner you're away from there the better."

"There's more, I'm afraid. Lemonis appears to be missing. Mrs. West has tried several methods of contacting him and he isn't returning her calls; she's concerned that something has happened to him. He went out at midnight and hasn't been seen since."

"He's safe and well. We put someone onto him as soon as you told us about the other woman. He's attending his youngest daughter's Christening. It's a big Greek event; over a hundred guests according to our people outside her home."

"I'm thinking that sending a guy to Seattle with Judith and having him travel to the UK with her when she's ready to join us. First to keep her safe and second to add to the security detail over there."

"Good idea, who?"

"Atticus."

"Are you sure you can trust him?"

"As sure as it's possible to be at the moment, he's not thrown me any dummies so far, and there's no reason to suspect that Judith is a threat."

"Okay, I'll arrange another ticket and a UK license."

"Great I'll be in touch."

"There's something else you should know. Rupert Loughty's been murdered, at his sister's house in Donegal."

"The stinking scum. He'll pay for this if I discover who did that."

He ended the call.

"What was that last bit about?" Anna had overheard.

"Rupert Loughty is dead."

"Dear God, won't this ever end?"

"Mr. Lemonis is safe, but I can't give you the detail at the moment."

"There's something else you're not telling me. What is it?"

"I'd rather not say, ma'am. It's not my place."

"A minute ago you were telling us that I'm your employer. If you have information which impacts on my personal life, I believe it is precisely your place to tell me."

"I understand he's at a Christening near Venice Beach, ma'am. He has probably got his phone turned off."

"A Christening? Whose?"

"I believe it's at the home of a lady called Ariana Georgiou ma'am."

"We don't know anybody called that."

"Perhaps she's a work colleague, ma'am."

"I don't think so. I'm going to look into this."

"Ma'am, if you'll forgive me from saying so, you're still in shock. Maybe it would be better to wait."

"Bollocks," she said, just as Cassie re-entered the room with the coffee.

"Mummy, you said it again."

"It's been a bad day. Sue me." Then to Drew, she said, "Thank you for everything. I really can't thank you enough."

"You don't need to thank me, ma'am."

"We're not getting into that again. Can you leave me for a few minutes. I need to make some calls?"

He took his leave and went to speak to Mockingbird. After giving him a rundown of the events of the day, he waited for the reaction.

"We gotta get these bastards, Drew. I didn't know Mickey before this but he seemed like a good guy. Whatever, he was one of the team. So was Gates, and you don't kill your own."

"I agree, but this may be much bigger than we can handle ourselves. I can't tell you everything, not least because I don't know it all myself. What's more we mustn't lose sight of what we're here to do. Having said that, if Gates puts his head over the parapet again, he's mine."

"I'm with you, pal."

"One last thing, we're relocating tomorrow. I want you to come along."

"Just me?"

"For the time being, yes."

"Can I know where?"

"Seattle."

"Sure, what time?"

"LAX to Tacoma 06:25. Pick up Judith from her home by cab 05:00. Business class so dress smart; if you can," Drew added with a grin.

"Cheeky bastard. I always take a suit when I'm doing close-protection work."

"Drew, Drew! Come quickly Mummy's not well."

He ran to the dayroom where he found Anna clutching her stomach, rocking back and forth, as she wailed. Sitting beside her he pulled her into his arms and held her tight.

"Sit the other side Cassie and hold her."

"What's the matter with her?"

"She's just had some horrible news, and on top of everything else it's just too much."

Mockingbird came to the door, "You want me to get a doctor?"

"Not yet, I think she'll be okay in a while."

He stayed with her for the next hour or so until she stopped crying and fell asleep. Then he lifted her in his arms, carried her to her room, and laid her on the bed.

"Will she be alright?" Cassie asked.

"I think so. Your Mummy's strong woman and she's had some real bad things happen to her, but she'll pull through for two reasons. First because she's got you, and second because she's got you too."

"What does that mean?"

"She'll get better because the person who she loves more than anything in the whole world needs her to get better; and she'll get better because that person loves her just as much. Stay with her and if either of you want or need anything just call."

In the control room he found Mockingbird bringing Frenchie and Mac up to date. They appeared as horrified and angry as anyone would expect, vowing terrible retribution on Gates and his accomplices.

"We'll be getting our own chow tonight. Alejandro quit when I told him about the events of the day. He said it was too dangerous, and Lemonis was an asshole anyway," Mockingbird told them.

"Can't fault him on any of that," Mac said.

It was after nine p.m. when Lemonis returned and Drew wondered if his wife would confront him with what she'd learned. The absence of shouting probably indicated that she hadn't. If that were the case he doubted that she'd told Cassie either. He had anticipated that Lemonis would at the very least have wanted to talk to him about what had happened...but nothing.

By eleven his walk around the house suggested that the three principals had retired for the night. Cassie's open door indicated that she was spending the night with her mother.

He stepped into the youngster's room, picked up her small purse and searched it."

Fourteen

The vibration of his phone at 04:15 woke him from a shallow sleep, he was on his feet and in the shower in moments. Minutes later he was in the control room with Mac, Frenchie and Atticus. By 04:40 Anna and Cassie joined them clutching their bags.

"Mac, grab the keys to the third Navigator. You can take us to the airport."

"I thought you were taking the cab."

"Last minute change of plan. Let's go."

Two minutes later as they were driving out of the gates, Drew turned to see Lemonis standing at the front door with a face like thunder.

He pulled down the sun visor above his head, ripped off the listening bug discreetly taped to it and threw it out of the window.

"Stay within the speed limit but get us there as quickly as you can without going the normal route."

"Are we being followed?" Mac asked.

"I don't know, but we are being tracked. When we get to the drop off point, we'll all leap out, you drive off and take a really roundabout route back to the house. Cassie pass me your purse." He took it from her, opened it, took out the tracker and stuck it to the sun visor using the tape still there from the bug.

"I'm getting that I'm some sort of decoy, right," Mac observed.

"Yeah, sorry. It won't fool anyone for very long, but every little counts."

"I won't ask where you're going."

"Best not. Once Lemonis realizes we're gone, he'll find he doesn't need your services any longer. Just make sure you get paid for the full six months."

Anna leaned forward and handed him her card. "If Theo decides not to pay you, call the UK number on there and I'll make sure you get your money."

They were the first words he'd heard her speak since her crisis the night before, although they'd exchanged a few texts about last minute changes to their arrangements.

The trip to the airport took thirty-five minutes by the route that Mac chose and they spotted no obvious evidence of a tail. They pulled up in front of the terminal and quickly climbed out. Mac wished them luck and pulled away having been stationary for mere seconds.

Inside the terminal they caught up with Atticus and Judith who greeted Anna and Cassie with affection and concern. They didn't spend time exchanging pleasantries. Anna handed Judith her ticket, boarding pass and the tracking device from her own purse. She then handed over Mockingbird's ticket and the boarding pass her contact had emailed to her.

"Is there something else I should know, Drew?" he asked.

"Yes, we're not travelling to Seattle with you. We're going elsewhere. you and Judith will join us later. It may be days or it may be a week or two. For the time being your job is to keep this lady safe. She knows your destination near Seattle. We'll be in touch. Thanks for this."

They shook hands, Anna, and Cassie waving a tearful farewell to Judith as the two headed to the domestic departure gates.

Before they made their way to the international gates, Drew and the girls headed to the left luggage lockers where he deposited his guns, unsure when or if he'd see them again. By the time they'd passed through passport control and security and made their way to the boarding gate they had only a tense fifteen-minute wait until boarding started.

He didn't relax until the enormous Airbus 380 began racing down the runway.

Fifteen

Drew had never flown first-class before. When flying, he was more accustomed to being strapped to the wall of a C-130 and sharing the cabin with a military vehicle or two before free-fall HALO parachuting to the ground, or abseiling from a Black Hawk, or dropping out of a Chinook ten feet from the ground, or low-level jumping from a light aircraft. This was weird. The ten-hour flight would be endured in luxury unlike anything he'd experienced; completely outside his comfort zone.

Looking across at his two charges though, he could see they were entirely at ease.

Anna still hadn't spoken to him in any substantive way since she discovered the news about her husband. He worried that the psychological effect could be devastatingly permanent.

They hadn't been in the air long before he was being offered food and drinks, offers he gladly accepted but when they arrived he was disappointed; the portion sizes were pitiful. A comment to the cabin crew prompted the offer of a second serving and he settled for that.

After they'd eaten the others were very quickly asleep, but it was more than two hours into the flight before sleep overcame Drew. He dreamed of the disastrous operation to capture Mbuti, but it somehow morphed into the recent hijack, and after disappearing into the trees Gates returned to kill Anna and Cassie while he found himself powerless to move.

He woke with a start when someone shook his shoulder. He was instantly alert.

"I'm sorry to wake you but I thought now Cassie is asleep, we should talk." Anna was speaking extremely quietly. "Can I squeeze in beside you?"

"Sure."

Even with the extra wide luxuriously upholstered seat it was a tight fit and pressed so tightly against him, with the faint scent of her perfume in his nostrils, made him conscious for the first time that she wasn't just his charge, but a beautiful adult female. It was more than a year since he'd been with a woman, and he couldn't help becoming aroused.

"I'm going to say it once more, and then I'll try not to mention it again. I will never be able to thank you enough for what you did yesterday, and I don't just mean for saving our lives in the street, as if that weren't enough. I heard what you said to Cassie about how we need each other. It was beautiful and profound, and it was exactly the right thing to say to a traumatized eleven-year-old. I think at that moment I was on the brink of the abyss, and it brought me back."

"It just seemed the right thing to say at the time."

"I'm trying not to be insulting here, but it wasn't the sort of spontaneous thing I'd expect from someone in your profession."

"Yeah, but don't let it get around; it'd ruin my reputation.' He laughed it off, but the truth was he'd often been ribbed by teammates when he got emotional about things, particularly when children were orphaned or injured.

"There'll be a car to meet us at Heathrow. It will be the middle of the night there. UK border controls are notoriously unpredictable so we could be through immigration and customs in twenty minutes or it could take over an hour. My home's about fifty minutes away."

"What accommodation do you have? I mean I've looked at it online, but there's no floor plan."

"If you're asking where you'll sleep, then I'd like you to take a room on what you would call the second floor, near Cassie and I. Perhaps you could use Theo's room. I've never had a bodyguard before so the issue of where to accommodate one hasn't arisen."

"What about Judith. Where does she sleep?"

"She sleeps in what we call the coach house. I know, pretentious isn't it, but it's the name the architect gave it and it stuck. In reality, it's just the garage with rooms above, linked to the main house by a covered walkway."

"What about Mockingbird. Where will he sleep?"

"There's the groom's room in the stable block. It's not in use at the moment. Would that be okay?"

"How far from the house is it?"

"Only about a hundred feet. There are only four horses at the moment; we've had six in the past. Do you ride?"

"I can ride, but it's not something I've done regularly. Getting back to accommodation, do you have any other staff?"

"Only Jason the housekeeper. He sleeps above the coach house too."

"Are he and Judith an item?"

She laughed. "Definitely not. Judith and Jason are brother and sister, twins, and he's gay. They have separate rooms."

"Is he in a relationship?"

"Yes but they don't want to live together. I don't think his other half has come out yet, I don't ask."

"Does Judith have any sort of significant other?"

"Judith and I were at uni together. She had an affair with one of our tutors and became pregnant. When the news got out, he lost his job and his wife threw him out. He blamed her for leaking it and tried talking her into having an abortion. She refused but in the end she lost the baby anyway. She's been told that the likelihood of her carrying a baby to term in the future is very small, I don't remember why. She's godmother to Cassie and was to Izzy as well. After the baby died she took a year out, before going back, finishing her degree, and getting a DPhil in Education at Oxford. She absolutely adores my two girls, so when Henry died, and Cassie got a bit agoraphobic I asked her if she'd be interested in tutoring them both, not believing in a million years that she'd take the job, but she practically bit my hand off. She's had the odd relationship but she has big trust issues with men, and she's a bit of a loner these days."

"Does she know about Theo yet?"

"Not yet. That's not going to help with her trust issues when I tell her either."

"What about domestic staff?"

"The full-time staff are Toby the groom, Marilyn, the cleaner, Josh the groundsman and he hires casual workers if there's extra work to do in the spring and autumn."

"What sort of intruder alarm do you have?"

"Just the basic, but it's quite modern I think. We had a break in about two years or so ago, so we had it replaced."

"I think you should have a complete review as a matter of urgency; maybe consider something more elaborate. Mockingbird and I will need all the help we can get."

"Okay, but can we agree to just call him Atticus?"

He laughed. "Okay."

They were silent for a few minutes.

"What about you, are you really not leaving a weeping lover back in the states?"

"Life in special forces doesn't lend itself to long-term relationships, ma'am. The few that happen normally end with either the wife or girl walking away, or the operator leaving the unit."

"What about the females?"

"Same goes. There aren't that many, and I've only known three that were married, one to a guy in another squadron. They rarely saw one another so they ended it. Another one's husband couldn't take not being the macho one in the family and walked, and the third one's wife wanted kids so she left."

"Aren't there relationships between the operators?"

"Apart from the fact it's against regulations, it would be very rare for anything meaningful to happen in my experience. There is the odd hook up but even that's frowned upon by the rest of the team. It could put lives at risk on an op if someone's not completely focused on the job.' Changing the subject he said, "Your home looks kinda big for a relatively modern building."

"My father had it built for us as a wedding present. It's a sort of twenty-first century version of our family home in Surrey. It's way too big for us really but I can't bring myself to part with it. Same with father's home; I've turned that into a small hotel."

"Jesus, that's some wedding present."

"Knowing my dad there will have been some kind of inheritance tax dodge involved but don't ask me to explain."

"Your old man must have been pretty loaded."

"He was a banker like most of his forefathers; his family had been minor league aristocrats until the early twentieth century. My great-grandfather expanded the family wealth between the wars, I don't know the details of that. He claimed to be a socialist and renounced the family title. Daddy clearly didn't have his grandfather's socialist principles. Having said that, when he died, he left sixty percent to me, twenty percent to charity, five percent to his employees and the rest to the Labour Party."

"What about your first husband?"

"Henry and I met at uni; he was doing his PhD while I was a fresher. He worked alongside some of the world leaders in computer chip technology but working for other people was restricting him from developing his own ideas and he wanted independence. My dad offered to put up forty-one percent of the startup costs in his name, and ten percent in mine, if he could raise the rest, but only on condition that I worked in the company. My dad was a bit of a bully where I was concerned, but we didn't mind because Henry and I had already decided I would work with him to get the venture off the ground. We worked well together. I didn't do any of the technical stuff of course. I was more managerial."

"What was your degree then?"

"English Lit, and classics, hence Isolde and Cassandra."

"Can I come and sit with you, Mummy?" Cassie asked.

"You'll have to sit on Drew's lap if you do. Is that okay, Drew?"

"Er maybe not just at the moment. Later perhaps."

Anna looked puzzled for a moment, then glanced down.

"Oh yes, perhaps we should let Drew get some more sleep. Come and sit with me in my seat." She stood, leaned down to him and whispered, "Sorry, I didn't think."

Two hours later the pilot announced that they had started their descent into Heathrow. Anna sent Cassie back to her own seat, and looked across to Drew. "Everything okay now?"

"Fine thanks."

The aircraft had barely come to a halt let alone hooked up to the jetway when people started hassling cabin crew to help pull hand luggage out of lockers. Drew couldn't understand what the rush was for those in first-class, there were only twelve of them and they were going to be allowed off first anyway.

Immigration amounted to little more than scanning their passports and comparing their faces with the photos. Customs was slightly more involved; they insisted on searching everything, but with their small bags it only took minutes before they were out the other side.

"Lady West, Miss Cassandra." A short, prematurely gray man in his late forties greeted her with a wide smile as they emerged into the arrivals hall.

"Uncle Percy!" Cassie shouted, running to him and engulfing him in a hug, "It's been ages."

"It's lovely to see you both. You must be Mr. Parker. I'm so pleased to meet you face-to-face. I know it's only been a few days since you joined Lady West but it seems so much longer."

"Percy, how many times do I have to ask you to drop the title?"

"I know, ma'am; force of habit. I'll try to remember, ma'am. Isn't that what I'm supposed to say?"

"You can drop the ma'am too; we've known each other far too long. It's Anna."

"Can we get away now. I'm uncomfortable in open public areas until this business is under control," Drew told them.

"I've texted Toby to bring the car to the front.

"What car is it?"

"BMW X7, about two years old. Silver-gray."

"Good choice."

At the door, Percy checked to see if Toby was there and signaled he was. Drew went out, scanned the area, ushered them across and directed their seating arrangements. He wanted Percy in the back row, Cassie behind the driver, Anna beside her with himself in the front passenger seat.

"Would you like to drive?" Toby asked.

"Not today thanks. Let's go, not too slow, lock the doors, and try to keep it about five miles an hour below the limit on the highway please."

"Yes sir."

"You don't need to call me, sir. Drew is fine. We're just colleagues with different responsibilities. What do you do?" He asked still scanning the vehicles in front and behind.

"I'm Toby, the groom, I don't normally work at night but Mr. Belton asked me to come in especially."

"We're really grateful for that, Toby, thank you," Anna said.

"That's alright, Mrs. West. Any time."

The journey to the house took about fifty-five minutes. Toby opened the gate with a remote control from the central console, they sped through and he used the remote to close it again. The car came to a halt next to the front steps, Toby unlocked the doors, and Drew jumped out.

A small thin man rushed to meet them. "Anna, Cassie, I've missed you so much."

After thanking Percy and Toby, Anna hustled them all inside.

"You must be Drew; lovely to meet you. I'm Jason. I'm making everybody some breakfast; can I get you something."

"Thanks, Jason. If you sort everybody else out, I'll get myself something later. I need to have a quick look around first, get my bearings so to speak. Do you mind if we sit down for a long chat tomorrow? As the housekeeper, you probably have a better idea about what makes this place tick than anybody."

"Do you really think I would be able to help. I never imagined…" He had only a mere hint of camp in his accent.

"In my job you learn that people who live, work, and play somewhere are the richest source of useful intelligence, and often they're not even aware of it. Over the next few months, I'm going to be relying on people like you, Judith, Percy, and Toby to work with me to build a metaphorical wall around Anna and Cassie."

"Will it be dangerous?"

"No, that's not what I mean. I'll explain more tomorrow."

Walking through the big house gave him a much better idea how big it was. It wasn't just the size of the rooms, but the sheer number of them; drawing room, dayroom, family room, dining room, cinema room, library, study, gym, conservatory, kitchen cum breakfast room, laundry room, utility room, plus two washrooms. On the next floor up were five bedrooms, each with their own ensuite bath or shower room, a family bathroom, and stairs to two attic rooms each with their own shower room.

The house was luxuriously appointed with modern furniture and fittings. Not minimalistic but not cluttered either. It was decorated in neutral colors and the walls were hung with an eclectic collection of photographic prints, limited edition lithographs, and modern oils.

On his way through the kitchen, he was stopped by Jason. "I know you said not to, Drew, but I made you an English breakfast. Mrs. West told me how you like to keep your strength up."

"That's great, thank you. Have I got time to have a quick look through the coach house before I eat?"

"Go ahead. I'll wait to put your eggs on with mine."

He was back at the table to join Anna and Cassie within ten minutes. Jason put a plate in front of him with every conceivable ingredient of the iconic full English breakfast and served himself last with a slice of toast, one egg and a single slice of bacon.

"So what do you think of our home then, Drew?" Anna asked.

"It's very big, and my first impressions are that you will need to spend a lot of money to make the alarm even close to leakproof without a security team."

"I'll ask Percy to recommend someone."

"With respect to Percy, I'd prefer to find someone myself. Is that okay?"

"Oh yes of course."

Anna's phone vibrated in her purse, she lifted it out, looked at it, and promptly put it on speaker. "Hello."

"Anna, I've been trying call you for hours, where the hell are you?"

"In Pangbourne."

"I thought you were in Seattle."

"Did you?"
"You crept off this morning without saying anything."
"You were asleep."
"We need to talk."
"We can talk next time I see you."
"When will that be?"
"When Hell freezes over."
"What did you say? What do you mean?"
"Exactly what it sounds like."
"Look, I'm sorry I wasn't around yesterday, but my phone went dead and I didn't realize."
"I guess Manos' and Pavel's phones were both dead as well then."
"We were all so tied up with everything…"
"I understand, baptisms can be so hectic."
"How did you…? Okay, I'm sorry, but it was Manos' granddaughter, and I know you're not fond of him…"
"Have a nice life with Ariana and your two lovely daughters, Theo. Oh and Theo…"
"What?"
"Fuck off."
She ended the call and slammed the phone on the table
"Mummy! You said the *F* word."
"I know, sorry sweetie; extreme circumstances call for extreme responses."
"Mr. Theo has got daughters?!" Jason exclaimed.
"Not just daughters, but a wife or mistress of nearly twenty years apparently. The shit has been keeping them secret from me the whole time I've known him."
"I just knew he wasn't gay. My gaydar is usually infallible and I've never picked up any vibes from him."
"Come on, Drew. Let's show you your room." Anna led the way up the stairs and opening one door, said, "This is my room. I'd like you to have this one next door. That's Cassie's just across there. Is that okay?"
"I guess; if that's what you want."
"It is. I'll get Jason and one of the cleaners to move Theo's things out later. I expect you want to take a rest now, like us."
"I've still things to do. My experience with jet lag has been to just work through it. When do you plan to get Judith and Atticus over here?"

"Whenever you give the go ahead. I've asked her to get someone to get all our things packed and shipped over. I don't know how long that will take."

They left him alone, and he examined his surroundings. There was a king size bed with night tables on either side, a sofa, a small breakfast table with chairs, a tall wide set of drawers, and a dressing table. The walk-in closet had rows of suits, jackets, shirts, ties, and shoes. There were more drawers and a small safe. The bathroom had a wet room shower and a bath.

He wondered about the connecting door between the room and hers. For security purposes it would be best to keep it unlocked, but for personal privacy she would probably prefer it not to be. The close-protection course in Maryland hadn't fully prepared him for the politics of gender sensitivity.

By the time he'd changed into training gear and made his way outside it was getting light. He decided the garage and vehicle inspection could wait and began a steady jog around the perimeter checking fencing and walls. Anna had told him that the grounds were approximately forty acres in total and he calculated that that made the perimeter about a mile. After the first lap, he speeded up and kept going through the tiredness caused by nearly a week of limited sleep and exercise, coupled with the effects of travelling back through eight time zones. He was nearing the end of his fifth lap when he saw a man approaching him from the stable block.

"I'm sorry sir, this is private property. I'm going to have to ask you to leave."

"I'm aware…"

"I don't want any arguments. I've asked you once. If you don't leave now, I'll call the police."

"I'm Drew, Mrs. West's new close-protection officer."

"Nobody told me about that. How do I know you're telling me the truth?"

"Maybe speak to Toby, or Jason."

"Toby's not in yet, and I don't know where Jason is."

"That's probably because they were up for two or three hours in the middle of the night collecting Mrs. West, Cassie, and myself from the airport."

"Mrs. W is back? Why weren't we told?"

"It was a last-minute thing. I'm guessing you're Josh,' he said offering his hand.

The guy tentatively allowed his small hand to be encased in Drew's huge one. "That's right."

"Good to meet you Josh. Let's go get a cup of coffee."

"I don't normally take a break until ten thirty. It's not nine yet."

"I'm sure it won't matter just this once. We need to have a chat."

In the kitchen Jason had just come in from the coach house. Morning Josh, I see you've met Drew."

"Yes, why didn't anyone tell me they were coming home?"

"That's my fault, Josh. Sorry but it's been a bit of a rush," Jason told him, "There's been another attempt to kidnap or kill Mrs. West and little Cassie. Mr. Parker here saved them again."

"Have you got time to join us for coffee and a talk Jason?"

"Anything we can do to help."

An exhausted looking Toby joined them while the coffee was being poured and Drew spent the next fifty minutes grilling them for information about the activities and routines of the estate, the trades people, and the security, before explaining how they could alter things to improve protection and work together on revised routines.

"Just remember, we're a team, and together we can keep this place running smoothly and safely. I won't tell you how to keep the household business order, keep the grounds looking spick and span, or managing the horses, but I can't do my job without your help. I don't want to overstate the case, but these security precautions are for all our safety, not just the family. The people who might come to threaten them won't give a fuck if anybody who stands in their way isn't one of their targets. You can come to me with questions and suggestions at any time. Also you need to know that I'm on duty 24/7 the whole year round. Put my number in your phones. I'm going to arrange personal radios for on-duty staff."

The other three's eyes followed him in awe as he stood to leave the room to finish his exercise routine, but as he went through the door a bell rang on the kitchen wall.

"What's that?"

"Oh that will be the school. They use the swimming pool on Friday and Monday mornings, I forgot to mention them. Sorry."

"Okay, anybody else?"

"Just the disabled riding club on Saturday mornings."

"Okay. I'll be in the gym."

An hour in the gym, left him feeling the cumulative effects of everything. It was approaching ten-thirty when he emerged from his room showered and dressed.

Anna was in the kitchen when he came down.

"Morning, ma'am."

"Good morning, Drew. How was the bed?"

"I haven't used it yet. I've been busy finding my feet."

"You must be exhausted."

"I've had no decent exercise for nearly a week. I can't afford to let myself slip. I actually came down to get the Wi-Fi password, I've some things I need to do online today."

Jason ran to fetch the card from the router with the default password on. "That's great Jason. I'll need to change those passwords, but I won't do it today."

"Why don't you take over the study, Drew? I always use the library if I ever need to do any work that requires a desk."

"I'm quite happy to just work in my room, ma'am."

"Drew, the study was only ever used by Theo, and Henry before that. Theo is only coming back here over my dead body, and not even then after I've changed my will."

"Okay then, ma'am. If you're sure."

He spent the next hour web searching and making phone calls, then went to find Anna.

"Ma'am, can we talk?"

"Of course, Drew."

"I need to spend some money."

"I understand, how much do you need?"

"At the moment I can't be sure. In the next day or two maybe only two or three thousand pounds. I need to buy a radio communication system for myself and the other staff. Cellphones aren't really suitable for the purpose. What I can't assess is the cost of a total upgrade of the alarm and intrusion system. I know you said it was only installed a couple of years ago, but in terms of protection against the kind of risk we're now dealing with, it's completely inadequate. It needs to be state of the art and designed specifically for these buildings and the anticipated threat. I've spoken to a couple of companies and even without seeing the place, the ballpark figures are pretty huge, well into six figures.

"That's okay, whatever it takes."

"The other thing that worries me is the time frame they're suggesting for actually doing the work, they're saying six-months or more. That's far too long."

"This is the UK. That's often the way of things I'm afraid. Do you mind if I suggest something?"

"If you can, ma'am, please."

"I know last night you didn't think much about my idea of talking to Percy about the alarms, but Silico is in the defense industry, and as such their security has to be world class. I'm sure that anybody he suggests would be able to cope with anything you propose. What's more he should be able to put pressure on them to get on with the job as soon as possible."

"That makes complete sense. I feel pretty stupid, ma'am. Until now I've just been a simple grunt doing what I'm told. Procuring hardware and services has been outside my purview. I sorta exposed my ignorance a bit there."

"Drew, you may be many things but none of them are simple or ignorant. I didn't employ you for your business acumen. I employed you for your skills as a bodyguard at which you have already proven yourself world class. I'll put £10,000 in your account today to cover immediate expenses. If you need more please just say. If you can keep a rough tally it would be a help. I don't want you dipping into your own money to pay for anything. Nor do I want you paying tax on expenses that I reimburse. Whatever the cost of the alarm upgrade, it can be invoiced direct to me, and whatever it costs will be fine. Does that help?"

"That would be really helpful, ma'am."

"I'll give Percy a call now. I've got a favor to ask you too."

"Whatever I can do, ma'am."

"It's not for me, and it's not for now. It's for Cassie."

"If I can I'll do it, ma'am."

"She wants to learn self-defense."

"It's not my area of expertise, ma'am. Doing enough to defend yourself and to deter an attacker, is not the same as being prepared to put yourself in harm's way or maybe use deadly force to defend yourself or another person. They are two completely different things."

"I don't think that she wants that. I suspect once she finds out that there's a chance she could get hurt herself just by learning she'll lose interest. I was thinking of some simple moves to discourage others from doing things she doesn't want. She'll be a teenager in a year or two and boys will start to become part of her life."

"The other thing that crosses my mind though, ma'am, is that in order to engage in that kind of training it would mean quite a lot of close physical contact. Some might find that inappropriate."

"I trust you, Drew and I know she does."

"Why?"

"What do you mean?"

"You've known me less than a week. I came as part of a team that was at least thirty percent corrupt."

"When I married Theo I'd known him for at least two years and I've been married to him for two more but that didn't make him any more trustworthy. I've watched you; I've seen you with Cassie; I've seen how you've behaved with me; I've watched you put yourself in front of gunfire to protect me and her. Furthermore, since Henry died, Cassie has been really introverted and withdrawn in the company of most of the men in her life. After the first hijack I feared that she'd become even more so, in the same way Judith did, but you managed to make a connection with her that no-one else has. I trust you, Drew."

"Okay, but it can't be until we've got things under control here."

"Understood."

"Also you might not find some of the moves I teach her in any textbook."

She laughed, "I bet I wouldn't. It's about time for some lunch. Will you join us?"

"Thank you, ma'am."

"It won't be anything special. I was still too tired to do any preparation."

"Will you be making lunch yourself then, ma'am?"

"I prefer to cook, otherwise I'd have no function at all. Theo disapproved of me cooking and behaved as if he was doing me a favor getting a cook in the States. Jason is a brilliant housekeeper but cooking is not his best talent. Give me a minute to speak to Percy, and I'll be right through."

"Did he say yes, Mummy?" Cassie asked coming in from where she'd been hovering outside the door.

"Yes, he did. You know he did; I saw you loitering outside the door."

"Thank you, Drew, you're the best bodyguard in the world."

"Probably not, but I do my best."

A few minutes later Anna announced that a security system design engineer would be there at ten-thirty the following day.

"Can I use the pool this afternoon, Mummy?" Cassie asked.

"If you're not too tired."

"Do you want to come, Drew."

"I've a few things I need to do and then I'm going to grab a couple of hours shuteye. I don't swim for fun. I use it to iron out a few knots in my muscles after exercise, and I prefer to do my swimming early in the day if possible. Sorry."

"Can I swim with you, if I'm up early enough then?"

"If it's okay with your Mom."

He spent the afternoon doing a full survey of the outer buildings, the stable block, the groundsman's equipment building, the garage and vehicles. He ran his eyes over the poolroom, which was accessible from the coach house walkway. After he'd finished he felt he had a good handle on what needed protecting.

He'd expected it to feel awkward, eating with the family, but if anything the evening meal was more like eating with his sister's family. Percy had joined them while Jason was hugely funny, and clearly a great favorite with all the others. Anna behaved a bit like the wholesome mothers do in afternoon TV movies, serving the food, controlling the conversation if it flagged, and making sure that nobody was left out. Jason and Cassie both tried to pump Drew for tales of his adventures in the army but he managed to fend them off without upsetting anyone.

Percy revealed that he'd had several calls from Theo trying to get information or to pass messages to Anna but he'd stoically resisted them all.

"After all this time he still hasn't figured out the relationship between us has he, Percy?"

"I don't think he has, Anna, no."

"Percy was my father's right-hand man for a number of years, Drew. He's like the dear uncle that I never had. There's no way on this planet he would act in any other way than in my best interest. He's the main reason that you were on that security detail. Manos insisted on selecting the final short list of ten, but Percy overruled enough of them to make certain you would be on the team. Rupert recommended you, Mickey, and Atticus. The others were all selected by Manos."

"So where did you get my name from, Percy?"

"We asked Rupert to draw up a list of names. Yours was among them. He asked your colonel which of the names he would pick first out of all of them, and he picked yours without any hesitation. I'm afraid you were a marked man as far as we were concerned."

Drew waited for Anna to go to bed before doing so himself and setting his alarm for 05:30.

Sixteen

When he woke, his muscles were stiff from the exercise of the day before. He wasn't going to allow that to stop him from doing all he could to get back to peak trim. He'd estimated that he had at least one more day before Lemonis could coordinate another attempt at whatever he was trying to do.

He dressed in his unwashed training gear from the day before and left the house through the back door via the kitchen and utility room. After the first lap it started to rain heavily, so he sped up and did two more laps before returning to the house soaking wet. After leaving his shoes in the laundry room, he ran upstairs to change into a clean training suit and fresh sneakers, grabbed a towel and a pair of speedos, and went to the gym. He'd exercised on the various pieces of equipment for more than forty minutes and was changing the weights on the squat rack when he spotted movement out of the corner of his eye in the mirrored wall.

"You can come in if you want, Cassie."

Shyly she pushed the door open enough to step inside. "I'm sorry, I didn't mean to be rude. I was wondering if you were still going to swim."

"Cassie, this is your home. I just work here. I wasn't doing anything that needed to be private. You're always welcome to come in when I'm training. Do you want to use any of the equipment while you're here?"

"I've only ever used the treadmill before."

"Well why not do that. Another day I'll teach you to use some of the other things if you want."

"Okay."

Over the next fifteen minutes he stuck to various weightlifting routines under the watchful eye of his young protegee. Once he'd finished, he put the weights he'd used away and rubbed himself with the towel.

Cassie stopped the treadmill. "Are you going to swim now."

"Yes, but you didn't have to wait for me; if you're safe to swim on your own that is."

"I know but I wanted to swim with you. I got my Level Four swimming certificate last year."

"That sounds great, well done. Let's go then. Don't you need to get your swimsuit and towel?"

"I've got my swimsuit under my clothes, and there's a towel cabinet in the changing room."

"Okay then."

The changing room had four dressing cubicles but the showers were open. They each went into a cubicle to change and by the time he emerged in his Speedos she was waiting for him.

"You didn't need to wait."

"I wanted to. Is that okay?"

"Sure. I'll just rinse some of the sweat off before going in the pool though."

Cassie watched as the water cascaded over his huge muscular body.

"Are those bullet wounds?" She meant the scars in his side and on his shoulder.

"Yes."

"What happened?"

"A coupla times I got to find out I weren't as good as I like to think I am."

The pool was about twenty meters by ten, big by private standards anywhere in the world. The polished timber lined structure had glazed sliding doors onto a patio that looked out across the mown grass and well-tended beds of plants and shrubs.

He dived in, swam under water to the other end, turned and swam back before emerging where he'd started.

"Wow, I can't swim underwater anything like as far as that!"

"It is all about lung capacity, and you're still small. The more you exercise and the more frequently you practice, the more your lung capacity increases so the easier it gets. Swimming underwater can be less strenuous than swimming on the surface. The trick is to go for distance rather than speed; that way you can conserve the oxygen in your blood. Try it."

She gracefully dived in and managed to reach about seven feet from the end before she had to surface, wiping the water from her face. She grinned at him. "You're right, it is easier if you don't try to go too fast. That's the furthest I've ever done.

"Keep trying and you'll find your right pace. I need to do my laps now."

After about twenty lengths, Cassie started trying to keep pace with him so he slowed for her to swim alongside. She had really good technique. Whoever her teacher had been, had clearly been very good. At fifty laps he stopped.

They stood at the shallow end. She looked up at him and smiled, "That was fun."

"You're a good swimmer."

"I had private lessons."

"Don't you miss having kids your own age to hang around with?"

"Sometimes, but I'm used to it now. Being tutored by Judith is brilliant; she's so clever, and such a good teacher, she makes everything fun. Izzy was doing brilliantly under her, she wanted to be scientist. After Mummy and Theo got married, we started spending so much time in LA and Stillwater, I lost touch with most of my friends."

"Perhaps you can get back in touch with them now."

"Mummy says I should wait until we're sure we're safe."

"That's a good idea. I hope it won't be too long."

He climbed out of the pool. She followed suit, and they went to shower and change.

She watched him clean himself without using the shower gel, as she smothered herself with it while still in her suit. She quickly shampooed her newly bobbed hair and hurried to keep pace with him. When she opened her cubicle door, he was waiting for her.

"I expect you're tired now."

"A bit, I don't normally swim for that long."

"And you've probably got some jet lag. Shall we get some breakfast?"

In the kitchen, Anna was talking to Jason as they drunk coffee.

"Did you have fun, darling?"

"Drew taught me how to swim long-distance underwater, I went nearly a whole length."

"Well done sweetheart."

"And I swam thirty lengths without stopping."

"Gracious. What do you want for breakfast?"

"What are you having, Drew?"

"I'll sort my own out if I'm not in the way. Is that okay, Jason?"

They watched him take a fry pan from a hook, a box of eggs and a pack of bacon from the fridge, before silently preparing himself four eggs and four slices of bacon with three slices of toast, serving it all up with a big glass of orange juice.

The others all had cereals and toast.

"Is that what you have every day?" Cassie asked.

"When I can. I've a big frame and to keep it in good shape, I have to exercise more than most people, and nutrition is important to maintain that level."

"I'd better upgrade our grocery order, Anna," Jason remarked with a smile.

"Will Atticus have similar appetites," Anna asked Drew?

"I expect so. We're an odd breed. I was going to ask if you could show me how to use the wash machine Jason, it looks completely different to US ones."

"You don't need to wash your clothes, Drew. It's my responsibility to see that's done. One of our staff does it Mondays and Thursdays. Anything needed in between I do myself. Just leave your dirty laundry in your hamper."

"In that case I'm going to need to buy a lot more clothes. What's getting delivery of online purchases like here?"

"Pretty good; depends on the retailer."

"Will they take American Express?"

"I expect so, but if you have trouble you can use Jason's household card. In fact, do that anyway and I'll arrange a card of your own," Anna told him. "In the meantime, Jason, can you put some of Drew's things through the wash so he's got something to wear until he gets some more clothes?"

"No problem."

"Thanks all of you."

"Drew has got bullet wounds, Mummy."

"That must have been horrible, but I don't expect he likes to talk about it."

"That's right, ma'am."

He went to clear his things away and Jason stopped him. "Leave those, but can you bring your laundry down when you come?"

"Drew is really strong Mummy; you should have seen the weights he was lifting."

"He was in the army until very recently. I expect they have to stay very fit."

"I think he must have been one of those special forces soldiers. I don't think it would be a very good idea to upset him," Jason said

"When we went shopping one day, there was a man following us, and Drew guessed it was one of the horrible people that have been trying to hurt us. He made him stop, punched him on the nose, pulled him out the car, and lifted him off the ground with one hand! The man even had a gun! He's really brave."

"Yes darling he is and we have to very grateful for that, but he might not want us to keep talking about it in front of him."

"There's a safe in my closet, ma'am. It might hold some of Mr. Lemonis' things?" Drew suggested when he came down.

"That's a good point. Let's go and look."

"Do you know the combination?"

"It's my birthdate."

They went up to his room, and in a few seconds it became clear that the combination had been changed. They tried different variations, then variants on Theo's birth date, and none of them were successful.

"Ma'am, why not ask Percy if he learned about your husband's other family birthdates?"

"Great idea."

After a brief phone call they received a text with three dates for them to try. A few minutes later the safe was open deploying Ariana's birthday in the American way.

"Bastard!" she said, "One of his children was born the week before we got married."

"Don't complain, it's a dumb way to choose a password, making it easy to guess. What's in there?"

Anna reached inside. There was a folder full of papers, a Russian passport, and a gun.

"A gun. I didn't know he had a gun!"

"I think there were a lot of things you didn't know about your husband, ma'am."

"You're so right. How could I have been so taken in?"

"Show me the passport."

She opened the booklet and handed it over with tears in her eyes. He took it and looked at the photograph. Although it was Theo, the document was in the name of Oleg Sorokin. It was current and stamped as having been in used twice in the previous twelve months. "What's in the folder?"

"Let's take it down to the study to look it over. I'm not touching the gun."

"Just leave it in the safe and lock it."

The first thing they found were two wills, his and her own.

"What's my will doing in there?"

"Read it."

She did as he suggested. "This isn't the will I signed!"

"Are you sure?"

"Absolutely certain. There's no sign of a bequest to my girls, and it names him as their guardian. Judith and Percy were to have been their guardians."

"What about the date, and your signature?"

"I can't remember the date, but it was about that time. Theo made a new will at the same time and I'm pretty sure those people were the witnesses. As for the signature it certainly looks like mine."

"Call the lawyer."

"I'll ring them now."

Twenty minutes later she turned to him ashen-faced, "The lawyer that drew up those wills is dead. The senior partner says that two months after the wills were signed, he and his wife were killed in a home robbery, they were shot. He also says that the firm weren't asked to store the originals, and for reasons he can't explain, they have no copies on file."

"Do you have a copy?"

"Yes, just a moment." She hurried through to the library safe and was back very quickly. "It's gone."

"Ma'am, this is big, very big. You can't sit on this."

"What should I do?"

"You need to get a lawyer here, today if possible, and write up a new will that says what you want it to. And I'm guessing that Percy has contacts in MI5 or something. This is clearly an international conspiracy, it looks like an attempt to gain control of Silico or the military secrets it holds. It's far too sophisticated to be anything else."

"You don't think they could have been mixed up in Henry's death do you?"

"I've no way of knowing, but I wouldn't rule it out."

"Oh my God!"

"I'll call Percy, you call a lawyer."

"I haven't used a personal lawyer since those wills were drawn up."

"I'll call Percy."

He texted Percy, *Urgent call, right now!*

When he called the number Percy answered immediately.

"Are you alone?"

"Just a moment…What's happening?"

Drew went on to explain what they'd found. Percy said he'd get a lawyer to her by the afternoon, and he'd speak to *relevant people* about the whole business and get back to them.

"What have we ever done to deserve any of this?" Anna cried.

"What's the matter, Mummy?" Cassie came into the room.

"We've just discovered something else about Theo darling, something terrible. I'm so angry, I can't tell you. I'm angry with him and I'm furious with myself for falling for it."

"He's gone now, Mummy. Please don't cry, I don't like it when you cry. Drew will keep us safe."

Anna wiped her eyes with a tissue.

"Excuse me, ma'am, but should we look at the rest of the papers?"

She flipped through them. "They're mostly in Cyrillic script and Greek. They mean nothing to me."

"I'll put these back in the safe until we know what to do about them,' Drew said.

In the kitchen, Jason was making sandwiches for everybody. Toby and Josh were sitting at the breakfast table already consuming theirs. "Morning Mrs. West," they announced almost as one.

"Hello boys. Jason you're a sweetie, making lunch for me."

"I saw that you were busy."

Lunch was a quiet affair, apart from Toby announcing that the disabled riders would be taking the following two weeks off because the instructor was going away. Josh complained that the badgers' sett at the rear of the property had disturbed the fence posts again.

"I never liked Theo Mummy; he was always horrible to me if he caught me listening."

"What did he say?"

"The last time was when I heard him speaking a funny language on the phone one day. I asked him if it was Greek, and he shouted at me really loudly and told me if I kept being nosey, he'd hit me so hard, I'd wish I was dead."

"When was that Cassie?" Drew asked.

"We were at the Stillwater ranch. It was before Izzy died, because I told her about it and she said that Mummy would never let him hit us."

"Can you remember anything he said at all?" Drew asked.

"Not really, but he mentioned Mummy's name, and a bit later he said mine and Izzy's names as well."

"Okay, sweetie," Anna told her.

When Anna's phone began to ring she jumped. "Percy…Okay…No, if you tell me she's good, then I'm sure she's great. What time?...You will? Thank you, you're such a darling. What would I ever do without you? Would you still be okay to continue as guardian?…I thought you were over that…Oh dear, that's horrible.…Do you think so?…I've no idea…Okay, what are they going to do?…I suppose not. I'll see you soon."

"What's happening?" Drew asked.

"Percy's asked someone from his own solicitor's firm to come this afternoon. She'll be bringing her secretary with her. They'll be here within the hour. I'll ask Toby and Jason to be witnesses."

Drew breathed a metaphorical sigh of relief that she hadn't asked him. "What did he say about MI5?"

"He just said that he'd informed the only people he knew, and they thanked him for the information. Percy's coming over."

"Okay, I hope your spooks over here in the UK are on the ball. It's clear these psychos are playing for keeps. I've been thinking about this. By now they must know that there's more than a small a chance of their main game being exposed. They've made their play now and it's too late to pull out. The thing at the top of their agenda now will be avoiding Lemonis being exposed as a foreign agent. You and the things in that safe are a threat."

"I think you're right." She paused. "Drew, I'm about to ask you an enormous favor. I feel really guilty asking, but at the moment there's a time imperative."

"What is it ma'am? If I can, I will."

"My two preferred guardians have always been Judith and Percy, but he tells me that he has health issues of his own, and he thinks I should have a spare. Drew, I can't think of anybody else that I would trust to put Cassie's welfare first."

"Ma'am, are you asking me to be a guardian for Cassie in the event of your death?"

"Yes."

"You can't be serious; you've only known me a week, and I've no experience of looking after kids. That's crazy!"

"I'm not suggesting you would become her new father; I just want someone who will help act in her interest in the decisions about the running of her affairs alongside Judith and Percy. There would be a trust fund board on which all three of you would have a seat. Judith would be her principal carer."

"But what the hell do I know about deciding what to do with however many goddamned millions you've got. I've had my sister managing most of my financial affairs for the last ten years. Sorry for cursing, ma'am."

"You don't need to know about managing money. You just have to use common sense to help make the right collective decisions about her health, education, housing, and welfare. The pounds and pennies stuff would all be dealt with by the trust. The members would include lawyers, and investment management experts, but none of them know her from Eve. And of course if I stay alive, this is all hypothetical anyway."

"I'll have to think about it."

"Well don't take long. The solicitor will be here soon."

"Maybe you'll find a new partner, or someone more suited."

"Maybe, but if that were the case, I would change my will anyway, but I'm not in any hurry to go looking for romance. Drew I've watched you with my daughter; she trusts you; she's besotted with you, and you're the first man she's been able to connect with since her father died."

"What about Jason?"

"I asked him once before. He said he was terrified at the thought."

"Okay then, I guess."

"Then you better make a good job of keeping me safe."

"Yes, ma'am." He stood up to leave the room."

"Seven-hundred and fifty-four by the way," she said.

"Sorry, ma'am?"

"The number of goddamned millions I've got, as of about three weeks ago." She smiled.

"Jesus H Christ."

The gate alarm sounded and the callers gave their names as Mrs. Patricia Spenser, and Mr. Gerald Seymour of Ruskin and Firth Solicitors. Drew looked to Anna for confirmation, she nodded and he pressed the control to open the gate.

The two solicitors showed their driving licenses as ID, gave Drew their cards, and he showed them through to the study, closed the door, and left them to it.

A short while later, the gate alarm rang again. It was Percy, but before he'd even got out of the car it rang a third time. The caller was the alarm system designer apologizing for being nearly three hours late. When he got out of his car Percy verified it was the guy he was expecting and asked Drew to show him around the property. It took over an hour to do that, but then the man asked Drew to leave him alone to finish the detailed survey.

The gate bell rang a fourth time with two men who gave their names as Firbank and Graves and there to see Mr. Parker.

"That's me, what can I do for you?"

"We're from NatWest Bank Fraud Prevention Branch. We understand that you've noticed suspicious activity in your foreign investment account."

"Oh yeah, come in." He opened the gate for them and went outside to meet them.

The graveled turning circle at the front of the house was now filling up with cars, what with Percy, the solicitor, the alarm guy, and now this one. The guy in the passenger seat got out and offered a hand to shake discreetly proffering a warrant card. "Detective Chief Inspector Firbank SO15 Branch Scotland Yard. Is there somewhere we can go to talk, Mr. Parker?"

"Sure. We can go in the study." Anna was just coming out of the library as he led them through the door. "Two police officers, want to speak to me about that business earlier, ma'am."

"Oh, that's good. Thank you officers. We're just tying up loose ends in here if you need me."

"Okay, ma'am."

"Take a seat,' he said to the cops.

"Who are those people with Lady West, Sir?"

"Lawyers, she's drawing up a new will."

"Good idea, given the circumstances, if what we're being told is true. This is Sergeant Graves. We work together." They nodded an acknowledgement to each other. "Right give me a full account of what's been happening from your point of view. Sergeant Graves will record it, if that's okay."

"No problem." In his career he'd given hundreds of verbal reports of operations, and narrating a chronological account, whilst omitting assumptions and third-party information, was second nature to him. He finished twenty minutes later, with very few interruptions from his listeners.

"That's extremely interesting, Mr. Parker. What can you tell me about your selection for inclusion in that security detail?"

"Over and above what I've already told you, nothing. Mr. Belton may have more; he's the guy who selected me and who passed my concerns on to whoever brought you guys in. He's in the kitchen now. Mr. Belton is…"

Graves spoke for the first time, "We know who Mr. Belton is."

"Mrs. West may have more information."

"When you finally gained access to the safe, tell me more about that."

"Inside we found a handgun, a Russian passport, and a folder full of documents, most of them appearing to be written in Cyrillic script, could be Russian I guess, or any one of a number of languages. A couple were Greek. We opened the passport, it was in the name of Oleg Sorokin, but the photo was unmistakably Lemonis. That's when I advised Mrs. West to report what we'd found and she called Mr. Belton."

"What sort of gun was it?"

"9mm Glock 19."

"Did you touch it?"

"It was on the top shelf, there was no need."

"That's good."

"Do you think Mrs. West will be long?" Firbank asked.

"Would you like me to find out?"

"Yes, please."

Anna was in the process of showing the solicitors out of the door. "I'll sort the gate, ma'am. The cops would like to speak to you now."

The alarm guy was in the kitchen with Percy, Jason, and Cassie. "How did it go?" Drew asked the alarm specialist.

"I think I've got all the information I need. Let me talk you through what I propose." It took forty minutes for him to explain the intricacies of his recommendations for a new system and for them to agree on the preferred options. Throughout Cassie had stood by his side holding his arm and listening to everything that was said.

"I've designed in as much of the old equipment as possible, but much of it won't be suitable."

"I doubt that will be a problem."

Percy confirmed that it wouldn't be because it would be regarded as a company expense.

"I can't give you a precise quote right now, but I can give you a reasonably accurate estimate."

Percy stepped in, "We won't be looking elsewhere, so take it as read that you've got the contract. It's when you can do it that's most important at the moment. There have been a number of attempts on Mrs. West's life in the last few months, and we need to get this done as soon as physically possible."

"I'll need to confirm, but I'm hoping we can start in about a week to ten days and have the job completed by the end of the month. It will take four engineers working all daylight hours. We can't start earlier, because the main control panel has to be assembled to order and shipped from Germany."

"If that's the best you can do, then it will have to be good enough."

After the guy left Percy asked, "How is it going with the police?"

"I doubt very much if they're cops. Said they're SO15, Special Branch, but my guess is they're MI5."

"I suspect you're right."

"I guess they'll want to speak to you next."

"Are those men spies?" Cassie whispered.

"More like counterspies, people who catch other people's spies."

"This is very scary."

"Now that these people are involved they'll get to the bottom of it, Cassie," Percy told her.

"I'm worried about Judith," Jason said. "I miss her, and I know she'll be missing Anna and Cassie."

"Lemonis doesn't have any beef with Judith as far as I know. As soon as she's had all their things shipped, she can hop on a plane and be right here."

"She told me last night that the shipping company are coming later today."

"When they all had to sign her new will, Mummy asked me to film it on my iPad."

"That was an important job. It shows how much your mom trusts you," Drew told her.

"I saw the bit at the end, where it said if anything happens to her, then you, and Judith and Uncle Percy will look after me."

"It would be mostly Judith who would be your caregiver, I expect."

"You would still be around to keep me safe wouldn't you?"

"Of course, unless you fire me." He smiled.

"Apart from Mummy, the people I love most in the world are Judith, Uncle Percy, Jason, and you."

"I think we're all very lucky that you think so highly of us," Percy said.

Graves appeared at the kitchen door, "Mr. Parker, could you join us in the library? Mr. Belton, if you can wait around for a while longer we'll need to chat to you before we go if that's okay."

Drew followed Graves back to the library.

"Mr. Parker, we have a difficult decision to make and Mrs. West says she needs you to help her make it."

"Ma'am?"

"I'll let Inspector Firbank explain."

"At present, Lemonis isn't aware that the contents of that safe have been discovered. We believe that gives us two ways to deal with the current situation. The first is to play it the way I'm sure Lemonis would prefer, that is grant him access to the safe and pretend that this is just a domestic dispute, only about his infidelity, unrelated to the recent violent episodes. Telling about the new will would, in effect nullify his attempt to seize control of Silico and essentially remove the immediate threat to Mrs. West."

"What's wrong with that?"

"It would make it difficult for us to identify who else might be involved in this affair."

"So what do you suggest?"

"That we leave the contents of the safe as they are, so that when Lemonis comes here to retrieve them, he'll take them away, hopefully believing that nobody has any evidence of his Russian connections and that his plans remain achievable. However, because he won't know that Mrs. West has already changed her will, there would remain some degree of risk."

"Are you proposing that we allow Lemonis in this house, to go to that safe and remove the contents so he's the only one in the building with a gun?"

"Ah yes, that is a good point." Firbank conceded.

"I've got someone on their way with a replacement, because the one that's in there may have his prints on it, and we may be able to connect it to a firearms incident that we believe is possibly associated with this business."

"Are you talking about the deaths of my previous solicitor and his wife?"

"Yes, ma'am."

"What do you think, ma'am?" asked Drew.

She put her face in her hands while she thought, then looked up. "Obviously, I want the risk removed as quickly and effectively as possible, but I don't want that worthless individual free to cause any more damage to people like me, to the security of our country, or to yours Drew. I'd prefer for him to feel the full force of the law. He's responsible for the death of my daughter, Rupert Loughty, and Michael Maus, and probably that lawyer and his wife. He's threatened my life and Cassie's, and he's stripped me of every ounce of my dignity. He needs to be locked away, but only if it's possible to manage the risk."

Drew thought for a moment, "The gun that's on the way here, is it functioning and loaded?"

"I imagine so." Graves replied.

"We can't be sure that he'll come here though Drew, can we?" Anna asked.

"He's in the air as we speak, expected to land at Oxford Airport at about 20:10 hours," Graves told them. "Whether he'll come straight here or leave it until tomorrow we have no way of knowing, but I think we can be pretty confident he'll come."

"Are you proposing to give me any back up here?"

"We could be on dodgy legal ground there," Firbank said.

"So it's okay handing over a loaded weapon to a known foreign agent with proven deadly intent, but not to provide protection to a citizen of your own country."

"The problem is that the crimes you are accusing him of are unproven or in another country."

"For fuck's sake, excuse me, ma'am. I mean, what the hell?"

"It does sound ridiculous, Inspector," Anna said.

"Anyway, ma'am, providing Lemonis comes alone, I think there might be ways to make the risk more manageable, so it's up to you? Is there anywhere that we can send Cassie overnight?" Drew said.

They heard the gate bell ring.

"I might be able to find one of her old school chums to have a sleepover. If not she can stay in the coach house or the stable block with Jason until he's gone. We are only talking about Theo, aren't we?"

There was a knock on the door. It was Jason. "There's a gentleman to see Mr. Graves."

He left the room and was back in seconds holding a gun in a clear plastic bag.

"So can we assume we're going with option two then?" Firbank asked.

"Okay then, Inspector, I suppose so. Is that okay, Drew?"

"If that's what you want, ma'am."

"Let's go and have a look at this safe then," said Graves, moving toward the door.

"Wait a minute, give me that gun."

Graves handed it over and Drew stripped it to its component parts in seconds and lifted the firing pin mechanism. "Have you got a paper clip and a pair of strong scissors?"

Anna opened a drawer and handed him what he'd asked for. He took a paperback from one of the shelves and put it the desk. After straightening the clip he put it between the blades of the scissors and held them on their side on the book. By hitting the back of the upper blade with the heel of his hand, he created a weak spot in the pin enabling him to snap the metal where he wanted. Then taking the small piece he'd broken off he used the scissors to make a small hook at the end. After tearing off a corner of a page from the book, he chewed it and used it to hold the little piece of metal in the spacer sleeve while he put the slide assembly back together.

Even including the meticulous wiping of prints, reassembly of the weapon took just a few more seconds. After opening a window, he pumped a round into the chamber, aimed the gun at a huge oak tree, and pulled the trigger. The result was just a click so he pumped the slide again ejecting the round and putting a new one in the chamber. Then he repeated the exercise twice more with the same result. The others watched him pick up the rounds and inspect the primers to assure himself they were unmarked, before wiping them of prints and reloading them into the magazine. The others watched silently as he used the scissors to make a scratch on the nose of the gun. He then wiped his prints off the barrel and stock with his handkerchief and handed it back to Graves.

"You've done that before."

"No, just heard about it."

"You ready now?"

Drew nodded.

The cop took a pair of purple nitrile gloves from his pocket and pulled them on. Firbank did likewise, and they both followed Drew up the stairs. He pointed out the safe to Firbank and Graves took out his phone to record what was happening. Drew gave Firbank the combination and watched him go through a forensically secure method of removing the documents one by one, photographing them, and replacing them in the safe. Finally he took the gun from the safe, put it in a plastic bag, and replaced it with one Drew had spiked.

The inspector closed the safe, Graves stopped his recording and they all returned to the ground floor. They asked Percy a few questions, gave everybody an anonymous looking card with nothing other than a telephone number on it and then advised them to put it in their phones under 'Helpful Friend'. After wishing them well and instructing them to call the number before speaking to the regular police about any developments, they left.

"You sure do things different over here. That has to be the most bizarre spook encounter I've ever heard about," Drew told them.

Anna said, "Most of us never get to have spook encounters."

Seventeen

At about seven-thirty Drew's phone buzzed. He glanced at it and said, "I'm going to take a quick look around the grounds. Won't be long." He wandered out into the dusk and began walking the perimeter fence. The grass was still damp from rain the day before and blades of recently mown grass stuck to his shoes. As he approached the oak tree that had been his target earlier in the day the silhouette of a figure briefly showed itself.

"You're losing your touch Babychamp; you had no idea I was here." The man was using Drew's nickname from his rookie days in Delta, when he wanted to win at everything, and usually did.

"In your dreams Sweeney. I made you two hundred yards back. Everything okay with you these days?"

"Not bad. Got a contract doing security for a chain of casinos; pay isn't fantastic but it's easy money. What about you? Have they let you loose on the free world at last?"

"Yeah, doing close-protection work."

"That's a bit tame for an action junkie like you."

"Maybe but perhaps I've changed."

"Believe that if I see it."

"Did you manage to get what I wanted?"

"Sure, a Browning. I doubt it's clean though. Short notice." He handed it over.

"No problem. What do I owe you?"

"Just give me what I paid, two hundred."

"I haven't had time to get UK currency yet. Here's five hundred bucks. I'm covered for it."

"If you're sure, thanks. I'll hang around and keep my eyes open until 09:00 but I can't get directly involved I'm afraid."

"I know that. I'm grateful for all you're doing."

"I'll let you finish your walk. Stay safe buddy."

"You too and thanks."

Back indoors he cleaned the bottom of his shoes in the laundry room then put them back on. Joining Anna and Cassie in the family room carrying a pint glass of milk he asked, "How are you both?"

"I'm a bit scared, Drew," Cassie replied.

"Me too, to be honest," Anna said.

"I'm nearly peeing my panties," Jason contributed, as he carried in a tray of drinks.

"I'm told Lemonis landed about ten minutes ago, so if he's coming straight here, he'll be here in about forty or fifty minutes I'd guess. When he arrives, Cassie, I want you to go to the coach house with Jason and stay there until I tell you to come down."

"Is it going to be dangerous?"

"I doubt it, but it might be unpleasant. If that's the case, the less people involved the better."

"How do you learn to be brave like you? You're never frightened."

"Who told you that? Of course I get frightened. If you don't get scared in dangerous situations it probably means you're a bit dumb. You just have to manage your fear by telling yourself that whatever it is that scares you doesn't really care if you're frightened or not and won't change its behavior because you are. You just have to do whatever you can to remove the threat. Sometimes that means running away, but often it means confronting the problem. When it's a person threatening you, they'll feed off your fear and rely on it to force your submission, so often it's best to do something to confuse them, something they're not expecting. Sometimes it can give you moments to change the course of events."

"How do you mean?" Anna asked.

"Well for example, they might expect you to run away, so if you attack them they have to rethink what to do. Or if they'd expect you to struggle you can just go limp and make yourself a dead weight. The main rules are don't give them time and fight dirty; use any tactic or any object to hand as a weapon if you're struggling at close quarters. Laugh, say something stupid, say anything that comes into your head, even if you don't believe it."

Three quarters of an hour later the gate bell rang.

"Don't panic any of you. Jason take Cassie to your room. Mrs. West wait in the family room."

Drew waited until the bell rang a second time before answering. "Can I help you?"

"It's me, Mr. Lemonis. I want to speak to my wife."

"One moment." He paused. Anna watched from the family room door. "Mrs. West doesn't want to speak to you."

"Look there's been a huge misunderstanding. I can clear it up in just a few minutes if I can just speak to her."

"Do it through your lawyer."
"That really isn't necessary if…"
"I've made Mrs. West's position clear."
"At least let me collect some of my things."
"Tell me what you want, and I'll have them sent on."
"There are some things that I need urgently."
"I'll bring them to you at the gate."
"They're in the safe in my room."
"Tell me the combination and I'll get them for you."
"Do you think I'm stupid. They're highly confidential, I'm not letting you see them. I need them for an important meeting tomorrow. Just let me in long enough to get them and I'll leave."
"Just a minute." He paused again. "Are you alone?"
"Pavel is with me."
"Leave Volkov in the car at the gate and walk up the drive."
"Listen to me you fucking oaf, you don't tell me…"
"If you want to come in here then that's exactly what I do. So what is it?"
"Okay then, just open the gate."
Drew pressed the button to open it and immediately closed it again so the car wouldn't have the opportunity to drive in. When he opened the front door, he immediately saw that Volkov had come through with Lemonis and they were walking together toward him.
He waited for them to get close.
"I said for him to wait in the car."
"Well he's here now."
Volkov silently smirked.
"Yes he is, isn't he?"
"Well let me in then."
"Not until Volkov is in the car."
"Don't be ridiculous. I want him here for my protection."
"Why do you need protection?"
"From you."
"You don't need protection from me at the moment, but you will if you try to come in without my permission. So unless you want to stand out there all night he goes back to the car."
"How do I know I can trust you?"

"Because I'm not a lying duplicitous asshole, like some people I've had dealings with lately. I won't hurt you unless you do anything to endanger Mrs. West or Cassandra."

"That's absurd, why would I do that?"

"I refer you to my remark about lying duplicitous assholes."

"You insolent scum."

"Yeah well. Is he going or not?"

Lemonis turned to Volkov and shook his head toward the gate.

"Well let me in then."

"When he's in the car."

They waited until he reached the gate and Drew opened the gate just long enough for Volkov to step through, then opened the door and stepped aside for Lemonis to enter.

"Wait there Lemonis, I need to check you for weapons."

"That's Mister Lemonis to you."

"Mister is a title of deference or respect, neither of which apply in your case."

"You bastard, I'll make sure you come to regret this," Lemonis said as Drew frisked him.

"I'm trembling. I'm a close-protection officer, Lemonis, it's what we do. Unlike most of the amateurs that you hired to protect your wife. Sorta makes me wonder why."

He searched the man's attaché case and handed it back.

"Anna," he called. "None of this is necessary if you'll only let me explain."

She came to the door of the family room, "Get your things, then fuck off out of my life forever Theo. I'll never forgive you for the lies and humiliation. The rest of your stuff is in the garage. If you want it, send a van by the end of next week or it will go to the charity shop." Then she stepped out of sight.

"Please don't waste time, Lemonis. Mrs. West has had a busy day."

When he reached the door of what had once been his own bedroom he stopped and turned. "You can wait here."

"Wrong, Lemonis. I can wait wherever the hell I like."

The man turned, stomped into the room, straight to the closet and stood in front of the safe so as to hide what he was doing. It took him less than a minute to empty the contents of the safe into his case. Then he pulled opened the shallow jewelry drawer to find it empty.

"There was a Rolex in here and a gold signet ring, I suppose you've stolen them."

"Do I look like a man that has any use for either of those things. If they were there, then they're now in the garage with the rest of your things."

"If you think that by moving into my room you will end up moving into my wife's bed you're in for a disappointment. She's a cold frigid woman."

"Lemonis, I'll say this as politely as I can. My position here is as a close-protection officer, and in that capacity, sleeping with her would be a violation. My role does not include defending her against verbal abuse from lying duplicitous assholes. However in my capacity as a respectable human being, if you use such filthy derogatory language about her again in my presence, I'll put my hand down your throat and rip your lungs out. As long as that's clear, and you've got all you need, you can leave, and I don't expect to see you on these premises again."

Lemonis looked at Drew with pure malevolence and turned to walk back down the stairs.

"You have a nice night *Mister* Lemonis, won't you?" Drew said as he followed him and watched him walk out the door and along the drive to the gate.

When they drove away he closed the door and joined Anna in the family room.

"I heard what you said to him, what did he say about me?"

"I'd rather not repeat it, ma'am."

"Thank God that's over though," she said, as Jason and Cassie came into the room.

"I'm sorry, ma'am but I don't think it is over."

"What do you mean?!"

"There was no point in him pressing the point about Volkov. There are no innocent reasons for his pet ape to be here. He knows I'm no threat to him unless he threatens you. I think that he wants to bring this to a conclusion as soon as possible. I don't know the reason for that, but I believe he'll be back, probably with Volkov. I may be wrong, but I don't want to take any chances,"

"Tonight?"

"I don't know. Possibly, because Judith and Atticus will be here by tomorrow night."

"What are we going to do?"

"Just in case, I want you and Cassie to spend the night in the coach house with Jason. I'll take care of them."

"On your own?!"

"That's my job, ma'am."

"Would we be better in the stable block?"

"I think you might be more vulnerable in the stable block."

"Oh God. I don't understand why the police can't help."

"Because we've no evidence, and all the crimes he's committed have been in the US, and even they aren't proven. But they won't do anything until he thinks we've all gone to bed."

"What if we all just sit up all night?" Cassie suggested.

"It would be one way to deal with it I guess, but we can't stay awake every night."

"We need to get him out of our lives," Anna said. "I just feel guilty at you having to take all the risk."

"Like I say, ma'am, it's my job."

Cassie reiterated her fears, "This is scary."

"Try not to be too scared, Cassie. These people are amateurs,' he told her.

"Who will he have with him though?" Jason asked.

"Volkov almost certainly but he isn't a professional soldier; he's just a thug. I wouldn't be surprised to find Gates there. He's not a soldier either, or if he is, not a particularly good one, not if his inept handling of whatever he was trying to achieve in Santa Monica is anything to go by."

"But you're on your own."

"What I want you to do is think about how best the two of you can use what's in Jason's room to barricade the door, but make it look as if you're in Judith's. I very much doubt they will get the chance to go anywhere near you in there though. I'm going to make a few little preparations. I'll be back in a bit."

Eighteen

The garage was Drew's first destination where he rummaged through Lemonis' belongings until he found the Rolex and the signet ring that he'd been accused of stealing and slipped them in his pocket. Then he emptied one of the suitcases of its contents on to the pile and took it with him.

Next he went to the study where earlier he'd seen three unused prepaid burner phones in one of the desk drawers, after removing the packaging he turned them on and made sure they were all charged, before putting them all on silent and vibrate. After marking them, *1*, *2*, and *3* with a permanent marker, he called his own phone with each of them, and recorded their numbers in his contacts.

In his own room, he put the Rolex and the signet ring in its case on the top of the set of the drawers near the closet for their distraction value. In Anna's room, he put the suitcase on the bed and began to fill it with her clothes, but left it open on her bed with some spilling out.

Making his way to the attic rooms he opened one of the small access doors into the roof space and placed phone number *1* onto the particle board floor, called it with his own, and let it vibrate long enough to satisfy himself it could be heard from inside the room with the door closed. Across the room, the small free-standing closet was just big enough for him to fit inside once he'd removed the box of children's toys that was inside. He placed that on the floor next to the roof space door and returned to the ground floor.

Slipping out the back door he went to the stable block, turned on the light in the tack room, closed the door and returned to the house. Looking back, he saw that the strip of light beneath the door was just visible.

In the kitchen, he put a pan of water on the cooker on the lowest available heat setting. Then taking another pan, he put phone number *2* inside it and placed it on the tiled floor of the downstairs washroom opposite the study and closed the door. He locked it from the outside using the emergency access facility of the lock. He briefly called the phone and waited until he heard the satisfyingly loud noise of its vibration.

Returning to the family room door, he silently attracted their attention and held his finger to his lips, before speaking, "We need to find somewhere for you to hide, ma'am." Then, using his right hand as if he were operating a sock puppet he indicated that he wanted them to keep talking. "It needs to be somewhere they wouldn't think to look if possible."

Leading them out of the room. Anna said, "I can't think of anywhere."

"What about the kitchen store cupboard?" Jason offered, catching on, "I tidied up in there last week."

"Too obvious, same goes with bedroom closets."

"There's the pool room." Cassie suggested.

"The cubicle doors have that big space at the bottom."

When they reached the gym they went inside and closed the door.

"We can't hide in here, we'd be found right away, they'd see us through the big windows."

"You're not going to hide in here."

"Are they here already?"

"Not yet Jason, but I doubt it will be long and definitely tonight if they're coming. Lemonis needs to make sure you don't make another will."

"Why did you do all that with the hand signals Drew, are they listening to us?"

"I think they were, Cassie. On his way out of the house earlier Theo pressed a listening bug to the inside of the lower staircase newel post. They won't be able to hear us from in here."

"Why didn't you tell us, or take it away?"

"Because I wanted them to hear, and I wanted what you said to sound natural. Once he's run his colors up the flagpole, it's a straightforward crime so the local police force can get involved, as can the press. So if anything else happens in the future, suspicion will immediately fall on him. We just need to get through the next hour or two. I've prepared a few little surprises for them."

"Do you mean booby traps, like in the *Home Alone* movies?" Cassie said excitedly.

"Maybe not marbles on the floor, blowtorches, or paint cans on a string, but you're getting the idea. Now listen, the things I've done are to confuse them and hopefully split them up, making them easier to deal with. None of you are going to hide in the coach house, stable block, or any of the places you discussed earlier. All three of you are going to hide in the very last place they'll think of looking."

"Where's that?"

"Behind the big sofa in the family room."

While he was talking he lifted one of the one-handed multi-weight dumbbells, removed the weights, assessed it for suitability as a weapon, and nodded his satisfaction with the heavy iron bar.

"Jason turn your cellphone off. Mrs. West put yours on vibrate only and give it to me. Cassie make sure yours is set to ring and give that to me as well."

"The ringtone is *Hakuna Matata* is that alright?"

"So much the better. Make sure the volume is turned up."

"But we won't have any protection behind the sofa."

"Jason, I doubt that they'll even do more than poke their heads in the door so if you stay still and keep quiet you'll be fine. They'll be far too busy to do much more."

His phone vibrated in his pocket. He read the incoming text, *SUV 5 occs just arrived. One getting out.*

Drew acknowledged it. 'Five. More than I was expecting.' He thought. "Okay, go where I told you, leave the lights exactly as they are, and keep quiet."

He put Anna's phone in the library, ran up the stairs, and threw Cassie's phone on her bed before going to the back door to watch the shadows for movement. After a minute, light from the half-moon showed a figure approach the far end of the stable block. He flipped the switch that provided power to the stables and watched the tack room light go out. Slipping outside he crossed to the stables. The guy was looking back the way he came allowing Drew to creep up close behind him unnoticed.

"They're in the stables, they just switched the light out." The guy said into his cellphone. "Okay I'll wait."

But Drew didn't wait, he stepped behind him and two seconds later he was on the ground with a broken neck.

His cellphone buzzed. *Three more dismounting.*

He opened the tack room door and dragged the body inside. It was Priest. He picked up his gun and ran back to the house where he left the door open, and turned the power to the stable block back on. Turning up the heat under the pan a little as he passed through he went to the study and waited.

Three minutes later he heard voices. "It looks like they fucked off after taking out Priest."

"Fuck! Let's not take it for granted. You search down here. I'll look upstairs."

"Where's Gates?"

"Searching the coach house." Footsteps disappearing upstairs followed.

Drew waited and called the phone in the washroom, moments later a man appeared and grabbed at the washroom door handle with his left hand. He held a gun in the other. Drew brought the dumbbell bar down on the guy's head so hard that it fractured his skull. Pleasingly it was Volkov.

He kicked Volkov's HK45 away and stepped over his body. He ran up the first stairs where a man he recognized was in Anna's room fondling her underwear. Taking advantage of the diversion, he quickly continued to the attic rooms.

"Where are you?" he heard Gates' voice call.

"Main bedroom. Looks like they've gone."

"Don't take any chances. Keep looking."

In the room where he was waiting he heard Gates shout, "Have you looked everywhere?"

"Not the top floor yet."

Seconds later he heard a blast of *Hakuna Matata!'*

"Where's that coming from?"

"The kid's bedroom, but she ain't in there." The man was slowly climbing the stairs.

Drew waited in the tiny closet with the door closed all bar a quarter inch while the man searched the other room. Then he saw the man appear in the doorway. It was Frenchie. He looked around the room and moved towards the closet. That's when he called the burner phone in the roof space expecting it to buzz straightaway, but nothing happened. He braced himself for discovery as Frenchie's hand reached for the door, and then at the last second the phone began to vibrate.

Frenchie's head snapped toward the roof space door, distracting him enough for Drew to burst out and punch his former teammate in the side of the head with a fist gripping the dumbbell bar. His victim dropped to the floor as his finger pulled the trigger and fired a single suppressed shot into the wall.

Drew took the silenced HK45 out of Frenchie's hand, put it to one side, and extracted a vicious looking knife from his belt. After stripping the sheet from the bed he cut it into long strips and used them to tie and gag the unconscious man.

"Where the fuck are you Frenchie?" Gates shouted up the stairs.

Drew waited to discover what the treacherous bastard would do next.

Several minutes passed during which he heard nothing. Then suddenly he heard Cassie scream. Gripping the gun he'd taken from the tack room guy, he headed down the first stairs.

"Drew, he's got Cassie!" Anna screamed.

"Get down here, Parker now. Or I'll kill the pair of them."

"Where are you then, you worthless piece of dogshit?" he asked from the top of the final stairs.

"In the kitchen."

"Okay, I'm coming."

"Throw down the gun."

From halfway down he threw Priest's weapon and watched it skid across the carpet towards the front door. Jason staggered out of the kitchen, clearly having been pushed from behind. He could hear Anna crying inconsolably, and when he stepped into the kitchen doorway he found Gates gripping a terrified, struggling and weeping Cassie around the waist, and pointing a 9mm Glock at him.

"Not such a smartass now then, Parker, eh?"

"I'm not the one having to hide behind an eleven-year-old girl though a.m. I? You're such a loser."

"The only thing that matters is who wins the endgame so when you're all dead, I won't be a loser then will I?"

"Is that your plan then, to kill everybody?" Cassie screamed and struggled more violently than ever.

"Who's to stop me?"

"I am. Don't panic, Cassie. Remember what I told you earlier.

"How exactly are you going to stop me?" he laughed, pointing the gun at him.

"I don't know, maybe with this,' he said, taking the Browning that Sweeney had acquired for him out of his pocket.

"While I'm holding the kid? I don't think so."

"What do you think, Cassie, will he be able to stop me with that *limp*?

"Fuck this, life's too short,' Gates said. "You'd better get behind me your ladyship, if you want your little bitch to live."

Anna did as he said, but at that moment several things happened simultaneously. Gates pulled the trigger and his gun misfired. Anna screamed. Cassie allowed herself to go completely lifeless causing him to lurch to one side so the shot that Drew fired instead of penetrating the rogue bodyguard's forehead grazed his ear instead.

Gates dropped Cassie and pulled his trigger again. On the second occasion it didn't misfire, and the bullet took a small piece out of the inside of Drew's left arm. Thankfully the third and fourth attempts resulted only in a dull click, and he threw the gun at Drew, turned, and ran for the back door. With Anna rushing to her daughter's aid, Drew stepped over Cassie and ran after Gates, firing again on the run.

Almost shaking with a rage he hadn't felt for many years he stopped, took aim at the figure disappearing into the darkness, and fired. Gates cried out, staggered, and grasped his leg before disappearing away into the night.

Drew went back inside, closed, and locked the door.

"Are you all okay?" he asked.

"Yes, I think so." A tearful Anna was clutching her daughter to her side.

"What about you Jason?"

"I don't…' he said and fainted.

"Has he been shot?" Drew asked.

"I don't think so but Gates hit him really hard with his gun."

For the first time Drew noticed the blood running down Jason's face and neck. The left shoulder of his tee-shirt was drenched in blood.

"Can you get something to dress that wound, ma'am?"

"Is it over?"

"I'll tell you soon."

He took his phone from his pocket and texted Firbank. *Our friends came back to play 5 this time and decided to play rough 2 won't be playing again 1 is taking a break I persuaded him to wait around to talk about it 1 got hurt like he did in US and team owner didn't get out of the team bus Medics could be helpful for post-match treatment local referees useful to decide score help with post-match pitch repair may be necessary.*

No sooner had he finished typing than the phone vibrated in his hand. It was a text from Sweeney.

SUV just drove off at speed with two. Passenger appeared to have leg wound. Got windscreen pic of them in headlights of another car. Send it next. That's me done; Hope you're all okay. Good luck.

He texted back. *All good, thanks. I owe you one.*

The phone buzzed again with the incoming picture which clearly showed Lemonis and Gates in the front seats of the SUV.

"The bastards have gone now. I've told Firbank, he'll send cops and medics. How's Jason?"

"He's coming round now," Anna said, and looked up at him, "Drew, you've been shot!"

"Can you get something to wrap around it to stop me bleeding all over. I've got things to do before the circus arrives. A tea towel would probably do the job."

Anna leapt into action.

"How are you now, Cassie?"

His words shook the child out of a stupor. "I'm scared. Have they gone forever?"

"I can't be sure what they were trying to achieve, but I don't see them finding a way back from this."

While Anna wrapped his arm his phone buzzed again. *Local referees and medics on their way. Please decline post-match interview until refs have been briefed by FIFA reps. Stay in touch we may have more info in next 24.*

"Cassie, I need your help. Do you know what duct tape is?"

"No."

"What about cloth tape?"

"I know what that is."

"Do you know if you've you got any around here?"

"I think there's some in the laundry room. Shall I get it?"

"That would be great."

She was gone and back in seconds.

"That's fantastic. Now I need you to stay here with your mom and help her keep Jason calm. I'm just going to step outside for a few seconds, and I'll be right back."

He picked up Sweeney's gun, ran outside to the tack room, put the gun in the dead man's hand to make certain it had his prints on it as well as his own, then took it back inside and left it on the kitchen worktop. As he ran back inside he heard the first sounds of emergency sirens in the distance.

"Will you three still be okay on your own for a second while I do something upstairs. Don't go into the hall."

He pressed the button to open the gates and then quickly put the gun he'd taken from Priest in a drawer in the study along with Frenchie's knife, before taking the stairs two at a time, carrying the roll of duct tape.

When he got to the attic room he was just in time to prevent Frenchie freeing his hands from their makeshift ligature.

"Hi Frenchie, nice of you to visit. Next time it might be better to call ahead. I hope you weren't thinking of shooting off before we had a chance to chat."

The man was making all sorts of attempts to communicate something to Drew, but he wasn't interested, and replaced the gag with tape

Tape was as good as cable ties when it came to restraining somebody and in minutes Frenchie was more immobile than ever.

"Make yourself comfortable, my friend. There'll be someone along to chat with you very shortly."

Drew was back on the ground floor to open the front door to the first cops where he offered his hands for handcuffs. "There's been a shooting. There were four intruders and a getaway driver, two intruders are dead, one is injured and restrained on the top floor, the fourth one escaped with gunshot wounds. One member of the household has a blunt force injury and two psychologically traumatized females in the kitchen, and myself with a minor gunshot to my arm. One body is in the hallway behind me, the other is in the stable block. There's one gun on the top floor on the dressing table, one on the hallway floor near the body, another on the floor by the kitchen door, and one on the kitchen worktop."

The first cop dragged him outside and cuffed him. In common with most British police they were unarmed.

"Mrs. West, the police are here, it's safe for you and Cassie to come out. Jason too if he can."

Anna emerged supporting Jason, preceded by Cassie. All were looking pale and shaken in the police car headlights. At that moment two more police cars and an ambulance pulled into the drive. A sergeant leapt from one car and asked for a sit rep from the first two, who between them gave a garbled rendition of Drew's words when they'd first arrived.

The sergeant dispassionately looked Drew up and down, "Put him in the back of your car for the minute." Then turning to Anna, he asked, "Tell me who you are, miss."

"My name is Lady Annabelle Astley-West. This is my house, and these are my daughter Cassandra West, and Jason Yates my housekeeper. The man you have handcuffed and locked in that police car is Drew Parker my close-protection officer who tonight has single-handedly fought off the latest attempt to kidnap or kill me and my daughter. This time there were three or four armed men and it was the fourth time in less than three months."

"Tell me what happened here tonight, ma'am."

"I heard Mr. Parker give your officer all the information you need for the present, and I'm not prepared to supplement that for the time being. Before you proceed further you should refer to Detective Chief Inspector Firbank of SO15 Scotland Yard. I have his number somewhere if it helps."

"That won't be necessary for the moment, thank you ma'am."

An armed response vehicle arrived a short while later, along with an inspector, who instructed the team to ensure the building was safe, whilst the paramedics treated Jason and Drew. Both Drew and Jason were told they needed hospital treatment. Drew refused to go until SO15 arrived, and Jason insisted on waiting for Drew. Anna and Cassie were advised to seek treatment for shock, but they also refused to go anywhere without Drew.

When the armed cops had given the all-clear, they verified the situation corresponded exactly with the information that Drew had given the first responders as recorded on their bodycams.

Over an hour later, Firbank and Graves arrived and had a long conversation with the inspector in charge. The drive looked like the set of an action movie and there were two TV vans in the roadway. Anna, Cassie, and Jason were still shivering on the front steps, wrapped in silver foil blankets and continued to refuse to leave without Drew. One cop had been dispatched inside to get coats for them, but the after effects of shock were still affecting them.

Percy had finally been alerted and offered to put them up until the police had finished with the crime scene, but Anna indignantly declared that she wasn't going *to allow that asshole of a husband the satisfaction of seeing me driven from my home.* She didn't care if it meant sleeping in the garage.

After an intervention by Graves, the four occupants of the house agreed to be taken to hospital for treatment after an assurance they would be back in time to meet Judith and Atticus when they arrived.

The ambulance had been sent away, and the four injured and traumatized people were transported to and from hospital in a police van and treated away from the general public by doctors and nurses asked to sign an Official Secrets Act declaration beforehand.

Drew's gunshot wound had made a gouge about half an inch wide and an inch and a half long on the inside of his upper left arm. They stitched and dressed it, and gave him pain killers.

Jason's head wound was going to leave a scar near his hairline, and the bruising along the side of his head seemed to be getting worse every minute; with the bandage he looked like the survivor of a war.

Anna and Cassie were examined for immediate signs of PTSD, given sedatives, and advised to speak to their own doctor.

They returned to the house in little more than an hour. Each of them was to be interviewed under caution but the circus outside the house had already been reduced to a single police patrol car, an unmarked CID car, the car Firbank and Graves had arrived in, and a small hatchback belonging to the most recent arrival, a defense solicitor. Percy had been asked to leave but before going had ensured Ruskin and Firth sent for the lawyer to be present when one by one the adults were interviewed

One uniformed cop manned the gate, and another was in the house.

The press had been told that there had been an armed intrusion and a man was *helping them with their enquiries.* There was no mention of dead bodies, or gunshot wounds. The CSIs had been urged to be thorough but quick and to treat each area of violence as a discrete crime scene rather than the whole house.

The house occupants all gave truthful narrative statements of the events of the night without being pressed for explanations or references to previous events, apart from Drew who deliberately omitted a few details. To the bewilderment of the lawyer, none of it was challenged by the police and she was back in her hatchback and on her way home a great deal quicker than she had imagined she would be. Involvement of SO15 had made the whole thing much simpler for the local police although they clearly hadn't been happy about it.

By five a.m. the household were sitting in the kitchen together drinking coffee or hot chocolate. None of them discussed the events until Jason spoke up.

"If nobody else is going to say it, I will. Drew, you're a fucking miracle. Sorry for swearing Anna, but if it weren't for him maybe none of us would even be alive right now. Thank you so much not just for saving me, but for saving two people who are more precious to me than you can possibly know."

Anna said, "Jason's right, and I've been trying to find the right words to say how I feel, and they wouldn't come, but I agree Jason, you are a fucking miracle. While we three cowered behind the sofa, you went out alone, and tackled four armed men. Without weapons or support, just courage, and your wit. I doubt I'll ever be able to find the means to thank you properly."

Cassie stood up, put her arms around Drew's neck and kissed him long and hard. She pulled back and stared in in his eyes, "I think you're a fucking miracle as well. I love you. Thank you for saving us. You don't say very much, and you have to do some nasty violent things sometimes, but I can tell that inside you are a kind gentle man." She kissed him again and went back, giggling, to sit beside her mother.

"What are you giggling about?" Anna asked.

"I said *fucking* in front of you."

"Yes well, we'll give each other a free pass this time, but we won't make a habit of it, okay?"

"I wasn't unarmed and I didn't do it alone,' Drew stoically pointed out. "And I fouled up."

"What do you mean?"

"I had a gun that a buddy acquired for me and he acted as a pair of eyes for me. He let me know when they arrived. I underestimated how many people there would be, and when I doctored that gun I obviously didn't do it well enough."

"Oh well in that case, I take it all back. You had a guy watching and you knew what time they arrived. Big deal! You outwitted, outfought, and overcame four professional gunmen on your own. Please don't try to belittle that. There was me thinking you were clairvoyant and able to predict the precise numbers of adversaries every time before you go into action, and you're only prepared to stand in front of a loaded weapon aimed at you if you know in advance that it's been deliberately deactivated so it won't fire. For God's sake, you didn't even know that the gun was the same one you'd tampered with."

"I had a pretty good idea, that it was. It was the only G19; the others were all carrying suppressed HK 45s."

"I don't care if it was a bloody flintlock pistol." Anna stood and came round to Drew, to kiss him too. If anything it was a more intense kiss even than Cassie's. "We probably shouldn't make a habit of that either."

"No, ma'am."

"Can I…" Jason added.

"I'll pass, if that's okay Jason."

Everybody laughed, looked at each other then began to laugh again until they were helpless.

"Haven't you got anyone special in your life, Jason?" Drew asked in, what was for him, a rare moment of personal conversation.

"If you're asking a.m. I in a relationship, the answer is yes I suppose. I have a friend who I see two or three times a month. His name is Paulo, he lives in Reading and works in an Italian restaurant. He likes to play the field a bit too much for my taste, so it won't amount to anything. But I do have special people in my life. One is on an airplane on her way here right now, and two others, or maybe three now, are at this table."

"He'll be worried about you, if what happened is on the news this morning."

"I know, I'll speak to him later. He won't get out of bed until nine, unless he's with one of his other *buddies*." He made air quotes with his fingers around the last word..

"Cassie and I are going to lie down for an hour or two. What time can we expect Judith and Atticus?"

"She hopes to be here about eleven," Jason told her. "I'm going to give these poor police people a cup of tea and then I'll have a little shut eye myself. What about you, Drew?"

"I'll have a doze in the family room if that's okay." He didn't tell them, but he had other things he wanted to do. The gun and knife he'd locked in the study drawer, might be useful additions to his personal armory; he wanted to check them out. He was convinced this wasn't over yet, and with the UK's strict restrictions on weaponry, he needed whatever edge he could give himself.

He went to the study and recovered the gun, stripped it to its component parts, carefully examined every piece before reassembling it and satisfied himself that it worked. He examined every round and reloaded the magazine. Making a mental note to acquire some ammo, gun oil and a cleaning kit, he locked the weapon away in the drawer and took the knife to the kitchen where he searched the drawers for a sharpening stone. He found one without difficulty. It looked as if it had never been used.

As he set about giving the knife an edge that met his exacting standards, his phone vibrated in his pocket signaling an incoming call. He glanced at the screen before answering. "Firbank. Is there a problem?"

"Possibly. I hope I didn't wake you."

"Go on."

"First I should tell you that the Gaston Doucette, the man arrested by our regular colleagues, escaped from hospital about an hour ago."

"Put me down as surprised."

"We sort of anticipated it might happen and put a tail on him, unfortunately he gave them the slip within minutes."

"Change that to shocked."

"That's not the worst of it. Is Mrs. West around at the moment?"

"She's gone to bed. Don't tell me there's another problem now?"

The counter-terrorism officer explained and added, "First of all we can't be sure if it's true; second, we're not sure whether it matters even if it is true; and third, neither are we sure that if it does matter that there's anything that can be done about it.

"Shit, as if she hasn't had enough to contend with. I'm guessing that you want me to talk to her about it."

"Yes."

"Thanks a bunch."

"How's the wound?"

"I've had worse. I'm guessing that you've no idea what happened to Gates."

"No, the car was abandoned about five miles away. There was a lot of blood, but unsurprisingly there are no reports of hospital admissions."

"The ear wound looked superficial but I expect will have bled a lot. The leg wound was a thigh shot, so unless I hit a femoral artery the bleeding won't have been excessive, but the combined debilitating effect of the fresh wound coupled with whatever injury he still had in the other leg from the collision… well, he'll be struggling."

"We should be able to pick him up then."

"He's got help, and with Lemonis' resources, I'm not so sure. As much as I'd have liked to have killed the worthless pieces of shit, they're still in the wind. I'm not confident that Lemonis and the Ruskies are finished yet. There's too much at stake from what you say."

"I tend to agree with you."

"Are you still determined not to pick Lemonis up, even though there's plenty of evidence of his involvement in domestic crime?"

"We're collaborating with your people across the pond. They speak very highly of you by the way."

"Not sure that's a good thing, I've no intention of making this a habit. That's why I hung up my boots."

"Hmm, maybe."

Drew went back to the task of sharpening the knife. When he'd done, he put the knife back in the drawer with the gun, took a seat in the family room, and finally gave in to fatigue.

Nineteen

Sometime later he woke to find Cassie curled up against his side in her nightwear. He attempted to get out of the chair without disturbing her, but as soon as he moved she opened her eyes.

"You should probably be in bed,' he told her.

"I was but Mummy got up to have a shower so I came down to be with you. Is that okay?"

"Yes of course. Where's your mom now?"

"She's in the kitchen with Judith and your friend."

"They're here! What time is it?"

"Nearly twelve o'clock."

They walked through to the kitchen.

"Catching up on your beauty sleep then, Parker," Atticus said with a smile.

"Yeah, I thought since you'd been having a holiday, it wouldn't hurt if I took a break as well."

"Mrs. West and Jason here have been catching me up on your adventures. Been a bit busy eh? What is it with that Gates guy? I know some of our lot go astray a bit after they ship out, but I don't remember anyone going so rogue as to start trying to kill some of their own team."

"Me neither, but what do any of us really know about him? Maybe he was always crooked. He was recruited by Volkov, who was almost certainly Russian, and we only have his word that he's ex-SAS. The Brits are being pretty closed lips about him. I came across him a couple of times when his head popped up on ops, but who he was actually working for I don't know."

"True, although maybe we're past the point where it matters."

"I guess that's also true. How are you, Judith?"

"I'm fine. Anna and Jason have been telling us how you saved their lives, again."

"Just doing what I'm paid for."

"He's done much more than what he's been paid for Judith. He's managed to help us to maintain our sanity as well. I'm going to have to keep an eye on him though, he's bewitched my daughter."

"Muuummmy!"

"We need to have a bit of a chat when you've got a minute, ma'am?"

"Okay, but let's have something to eat first. It'll only be sandwiches for the moment; everybody's still exhausted."

"I don't understand how what happened last night isn't all over the national news," Judith said. "Home of a titled extremely wealthy woman invaded by armed intruders, two people dead, one of the perpetrators arrested then escapes from hospital, and another with gunshot wounds on the run. That's without mentioning the involvement of the woman's husband, and the threat to her child."

"There are things involved that we can't speak about yet, and it's in the interests of the security services to keep it all under wraps for the time being," Drew told her.

"Are we saying that this isn't all over then?" Atticus wanted to know.

"We're saying that we don't know yet. Is that right Drew?" Anna said.

"Yes, ma'am. For the time being it's best that we assume it isn't, so Atticus and I will try to maintain a 24-hour watch until it is. That okay with you buddy?"

"Sure, no point in me being here otherwise."

"Can we go and have that talk now, ma'am? Is the library okay?"

"If that's where you prefer."

Cassie stood up to follow.

"It might be best if you sit this one out, Cassie. I'll let your mom, decide whether this is the right time for you to know what I'm about to tell her."

She looked hurt. "Uh…Okay."

Anna started to look concerned, as she led the way.

"Surely there can't be anything else," she said as she closed the library door behind them. "I try not to have secrets from Cassie. She's insecure enough as it is."

"I'm sorry, ma'am, but I don't think this is something it's my place to reveal to her."

"Okay then, what is it?"

"First, can I ask you about your marriage to Lemonis. Where was it?"

"It was a civil wedding at a hillside villa on Corfu owned by a member of his family. There were over a hundred guests, it was beautiful. The ceremony was conducted in Greek but with an interpreter."

"Did you have to sign anything?"

"Yes, afterwards we went inside, and there was a Greek official, a registrar I suppose, and there were quite a number of documents to sign because I was a widow and a foreign citizen."

"Did the registrar speak English?"

"No, and it made the whole thing painfully slow. Theo kept apologizing for the time it was taking."

"Who interpreted the documents for you?"

"The same interpreter."

"And as far as you know, the documents were only to do with the marriage?"

"Yes of course. Tell me what's going on; you're scaring me now."

"As you know, the documents we found in the safe, weren't all in Russian. Two of them were Greek. The Greek ones were adoption papers for Isolde and Cassandra."

"What!"

"They agreed to Lemonis' adoption of your children."

"Oh my God! What does this mean?"

"Firbank says he doesn't know what the implications of it are at the moment; or to quote him more precisely, *They can't be sure if it's real; they're not sure that if they are real, that it matters; neither are they sure that if it does matter if there's anything that can be done about it.* But he suggests you take advice about it as soon as possible."

"What does all that mean though?"

"I'm guessing that it means that he doesn't know if the documents have legal standing if you didn't know what you were signing. If the registrar believed you signed them in full understanding, and if they are accepted as legitimate in Greek law, is there any way they can be quashed, if so how quickly. He also questions whether it makes any difference if they can't be nullified. In my opinion it makes a huge difference, because it would probably nullify the arrangements you've made in your will for Cassie's guardianship by making him her legitimate parent at the very least. At worst, in the event of your death, she would become a direct target because Lemonis would be her only surviving next of kin."

"Oh my dear God, I've been such a fool."

"Excuse me for saying so but you're no more foolish than hundreds of thousands of women who fall foul of manipulative, controlling and dishonest men. Lemonis was a family friend; you had no reason to distrust him, much less any reason to suspect that he was acting as an agent of a foreign state. There's no way he could have set this up by himself. This is not just a scam to defraud you. This is a sophisticated attempt to gain control of an important defense manufacturer and its military secrets. There's no way you could have suspected what was happening."

"Why didn't I suspect though, when Theo didn't want to make love?"

"It would be more reasonable to ask why the British security services didn't tell you?"

"What do you mean?"

"When did he tell you about his sexuality?"

"He indicated that he might be gay to Henry several months before Henry died but was too scared to come out. I suppose it was one reason that Henry didn't question when we spent so much time together when he was away."

"Doesn't that seem strange to you now, if he was so fanatical about keeping it quiet?"

"Now you mention it yes. In the months after the funeral, he was rarely away from here if he was in the country. We both told each other how lonely we were, and then we decided that we wanted to formalize our companionship. I don't remember much about what went through my mind at the time."

"It didn't feel strange?"

"Not really, and it isn't that unusual."

"Do you still believe MI5 wouldn't have known of his claim to be gay until now? He would have been on their radar and they would have known his sexuality and also about Ariana for years. It would be my guess that that is the only reason why someone with the credentials of Rupert Loughty ended up taking a job as bodyguard to someone who at the time had no reason to suspect she was in danger. The death of your first husband will have raised all kinds of red flags. Where was Loughty supposed to have been when the first hijack took place?"

"He'd been in Ireland visiting family. His mother had a suspected heart attack. He returned as soon as it was confirmed as something much less serious."

"I suspect that your first husband's death was no accident. He could have been killed as part of a sophisticated long-term strategy to seduce you into marrying Lemonis and one way or another taking over Silico, which at the time was becoming a big player in military tech. When they eventually felt the time was right, they lured Loughty out of the country, but didn't reckon on him getting back as quickly as he did, or on his intervention in the hijack."

"But Percy recommended Rupert. Did he know?"

"I doubt it. I imagine that he was pressured to give you the best protection by the security services, and Loughty was their chosen man."

"I remember Theo being upset that I'd insisted on Percy's recommendation. He wanted Pavel all along."

"It was Firbank's buddies who were responsible for me being in the team as well."

"So all this time I've been an unwitting puppet for British security services, putting myself and my children in the line of fire, the bastards."

"I doubt they knew about the adoptions or the wills until it was done, and they may not have been certain that your husband's death had been deliberate, if it was. But this is normal M.O. for secret services, I suspect the F.B.I. would have behaved much the same."

"So if what you're saying is true, or even partly true, and there is no way out of this, Cassie and I will always be at risk."

"I know nothing about law, and issues arising out of conflicts of laws between different states are probably even more of a minefield. But it would seem to me that the only way that risk would vanish would be if Lemonis happened to die."

"Are you suggesting…"

"I'm not suggesting anything. Except, if the various powers that be really gave a shit about your and Cassie's safety, Lemonis would be six feet under right now, and at present it suits their purpose to allow this charade to play out."

"Have you talked to Percy about this?"

"Not yet. I haven't had time to think it through properly. I only spoke to Firbank a few hours ago and I've only known Percy a few days, and I can't be sure how much he trusts the security services. It wouldn't help if I told him my suspicions and he went running to them, because they'd just invent some bullshit story to put his mind at ease."

"Do you think I can trust Ruskin and Firth, those solicitors?"

"I'd be surprised if they weren't okay, but you need to find someone used to dealing with family law across international borders. There are probably companies that specialize in that sort of thing."

The door opened; it was Cassie. "I'm scared Mummy, I don't want us to be killed, and I don't want Theo to be my daddy ever. He's a horrid evil man. I hate him."

"Have you been listening again. You know you're not supposed to do that."

"I know but horrible frightening things keep happening. Can't we just run away and hide somewhere they can't find us?"

"I'd like that, but I don't know where to or if it's even possible."

"It is possible, ma'am, but you'd need to think through the practicalities of it before you committed."

"Tell me how first."

"Not here."

"What do you mean?"

"While we were at the cop station, Firbank and Graves, had free access to this whole house. Who's to say they didn't plant bugs anywhere they want. Let's go somewhere they can't hear us. Grab a coat. It's cold today."

He took her purse from her hand and laid it on the desk, put his phones on the desk beside it and held out his hand for Cassie's. Then he led them out the back door to a bench in the rose garden,

"Tell us how we can disappear for a while, without achieving my ex-husband's job for him, stay undetected, and yet remain in control."

"The first bit's easy. Not so much in the UK, but in the US or Canada going off-grid is relatively easy. Remaining undetected, takes a bit more effort, and it means having a very small circle of people who you trust implicitly, and who trust you not to ask too many questions about what's happening. Staying in control needs the cooperation of someone who you can trust absolutely."

"I think all that sounds achievable."

"The other things it would take in your case are, firstly total discretion and by that I mean you don't tell anyone at all about your whereabouts, not even what country you're in. Nobody at all, no friends, relatives, brothers, sisters, B.F.F.s - nobody. Imagine you're in witness protection where a single word out of place could be the difference between life and death, because in this case it could mean exactly that.

"It would mean self-discipline and an acceptance that the comfortable and luxurious lifestyle you're used to would be something you'd have to put to one side for the duration. No email, Internet, cell phones, or servants. We'd have to live simply."

"Where?"

"I have a friend who lives for much of the time in a remote cabin somewhere in North America, fifteen miles from the nearest town. We exchanged emails last month, and he mentioned that he'd be leaving the cabin empty for a few months to go travelling. I'm confident he'd allow us to use it while he's away. If not he could point us in the right direction of another one we could use."

"How soon can you set something like that up?"

"A day or two I expect."

"Have you been to this cabin?"

"Once, more than three years ago now. He'd just begun the process of renovating it, so it was pretty basic back then. I expect he's got a bathroom and running water by now."

"You expect he's got a bathroom? What did he do beforehand?"

"He washed in the stream and used a pit latrine."

"What's a pit latrine?"

"In this case, because it was a short-term solution, it was a hole in the ground where you do your business then put a shovel of earth over your leavings until the hole is nearly full. Then you dig another hole."

"That's disgusting, there's no way we could do that."

"As I say he's probably got plumbing by now. It was one of his priorities - that and electricity."

"Where's he going?"

"He goes walkabout, as the Aussies call it, normally hunting in the early winter, but this time he could be anywhere in North America."

"Then how could you contact him to ask?"

"He leaves a line open for one or two people including me."

"Can you find out a bit more about it before I commit. To be honest I'm not sure I'm the frontierswoman sort of gal. Even less sure about Cassie."

"I don't mind, Mummy. I can learn. I just want us to be safe."

"You'd have me with you, arrangements to stay in contact with Percy, and methods of calling for help in an emergency."

She went quiet for several minutes, her brow furrowed as she considered what he had said.

"How many rooms does it have?"

"Main room, two other rooms, and the bathroom by now I expect."

"Can you find out as much as you can about it before we decide on anything?"

"Sure, give me an hour or two, but in the meantime don't discuss it with anybody at all."

"Okay, let's go inside."

In the kitchen Jason was alone, preparing something for dinner.

"Where are the others?" Anna asked.

"They've gone to get some sleep."

"Mummy, I want to show you something?"

"Okay, sweetheart. What is it?"

"It's something that Judith asked me to do for homework." She handed her mother a notebook. She'd written, *I want to do it Mummy. I'm frightened to be here. Drew knows how to keep us safe but they can keep sending people here to hurt us, and it would only take one bullet to kill him. I love him, I don't want him to get hurt either. If we're somewhere that they don't know, they can't hurt any of us.*

Anna took her daughter's pen and wrote, *Let's go outside.* They walked out the back door and she turned to Cassie. "Darling, what Drew has done for us has been amazing, brave, and selfless. Nobody appreciates that more than I do. But he's more than twenty years older than you, There's no way you can have a romantic attachment with him, no matter how much you might want to."

"I know that Mummy. That's not what I mean. Since Daddy died he's the only man I can speak to, the only one I like, apart from Jason and Uncle Percy, Toby, and Josh, but it's not the same with them. Drew explains things to me and treats me like a small human being rather than just a little girl. I know he's handsome and brave, and clever and if I can find a husband like that when I'm older I would think I was the luckiest girl in the world. I think he would make a lovely new daddy if you married him."

"That's a very romantic idea my darling, but I don't know that I want to get married again. Neither of us know if Drew wants to get married to anyone let alone me. He's my bodyguard. He might want to move on after this is all over. I don't want him to. I hope he stays, but we have to remember that he's a man of action. He's spent the whole of his adult life fighting. Life with us would seem pretty tame."

"I know you're right, but I still want us to go."

"If it can be done safely, then so do I. We'll wait and see what Drew's friend has to say."

They didn't have to wait long, Drew approached them from the stable.

"Ma'am, can we talk again?"

"Certainly. Let's go sit in the rose garden again."

Anna took one end of the bench, Drew sat at the other with Cassie in the middle.

"I was lucky, my buddy was able to talk straight away, he said we can use the cabin until the end of September and use whatever stores we need to while we're there. Even better, he confirmed it now has a shower room, running water, solar power electricity, and satellite internet."

"What do I have to do to make it happen then?"

"Nothing very much. Hand write letters to Percy, Judith, and Jason explaining that we're going off-grid until this whole business is sorted out. Don't say where or for how long. Tell them we'll inform them of contact details as and when we have them. Pack a bag with only the barest essentials for you both. Passports, driving license, birth certificates. Leave phones, and laptops at home. Bring as much cash as you can practically and legally carry and be ready to travel at very short notice, and by that I mean within an hour."

"When are we going, and where?"

"Do you trust me?"

"Absolutely."

"We will be out of contact of any sort from anyone you know for at least forty-eight hours unless we choose otherwise."

"Can't you give us any idea where or when?"

"At present you don't need to know where. As for when, before seven a.m. tomorrow if I can tie up a few loose ends."

"As soon as that! Oh God now I'm scared."

"This is risk-free, no need to be scared."

"If you say so. Okay let's go for it. I'd better go and decide what to pack."

"Remember, no mention of any of this inside the house. Go to bed as usual. I'll wake you when it's time. It might be better if you sleep together. I've got a few calls to make. Give me a shout when dinner is ready."

"Okay."

He took the burner he'd been using from his pocket and called a number he had committed to memory years ago. It was picked up after the third ring. "Hi Sis, how's it going?"

"Oh hi Bro, how's life in Hollywood?"

"I'm not in Hollywood, I'm in the UK at the moment but not for long."

"I didn't really expect you to stay in the same place for more than a week."

"I've got a big favor to ask?"

"I somehow guessed you hadn't just called to say you love me at this time of the morning."

"Have you sold my pickup yet?"

"Not yet, we've been too busy."

"Can you let me borrow it back for a while?"

"No problem."

"One other thing, and this is the biggie."

"Go on, I knew it couldn't be that easy."

"I need you to drive it to Pittsburg to meet me."

"As in Pittsburg PA you mean?"

"That's right."

"When?"

"Can't give you a time or place to meet yet, but within the next 72 hours. I'll text you when I know our flight."

"Where are you flying to?"

"Washington and we'll get a train to Pittsburg."

"We?"

"My principal, her daughter and me."

"What's going on Drew?"

"She's in danger, and she needs to disappear for a while. I can't tell you anymore at the moment. Can you do it or not?"

"Of course, I'll stay over and do some shopping."

"Why not stay with Cousin Noah – Morgantown's on route."

"Great idea."

"I'll text the details to this number. Love you Sis. See you tomorrow or the day after."

As soon as he ended the call he used one of the burner phones to send a long text to his sister's second phone, which was also a burner. Much of the message contradicted what he'd told her on the phone. It also told her to ignore the next text he sent to the other phone with a fake itinerary.

The next thing he did was transfer a chunk of money from his deposit account to a cash account that he kept for use on special ops. It had been dormant for over two years with less than two thousand dollars in it. The method he used to transfer the money was one he'd learned from a C.I.A. agent five years earlier that made it virtually impossible to trace the destination of funds after they left the account.

He booked a cab to pick them up outside the gate at 05:30 the next day, before going to his room and packing his bag ready to leave.

"Drew, Mummy said dinner will be ready in about ten minutes," Cassie told him from his bedroom door.

"Okay, Cassie. How are you doing today?"

"I'm still scared."

"I understand, but Gates has got at least two gunshot wounds. He seems to have been mixed up in everything, but I doubt he'll be fit for anything very much for a while, and Theo is too much of a coward to try anything on his own."

She showed him her notebook and she'd written, *Please don't ever leave us, we need you. XXXX'*

He took it from he and wrote, *I promise not to go anywhere until your mom tells me to, okay? I'll keep you safe.'*

She smiled and nodded before hugging him.

Judith and Atticus were awake for dinner, and Anna felt bad that they were going to be abandoning them without saying they were going or how long they'd be away.

Anna and Cassie legitimately claimed tiredness at eight pm, as did Judith still jet lagged from the flight. Drew stayed with Atticus and gave him more detail about the most recent attack. He told him that Lemonis' main target was Anna, with Cassie as a secondary. He didn't mention the Russian involvement. He just told him that the motive was greed, an attempt to gain control of Silicon, and there were complications that prevented Anna from telling the whole story to the police for the time being.

After setting his phone alarm, he was asleep in minutes.

Twenty

When his phone vibrated at 04:30 he was instantly awake.

After a quick shower he dressed and went through the door into Anna's bedroom. She and Cassie were asleep in their clothes. *How the fuck could anyone want to kill this naïve child and her mother?* he thought. He had already resolved that one way or another Lemonis and Gates were going to die.

Gently shaking Anna's shoulder, "It's time,' he whispered, holding a finger to his lips.

She nodded sleepily. "Okay, give us a couple of minutes." She whispered back, causing Cassie to stir and open her eyes.

At five-fifteen the three of them went to the kitchen, where they found Atticus making himself coffee. He looked up and was about to speak when Drew hushed him and beckoned him to the front door and pressed the button to open the gate.

Outside he told Atticus that the house was bugged and that they were going to go dark for a week or two. He explained that Anna had left letters for Jason, Judith and Percy in her room, and he would be in contact in two or three days.

"There's a cab due any minute. Get yourself a bug detector and use it to locate and destroy any devices you can find. It would be better if you didn't mention, we've left until you've done it, or not in earshot of the bugs if you haven't."

They walked to the gate and got there just as the cab arrived. Atticus had opened the gate, and Drew watched it close again as they took their seats.

"Heathrow then is it then sir?"

"That's right, Terminal five."

"Holiday?" The driver asked.

"Something like that."

"Where are you off to? Somewhere exotic?"

"Brazil."

"Wow! That is exotic."

"Our daughter wants to see rainforests, isn't that right, Cassie darling?"

"Eh? Oh yes, I want to see marmosets and opossums, I learned about them in school."

"I took her to the zoo, but it's not the same, is it? What else was it you wanted to see; leopards wasn't it."

"No daddy, jaguars. Leopards live in Africa."

"Can we just rest now; we're not used to being out of bed at this time of day," Anna said.

The cab dropped them outside the departure hall on level three of the huge building, and Anna paid him with cash.

Once they were inside, Drew asked them both, "Promise me that neither of you have brought a cellphone, iPad or laptop."

"I've still got my phone. I've turned it off though, so it can't be tracked," Anna confessed.

"Give it to me."

She handed it over. He took it removed the case, and to the astonishment of the other two, he twisted it until the SIM card draw popped open, allowing him to remove the tiny object. Then he put the phone on the floor, stamped on it, and kicked it against a wall.

"Give me your purse." She handed it over, and he waved his bug detector over it, and it beeped immediately. A few seconds soon revealed a tiny device a little smaller than an Alka Seltzer tablet. He repeated the exercise with Cassie's purse, turned and bumped into a man who was marshalling his family in readiness to check in for their flight.

"I'm really sorry buddy, are you okay? I'm such a klutz sometimes." Patting him on the shoulder with one hand and the side with the other."

"It's fine, don't worry about it," the man replied.

"Have a good trip," Drew said.

"And you."

Then, following the signs, Drew led them to the ground floor arrivals hall.

"Where are we going?" Anna asked.

"To get another cab,' he replied without elaboration.

"Did you just put those things in that man's pocket?" Cassie asked.

"Yep, they won't do him any harm, but it might confuse whoever's trying to track us for a while."

At that time of day, there was no shortage of cabs. They climbed into the first one, on this occasion a London black cab enabling Drew to sit facing them.

"Gatwick please, North Terminal, he told the driver."

"What's going on?" Anna asked.

"We're going to catch a plane."

"Where to?"

"I haven't decided yet."

"What!!!"

"I know where we're headed, I just haven't decided how we're getting there yet."

They lapsed into silence for the fifty-minute drive to the other airport. When they arrived outside the terminal, Anna paid the driver and turned to Drew. "Now what?"

"Let's go buy some tickets and hope we can get three seats on the same plane without having to wait too long."

"Which airline, which airport?"

"It's not that important, but Washington is my preferred East Coast destination. Alphabetically Aer Lingus are at the top of the list that fly from here. American next I guess. From the board, it looks like Aer Lingus have two flights to Dulles this morning. Let's give them a try first.

The desk clerk offered them a choice of three individual seats in Economy on a flight at 08:40, or three adjacent seats in Business class at 10:15. "We'll take the 10:15," Drew told him.

They handed over their passports for him to take their details. "That would be six thousand, one hundred pounds. How would you like to pay Sir?"

Anna went to look in her purse for the wad of bank notes she had bought with her.

"Take it from this," he said, handing him a card.

Anna looked at him in astonishment. The man took the card. "You will need to authorize the payment with your bank sir."

"That's fine, go ahead."

A few minutes later a cellphone in his pocket vibrated. He took it out and opened it with his fingerprint, opened an app and authorized the payment.

"That's all gone through okay sir. If you'll give me a moment, I'll print your tickets and boarding passes. If you proceed to baggage check and passport control you'll have plenty of time to take refreshment before boarding. Have a pleasant flight,"

They moved away from the desk. "I thought you told us we couldn't use phones or cards," Anna said accusingly.

"I said that *you* shouldn't use phones or cards. The phone I'm using is registered to someone else. The card I used is in someone else's name too."

"It was over eight thousand dollars though."

"You can reimburse me when we're out the other side of this."

"I feel completely helpless."

"You don't need to be in control at the moment. That's what you're paying me for. Let's go through to the departure lounge and we can get something to eat."

They checked their bags and meekly followed him through passport and security controls. Finding a seat in a restaurant, Anna insisted on giving the orders to the waitress. Drew did his normal trick of ordering enough food for two people.

"There will be food on the plane you know," she told him.

"I know, but I want to spend the time sleeping if I can."

"What sort of soldier were you? Most soldiers I've ever heard of don't have secret IDs, bank accounts, and phone numbers."

"Some of the things I did were slightly outside traditional roles I guess."

"Are you still in the army?"

"No, that's all behind me, but because of my special skills, I've no doubt they may come to me from time to time to ask me to do something specific."

"Is this *something specific*, you working for me?"

"No, ma'am. I'm working exclusively for you. I will never lie to you; I may be economical with the truth if I think there's something you don't need to know. If you ask me a direct question, I'll always answer it fully and truthfully."

"Thank you, Drew. I trust you."

"Were you one of those special forces soldiers then?" Cassie asked.

"Some people call us that."

"I don't think Drew is allowed to say very much about it, Cassie."

"Your mom is right, but you probably wouldn't find it all that interesting anyway; it's nothing like you see in the movies. When we were on stand down, sometimes we would watch those action movies as if they were comedies."

The wait for their flight seemed interminable. Drew kept Cassie entertained by telling her tales of amusing things that happened during his service. Sometimes she laughed so loudly she attracted attention from people around them, while Anna looked on with a smile, relieved that her daughter wasn't scared for a few minutes at least.

By the time they were eventually called to the boarding gate, they were already tired. So it wasn't long into the flight before all three of them were asleep. Cassie had asked to sit next to Drew with Anna across the aisle. Five hours into the flight, one of the cabin crew asked if he wanted food. He said no, and looked at Cassie. She had earphones on and an animated film was playing on the screen in front of her. Looking across at Anna she was smiling at him. "You've definitely earned yourself a big fan award," she whispered.

"The novelty will soon wear off."

"Maybe."

They slept an hour or two longer and after missing the scheduled meals, they ordered significant quantities of food from the snack card, confusing the server when they insisted on paying with cash.

The plane touched down at just after five p.m. local time. It was gone six by the time they were through immigration and baggage collection. Drew hustled them across the airport to the Hertz desk where he hired a rental car using a fake driving license, giving Pittsburg as their destination.

"Is that where we're going then, Pennsylvania?" Anna asked.

"No Richmond, and it's just a stop along the way."

The drive time was another two hours and it was past eight p.m. when they arrived at the Richmond International Airport Hertz drop off point, where they left the car without offering an explanation. Then they caught a cab to a motel only a mile or two away. A room had been reserved in the names of Mr. and Mrs. Branson and daughter Erica.

"One room eh?" Anna remarked.

"You're not worried are you?"

"No, just curious."

"If you think I'm going to let you sleep in a different room in a crappy little motel like this while you're paying me to be your bodyguard while all this is going on, ma'am, you're nuts."

There was a knock on the door, "Pizza delivery for Mr. Branson," a female voice called.

"Oh God, who knows we're here?"

"Don't worry about it,' he said. Then, "I'll be right there sweetheart, don't you worry your cute little butt off."

Cassie gasped and her jaw fell open.

"You better get your ass out here quick pecker-head or this package is going right in the trash."

He laughed and went to the door to find a blonde woman, about thirty-five years old wearing jeans, a check shirt, cowboy boots, and a fur-lined jacket.

"Hiya, Sis. How are you?" They hugged and exchanged kisses.

"I'm good. Are you going to invite me in, or are we going to stand out here all night and embarrass the hell out of everyone while you make out with your sister?"

"Come on in, Sis. Let me introduce you to Mrs. West and Cassandra. We're travelling together."

"If I'm going to say a proper hello to your friends you'd better take this freaking box. It's heavy."

He took it from her arms, and she went to Anna.

"Hi there I'm Carolina but most people just call me Lina. How are you? Tired I'm guessing. You've been travelling one hell of a long time. It's good to meet you. Great that someone's finally got this dumb hunk of muscle lined up."

Glancing at Drew, Anna blushed.

"Anna is my employer."

"Yeah, if you say so. And this cute little thing is your daughter? You English always did breed 'em pretty."

Cassie blushed and smiled.

"Don't let the good ole cowgirl act fool you, she's a hometown, wholesome Yankee."

"Yeah well, when I got my boots on I gotta make like I mean it. You eaten yet?"

"Not yet," Anna replied.

"Let's go and see if we can still get something. There's a bar and grill a block or two away. We can walk there."

"Is that okay with you, ma'am?"

"I think we can drop the whole *ma'am* thing now, don't you? It's just Anna from now on."

"There you go then, I wasn't so far out, was I?"

Anna blushed and Cassie grinned like the cat that got the cream.

Drew had opened the package that Lina had brought, strapped on a shoulder holster and was checking out a handgun.

"Are they what you wanted?"

"Perfect, Sis, thanks,' he said, strapping an ankle holster to his right leg. Did you get the other thing without any trouble?"

"Sure, it's outside in the lot. Right near the top of what you said in the end."

"What is it?"

"2017 Ford F-150 XL Super Crew 4x4; about forty-two thousand on the clock, good tires, satnav, with front and rear dashcam. Couple of minor scrapes, which they offered to put right. I told them to leave 'em and take a grand off the price." She handed him the key.

"Perfect, keep the change. Put it in Ben's college fund with whatever you get for my truck."

"See that Anna, I told you he was dumb. Gives money away like it's free."

Cassie rushed to his defense. "He's not dumb, he's the cleverest man I've ever met. You should have seen what he did to save our lives."

"Shush, don't tell him that, he'll get a big head. When you let 'em get a big head they're difficult to control."

"You're funny," Cassie said.

Drew pulled a jacket on, slipped the gun in the holster and led the way out.

"That's it over there in the corner," she said pointing to a white double cab pickup. "It's got a full tank and had a full service this afternoon."

In the bar they ordered food and drinks and talked while they waited.

"So, Anna, how much danger are you in, if you need to hide out with my little brother by your side?"

"How much is it safe to tell her, Drew?" Anna asked.

"Nothing to do with the Firbank and Co side of things for the time being, but you're pretty safe with the rest. I need to use the john. I'll be back in a few."

"I'll use the ladies' room at the same time." Cassie said, getting up to walk by his side. "I like your sister, she's really nice."

"Yeah, she ain't bad is she? We don't get to see too much of each other though, what with my work."

"I suppose. I miss my sister since she's gone."

"You go in while I'm in the gents, and I'll wait out here for you to come out."

He didn't have to wait long. "There was a girl in there injecting something in her arm. She told me to eff off."

"We won't be spending too much more time in places like this. Just forget about it."

As they came out of the washroom area the waitress arrived.

"Enjoy your meal."

"Anna's been telling me what's been going on with that asshole of a husband of hers. He needs sorting out, big time."

"If he dares to show himself in my presence anytime soon he'll find himself absentis penii."

Cassie started giggling. "I worked out what you meant. Missing penis."

"She's sharp this little one, ain't she?" Lina said.

"These last few months have been a steep learning curve for her. If it weren't for Drew I think she'd be struggling. Me too probably."

"Yeah my little bro is useful sometimes. What's your plan for tomorrow, bro?"

"Hit the road about sunrise. Hope to be in Slade about three or four. Did you book the room for me?"

"Yeah, Black Bear Lodge Motel. Used the same names to register you. You gonna be meeting up with your pal from when you worked building log cabins?"

"Yeah but he won't be there; he's loaning me the cabin. He says we can have it until September but I hope we won't need it for anything like as long as that."

"Where's he then?"

"They've gone to spend some time with his step-daughter's family somewhere in the reservations."

"He's married?"

"No, the girl isn't really his step-daughter, he's her guardian. I don't know the whole story, but her parents were killed when their shop was raided or something, and he was named as guardian in their will."

"How old is she?"

"About twelve or thirteen I think."

"I don't get that. Everything you told me about him didn't give me an inkling that he'd be the sort to bring up somebody else's kid. Do they live in that cabin out there in the wilderness by themselves?"

"I guess so. I didn't expect it either."

"Poor kid."

"From what he told me, she loves it. Doesn't want to live anywhere else. She even goes out on hunts with him. Two or three nights sleeping under the stars all weathers."

"Just as long as you're not expecting me and Cassie to do that."

"So what do you do then, Anna?"

"I'm ashamed to say at the moment, not very much. When my first husband was alive, I worked alongside him in our company. He provided the technical expertise and creativity, with a great deal of advice from my father. I added my business skills. Henry was a genius. He designed a new way to make computer chips work, and the company has gone from twenty-five employees with a turnover of £250,000 a year to more than three hundred employees and a turnover of £750 million in eleven years. My father provided much of the startup money. I'm still a majority shareholder, but nowadays I don't have an executive role. When Izzy was killed, I just couldn't bring my mind to anything, and tried to concentrate on being a good wife to Theo."

"Wait, hold on. First of all who's Izzy?"

"She was my eldest daughter. She was kidnapped and killed in the first hijack."

"First hijack!? Just how many have there been?"

"If you count what happened a few days ago, five attempts now I think. Some more serious than others."

"Are you saying that this husband who you were being *a good wife* to has been responsible for the murder of your daughter and five attempts on your life? Why the fuck is this piece of shit even alive?"

"Apart from the day before yesterday, he's always managed to be somewhere else when it happens, although Drew had his suspicions after the first time, but we couldn't be absolutely certain until a day or two ago. I've lost track of the days now with all the travelling and time zones."

"I don't understand why he's so intent on killing you though or this little cutie either for that matter."

"There's more to this than we can say at the moment."

"They raped my sister before they killed her," Cassie said through her hands.

"Oh my darling," Anna said, putting her arms around her. "I didn't know you knew about that."

"What a worthless asswipe!"

The waitress came back to the table. "Can I get you anything else?"

"No, thanks. Just the bill," Drew told her.

She printed the bill from her handheld machine and gave it to him, expecting him to give her his card. Anna took the piece of paper from

Drew's hand, glanced at it, and handed over a $100 bill, telling her to keep the change.

"Thank you ma'am, that's very generous. Will you be needing the table for much longer?"

"No thanks, we'll be leaving in a few," Drew said.

"Can we go back to the room to talk?" Lina suggested.

"That would be lovely, wouldn't it, Cassie?"

"Until the first hijacking, I'd never even seen a fight, let alone been anywhere near when a gun was fired," Anna said as they got back to the room.

"Jesus lady, you must have led one hell of a sheltered life," Lina said.

"I guess you'd call me a poor little rich girl. Private school educated until I was ten, then home tutored until uni. Lived at home throughout my degree course, fell in love with the first boy I agreed to go out with, married him and, well you know the rest."

"That sure was a rarified existence up until you married that skid mark of anal mucus."

Anna laughed. "You Americans have such a colorful vocabulary when it comes to describing people you don't like. In the last week or two I've learned asshole, asswipe, piece of shit, anal mucus, anal snot and probably a few more. In the UK I'd probably normally say bastard with the *F* word. After extraordinary provocation I might resort to the *C* word."

"What's the *C* word, Mummy?"

"Something I hope you never need to use, darling. Anyway changing the subject, Drew, am I right that in order to get me and Cassie over here and find us a secret hideaway, you've paid for our flights, food, overnight accommodation, and bought a car?"

"So far that's about right."

"And don't forget about the guns," Lina said.

"How did you know that I'd pay all of that back?"

"I didn't, but you trusted me. I trusted you."

"Why didn't you just ask me to give you the money before we left?"

"If I'd told you, I could find you somewhere to stay, but you have to front me a hundred grand first. Would your first thought have been, *Yeah that sounds like a bargain go for it*, or would you have thought, *Maybe but let me think about it for a day or two*?"

"Okay, but how can you afford all that. The army doesn't pay that well, does it?"

"My brother doesn't spend anything that's why. He's not just tight, he's tight like a duck's ass, watertight."

Cassie found that hilarious and was rolling around on the bed laughing for several minutes to the amusement of the others.

"My daughter's education in the ways of the world is being broadened further as every day goes by, and mine for that matter. I doubt in our previous existence that the subject of penises would have arisen in any conversation I might have had, let alone Cassie's. What about your family, Lina?"

"Like Drew, no college after high school; got a job and did evening classes to get a degree of sorts, met Curtiss in the burger bar where I worked. He's a bit older than me and works selling insurance. He got offered a job managing the company office in Wilmington so we got married and moved. I work at the high school in the principal's office. I guess you'd say I'm a soccer mom, with one kid, Ben. He's great, nine-years-old going on nineteen, and thinks the sun shines out of Drew's proverbial."

"I'd love to meet your family one day."

"I think I'd like that too."

"Perhaps you could visit u…I mean me in England."

"Ben would bite through doors to get that to happen."

"I think we'd better start thinking about getting some sleep," Drew interrupted.

"Okay, bro, I'll let you and these lovely people go. Just make sure y'all stay safe d'yer hear?"

She hugged and kissed her brother, did the same with Cassie and told her she was a great kid, but when she got to Anna she held her close and whispered, "I heard what you nearly said back then. You could do worse you know, and I doubt he'd be hard to catch. I've seen the way he looks at you and vice versa."

Anna blushed but said nothing.

They took turns using the bathroom, and eventually turned the lights out.

Anna found herself thinking about what Lina had said, as she watched him come out of the bathroom; his impressive physique, his arm marred by the blue and yellow bruising from the bullet wound emerging from behind its four-inch square waterproof dressing. After admonishing herself for thinking like a schoolgirl, she turned over and put her arm around Cassie.

Twenty-One

She had a disturbed night, having woken three times in the midst of erotic dreams, something she couldn't remember having had since her days at uni.

It was just past five when she woke the third time to find herself in bed alone. It was still dark but there was enough light from the parking lot lights creeping around the edge of the curtains to see her daughter asleep in bed beside Drew. At first she didn't know what to think, but the untroubled look on Cassie's face was enough to put her mind to rest and she fell back to sleep.

When she woke next, Drew's bedside light was on and Cassie was already stirring. Drew was nowhere to be seen.

"So you're sleeping with men now are you?" she teased.

"You kept fidgeting and waking me up, so I came to sleep with Drew, that's all. We didn't do sex things."

"Oh God, I didn't mean to suggest you did, I'm sorry, and I'm sorry for disturbing you. I kept having strange dreams. Where's Drew?"

"I don't know."

"Do you want to use the bathroom first?"

"No you go. I just want to lie here a bit longer."

Before she could go, the door opened and Drew stepped in with arms full of sandwiches, snacks, and drinks.

"I brought breakfast; well first course anyway."

"First course?"

"I won't want to do a seven-hour drive with just a sandwich and a packet of potato chips inside me, so when we've been going for a couple hours, I'll try and find a diner for refueling."

"Have you used the bathroom yet?"

"No, not yet. Why don't you go first? We can eat our breakfast while you're in there."

The sandwiches from the vending machine were dry and barely edible. Anna and Cassie barely ate half. The coffee wasn't much better, so they made do with a bottle of water each."

"Next," Drew announced as he came out of the bathroom.

Anna self-consciously stood up in her nightie and panties, and he turned away so as not to embarrass her. Lying on top of the bed, Cassie watched the body language of the two adults, sensing that something unspoken was happening, but not understanding what it was.

"Mummy's pretty isn't she?" she said, after Anna had disappeared into the bathroom.

"I guess."

"Why haven't you got a girlfriend?"

"My life hasn't been the sort of life that makes it easy to have a girlfriend, like I told you before, and I'm not a one-night stand sort of guy."

"You're different. From the things I read, most boys only want to do sex and then go away again."

"These days a lot of girls are like that too."

"I suppose so, but I don't think that's the way it's supposed to be."

"I agree with you, but we don't make up the rules, do we?"

"Will you never have a girlfriend?"

"I hope I do, some day."

"I read somewhere men have psychological problems if they don't have sex."

"This conversation is getting a bit weird, don't you think?"

"I guess so, but I don't have anybody to talk about stuff like this. I tried with Judith. She goes all shy and says we'll talk about it another day, but we never do. Talking about it with Mummy would feel weird too."

"I think your mom is exactly the sort of mom to be able to talk about things like this. It's not that I mind talking with you about anything really, but your mom might be uncomfortable if she thought you were coming to me about intimate things rather than her."

"I suppose so. I used to talk to Izzy about this sort of thing. She had a boyfriend that Mummy didn't know about, and I think that they sometimes did things together. She told me that she would die of embarrassment if she talked about them with Mummy."

"I don't think you're doing your mom justice. She seems quite broad-minded to me, in spite of her sheltered background."

"I don't know if you two realize it, but the wall between this room and the bathroom is paper thin."

"Oh my God, Mummy, did you hear all that?"

"Pretty much," she said emerging from the bathroom. "I have three observations. First, I'm grateful for your endorsement, Drew; second, Drew is right I'm the right sort of person to talk about these things and please don't feel weird about it; and third, I don't mind if Cassie talks about things with you Drew, as long as you're both comfortable with it. I only wish I'd had somebody I could have talked to."

Cassie walked past her mum to go to the bathroom. "Sorry, Mummy."

"No need. I should be more open and make myself more approachable. I didn't realize that Judith found those things difficult to talk about. Hurry up though, darling. Drew wants to get on the road."

"Didn't you want those sandwiches?" he asked.

"They were disgusting, and so was the coffee. Thankfully you bought water as well."

"The water was for the journey, but it doesn't matter we'll get some more on the way out. Bring the bottles. We can fill them from the dispenser."

"Sometimes you make me feel inadequate. Of course the water was for the trip. Why didn't I think of that?" She watched him pull his pants on and thought how strange it felt to be in such intimate proximity with a man again.

Drew helped himself to the sandwiches that hadn't been eaten.

"Mummy, can you pass me something to wear?"

Anna passed her daughter some clothes, "I was wondering how we were going to manage with so few clothes."

"There's an outfitter in Slade. You'll need to buy some more. There won't be anywhere for you to launder things and if the weather's bad it might be several days before we can wash them ourselves."

"I hadn't even thought about that."

"Thought about what, mummy?" Cassie asked coming from the bathroom.

"Doing the laundry. I'm guessing there's no washing machine then, Drew."

"No, it'll be the sink or the stream I'm afraid."

"This is going to be another steep learning curve, isn't it?"

"I expect so. I'm not sure how good at female underthings an outfitter will be, so we'll go into Slade again in a day or two where you can buy whatever you need."

Ten minutes later they were climbing into the car.

It was 05:45.

"Which one's Lina's car?" Cassie asked.

"None of them. She drove to Richmond in my old pickup, which she left at the dealers. She'll get a cab back there later to drive it home."

"Why did you get her to buy the truck for you? Surely you could have bought a truck here yourself or in Washington for that matter," Anna asked.

"I could, but I don't know how much money they're throwing at this surveillance thing, and I can't be sure they haven't put a tracker on my pickup. Remember we're probably dealing with the Russians here. I doubt they're going to put a human tail on us but we already know they're trying to track us electronically. If they've put a tracker on my pickup it will confuse them. I'm just trying to use as many cutouts in our journey as possible."

"Could they be tracking this car?"

"I used my bug detector on it earlier and couldn't find anything. They still have no reason to believe that we're in Richmond as far as I know," he said, putting the car in reverse to pull out of the parking space, "They'll know we flew to Washington, and I guess they can figure out eventually that we got a rental. Whether they can figure out which one and where we went to with it is another thing. Even if they do track us to Richmond, by the time they do my pickup will be back in Wilmington and we'll be in Kentucky. Even if they knew that, it would be a dead end, because there's no way they can know about my connection with Brady."

Drew had maneuvered the car out of the parking lot and onto Interstate 64 without interrupting his conversation. It was nearly eight a.m. when he pulled off at Lexington, Virginia.

"We can get breakfast here," he said pulling into the parking lot of a Waffle House. "Not my preference, but it's body fuel."

They ordered breakfast, regular size for Anna and Cassie, twice that for Drew.

"There's a Walmart over there. Have we got time to go in? I'm a bit worried about the underwear thing," Anna said.

"Should be okay. Try to keep it to thirty minutes if you can."

"You can go and get gas or something while we get panties if you prefer."

"You haven't quite grasped this bodyguard thing yet, have you, ma'am."

Cassie giggled.

"Yeah, alright, and it's Anna."

Thirty-five minutes later they were back in the car, rejoining the Interstate.

"So how did you find your first experience of shopping for ladies' intimate garments?"

"It was okay, I guess, but that kinda sounds like a no-win question. If I say I enjoyed it that would make me sound like a perv. If I say I didn't enjoy it that might make me sound gay. If I say I like them better off than on, it'll sound like I was making a pass at you, and if I say I prefer them on rather than off it might sound like I thought you were unattractive."

"Smartass!" she said with a smile.

Cassie giggled in the back.

At that time of day, the traffic was heavy around Lexington and heading West and it was nearly twelve when Drew pulled off at Charleston, West Virginia. He found a restaurant not far from the Interstate where they bought a quick lunch and used the washrooms. They were back on the road in forty-five minutes, and three hours later he turned off the Interstate at Mount Sterling onto the highways and smaller roads.

"Are we stopping again?" Cassie asked.

"We're nearly at our overnight destination. We've made good time. We can go straight to the motel or stop at the outfitters first."

"What would you prefer?" Anna asked. "Does it make a difference?"

"I think I'd prefer to go to the outfitters first. There are a few things I need to get myself."

"Let's do that then."

It seemed like no time at all when they pulled into the parking lot at the *Davy Crockett Outfitters*.

"Okay girls, you each need two pairs of strong boots, four or five pairs of strong pants or jeans, at least the same of shirts, a good strong warm coat, and a lighter waterproof one for warmer, wetter weather, plus gloves, hats, and scarves. This ain't Walmart. A lot of things won't be on racks for you to help yourselves. You'll need to grab someone to serve you for a lot of it. They'll be used to tenderfoot tourists so don't be embarrassed to ask if you don't understand."

"What about skirts or dresses for going out?"

"Trust me, Cassie, you won't be needing to wear skirts or dresses while we're staying at the cabin. As for going out, our options will be limited, so wherever we go shirts, pants, and boots or sneakers will be just fine."

They spent more than an hour gathering their various purchases. The bill came to over twelve hundred dollars. Drew added a few things of his own and insisted on paying with his card. "You need to maintain your supply of cash for the time being, just to be on the safe side."

"All that came to less than when you take me to London shopping sometimes, Mummy, and it was in dollars not pounds," Cassie said as they got back in the car.

"You're right, but it's still not right for Drew to be paying for it."

"I'm confident you'll reimburse me when the time is right, ma'am."

"I most definitely will, and it's Anna!"

"Difficult to get used to after all my time in the military."

"Anna," she reminded him."

"Anna."

"That's better. Where are we going now?"

"Just one more brief stop."

He drove across town to an electronics shop he'd been directed to by a guy in the outfitters.

"I won't be long,' he told them and went inside.

"Are you Erik?"

"That's what it says over the door."

"I'm told that you're the go to guy for what I need. I need a satellite phone."

"You can get them almost anywhere around this part of the world these days, but I'm more than happy to help you out."

"I need advice as well and maybe something special."

"Tell me. I like special."

"You know how easy it is for people to track your location from a call you make. I want to be able to make a call using a sat-phone and not have people know where I was making the call from. Is it possible to put something like a VPN on one to stop it being tracked?"

"That's real cloak and dagger stuff you're talking about there. The short answer is no, I don't think so, but the longer answer is that they can't trace sat phones in the same way as normal cells. It's possible the source of a radio signal can be located while it's live, but if they don't catch it during a transmission they'll miss their chance. If the conversation were taking place over the Internet via a computer with a VPN, they'd have no chance. Mind you if you could set that up then you may as well use your cellphone down the Internet although you'd need an anonymous Internet address."

"Okay, I think I understand. How easy is it to direct the sat-phone signal via the Internet?"

"It isn't easy at all. I don't know how to do it. I only know one guy whose done it around here. My brother installed it for him."

"Would he do it for me?"

"I doubt it. He works on big industrial electrical installations these days. You could call him and ask."

"Who is the guy who had it done?"

"His name is Atkins, lives somewhere out there in the wilderness, I don't know where."

"Thanks, have you got two sat-phones?"

"No problem, anything else?"

"No, thanks."

"Okay," he said, as he got back in the car. "Let's go to the motel."

"How far is the cabin from here?"

"Not far; about twenty-five miles."

"Couldn't we just go straight there now?"

"If we went there now we'd have less than an hour of daylight to orientate ourselves. And if you'll forgive me for saying so, you two are probably not best prepared to cope if Brady's improvements aren't as advanced as I hope."

"You're right, as usual."

"I'm excited, but a little bit scared as well though," Cassie said.

"No need to be scared, Cassie. There are some simple rules you'll need to learn, but most of it will be common sense. We have to remember that in the forest, many of the things we take for granted at home won't be there, so we need to adapt."

The check-in at the motel was straightforward.

"I wonder why it's called The Black Bear Lodge," Cassie asked as she flopped on the nearest bed.

"This is the Red River Gorge, and we're in the Daniel Boone National Park. The area is famous for black bears."

"Bears! Are they dangerous?"

"They can be, but we'll not be behaving in ways to attract them or antagonize them, so we'll be fine."

"Are there any other dangerous creatures we need to be aware of?"

"Two or three types of rattlesnake. It's best not to pick berries unless you're sure what you're eating. The most dangerous creature in the wilderness is you."

"What do you mean?"

"I don't know the figures, but every year dozens of people die in US national parks, and the main cause is stupidity. People who don't listen to what they're told or ignore advice, tourists who've watched a few episodes of *Grizzly Adams*, or *Dual Survival*, and read a *CJ Box* novel or two and think they know everything."

"But we haven't even done any of that."

"That's what I'm here for, and we're not going to be exploring the wilderness on foot."

"Do you know all about that sort of stuff then?"

"I'm not a backwoodsman, but I've had to survive in hostile environments all over the world. The animals are different, so is the climate and vegetation but most of the skills are transferrable."

"What about your friend?"

"Brady wasn't born to this way of life, but he was always a loner and it didn't surprise me when I found out he'd chosen to live this way. He's strong as an ox, short but powerful. He could probably lift me over his head. Never saw him with a girl, so when I found out he was guardian to a kid you could have knocked me down with a feather."

"Did he build the cabin himself?"

"I think it was an abandoned home, and he took it over and made a lot of improvements. He told me that I'd be surprised when I saw what he'd done to the place. He said he'd come into bit of money that had allowed him to be a bit more ambitious, what with his new responsibilities."

"It's very nice of him to let us use it."

"He's a great guy, a bit taciturn if he don't know you, but absolutely harmless unless you do something to harm or threaten a defenseless person."

"Sounds like somebody else I know," Anna said, with a grin. "Is there a restaurant here?"

"Afraid not, Anna. The desk clerk told me the closest is a Tex/Mex place round the corner called La Cabana. He said it's walkable but doesn't recommend it after dark."

"Drew?" Cassie said.

"Yes."

"What are you going to do with the truck if you come back to England with us?"

"Sell it. The F150s hold their value quite well, so if I look after it, I won't lose out too much."

"If we're going to the restaurant tonight, Mummy, can I wear some of my new clothes so I can blend in."

"Of course, darling. I will as well. That's a good idea. I'll fetch some from the car, and we can wear the same things tomorrow. What are you smiling about, Mr. Parker?"

"The idea of you blending in."

"What do you mean?"

"Think about it, everything you'll be wearing will be straight out of the packaging and your complexions couldn't be more English rose if they were off a Waterhouse painting."

"What's wrong with our complexions?" she indignantly asked.

"Nothing, that's the point. They're perfect. They've never spent hours and days in harsh weather, or extremes of heat or cold. They're beautiful." Then he realized what he'd said. "Sorry, I shouldn't have said that."

"Why? It was lovely thing to say."

He couldn't think of anything more to add to the conversation. He blushed and felt awkward.

"I'm a bit surprised by the Waterhouse reference though. I hadn't put you down as a connoisseur of fine art."

"I'm not, It's just my grandparents had a print of his on their wall and I always wanted to imagine that's what my mom looked like. Just before I enlisted, there was a song going around about mothers called, *The First Lady in My Life Was You.* I told Lina that it made me think of that picture and that was when Lina showed me a photo of my mom. It was horrible. She'd been taking drugs for years at the time and she looked about twenty years older than she was. She could never have born any resemblance to the woman in the picture.

"Lina was furious with me and told me some stories about things I'd either forgotten or not known in the first place. She shouted at me. *You can forget any fantasy you might have about our mom; she was a selfish, child-abusing, drug addict who never gave two shits about either or us.* She pointed toward the kitchen where Grandma was making dinner. *That woman through there was the first lady in your life, mine too!* It was the first time I remember seeing Lina cry."

"What was the print called? Can you remember?"

"It was *Miranda 1875*. She's sitting on a rock gazing out to sea at a gathering storm and you see her in profile with the light on the side of her face."

"My goodness, that print must have had a profound effect on you. That was the most evocative statement I've heard you make since we met."

"What does the number mean, Mummy?"

"It's the date it was painted I think, because he painted her several times. I know the version you describe though - it's beautiful. Miranda is a character from Shakespeare's *The Tempest*, a beautiful and innocent teenage girl. You'd be perfect to play her, don't you think, Drew?"

"Eh? Oh yes." He had been staring at her while she spoke.

"I don't like reading Shakespeare. It's too much like hard work."

Anna and Cassie dressed in their new shirts and jeans."

"Should we have Stetsons?" Anna asked.

"In this area a beanie would be more in keeping I expect, but you look fine. Once your clothes and boots get a bit messed up you'll look a little less like line-dancing club fugitives or the chorus line from an episode of *Country Hoedown*."

"Is that a bad thing, looking like that then?"

"Not necessarily, but I remember what the Brits all said about Dick Van Dyke in Mary Poppins. It was a cliché. You're probably best if you don't try too hard. You're okay for now though."

The spicy Mexican food proved surprisingly popular with their English palates, and the girls said they would like to go again next time they were in Slade.

Drew, however, stuck with steak.

Twenty-Two

In the morning they discovered that the motel coffee shop could only give them coffee and Danish for breakfast, with chocolate bars, or potato chips if they weren't enough, and what was worse, nothing else nearby was open until nine. The girls were happy with that but Drew bemoaned the absence of an American diner, so he supplemented the meal with a couple of energy bars from the box he'd bought in the outfitters.

Nevertheless they were on the road to the cabin by eight-fifteen and by nine they were at the little grocery store in Pine Creek that Brady told him was their closest source for day-to-day supplies.

They all went inside where a black woman in her forties asked, "Hi there folks - what can we get fer yer?"

"We need to stock up on basic groceries. All the usual things - eggs, bacon, bread, butter, vegetables. The perishables - you know the sort of thing and I need to fill my tank."

"If you want to go ahead and fill up, I'll start putting together a box of the sort of things if that'll help. You staying around here?"

"Yeah, for a while. We're borrowing a friend's cabin while he's away."

"You ain't Brady's friend Drew are yer?"

"That's right."

"So this is Anna an' Cassie, is that right? He told me to expect yer."

"That's right," Anna said coming forward and offering her hand to shake.

"Shakin' hands. Proper manners. Brady told me you're English. I ain't met anybody from English land afore. Just a minute. MILLY!" she shouted. "I'm Ruby."

"What's up ma. I'm doin' my learning," a voice called.

Drew went outside to fill the car.

"Brady's friend is here with his English girlfriend and her little girl. Come and say hello," demanded Ruby.

"I'm not really his girlfriend."

"I know, you're still married to an asshole, like I was. Brady told me I got to keep it quiet. That's okay I understand. Did he beat up on you like mine did? I told Milly too, she won't talk about you."

"Something like that."

"Mine's back in state prison now, probably for life. Asshole; best place for him. Milly, are you coming?"

"Okay ma."

A small girl appeared by her mother's side.

"This my Milly. She's real smart, does all her learning on the interweb, all by own self an' she's only nine. These are Brady's friends he told us about. This your little un?"

"Yes this is Cassie. She's eleven."

"Hi, Cassie. I can't stay long cos I'm doin' about triangles again today an' it's real hard."

"I'm not bad at trigonometry, if you're still struggling I can help if you want. I probably can't do much today though we've got to get to the cabin."

"You'll like it - the cabin. Brady's got it fixed up real good."

"Show me what you're working on."

The two girls went through to the back.

"Is Brady a good customer?" Anna asked.

Ruby laughed. "You could say that Brady owns this store an' lets me run the business without payin' no rent. That's a secret too. I ain't s'posed to tell no-one."

"Are you and him an item?"

"How d'yer mean? Like goin' together?" She giggled. "No, I should be so lucky. Brady ain't got eyes for nobody 'cept Alice."

"Alice?"

"He's her guardian, an' he worships the ground she walks over."

"Can I help you get the groceries together?"

"No, you stay there. Won't take but a minute."

While she was gone, Anna looked around the small general store, surprised at the range of products.

Ruby soon returned carrying a big box crammed with everything that Drew had asked for and quite a few other things besides.

"I just did up an order the same as I do for Brady. Here's a card that Alice had printed with our email and phone number. If you want stuff an' you tell us early enuff, we can order it in. Milly does that - she's good at that stuff."

"Hey, Ma. Cassie's real smart. She showed me how to do some of those triangle things much better than that teacher."

"I think if you're doing trigonometry at nine years old then you must be quite clever yourself," Anna told her.

"I love your accent, Anna, it's real cute."

"Thank you, I like yours too. How much do I owe you?"

Ruby looked in the box and mumbled to herself as she looked through the contents. "Thirty-three dollars and fifteen cents plus for the gas. He's finished pumping now, so that's one hundred and forty-nine and 31 cents. I didn't put eggs in cos Alice's chickens are laying quite well at the moment. If you get too many, bring them to the store next time you come."

Anna handed her two one-hundred-dollar bills and refused the change.

"That's mighty generous, but we don't do tips here, 'cept for deliveries."

"Then put it in Milly's college fund. If she's learning trigonometry already, I'm sure she'll be off to uni before you know it."

"Brady's always sayin' stuff like that."

"There you go then."

"You city folks are a strange bunch."

"Ruby, I'm really outside my comfort zone, and a friendly face is more welcome than I can say. I hope we get to stop by here often."

"I 'spect you be plenty busy with that horny boyfriend of yours. You can always leave Cassie here for an hour or two if'n you need some quiet time you know."

"Thank you, Ruby, but I don't think that will be necessary."

"Oh okay, I guess you English people are more broad-minded than they say."

"No that's not what I meant…Oh never mind."

"You gonna feed the pig and chickens while you're here, save me from the journey every few days?"

"Oh okay. What do they eat?"

"There's a big bin of chicken feed, by the hen house. You just need to keep the feeder topped up; same goes with the pig. You can also give the pig any slops from the table. I usually save ours to take up there when I go. In fact you can take the bucket with you if you like."

"Okay."

"I'll fetch it, ma."

Milly disappeared out the back and reappeared a few seconds later carrying a bucket. "Here you go, Cassie. Stinks a bit but April, that's the pig, she loves it."

Cassie took the bucket with a wrinkled nose and handed it to Drew as he came through the door.

"You ready then?" he asked, taking it from her without comment.

They all said their farewells.

"Bits of that conversation were the most surreal I've ever had I think."

"How do you mean?"

"Never mind. She's nice though. I like her."

"Milly's nice too. No wonder she couldn't understand those trig questions. I don't think she's being taught properly. She got it straightaway when I told her the way Judith taught me."

The final twelve miles or so to the cabin went quickly.

"Wow he's even had the track made up since I was here. When they pulled into the yard, they found a smart tidy cabin with a water tower, a long outbuilding that had obviously once been a stable, a small log building at its side and another on the edge of the clearing its purpose unclear, and a huge table saw under a shelter next to that. A backhoe and a strange looking pickup truck were parked in front of the stable. There was also a chicken run with a henhouse, and a pig pen with a movable shelter.

Drew pulled the truck in front of the cabin. "I won't be a second, I'll just get the keys."

They watched him walk to a nearby pine tree and shin up it to the lower branches glance around and with one hand untie a leather thong before climbing down again.

"Well that beats leaving it under a flowerpot I suppose." Anna laughed.

He opened the door and tied the key around his neck before stepping inside to look around.

"It's cute," Anna remarked.

"Like Goldilocks' cabin," Cassie added.

"Except if bears get in here they won't be looking for porridge, and it will be because somebody did something stupid. We can talk about it a bit more later. Can you get our things from the truck. I need to light the stove or we won't be getting any hot meals or water?"

By the time they had everything inside the cabin and closed the door, the fire in the stove was burning fiercely.

"How long does the water take to heat up?"

"I don't know, the water in the tank may still be a little warm already. It depends how long Brady's been away, and how big the hot water cylinder is. Try the faucet. But we don't need to wait until the tank is warmed up to make tea or coffee. The coffee percolator is there, and there are coffee and tea containers on the shelf there. If you can get some hot drinks going, I'll see about getting the Internet and satellite phone working."

"Okay but before that, can we decide who uses which bedroom?"

"Just choose the one you two want, and I'll have the other."

Brady had given Drew the passwords for the laptop computers and Wi-Fi and he had them booted up and working in minutes. The internet connection kicked in straightaway, allowing him to call Brady and tell him they were there.

"Brady, this is something special you've created here, not what I was expecting."

"Well when you get someone special in your life your perspective changes, doesn't it? It's about time you found someone yourself."

"We met Ruby and Milly at the store. So you're a storeowner as well now as well?"

"She ain't supposed to tell anyone about that. I didn't want it to be general knowledge, but in small towns, nothing stays secret for long I guess. We're up visiting some of Alice's distant family in Oklahoma. She's only just discovered their connection. Not sure it will be long before we've outstayed our welcome, but I'll give you notice if we decide to come back."

"Thanks buddy."

"The meat store is still pretty full, we had a great hunting season last year, so help yourself it needs to be used. Likewise with the freezer and store cupboard. Have you met the forest ranger yet?"

"There was nobody there when we drove past the station. We've only been here about twenty minutes."

"He'll drop by before long, he's a good guy. Dry sense of humor. Runs a pretty tight ship with forest regulations, which is good in my book."

"I'll let you go now. Would be good to meet your Alice one day but I don't know when that's likely to be, it looks like I'm going to be in England for the next while."

"Stay safe buddy."

Anna emerged from the biggest bedroom. "There are two freezers in the storeroom, and they're both almost full of meat and vegetables. The meat isn't labelled though."

"It'll be things like deer, elk, turkey, bear, rabbit, or groundhog I expect. I doubt he shops for meat."

"Groundhog!" Anna exclaimed.

"Bear!" Cassie added, equally horrified.

"Of course. Brady doesn't hunt for sport; he does it to survive. It's one of the main reasons he lives like this."

"Is he one of those survivalists?"

"Not the sort that lives a twenty-first century lifestyle during the week and at the weekends makes plans to hide in a nuclear bunker and eat Spam until they die after the aliens arrive. He uses real life survival skills to only use what he has to, and to put back as much as he can - eco-friendly if you like."

"How will we know what we're eating?"

"I expect he'd recognize it by the color, shape, or streaks of fat, but does it really matter? Everything in the meat store will be smoked so it might taste unusual to you anyway, and the frozen meat once cooked will taste similar to what your used to. If I gave you a plate of groundhog stew and told you it was chicken you'd never know the difference."

"I don't want to eat bear. They're lovely animals; it's cruel to kill them."

"Brady doesn't hunt bear, but sometimes if you're in the forest and you're attacked by one, killing it is the only option. Also, sometimes hobby hunters might wound a bear, and not chase after it to kill it. If Brady came across a wounded animal, he'd kill it out of humanity, and regard it as immoral to leave it to rot. He'd bring the carcass back here. Eating it is like honoring it. That's a native American philosophy."

"Is he Indian?"

"No Russian descent, but I think Alice is at least part. Anyway, there won't be much beef or lamb eaten while we're here, so unless you're planning on going vegetarian, those meat varieties will be the only options, I expect."

"Okay, just don't tell me if we're eating bear, if you can avoid it."

Drew took a plate out to the heavily constructed meat store, surrounded by plants that deter bears. Using the hunting knife he'd bought in the outfitter store, he cut three good sized but thin steaks from what was probable an elk haunch.

"How does it stay fresh out there?" Anna asked.

"It's been well salted, smoked, and dried."

"Cassie, can you unpack our bags and the clothes from the outfitter and put them on the free shelves in the closet for me, please?"

The business of familiarization and settling in continued. Anna tried out the coffee pot using the water boiler on the stove, and Cassie unpacked everybody's clothes in the end.

"Is the bedding clean?" Anna asked.

"It looks okay to me, Mummy."

Drew checked the fuel tank for the generator and found it virtually full while Anna reported the water was hot enough to wash or shower after about an hour.

"Everything's so organized and clean; it somehow isn't what I expected."

"I've no doubt that Alice's influence will have been involved in that."

"Have you noticed that the initials *B&A* have been carved everywhere - on the cupboard doors, the chairs, even on one of the beds. It's a sort of logo," Cassie pointed out.

The others looked around them, noticing them for the first time.

"Brady must have been lonely without realizing it before Alice came into his life, and after she lost her parents, she would have had no-one either," Anna observed.

"Milly told me that when the robbers came into the store and threatened to kill them, her mummy shot one but the other one shot Alice's mummy and her daddy had a heart attack, so she took his gun and killed the other robber. She was only ten."

"My God, that's horrific!"

"Her Mummy had cancer and was in a wheelchair. Milly says that Brady, was the kindest and bravest man she knew. I told her that Drew was the same."

Drew didn't comment. He just went outside and began chopping wood. An hour later Anna called him in to eat.

"Thank God they've got aprons, whatever that fat and meat is, it really spits."

"I'm just having cheese, Mummy."

"I know, sweetie, but I think you should try it rather than dismissing it out of hand. Drew says it elk, which is just a big deer. You've had venison and liked that. Try a small piece of mine."

"Okay then."

"I'm going to make macaroni cheese this evening. That's simple. I've seen they've got all the ingredients, and I need to find my feet cooking with this range."

"Can we look around outside the cabin now?" Cassie asked.

"Good idea," Drew said. "Grab something to collect eggs in. I'll take the pig bucket."

They let themselves into the chicken run and lifted the lid of the nesting box to find about fifteen eggs gathered in a metal collecting basket that ran the length of the nesting box.

"This real clever. It's all automatic look. They feed themselves. The door is on a light sensor so it opens in the morning and then closes at night and there's a heater on a thermostat for the really cold weather," Drew enthused. "I expect they allow the birds to roam when they're at home."

Cassie collected the eggs, put them in the pan, and ran back to the cabin with them.

"They must have a dog. There's a big kennel next to the porch," she said when she returned. "Shall we feed April now?"

"Funny name for a pig," Anna said, as Drew tipped the bucket of slops into the pen.

"Well she made short work of that," Drew said with a laugh.

"There's a grave over there, look."

They walked over to see.

The wooden headstone had a circular emblem alongside a representation of a frontiersman chiseled in relief. The emblem said it was the Great Seal of the Chickasaw Nation, and below an inscription read, *Joe and Ellie Foster bonded by love in a partnership forged in adversity. Loving parents and loyal friends.* Then underneath was the first verse of *An Ashokan Farewell.*

With a catch in her throat, Anna observed, "That's so beautiful."

The nearby vegetable patch had rows of carrots, onions, kale and other vegetables at various stages of development, some clearly past their best.

"What's that thing?" Cassie said, pointing at a big metal box beside the house.

"That's the generator. I expect it automatically cuts in before the battery gets too flat if the solar panels aren't coping."

"For a backwoodsman, this place is very hi-tech."

"I expect having the responsibility of a child to care for caused him to have a bit of a rethink."

"Would you want to live like this?"

"For a permanent lifestyle, it's bit extreme for my taste, but I wouldn't object to going back to nature from time to time, a few weeks perhaps. Makes you appreciate things a bit more."

"What's your dream, it can't just be standing on the shoulder of rich people like me keeping them safe. Don't you have a personal pipedream?"

"I kinda liked the idea of a ranch. That's what my savings were for, but it's a bit unrealistic I guess."

"Where's the stream that you talked about?" Cassie asked.

"Along that path. I'll get my gun first and we can walk down there."

"Why do you need a gun?"

"I probably don't, but bears have not been out of hibernation that long, so they won't have had a chance to fatten up yet. Hungry animals can be unpredictable, and so can a sow with young cubs."

"Maybe we should leave the stream for a while then?" Anna said, "Where does the water come from?"

"The stream I expect. He wouldn't have gone to all this trouble and not have water pumped in. He's got a Klargester to deal with waste products."

"What's a Klargester?"

"It's a drainage system. It basically takes away all the unpleasant stuff out everything that goes in the waste, and the water that soaks away into the ground is almost clean. Then every year or two a big vehicle comes to pump out all the solid stuff. Let's have our little *staying alive in the forest 101* chat now?

"Okay, first rule. Never leave any kind of food lying around. If you do, a bear can smell it downwind from quite a way away, and will use great efforts to get hold of it. Did you see the marks on the door and front window? They were probably made by a bear after something made him believe there was something nice to eat inside.

"Second, If you're confronted by a bear, change direction or back away slowly, preferably back the way you came. Walk, don't run, and keep your eye on the bear so you can see how it reacts. In most cases, the bear will ignore you or flee. If the bear walks toward you, act boldly, yelling or throwing something at it. If you see a sow and cubs do everything you can to avoid approaching them, no matter how cute they are.

"Next, waste; everything that isn't consumed must recycled, burned, or taken into town to be disposed of. Not only is it the right thing to do, but it's strictly controlled and monitored. We passed the ranger station on the way in here. Brady tells me the one from there is a good guy but very strict. The incinerator is that thing over there. We'll put combustible waste in there and burn it once a week. That's the only place outside the cabin that anything gets burned. The food waste except bones we'll give to April. Everything else in that old oil drum is to be taken into town.

"There's no TV as you know it, but from what I've seen you don't watch much. We can keep abreast of what's happening in the world via the Internet. You must not try to contact any friends or family while you're here by any means. I have my phone, the one I can use to contact Brady, and anybody else not associated with any of this and I have these two satellite phones. I'm told if I operate them from here they'll be almost impossible to trace. Later on I'll use one of them to contact Percy and set up a system for him to talk with us that will be impossible for them to trace."

"Can I download books to my eReader?"

"Has it got an email function?"

"Yes, but I've never used it."

"That shouldn't be a problem then."

Anna went quiet for a while and then asked, "What do we do in the evenings?"

"What did you do in Santa Monica, or Pangbourne for that matter? I don't remember you watching much TV in either of those places."

"Fair point. Often I'd just chat with Judith or Jason. Cassie reads a lot, sometimes streams a movie."

"Nothing stopping the three of us chatting. Telling each other stories, asking questions, making jokes that sort of thing. That's what we do in the army when we're on an op. When we're on base a lot of them go to a bar, look for someone to spend time with, that sort of thing."

"You mean prostitutes, don't you?" Cassie said.

"Cassie!"

"It's okay, not usually. That would mean paying. Just someone generous with their affections, but not looking for a long-term relationship."

"Did you?"

"I did when I was a rookie, but to be honest I didn't enjoy it, and don't think people find me much fun."

"Why not?"

"I don't drink, and a lot of my buddies thought that was weird."

"Why don't you drink?"

"Because when I drink, I'm not a nice person."

"Being different must have been awkward in that environment."

"At first people used to think it meant I was soft and try to test me out by picking a fight with me. Got me in bad trouble once. It stopped after a while and they accepted me as I am."

"Why did it stop though?"

"Because I usually won the fights."

"How can you be so aggressive one moment and so gentle the next?"

"Don't know. These days I only get aggressive with assholes who pick on other people, like Gates or your husband."

Their conversation was interrupted by the sound of a vehicle on the track.

"Stay inside for the moment." He glanced out of the window and waited until a green Jeep Cherokee pulled into the yard. "It's the Ranger - no need to worry."

He stepped out on to the porch, and the others followed.

"Hi, you must be Ranger Reynolds, Brady told me to look out for you. I'm Drew Parker."

The two men shook hands. "Good to meet you, Parker. Atkins speaks very highly of you. Howdy ladies, how're you settling in?"

"Still finding our feet to be honest. We're just a couple of English girls and we're way out of our depth here."

"So I gather. Brady told me a little about your predicament. That's the only reason I gave the go ahead for you to come. The US Forest Service isn't big on the inholdings being used for short-term tourist rental."

"We're really grateful officer, and we won't stay longer than necessary."

"I got that, but if you're in danger, I won't be chasin' you out. And it's just Russ by the way, ma'am - until you do something wrong that is," he grinned.

"And I'm just Anna. This is Cassie."

"I'm pleased to meet you. I won't bother you too much but I'll drive through once in a while on my way up the track and back. Here's my card. If you need me just call that number - it's my cell. If I'm on duty I'll pick up. If I'm not it'll divert to one of my colleagues."

"Can I offer you a cup of coffee, Russ?" Cassie asked.

"You can if it's that good stuff that Alice gets in. That'd be right nice, thanks. You known Atkins long?"

"About fifteen years I guess. I'd never imagined him with kids."

"I never seen two people so devoted. They're good for each other. That girl had a lotta tragedy in her life. She deserves a bit of happiness. So does Atkins for that matter. He survived more than one attempt on his life."

"What was that all about?"

"He upset a dirty cop when he first got here and that kicked off a vendetta that last two or more years culminating in the deaths of Alice's parents. That's their grave out back. It's a long story, and I'm not sure I know the whole thing. One day when I got more time I'll tell you how the crazy S.O.B. got mauled by a bear, killed it with his knife, and hauled it and an elk thirty-five miles by himself rather than waste it. He was lucky to live."

"He was always the strongest man I knew."

Reynolds said goodbye and drove on up the track. An hour later he passed back through the yard, stopped and called Drew over. "I forgot to tell you. there's a sow and her three cubs doing the rounds hereabouts at the moment. Best be on the lookout. She won't be wanting company."

"Thanks for that, Russ. Have a good one."

The macaroni cheese, or mac and cheese as Drew insisted on calling it, was very popular especially in the light of the considerable improvisation called for from Anna to produce it.

"I'm a bit scared, but I'd really like to see the bear cubs," Cassie told them.

"If you see them out the window, you won't be any danger in here. Likewise if we're in the car. Once they've fattened themselves up a bit they'll be less aggressive."

"Won't we run out of stories to tell each other, if we're here a long time?"

"I'm not anticipating being here a long time. One way or another this is going to come to a head soon."

"Tell us a story from your days in the army."

He told them about an embassy siege in Copenhagen that had lasted three weeks and turned out be the unarmed ambassador's daughter trying to get her boyfriend freed from jail.

"That was a bit funny but not very exciting in the end," the young listener complained.

"The stories don't have to be exciting. In fact they don't even have to be true as long as you fess up at the end. What about you, haven't you got anything to tell us?"

"I can't think of anything though."

"I'm quite interested to know more about this boy that Izzy was seeing and I knew nothing about."

"It was that boy from the ranch next to ours at Stillwater; you remember, his name was Randy."

"But he was he was about twenty or twenty-one!"

"Izzy really fancied him and he used to ride over to the fence line to meet her and they'd go and do sex stuff in the winter shelter."

"What sort of sex stuff?"

"It's embarrassing."

"Not so long ago you were asking a grown man you'd only known for a week for advice about sex; I don't think you need worry about being embarrassed."

"She told me they were going to third base. I didn't know what that meant. So I looked it up on the Internet. I told her that I didn't believe her but she insisted and told me she played with his you know what, and he played with hers. I asked her if she liked it and she said that Randy wasn't very good at it."

"Did she have a point of reference?"

Cassie got up and whispered something in her ear.

"Oh, I see," Anna said.

"Was that alright?"

"Yes of course it was, well her reference was anyway. As for the rest of it, definitely no."

"It must be your turn now then, Anna.

"Well I haven't got anything quite as racy as that to tell in front of my daughter. Let me think."

"Tell us about your first boyfriend Mummy."

"You know who my first boyfriend was. It was your daddy."

"So was he the first boy you kissed."

"Well no, but he was the first boy I dated."

"So who was the first?"

"Uncle Samuel."

"Uncle Sam? Really?"

"We were quite young. Grandpa, Grandma, and I had been invited to his sister Leah's Bat Mitzvah celebrations. Sam and I were bored so he suggested we go somewhere to find something else to do. He took me to the summerhouse and asked me if I'd ever been kissed by a boy. When I told him I hadn't, he said he'd teach me. I agreed, but I didn't like it when he tried to put his tongue in my mouth."

"Was that all?"

"He wanted to play *you show me yours and I'll show you mine.* I wasn't that keen on the idea and agreed on condition he went first, with the intention of running away when it was my turn. It all went a bit wrong because he didn't just open his pants like I thought he would, he pushed them right down to his ankles, and started to play with it. I was so shocked I couldn't move. I just stood there while he did it. Just as he made himself squirt, Aunt Sarah came in the door and went bonkers. She hit him around the head, shouted at him, called him lots of nasty names, and told him to go to his room and he was grounded for a month. Then she helped me get the stuff off my dress and pleaded with me never to tell anyone about it ever. I agreed and until tonight I only ever told one person."

"That was a good story, Mummy. How old were you though?"

"About the same as you are now."

Cassie's jaw fell open.

"I guess that takes the story a notch or two up the excitement scale," Drew said.

"You saw a seventeen-year-old boy masturbating when you were my age!" said Cassie.

"I didn't really know what was going on."

"But he did," Drew said. "You were still a child and he was all but an adult. He could have been charged with a sex offence and ruined his whole life if you'd told anybody. What about you, what effect to did it have on you?"

"None really. Like I said, I didn't fully understand what was happening. A week or two later I told my girlfriend Jenny about it without saying who I was talking about. She thought it was great and wished it had been her. I never gave sex much thought again until Daddy and I started dating."

"That's weird though, thinking about your mummy and daddy doing sex things. I don't want you to tell me about that."

"I think that's enough stories for one night. I didn't mean this to turn into a session of true confessions. Perhaps we can keep our stories a bit further above the waist in future eh?"

"I'm tired now; can I go to bed, Mummy?"

"Go ahead, sweetheart. I won't be far behind you."

"I'll try not to disturb you when I use the bathroom," Drew said.

"I didn't think about that when we chose the bedroom, sorry; don't worry about it though. It's a strange layout isn't it?"

"This building is over a hundred years old. When Brady took it over it had just the three rooms and he intended to live in it alone. The bathroom and store were added at different times, probably when he found he would be having Alice with him. He'll have added the two rooms in the most convenient place at the time."

"Of course. That seems an unusual relationship though doesn't it? Almost like a couple rather than guardian and ward."

"I don't want to judge things I know nothing about."

"Absolutely, you're right. Do you want to use the bathroom first?"

"No go ahead, I want to check out Brady's arsenal before I go to bed, and I don't want to smell of gun oil when I get between the sheets." It wasn't entirely true, he just needed to think.

"Okay, I'll leave the door open."

It was over an hour later when he finally made his way to the bathroom to take a shower, and by the time he'd finished drying himself the towels were soaking wet. He made a mental note to find Brady's linen store and walked back through the bedroom wearing only briefs, and unaware that he was being observed by Anna through slitted eyes. A side lamp in the main room was casting enough light to enable her to admire him, even if she felt guilty for doing so.

Twenty-Three

At 06:40 the first glimmers of light were just beginning to appear between the treetops across the yard when Drew opened the shutters and went outside to begin a punishing workout. The last weeks had made it difficult to maintain his usual fitness regime, and he was determined not to allow civilian life to cause a drop in his standards.

At nearly eight o'clock, Anna emerged on the porch in sneakers and the thick bathrobe that she'd bought at Walmart, to find Drew doing laps of the property with a huge log on his shoulder that he'd cut for the purpose the day before. She was carrying the damp towels from the bathroom.

Drew dropped the log on the ground beside the steps, and breathlessly waited for her to speak.

"We need to hang these out to dry. I can't find any fresh linen. If there isn't any we might need to buy some."

"I haven't looked, but in the meantime there's a wash line around the back, I'll hang them out for you if you hold them while I do it."

Cassie joined her mother, similarly dressed. "Shall I get us some clean towels, Mummy?"

"Do you know where they are?"

"They're in that that big cupboard at the bottom of the water tower, I found them yesterday."

"That makes sense, it's where the hot water cylinder is," Drew told them.

The two adults hung the towels to dry then went inside.

"If you have your shower, I'll make breakfast. What do you want?" asked Anna.

"Eggs, bacon, and fried bread or toast please, but you don't need to cook for me if you're just making toast or cereal."

"I don't mind cooking for you. There isn't much else I can contribute here. I can't find any cereal, and there's no toaster."

"There are oats in that biscuit barrel, and the fork with a long handle by the fireplace is for toasting bread. If you open the range door you can do it there. I've put extra wood in the range so it should be good and hot by now."

"Thanks. How many eggs?"

Anna arranged the different breakfast choices so they could all eat together.

"This furniture is really nice, so perfect in this setting. Do you think he made it all himself?"

"I'd be surprised if he didn't."

"He must be really clever."

"He was one of the best craftsmen there was when we worked together."

"He must have acquired a bit of money from somewhere though. This would have been extremely expensive to set up, especially with all the hi-tech trimmings and buying the store."

"His old man was an Olympic weightlifter and owned a string of gyms. After he died Brady got it all."

"What are we going to do today?"

"I'll do the dishes and collect the eggs when I've had my shower," Cassie offered.

"And I'm going to figure out how to wash things by hand."

"I'm going to get some practice with a long gun. Brady's got a makeshift firing range out there."

"Have you got enough bullets?"

"Brady's got enough ammo for the siege of Leningrad, and more guns than I ever imagined. It's odd because he never owned a gun when I first knew him, and he only had two when I came here after he moved in."

"Won't the Ranger get worried if he hears of lot of gunfire?"

"I'll text him to tell him what's happening."

He collected an M16 from one of the gun safes in the bedroom and was about to go to the store to fetch a box of ammo, when he spotted Cassie at the sink.

"Don't bother washing the frypan, just wipe it with some paper. If you get them too clean, the eggs will stick."

"Okay. Can I watch you firing the gun?"

"You should wear ear defenders if you do. There's another pair in my room."

She finished and put the dishes away, grabbed a cooking pot, and went outside. Drew was loading a spare magazine at the table, and Anna was gathering clothes to wash.

Seconds later, Cassie backed through the door, white as a sheet. "B-b-bears," she whispered, starting to close the door.

"Don't close it." Drew told her.

"You're not going to shoot them are you?"

"Not unless they attack us, and they're unlikely to do that unless we annoy them. Where are they?"

"The babies are trying to look in the pig pen, and the Mummy bear is pulling carrots out of the ground. We can't see them from here."

"Let's just wait here for a minute and see if they come into view."

They didn't have to wait long before a cub came skittling across to Drew's pickup and start sniffing around the wheels."

"He's so cute," Cassie whispered.

A quiet grumbling sound preceded the mother's lazy, four-footed amble across the yard toward the path to the stream. Halfway across she stopped and briefly glanced at the three humans before continuing in the same direction, and two cubs rushed to catch up. The first cub hadn't finished examining Drew's car when the mother spotted he wasn't there, she turned and issued an impatient growl, causing him to rush to join the others.

They were almost out of sight when an ear-shattering roar, caused the bears to turn and hurry back in the direction they'd come. As they passed in front of the cabin, another bear, almost twice the size of the mother galloped into the yard and roared a second time. The cubs climbed the tree where Brady kept his keys, but the mother stopped and responded with a roar of her own. The mother's defiance prompted the new arrival to rise up on its hind legs exposing a big patch of bare skin on his belly. He roared a third time. The mother clearly wasn't about to give ground, and the enraged male dropped to all fours and began to rush her.

There was the deafening roar of gunfire as Drew fired five rapid shots of the M16. The two bears both stopped in their tracks before stampeding away, the male back up the track in the direction he'd come from and the mother toward the forest behind the henhouse. She stopped at the tree-line only long enough for the three cubs to clamber out of the tree and follow on behind her. The whole episode from start to finish couldn't have taken more than three minutes.

Silence followed, the three of them still frozen to the spot in the cabin doorway.

"Well you wouldn't get that in the zoo," Drew remarked with a grin.

"I was terrified, but I couldn't move," Anna said.

"Was that the daddy bear?"

"Maybe. It was a male anyway."

"Why was he being nasty?" Cassie asked.

"I read it's because they regard offspring as potential territorial challengers."

"Was he going to hurt them then."

"The article I read said that male bears, are desperate to pass on their DNA, so they try to mate with every female they find, and sometimes they kill cubs, forcing the female's body to stop producing milk for their young and become fertile again."

"That's horrible. Those babies were the cutest things I've ever seen."

"One or more of them may have been male cubs and will grow up like the big one you know."

"I don't want to think about that. I've got to change my panties now, I peed myself a little when he roared," she said indignantly.

"Do we have to stay inside now?"

"No, in some ways that may have been a good thing because that boar won't be back for weeks, maybe not the mother and cubs either. Although there's a chance that the mother may regard us as protectors, especially if this is a place where she'd always felt safe before, and she regarded the gunfire as an attack on the male rather than her."

Cassie came out of the bedroom, and red-facedly handed her damp underwear to her mum.

"Do you want me to show you how to do hand washing?"

"Yes please, I couldn't find any soap."

"The soap is that bar by the sink, and there's a hand crank washing machine in my bedroom that will be fine for small, lightly soiled items if you don't overload it. The bigger and dirtier items have to be done in the sink with the washboard. That's the wooden thing under the sink. The trick is to use the least amount of soap you can get away with or rinsing will take forever. Use the cheese grater on the soap for the washing machine."

"I've never seen soap like this before."

"It's homemade, uses less chemicals, and most importantly for Brady's purposes, it's unscented. Animals can smell you coming for hundreds of yards if you wear clothes washed in proprietary washing products or if you're wearing perfume or deodorant likewise. On ops in the army, we would never use scented soap; mostly no soap at all."

Drew picked up the M16, and a small-bore hunting rifle. "Do you still want to watch me shooting."

"Yes please. I don't think that daddy bear will come back if he thinks that siege of Leningrad thing you talked about has started."

"Okay, you carry those," he said handing her some magazines and three boxes of ammunition.

An hour later they both returned to the cabin, he was carrying the M16, and the small-bore rifle, Cassie the empty magazines and three ammunition boxes, two empty ones and one containing the brass casings from the discharged bullets. "Tip the brass in that bucket by the incinerator, Cassie. I expect Brady recycles them."

She came back inside as soon as she'd done it. "That was fun," she said with a big grin on her face."

"I thought you'd get bored after five minutes of watching Drew shooting bullets at an imaginary adversary."

"I didn't just watch. Drew let me shoot as well."

"You've been teaching my daughter to use lethal weapons; I don't know if I approve of that."

"She mostly just used the small-bore rifle. Not strictly speaking a weapon; it's for small game hunting. She was getting quite good by the end, and it's not something she'll have access to in the UK, unless she takes up sport shooting or biathlon."

"When can I speak to Percy?"

"I thought I'd call after lunch. I'll set it up now."

"I'll do it after I've finished hanging this washing on the line."

"I'll make lunch. I want a bacon sandwich. This bread is really nice," Cassie offered.

"All set. We'll call as soon as we've eaten. It'll give him enough time to be somewhere he can't be overheard."

"I don't understand what this system with the phones is."

"It's similar to the one you used in California. I use number one phone to message him that I want to speak. He calls me back on phone number two from a burner. If they're monitoring his phones the only number they'll have is for the sat-phone. If they want to locate where I'm calling from they'll have to do it when we're actually speaking, but if we're speaking from phone number two they won't know to track it."

"That's clever. I'll call Percy now."

"I'll do the dishes again," Cassie offered.

The two adults went outside. Drew took one of the sat-phones with him and selecting the only number in its memory, put it on speaker, and handed it to Anna."

"Percy"

"Anna, thank God! Where the Hell are you, I've been going out of my mind."

"I'm sorry about that. I was so terrified. I told Drew that I wanted to disappear for a while, or at least until Firbank or the lawyers have decided if Theo can take Cassie away from me or be her guardian if I'm dead."

"What!? What do you mean?"

"I haven't told you, have I? Apparently, among those papers I signed at our wedding, I agreed to Theo adopting Izzy and Cassie. So if I die any mention of guardianship in that will I signed a few days ago might be worthless."

"Surely that could be contested."

"Maybe, but because of all the implications and complications of cross-border legalities it could take years, and if I'm dead who would there be to contest it?"

"Me, of course."

"I know that, and thank you, but in a court we can't be sure that they would necessarily take your side against an adoptive parent."

"I see your point. But where are you? Are you safe?"

"At the moment we're as safe as it's possible for us to be if we all stick to Drew's instructions. Is there any news from Firbank or whoever you speak to?"

"Not a word. I tried calling him when you disappeared. He won't call back. Ignorant bastard."

"I'm not going to talk for long. Drew wants to speak to you too, so bye for now. We'll speak again in a day or two."

She handed the phone to Drew.

"Hi Percy, sorry about this, but Mrs. West wanted to go, and I agreed. The risks against her were stacking up and I needed to get her somewhere I could control the information flow and the battlefield."

"I understand but this is very frightening, both in personal terms and in terms of the business. That's not helped by the fact that I don't completely trust Firbank. It's not that I think he's working for the other side, more a case of Anna's interests are not necessarily his first priority."

"That's exactly what I think."

"What do you think will happen next?"

"I think now Lemonis has shown his hand. He knows that it's only a matter of time before he's discovered unless he can create his own endgame. I also think British or American security services will soon lose patience and take him out."

"Kill him you mean?"

"I expect so, I can't see any way he could be turned and used against the Russians now, do you?"

"Not really, but that's not my area of expertise."

"Nor mine, but spooks are a devious bunch of assholes."

"Okay I'll let you go now. Thank you for what you're doing. Rupert Loughty made the right choice when he picked you."

"Just keep to the protocol and they won't find us."

"Bye for now then."

"You think that MI5 or the F.B.I. will kill Theo?" Anna asked.

"It won't be the F.B.I. Assassination isn't their thing these days. The political risks are too high. It would have to be a private contractor. I don't think that the Brits are quite so squeamish about these things though."

"If it weren't for you, Cassie and I would probably be dead by now, and all the work that my Henry did would be in Russian hands."

"If it weren't for you I'd probably be begging for jobs as a nightclub bouncer. I'd prefer to be doing this."

"I'm not sure about the bears, but I'm quite enjoying the simple life here, but once again if it weren't for you we'd probably starve to death in a week."

"The look on Cassie's face as she watched the bears was a picture. If we had a video of that sequence of events it would be an overnight Internet sensation."

"Weren't you watching the bears?"

"Some of the time."

"I think there's a bit of a softie somewhere underneath that harsh exterior," she said, prodding him in the chest with a smile.

He shrugged but didn't speak for long moments.

"Don't you miss your luxury lifestyle?"

"You may see it as a luxury lifestyle, which of course it is, but I do make an honest effort not to take it too much for granted. It wasn't easy to do with Theo. He was always wanting to go to dinner with celebrities and ultra-rich people and he always seemed put out if they snubbed him for being considerably less wealthy than they were. He didn't say so, but I could tell he resented that the only thing that gave him a ticket to the door of that set, was my title and my wealth. Ninety percent of his assets are tied up in NorArm, so no super yacht for him. Even some of the things he claims are his, belong to Manos. I hate the socialite lifestyle. Most of it has no substance at all. Nothing they say is reflected in their eyes, and their lives seem devoted to getting themselves in front of a camera."

"How did you end up marrying him? In the few days I knew him I saw nothing to suggest you'd make a good couple. Not that I can be any sort of judge."

"And you would be absolutely right of course. Percy politely tried to dissuade me. But Leo had been there from hours after Henry's death. I was an emotional train wreck, but he took over and helped me begin to function. Then, whenever I started to fall apart, he'd be there again to prop me up. Izzy never took to him and I know he sensed it, although he didn't mention it. I never realized Cassie felt the same. Shows what a crap mother I must have been. But when he suggested we marry, for some reason it made sense."

"Did you hit the girls?"

"No, of course I didn't. What are you saying?" Her eyes flashed with anger.

"Did you go out on the street and leave a seven and four-year-old alone without food. Did you bring guys back to the house you only met an hour earlier, have sex with them for money, or for an extra bonus let them sexually interfere with your daughters? Did you ever walk out on them for three days, so they had to beg strangers for food?"

"No, you know I couldn't have done any of that."

"That's what our mom did. Please don't tell me you were a crap mom. I've seen nothing but love, compassion, empathy, and understanding from you with Cassie in the time I've been with you. Most moms would have balled me or her out for some of the conversations we've had in the last week which would have left her hurt and confused. Not you, you allowed her to use the distraction to shed some of the distress and guilt that she's been feeling ever since that first hijack. She's damaged, but you didn't wheel her into a shrink's office and say, *Fix this kid*, like most parents with your sort of money would have done. You've nurtured her, gained her trust, and given her the foundations she needed to rebuild her life. After everything else that's been happening you must have been hovering on the brink of becoming basket case material yourself for much of the time. That you aren't is little short of a miracle. Give yourself a break."

"I don't know how to respond to that. I'd gathered your childhood wasn't all milk, honey and roses, but that's awful, how did you and Lina turn out such great people after that?"

"Thankfully I don't remember most of it, but Lina does. Our grandparents - they were like you, tolerant, open, and kind. But in my case the army helped kick my ass into shape."

"What did you mean about Cassie feeling guilty?"

"Survivor's guilt, they call it. I've seen it a dozen times when we've lost guys. It affects different people in different ways. Some go to pieces, some turn nasty, a lot just bottle it up. That's what I did at first. Now I seem to have developed what the army shrinks call a coping mechanism. I sit down and ask myself; if I did all I could have done, would they have expected me to have done things differently, did we make a mistake and if we did, did it make a difference, did any of us have the choice to do things another way, and would I do things differently in the future.

"They made us see psychologists who spent most of the time asking us to tell them all the things that were wrong with us as if that was going to bring some sort of cathartic epiphany and make me feel better about myself. Instead it made me feel worse, so I just told them what they wanted to hear and stopped going. What about you? Did you ever speak to anybody else about it, like a psychologist, friends or relatives."

"I saw a grief counsellor for a while but I couldn't bring myself to open up to her. I don't have relatives other than Cassie now. I tried to talk to Judith, but she has issues of her own, and Percy just didn't seem the right sort to pour my heart out to. You've been more help than all of them. I've learned more about myself in a week than in the last three years."

"I don't normally do a lot of talking. I don't know what made me say all that."

"I'm glad you did," she said, and they were quiet for a while.

"I know it's a nuisance, but could we go into Lexington tomorrow. There are things I want to buy, which I don't think the store will stock. I was singularly unprepared for this trip, but I think I'll get the hang of it."

"That shouldn't be a problem. We can go straight from breakfast."

"That would be great. I'm going to make a chicken curry tonight. I've never made one before but I looked a recipe up on the Internet and they have almost all the ingredients here. I took the meat out of the freezer first thing. Will that be okay?"

"It's fine for me. I like most curries."

"So do we."

Later, Anna asked them what they thought of her first curry.

"It was really nice, Mummy. It was like when we went to the curry house in Reading."

"I couldn't make poppadums though."

"What are poppadums?"

"They're thin round crispy pancake things they often serve with curry."

"Oh yeah I know what you mean, but the meal was great as it was."

"Are we going to tell stories again?" Cassie asked.

"Why not, but tonight, let's try and restrict them to ones where everybody keeps their clothes on."

They spent the next two hours recalling anecdotes from their past until they decided it was time for bed.

Twenty-Four

The following morning was a repeat of the day before and when all was done and cleared away, they locked up and climbed in the truck.

As they passed the Ranger station, Reynolds came out and waved them down.

"Hi Russ, how you doing?"

"Good thanks. Hi ladies. Wonder if you can do me a favor, Parker."

"Sure, what do you need?"

"It ain't me so much, it's Ruby. She needs a couple of people to witness her signature on her will, and she doesn't trust too many folks around here. She asked me to do it but I told her it was supposed to be two people, an' they actually have to watch her sign the document at the same time, so I said I'd ask you both when I next saw you."

"No problem. We're on our way into Lexington. We can stop there on the way."

They pulled up outside the store. "Wait there, sweetheart. We'll only take a minute. Milly will be doing her schoolwork. You don't want to disturb her," Anna said.

"Okay, Mummy."

She watched the two of them run inside, but they were longer than a minute. She was about to go and find out what was taking the time when one of Drew's phones on the consul started to ring. She leaned forward, picked it up and answered it. "Hello."

There was no reply.

"Hello," she repeated.

Still no reply, so she ended the call and put it back where it came from.

Drew and Anna came out and climbed in the car. "Sorry about that, darling. Ruby's a bit of a talker. Everything okay?"

"Yes, I was reading my new book and the…"

"Is it good, what's it called?"

"It's great. It's called, The Haunting of Sunshine Girl. It's a bit creepy. But I think it's going to be really exciting."

"Do you think that reading creepy books is a good idea? I wouldn't want you having nightmares."

"I looked up the reviews and they're all really good. Judith said I should broaden my reading and not just read the stuff in the syllabus."

"And she's absolutely right, as usual."

"I miss her, and I miss my lessons. I know I'm supposed to be ahead, but I don't want to fall behind again, like after Daddy died."

"I'm surprised you remember that."

"I remember sitting in lessons and not being able to think of anything. My mind was just blank for months. It was only when Judith came I started to be able to think again. She made me work hard and I started enjoying lessons again."

"I wasn't much help back then, was I?"

"None of us were much use at anything back then. Theo helped you, but he wasn't much help to me and Izzy."

They got to Lexington in time for a quick lunch in a burger bar before heading to a mall to buy things for the two females, none of which seemed that urgent to Drew. Last of all, Anna made a brief stop at a drug store before they headed back to the car.

The phone that Drew had registered under his false ID began to ring. He answered it on hands free with the car Bluetooth. "Hello,"

"Parker, where are you?"

"Hi Brady, we're on our way back from Lexington about halfway between Slade and Pine Creek."

"You need to get to the store quick. There's two guys in ski masks with guns threatening Ruby with all sorts if she din't say where you are."

"Okay, I'm pedal to the metal right now. How do you know?"

"Never the fuck mind how I know for now just get there and do something about it. The cops should be on their way but they may be coming from Stanton or Clay City."

The phone went dead.

"Make sure your seat belts are tight and hold on."

The well-paved almost straight section of highway lent itself to driving far greater than the 55-mph allowed by law, not that he was concerned about the law at that moment and the vehicle soon soaked up the last few miles to Pine Creek at the speed he was travelling. He stopped as quickly as he could without locking the wheels about thirty yards short of the store, ordered the girls to stay in the car, to keep low and if the cops came, to wave them down, and warn them that he was in there. Ignoring their pleas to wait for the police, he leapt from the car, drew his gun and hurried to the store, leaving the engine running.

His approach to the building was both fast and cautious - staying out of sight of the front door as much as possible. There was a grey sedan parked outside the store facing away from him. There didn't appear to be anybody in it.

As he drew closer he could see the open delivery door at the side near the back of the building. Moving as quickly and quietly as he could he peeped in the door to find Milly cowering between the shelves of the storeroom.

"Milly," he whispered.

She jumped.

"Mr. Drew, there's bad people with guns in the store with my mom, I think they're looking for you."

"I know. I'm going to see if I can do something about that. I want you to go to my pickup. It's around there to the left, Cassie and Anna are inside. Wait with them. The police are on their way.

He watched her do what he'd told her, before creeping inside. With every step his new boots threatened to squeak on the smooth floor. He was making his way along the passage toward the front of the store when he heard Ruby say, "I keep telling you mister, I don't know who you're talking about. I promise, I swear on my mother's grave, I don't know nobody called Annabelle or Parker. I been in these parts all my life and there ain't nobody round here with them names. There used to be an Annika, she moved to Cincinnati, an' there were a Palmer, but he died 'bout fifteen years ago…"

He could just see part of a man's side from the shoulders down standing about where store counter ended. As Ruby spoke, Drew noticed a flickering in the corner of his vision. Glancing in that direction he saw a small office with an open laptop showing the security camera view of the shop from behind Ruby. He quickly stepped across the passage into the room. Now he could see the two masked men Brady had warned him about. One was standing beside Ruby holding a gun to her head, and the other was standing in front of the counter, also holding a gun but down by his side.

Drew picked up a dented tin of dog food from the desk, bent and rolled it around the doorpost into the storeroom so that it crashed into the metal shelving.

"Who's back there, you black bitch?" It was a voice Drew instantly recognized

"It's just my lil baby girl, Milly. She's only small. She ain't gonna hurt nobody."

"Go and bring the kid out here. If we knock her about, perhaps it will get this whore to talk."

Drew pressed himself against the office wall and waited until an outstretched arm holding a gun came past the doorway. Drew's left hand shot out and grabbed the gunman's wrist causing a shot to be fired harmlessly into the wall. Drew's other hand smashed the gun butt viciously into the man's face. The man fell to the floor with a thud and Drew stooped to take the gun from his hand.

The laptop screen showed the masked Lemonis pressing his gun tightly to Ruby's forehead. "Whoever's there, get the fuck out here or as sure as day follows night, I'll blow this bitch's brains all over this store."

"It's me, Lemonis, you fucking asswipe."

"Get out here now, Parker, unless you want this woman's death on your conscience. Throw your gun out first."

Taking the other man's gun he threw it towards where Lemonis must be standing.

"Come out where I can see you with your hands up."

"I'm coming," he said, watching Lemonis transfer his aim away from Ruby's head and towards where he expected Drew to appear, but instead of climbing over the unconscious man, Drew threw himself horizontally across the body bringing his gun to bear as he landed, and putting a bullet in his former employer's chest followed immediately by another in the center of his forehead.

It was only then that Drew realized Lemonis had got a shot off himself which had grazed the side of his head. The pain and shock of even that small head wound left him momentarily dazed.

"Oh my Lord Almighty, Mr. Drew, is that you? Thank you, thank you, thank you."

"Stay there, and keep down. I need to make certain the other guy's out of action."

He got to his feet, staggering slightly and turned toward the passageway in time to see the other man disappear into the storeroom. Still unsteady on his feet, Drew tried to chase after the man, but his foot landed on the loose can of dog food and he crashed to the floor. By the time he was upright again, the other man had reached the sedan and was speeding away with smoke billowing from his spinning tires.

The siren of an approaching police vehicle was close, so Drew put his gun on the ground and waited. As the two police patrol officers dismounted their car with their guns drawn. He put his hands in the air and kicked his own toward them. He was getting too used to this rigmarole.

"There's been shooting; one perp dead; one fled the scene; my gun is just there. I have another in an ankle holster. One uninjured hostage inside behind the counter; one in the car behind you."

"On the ground, hands behind your head with fingers locked together, now," the first officer shouted, keeping his gun trained on him. Drew did exactly as he was instructed, and waited while the second officer cuffed him, searched him for other weapons, and removed the gun from its ankle holster. Meanwhile his wound continued to bleed profusely until Anna got out of the car and ran toward them."

"What the hell is the matter with you. This man is wounded. Get him some help now," she screamed.

"Paramedics are on their way, ma'am."

"He could bleed to death before they get here at this rate. Don't they teach you first aid?"

"Yes, ma'am."

"Well use it. This man is a hero. He's saved my life at least five times this week."

"Yes, ma'am." He fetched his medical kit from the trunk of his car and began to make a pig's ear of dressing Drew's wound as he still lay face down on the ground. Fortunately, the paramedics arrived in quick order and took over.

Cassie moved solemnly up to join her mum. "Drew isn't going to die is he, Mummy?" She was close to tears but somehow holding them back..

"No, darling. Go back and sit in the car with Milly."

"Shall I turn the engine off?"

"Good idea, sweetheart."

"I want to see my Milly. Let me outta here!" Ruby's loud voice coming from the open door of the store.

"Are you mentally incapacitated?" Anna yelled at the cops. "That poor woman's been held hostage at gunpoint for I don't know how long and now you're keeping her from seeing that her daughter's safe."

"We told her that her daughter is safe, ma'am. We're just trying to preserve the crime scene. We don't want her touching the body."

"Body! You're keeping her in there with a dead body? Listen to me you demented halfwit, this is something I never do, but I'm an extremely wealthy woman, and if she isn't out here in ten seconds, I will do everything I can to support her in a lawsuit against you personally, and your department in general for whatever unlawful detention is called in this country. Do you hear me?"

"Yes, ma'am. Brewer, can you go lead the witness out of the building via the delivery door."

Ruby emerged shortly after and Anna pointed her to Drew's car where she was joyfully greeted by Milly."

Two detectives arrived and took over. Their assessment was briskly concluded.

"Have you print scanned him yet."

"No, Sarge. I haven't been trained on the scanner yet."

The detective rolled his eyes. "Well let's do it now then shall we, eh?"

The cop fetched the fingerprint scanner from his car, the sergeant demonstrated its use, and handed it to the patrolman. "Take that will you Brewer and let me know if it comes up with anything."

"Can I sit up now?" Drew said.

"Sure." The paramedic helped him up into a semi-prone position.

"Does he need hospitalization?"

"No I think he'll be okay. Just make sure he gets plenty to drink."

"Okay buddy, stand up."

Drew effortlessly stood despite being cuffed while Anna returned to the car to check on the two girls.

"Wait a second," the paramedic said. "Have you got a second wound?"

"No, that was from where I got shot a few days ago in England. I guess the stitches split."

"Have a look at it will you, Tony. See if it needs any treatment," the cop said.

"It's difficult to tell with the cuffs on."

"It's fine buddy. It'll just need a new dressing," Drew told the medic, "Leave it and let this cop get on with what he has to do."

"If that's what you want," the sergeant said. "Thanks Tony. Right then, let's do it. Name?"

"Drew Parker, address at present, Cabin 412, Daniel Boone Forest. Age, Thirty-three. All the details that come back from the print scan are correct. I hope you're going to record this because, I won't say it again. I know my Miranda rights, and I don't want a lawyer. What I say now is my full, and truthful statement about what happened here today. I won't give any background until I've been given clearance to do so by the F.B.I."

"What, you think you're *Jack Ryan* or something?"

"Sarge, you'd better have a look at this," the second detective said loudly from the patrol car.

"Just tell me."

"He is who he says he is. Drew Parker, thirty-three; address: classified; ex-military; close-body protection licensed; trained at the Secret Service Academy; two Silver Stars and Medal of Honor. Everything else is redacted. There's an F.B.I. flag."

"Okay, so you are *Jack Ryan*. You gonna tell me what the hell went on here today before I'm taken off the case by the Feebs or spooks?"

Drew spoke for twenty minutes without pause giving a complete account of events from the moment they left the cabin that morning until the first patrol car arrived.

"Okay. Are you going to behave yourself if I take the cuffs off you?"

"No problem Sergeant Rex. I'll sit in my car until you tell me it's okay to leave if that's okay."

"I'd prefer if you stood right there."

"Fine."

"Brewer, would you ask the storekeeper if she's happy to talk me through what happened here."

"Sergeant, it might help you to understand things better if I tell you that I think the whole thing is probably recorded on the store security system. I can send you a copy of the dashcam recording from my car too, if you want. You won't need a warrant but you'll need to wait until I can get to a computer to do it."

"That'd be real helpful."

"Ruby sells adapters and thumb drives I believe. If she'd allow us to use her computer, could we do that now?"

"Great idea. I'll get the memory card from your dashcam, you wait there."

Ruby and the second cop joined them.

"You okay Mister Drew?"

"I'm fine thanks Ruby, and it's just Drew. You're one gutsy lady, do you know that."

"That's a real compliment after what you did here today."

They went inside and about half an hour later they came out again.

"Ruby showed me the footage, and it supports things happening exactly as you said. She also says you can have whatever you need to transfer that file to me. So can we go do that now?"

"Sure. Have you ID'd the dead guy yet?"

"We took his wallet, if that's what you mean?"

"Is it Theodore Lemonis?"

"That's right."

"Then you should probably inform Mrs. West in my car. It's her husband."

"What!"

"My job is principally to protect her from him."

"Today is getting weirder and weirder. Okay, wait there."

That was when Rex's phone started to ring.

"Hello…Yes sir.…Yes sir, everything as usual…He made a statement voluntarily.…There's video evidence to verify everything both he and the storekeeper said.…It's the same store Sir…I will sir…No problem.…When.…No I understand.…Of course sir…Straightforward armed store robbery. That makes sense anyway, now I think of it.…Thank you sir."

"Why am I not surprised. Looks like you lucked out, and caught a pass. No charges, you're free to go. Will you hang around for a day or two in case you can help with anything?

"No problem. What about Ruby and her daughter? Have they got anywhere to go until you finish up here?"

"I don't know, I'll ask."

He walked over to Ruby and came straight back. "Apparently she's already arranged to go to her friend Patsy's but she's asking if you can take Milly overnight. She says she's going to tie one on. She's just going to fetch some night stuff."

"That's fine. I gathered from what you said that this isn't the first shooting here."

"No, but that's a whole other story. If we get to meet in a bar one night I'll tell you about it."

"I don't drink but thanks. Out of interest, what were you thinking of charging me with?"

"I don't know - reckless endangerment maybe, discharging a firearm without regard for public safety," he suggested with a smile.

"That would've been an interesting court hearing."

"I could still give you a ticket for speeding." He laughed.

"And that would be absolutely right. Send it to me care of 935 Pennsylvania Avenue, DC."

The sergeant laughed. "Fuck off before I give you a ticket for parking on the sidewalk. Oh and Sir, thank you for your service."

Drew laughed and walked away.

"Ma said I could do a sleepover at the cabin with you and Cassie." Milly said.

"I know. That's okay, isn't it Anna?"

"Finally he calls me Anna. Yes of course it is. Are you okay to drive?"

"Now you mention it, would you mind? My arm's a bit tender."

"I've never driven anything this big before, or on this side of the road but I'll give it go."

"That was easier than I thought," she said twenty minutes later, as they pulled into the clearing.

"It should have been, you never got out of third gear or over thirty the whole way."

"That's the speed I drive in England."

"Okay." He laughed, took the key from around his neck, and unlocked the cabin.

"Cassie, can you go inside with Milly. Drew and I need to have a talk, and can you fetch the first aid box from the store and a big cup of water for Drew?" To Drew she said, "Can you wait to get out of those blood-soaked clothes for a minute?"

"No problem. They make it all look worse than it is."

Cassie brought the first aid box, and Milly brought a stainless-steel bowl of water. "We couldn't find a big cup."

"That's the dog's drinking bowl I think," Anna said.

"That'll do fine," he said, and downed the contents in one long draught. "Thanks Milly that was great.

"Can you fill it with hot water now Cassie, and get me something to wash the worst of this blood off?"

The two girls ran to do what he'd asked.

"What do you want to talk about?"

"Is it over now?"

"For you, almost certainly. I can't see how there could be any sort of challenge to Cassie's parentage now, and there's no legal route left for the Russians to take control of Silico."

"Why do you say *almost* then?"

"The guy who got away today was almost certainly Gates. It's possible he could still be being paid by the Russians via Stamelis, although I can't see what they'd have to gain. But assholes like that rarely like to lose so he may want to try something else on his own, but it will be me he's got a beef with, not you."

"Oh God what have we got to do to make all this stop?"

"We just need to be vigilant. If he does come after me, I doubt he'll have the resources to pay for help. That comes expensive. So, it will just be me against him, odds nicely weighted in my favor."

"What do you mean?"

"He's an amateur; claimed to have been in the SAS. That's bollocks. the SAS are an elite force right up there in the top five in the world. He wouldn't have got through the first few days of selection. Everything he did included a catalogue of basic errors. We'd both be dead by now otherwise."

"I called Percy; I hope I did the right thing."

"It turned out to be exactly the right thing, otherwise I'd be spending a night or two in a police cell waiting for various people to speak to each other. What I don't understand is how they found us so quickly. Lemonis seemed so confident that Ruby would know where we were. We only used those satellite phones the once, and even then not from the store."

"I think I know. Cassie told me that when we were in the store signing those wills, one of your phones rang, so she picked it up but eventually rang off when nobody spoke. You won't tell her off will you?"

"Of course not. I was dumb for not telling her not to answer them. Best not mention it again," he said.

"Thank you."

"It still doesn't explain how they got to the store so quickly, though, but we'll probably never know now."

The girls returned with the bowl of water and one of Cassie's tee-shirts. "Will this be okay?"

"That'll be just great girls, thank you."

Anna began to clean his face. "It's no use we need this shirt and jacket off. Cassie, can you bring me that sharp knife by the range?" she called.

"You're going to need a new jacket."

"Most of it will probably wash out."

"If you think they're going to let you in Business Class in clothes that look like you're a survivor of Custer's last stand, you're sadly mistaken."

"Does that mean I'm not redundant?"

"Were you planning on going back to looking for night club doorman jobs?"

"Not necessarily…"

"Then you're not redundant you great lunk."

"How are you though. You were just widowed for the second time?"

"I feel as if a huge burden has lifted from my shoulders. These last few weeks have been terrifying on so many levels I can't explain."

After she'd cut the shirt off she told him to lift his arm and gently pulled the dressing from the wound. "This needs restitching. We should go to the hospital."

"The nearest hospital to here is in Irvine, about fifty miles away. No point in driving there when I can do it myself."

"Do it yourself!"

"Done it before. It's not a big deal. Are there needles and surgical thread in there?"

She looked and confirmed there were and then watched while he swabbed it clean and attempted to reclose the wound with his own stitches.

"That's going to look like the top of a potato sack."

"Do you want to try?"

"I'll hurt you."

"You think it doesn't hurt when I do it?"

"Okay, I'll try." Ten minutes later she'd finished but wasn't happy with her handiwork."

"Got bit of a headache. Are there any Tylenol in there?"

She handed him the bottle. He took four and they sat on the porch bench without speaking, just staring into the dusk.

"We made you some sandwiches," Cassie said. "I made a steak for Drew, bacon for me, and Milly made cheese ones for her and you, Mummy, is that okay?"

"How did you make a steak sandwich. I hadn't cut any meat?"

"Milly showed me how to slice it because she watches her mummy do it. It's a bit thick, sorry."

"It's perfect, Cassie, and you, Milly," he said.

"I'm going to help Ma run the store when I'm older like Alice used to."

"And I bet you'll be real good at it too."

The girls brought them both a cup of coffee and left them to it. The two sat silently eating for several minutes. Then Anna said, "When Cassie thought you might die, she sobbed and wailed her little heart out for so long, her little body must have hurt."

"It's just hero worship."

"Don't you dare belittle what she feels for you. She loved her daddy as any girl would love a good father, but she was only little and time can be a good healer as they say. Then she learned to lean on Izzy because I was useless. After Izzy died... She's always been endearingly naïve, but it was as if her maturity had stalled or even regressed. She became clingy, introvert, and timid. But since you came along she's started to blossom again like a desert rose after the rain. To contemplate her losing that again is more than I can bear. I know it's a lot to ask, but please stay with us."

"If you want me to stay, then I won't be going anywhere."

She began to lean in as if to kiss him and his phone rang again.

"Parker, it's Atkins. I spoke to Ruby; she gave me a rundown of what happened. She thinks the sun shines out your butt. Even said that the cops told her you're kind of secret agent, and she ain't allowed to speak to anybody about what happened ever."

"I think they've been talking a bit of BS. It ain't me who's the security interest here it's Anna, but that's all in the past now."

"I watched the video Parker, so no need to bullshit me."

"I was going to ask about that. That's a serious piece of surveillance you got going on there for a tiny little store."

"No point in doing something if you don't do it properly. Paid for itself several times over now."

"So talk me through how you knew about it before anybody else?"

"I got it set up so if anybody presses the panic button, then it sends a signal to my phone. I can see the video, and I can call the cops from wherever I am."

"So I'm guessing Ruby pressed the button then."

"No she said she couldn't reach it from where she stood. It must have been Milly."

"Ruby's got some cojones though, that's for sure."

"She saw you send Milly out the back on the little repeater screen on the counter and kept talking to distract them so you could do what you had to do."

"Like I say cojones. Wish I could have got to see you while we were here and meet your Alice."

"You may yet. Our little trip to meet distant relatives hasn't been an outstanding success, we're on our way back. We're in Oklahoma City at the moment, we'll be home about midday day after tomorrow. So if you can hang around until then we'll get to see each other and meet each other's little ladies."

"She's not my little lady she's…"

"That's not what I heard. See you soon buddy."

He looked at Anna and even in the poor light from the cabin window he could tell she was blushing.

"Sorry about that. Ruby adding up two and two to make five."

She just shrugged. "Shall we go inside?"

"Who's going to sleep where tonight, Mummy?"

"If you and Milly take my bed, I'll sleep on the floor out here."

"You'll do no such thing. You'll sleep in there with me. I think I can be trusted not to molest you for one night."

"I don't mind sleeping on the floor. I've slept in a lot worse places."

"I mind. End of conversation."

Cassie was grinning like she'd won the lottery.

Milly wanted to know what they did in the evening without a TV and didn't understand when Cassie said they told each other stories about things that they'd done or experienced at some time in their past.

"Okay I'll start," Cassie offered. "When my daddy died I was only little and I didn't really understand very much, but I knew how bad it was because Mummy was really, really sad all the time, and that made me really sad too. My sister Izzy was sad too, but she told me we had to try not to be sad to help Mummy. Izzy was like my temporary mummy until our real mummy started to get better and decided to marry Theo. Izzy and I didn't really like him, but he was making Mummy feel better so we decided to put up with it, and because he was away from home a lot of the time it wasn't so bad.

"Izzy told me that Theo was a weirdo because he wouldn't go to bed with Mummy and told her he was gay, which is definitely weird because why would you marry a lady if you only like men. She told me that one day she went into his room without knocking and he was talking to a naked lady on Facetime and playing with his willy. He was really angry, shouted at her, and hit her around the head. She told me about it in the morning and she had a big red mark on her face. She didn't tell Mummy, and Mummy didn't see it because she was going to Seattle with him that day while we stayed at Pangbourne with Judith.

"After Izzy died I hurt so much inside, and I saw Mummy was hurting inside so I didn't tell her. We went to stay in California to be safe, but lots and lots of bad things kept happening until Drew came to stay with us. Every time somebody tried to do something bad to us, Drew stopped them or saved us. Me and Mummy should have been really, really scared, and sad, but somehow it wasn't too bad because Drew was with us. That's the end of my story."

Milly hadn't sensed the atmosphere in the room and broke the silence. "That was a really good story, is all that true about your daddy and sister?"

"Yes."

"I didn't think that rich people had crap like that going on in their lives like ordinary folks. My Pa wasn't a very nice person. He was always doin' dumb things like stealin' cars, or robbin' stores, or burglin' houses then he'd get caught and go to jail. When he weren't in prison he wouldn't get no job most of the time and he would take Ma's welfare checks to buy booze. He weren't good to Ma either he used to beat up on her sometimes an' make her do sex stuff when she didn't want to.

"Then one day Brady figured out it was him and some other guys robbin' all the stores around here an' he got sent to prison for three strikes. I don't know what that means, but Ma says it's a real long time an' we won't see him till he's an old man, an' that's good cos he's an asshole. But then things started to get good, because Alice's Ma gave my Ma a job even though Pa had been robbin' their store. After Joe and Ellie got killed, Alice let Ma run the store, an' move in so we didn't have to live in a beat up ol' shack no more. Ma says she's happier than a pig in shit. Sorry for cussin'. That's the end of my story.

"It's your turn, Drew," Cassie told him.

"Do you mind if I give it a miss tonight? I've got a headache so I'm going to get some fresh air before I go to bed," Drew said, standing up.

"Me too," said Anna. "You girls want to use the bathroom first?"

She followed Drew outside and joined him on the bench, and they sat silently for a long time, until finally she rested a hand on his leg.

Drew opened his mouth to speak but whatever he intended to say was thwarted by Milly.

"Shower's free, Miss Anna."

"Okay, be right there," she replied. "Do you want me to put something waterproof over the wound on your arm?"

"It'll be okay, it ain't bleeding anymore. Thanks though. I'll sit for a while after my shower, to let it dry properly before I put a clean dressing on it."

"Try not to be too long."

He waited for her to tell him she was done, but she didn't, and after what he thought was enough time he went back inside. She'd left a sidelight on in the main room, the bedroom light was out, and she lay beneath the bedding apparently asleep.

After a hot shower, he dried himself as thoroughly as he could and dressed in clean boxer briefs. The site around his arm wound was soon dry enough, but as he applied the dressing he could see it was inflamed.

After carefully sliding into bed beside her, attempting not to wake her, he lay staring into the half-light that spilled from the main room, his thigh lightly pressed against her butt. For the first time he noticed the night noises of the forest; owls, frogs from the stream, and the distant growl of a bear, but they weren't what stopped him from sleeping.

"Would you hold me?" she said.

"It's difficult at the moment."

"I wouldn't mind."

"I don't want to embarrass myself."

"Okay."

Twenty-Five

Neither of them slept well, but after dawn they were both unaware of the two girls looking in at them from the doorway, until Milly whispered something to Cassie and they both giggled.

Drew woke first, realizing that he hadn't set an alarm, and then that Anna had turned during the night, laid an arm across his chest, and a leg on top his. He looked up to see the girls looking at them with great curiosity. The bedding had been pushed down and his erection had returned making itself painfully obvious.

Disentangling himself from Anna's limbs he sat up and grabbed some pants. A quick trip to the bathroom rectified the noticeable causes of his embarrassment.

"Are you okay?" Anna asked as he dressed in training pants.

"I'm well thanks. You?"

"Yes I am; very."

Outside, a few minutes later, the two girls sat on the porch bench in their jackets and night clothes watching Drew go through his workout routine.

"Why does he do that?" Milly asked.

"He does it every day. It's how he keeps himself strong and fit."

"Looks like he's hurtin' hisself."

When he picked up the log and began running around the clearing, and just kept going lap after lap, Milly thought he was crazy.

"I bet he could lift us up over his head with one hand," Cassie said.

"Let's ask him."

"He's busy now. Wait until he stops."

They didn't get the chance to ask in the end, because he was interrupted by Reynolds driving into the clearing.

Drew stopped and dropped the log by his feet and breathlessly greeted the ranger.

"What the fuck, Parker?" was the response.

"How do you mean?"

"What is it about this place and that store?"

"I guess the shop has had more than its fair share of hostile activity."

"Yeah, and it's all connected to this place one way or another. Four dead people, in the store; five now, and one here. Then there was the shooting over the other side of the highway a year or two ago, and last night the stabbing in Campton. Jesus, we'll be needing our own cop station at this rate."

"I ain't sure where Campton is. What's it got to do with the store or this place?"

"Cops think it was the guy that got away yesterday. They found a rental abandoned not far away. He broke into a house, killed the owner, and went off with his car, but as he drove away, the owner's daughter came home, found her old man, and called 911. The cops have got an APB out on the car and guy now, and they've got a picture too. The daughter had one of those nanny-cams installed so she could keep an eye on him."

"You got a copy of that picture?"

"Sure." Reynolds took his phone out and after tapping it a few times showed him a photo.

Drew took the phone. The picture was black and white but the face was unmistakable. He identified him immediately. "He goes by the name of Gates, claims to have once been a member of the SAS. He was almost certainly the second man at the store yesterday."

"I'll call Rex, the sergeant you saw yesterday."

"Okay, you want coffee?"

"Sure, that'd be great."

Drew went back to the cabin.

"It might be a good time to grab your showers girls. The ranger will be here for a bit."

Inside the cabin, Anna was dressed and preparing breakfast.

"Have we got coffee for Russ?"

"Of course. He can have mine. I'll pour another."

"Morning, ma'am."

"Good morning, Russ; but it's just Anna."

"It's the way we do things around here, ma'am."

"I know. In the UK people wouldn't say that as a general rule, but because I have a title, they feel they have to use it all the time and I'm slightly uncomfortable with it I suppose."

"What are you then, a Duchess or something?"

Anna laughed. "No, I'm just a lady for what it's worth, but it's a nonsense because I didn't inherit it, and neither did I earn it. It's because I was married to someone who was knighted for his services to the computer industry. He's no longer alive and I've been married to someone else for two years, so it makes no sense to keep using it."

"That's one real peculiar system."

Drew's phone rang.

"Hello."

"That's right, absolutely no doubt whatsoever...No problem, glad to help....What time?...Fine, we don't have plans to go anywhere. But the cabin owner is returning tomorrow, and there won't be room enough for all of us....That'd be great. See you later."

"That the cop?"

"Yeah, he's calling by this afternoon to try and fill in some gaps."

"Why were these people after you?"

"You ain't supposed to know they were."

"Yeah well. Ruby don't seem to understand that too well."

"We're going to get the eggs," Cassie said, as she and Milly went out the door."

"Can I get you something to eat, Russ?"

"I wouldn't want to put you to trouble, Anna."

"No trouble. Then you can tell people you had breakfast cooked by the Duchess of Pangbourne."

"Well since you put it like that, how can I refuse."

The three adults sat and ate their food at the table while the girls ate porridge and toast on the bench outside.

"We were visited by some bears."

"Oh yeah, that's good. How many?"

Anna related the incident.

"Is that old boar back? I'm surprised he's still alive. He must be way over twenty years old." Reynolds said after they'd described what had happened. "That bald patch is from where a hunter got him with a shotgun and he didn't die. A conservationist found him a day or two later and insisted on calling a vet out to him. He and the vet operated on the creature on the forest floor for three hours, then they sat and waited until he recovered. Cost the tree hugger a fortune. Dumb SOBs the pair of them."

"Why, it was a nice thing to do."

"I guess but it could just as easy got them killed."

"What by the bear or other bears do you mean?"

"No, by hunters. Most of them are as dumb as cheese as well. They'll shoot anything that moves. Last year in the Daniel Boone there were a hundred and twenty-six injuries and deaths, including ten nonfatal and five fatal by gunshot. Giving them the benefit of the doubt, we'll say they were accidental. Given the choice I wouldn't let most of them loose with anything more lethal than a wooden spoon."

"Brady's coming back tomorrow, so one way or another we're going to be moving on. We hope to be given the okay to return to the UK. If not we'll have to put up in Stanton or Slade I guess."

"Well it's been nice knowing you all. Well done for putting that asshole down, scuse the language, Anna but that's the politest word I know for people like that."

"No need to apologize, Russ. I've thought a great deal worse than that about him in the last week or two, and it will take a long time for me to forgive myself for marrying him in the first place."

"So he was your husband. I thought Ruby was being fanciful when she came out with that."

"Regrettably, he was. It's a long story which we're not allowed to tell just yet."

Reynolds gave them his thanks and drove on back up the track.

As Anna gathered clothes to do some more laundry she spotted Drew about to start swinging an axe to split wood. "You can stop that right now, mister. You'll tear those stitches again and I've done all the emergency medicine I want to for the time being."

"Mister Drew? Cassie said you can lift us over your head with one hand. Is that true?"

"Maybe. How much do you weigh?"

"I'm guessing 'bout 65-67 pounds. Haven't been weighed for ages."

"Probably then."

"What about Cassie?" Drew asked Anna.

"I don't know, but not much more than Milly I expect."

"Could be."

"Show us."

"You haven't got any handles."

"There must be some way to do it," Cassie insisted.

"Okay, put your hands together like this, make your arms stiff and lock your elbows like you were leaning on a table wanting to lift your feet off the ground. Okay, now do it by the edge of the porch and I'll stand in front of you. Who's first?"

"You go first Milly," Cassie said.

After a couple of attempts at getting the balance right, he lifted her high above his head and held her there as she screamed with laughter, before bending his knees, heaving her up and catching her. Laughing and clapping she insisted he do it with Cassie, so he repeated the exercise for her with similar results.

"This is better than the strongman at Stanton Fair. He's just a fat ol' farmhand, an' he makes you give him a kiss after. Can you do it both of us at the same time?" Milly asked.

"I don't know, let's try."

After one or two failed attempts he managed to carry them halfway around the yard before tossing them away one at a time.

Their laughter had attracted Anna to the door and she watched them fooling around. "Do any of you want a drink?" she called to them, as she offered the dog bowl to Drew. "You didn't drink enough after losing all that blood. Coffee is no good for that."

"Thanks, you're right."

She nodded at his injured arm, "I see my concern for your stitches was wasted." She shook her head and smiled.

He looked at the dressing which showed signs of blood staining,. "It'll be okay. It doesn't feel like they've split."

"How's your head?"

"Okay I guess."

"Have we stopped you from doing your schoolwork, Milly?"

"It's Sunday. There ain't no schoolwork today."

"Is it? God, I've lost all track of time."

It wasn't long before Ruby arrived to collect Milly, and she came with a box of groceries. She refused payment no matter how much Anna tried to insist. "Anyhow they mostly gonna be for Alice an' Brady if they comin' home like you say, so it makes no sense you payin'."

"Ma, Cassie an' me are goin' to do talkin' to each other on the computer, an' she says she'll help me with my schoolwork if I don't understand."

"She's a right nice friend ain't she. Shame he has to go home."

"I don't know if we'll see you again, Ruby, but I'm proud to have met such a very brave lady."

"I sure ain't no lady. But I ain't never gonna stand by while some assholes hurt my lil Milly. You make sure you don't let that Drew go. He's a real good guy, and kinda horny too," she said as Drew lifted her daughter into the air one last time.

"Yes, he is, isn't he?"

No sooner had they finished lunch than Sergeant Rex appeared to ask questions. He did his best to wheedle out more detailed information about the events leading up to the shooting in the store but without success.

"I understand your professional curiosity Sergeant, but now Gates has committed murder, it's a domestic incident with no security implications so there's no need to pursue that line of inquiry."

"You're right of course. I doubt it'll be long before he's caught either. we've got the picture from the home video camera and one the feds got from the Brit police I think."

"I wouldn't be too confident if I were you. He may be getting some pretty high-powered help. I can't say much more I'm afraid."

"Okay, I get you. I'll leave you now. I'm not going to detain you anymore today. Word has come down that we're not to ask you to stay in the area, and I guess that'll mean that you'll end up going back to the UK, so you won't be available to be a witness if you're needed. I've got your guns in the car. You can have them back."

"That's great, thanks. I won't rule out coming back if necessary, and you've got my contact details, but I suspect that the question is moot."

"It's good to have met you, sir. Stay safe. Give my good wishes to the lady and her daughter."

He gave Anna the news about being released to go home. "Not that he had the power to stop us, but it's good to know they're happy for us to go. I suspect Gates will have too much on his hands to worry about me for a while. Rex said there's an APB out for him over five states."

"Thank God for that. How shall we go about getting back to the UK though?"

"Depends on whether you want to go through the three-day drive to DC and catch a flight from there, or if you want to drive to Lexington, Kentucky, fly from there to DC then another to Gatwick or Heathrow."

"The second option I think, but we've got to sell your car first."

"If we hang around long enough in the morning to leave things straight here and hopefully get to see Brady and Alice, we would still be able to hit the road and be in Lexington by evening - stay overnight somewhere. Then get the best price for the car I can in the morning before cabbing to the airport and catching the first available flight to DC. Hopefully, we should be able to be UK bound on some plane or other without having to wait too long."

"That sounds great. Shall I ask Percy to try and book flights?"

"All due respect to Percy, I doubt he's that familiar with cross state travel in the USA. If we can't make part of his pre-booked itinerary then we could end up chasing our tail. Same goes with a booking agent this late in the day."

"So we're talking ad hoc travel then."

"Probably best, although we won't be able to be too picky about our seating and accommodation requirements."

"That's fine with me, but let me speak to Jason and Judith, to put them on notice."

"Tell Percy as well though."

"Of course. I'll speak to him first. What about Lina, are you going to talk to her?"

"Definitely."

"Here, give me your phone. I'll call Percy now. There's something I need to rectify as soon as possible too; I definitely need my own phone."

She was on the phone to Percy for half an hour, and the same again to Jason and Judith before she gave it back to Drew. "You might need to put it on charge before you use it, sorry."

"It's okay there's plenty of time."

"Mummy, come quick the bears are back," Cassie called sotto voce, quietly half-closing the door.

"Here, take some pics." Drew said handing her the phone.

They all went to the window and watched the cubs play fighting and clambering over anything that could clambered over. One discovered the log that Drew had been using to exercise. He rolled it backwards and forwards until the other two decided it was their turn and the inevitable rough and tumble ensued. When mother bear lost patience and summoned them to follow, they scurried after her down the path to the stream.

"I wish I could stroke them."

"You wouldn't do it twice."

"I know but they're so cute. Why do people want to kill them?"

"I have no idea."

He looked at the phone and guessed there wouldn't be enough to charge to ring his sister, so he plugged the charger into it and then called.

"Hi Sis."

"Hiya bro. How's it going?"

"Not so bad, looks like we might be going back to lil ol' England sooner than expected."

"No time to come see your big sister and nephew then?"

"Not this time, sorry."

"You going to looking after Anna some more then?"

"Looks like it."

"You wouldn't happen to know anything about that incident in a smalltown Kentucky store yesterday would you?"

"I'm sure I don't know what you mean."

"Shame, I was kinda hopin' a certain lovely lady might now be a free woman."

"I'd better go now Lina before you say anything else to embarrass either of us. I'll let you know when I'm back in the UK."

"Say hi to your lovely travelling companions for me, won't you?"

"I will. Love you Sis."

"Must be a special occasion, my big lunk of a brother using the *L* word. Things are looking up." The line went dead.

Anna had overheard the whole conversation, although she'd made out she hadn't been listening. "How is Lina?"

"She's good. Said to say hi."

"It was a pretty short conversation."

"We never did waste words."

Cassie had been listening too and was grinning at them both with pleasure.

"I'm making spaghetti Bolognese tonight, but there isn't any spaghetti so I'm cooking baked potatoes instead. There's no microwave to thaw out the mince from the freezer. There isn't any beef so I'll have to use whatever meat there is, and there's no mincer so I'll have to cut the meat up as small as I can with that enormous, vicious looking knife. In fact there are almost none of the ingredients from the recipe I usually use so don't get your expectations up."

Drew cut and diced some meat for her, then sat and watched her going about the business of preparing the meal. Occasionally she'd say something or ask a question, and he would respond. Sometimes Cassie would add something but mostly she watched the interaction between the two adults.

When the meal finally arrived on the plate, everyone enthused and there was very little left for April in the morning.

Drew and Cassie cleared away and did the dishes, before they sat down for the evening in silence, with Cassie looking expectantly from one to the other.

To make conversation Anna said, "I'm going to wash the bed linen in the morning if it doesn't rain. I don't want to leave it for Brady and Alice to clear up."

"Good idea."

"How's your arm?"

"Okay, I guess." He lied; it was sore.

"Percy said something interesting when he was on the phone."

"What was that?"

"He suggested that if Theo hadn't made another will post-dating the one he made with me then it would mean that I'd inherit everything of his."

Drew laughed out loud.

"What' so funny?"

"Think about it. The irony if after all he did to take everything of yours, it ends up with you getting everything of his."

Anna couldn't stop herself laughing a bit. "Now you say, it is pretty amusing, but what about his other family, Ariana, and their daughters?"

"As I understand it, she's supposed to be Stamelis' daughter. If that's right, I'd be surprised if she weren't a Russian plant, only there to control him right from the start - a sleeper; with Stamelis as her handler. Either way, there's little doubt she'll be well cared for."

"There's a lot of pretty big assumptions in there."

"What was Stamelis' job. I don't mean his title but what did he actually do? I never saw him make a phone call or answer one or do anything else for that matter. Doesn't sound like any sort of Personal Assistant I ever heard of - one thing I'd bet on though - that he's the one who appointed Volkov."

"I didn't give it any thought before. I always left Theo to deal with his own affairs, but you're right about Pavel, and you're probably right about Manos too. I was always thought he was just lazy. Do you think I was in their sights right from the start?"

"I'd hazard a guess that back when he was in Greece, Lemonis was offered some sort of inducement to do something or other and they used that to get their hooks into him. Ariana was introduced into the plot, then the kids, making it increasingly difficult for him to get out. They would have forced him to sell his shipping interests and move his money into IT based stock in the US. Coming from a legitimate background in Greece, made it less likely to raise suspicion when he started buying into sensitive investment areas, and finally he gained control of NorArm. That would have been when Silico and Henry came into their sights."

"God what bastards, if that's true."

"As you say, pretty big assumptions, but is there anything in there that doesn't make sense?"

"No, everything you said makes perfect sense."

"If I'm right there are things you need to do as quickly as you can."

"What do you mean?"

"You need to offload NorArm to an American, British or other NATO country defense company. Isolate yourself and Cassie from it."

"I don't want it, any of it. I've more money than I know what to do with already."

"You can do some good with it. Some kind of charitable foundation perhaps. Don't ask me though, the most I've ever been able to give to charity has been a few hundred bucks from time to time, but for you It would be the final nail in the coffin of their plans."

"You're absolutely right."

"Can we tell stories now?" Cassie asked. "I don't want to talk about Theo."

"Alright but you have to start, and only happy stories tonight okay?"

One after the other they told tales from their lives that were sentimental or funny.

Eventually Cassie told them, "I'm tired. I'm going to have a shower and go to bed."

"I think she's anxious to get home," said Anna.

"Probably. These last few weeks must have been difficult for her, everything she knows turned upside down, not knowing what was going to happen.'

"You say that but she's changed, and I don't mean in a bad way. All her beautiful endearing features are still there but she's matured so much."

"She's very easy to like. But being around so much death and injury, and subject to prolonged threat would change most people, even soldiers sometimes."

"You're right. I like your idea about a charitable foundation. I'll need to give some thought to what cause I want to espouse. Have you got favorite causes?"

"Child poverty and exploitation I guess. Over the years I've been in so many places in the world where kids get the butt end of everything in life and I'm never been around long enough to do anything to help. It ain't always been outside the USA either. Makes me think of my own childhood and what it must have been like for Lina."

"You're a good person, Drew."

"I ain't always done good things."

"It doesn't change my mind."

"Okay bathroom's free," Cassie said, walking straight through to the small bedroom.

"Where are you going?"

"I'm sleeping in here tonight. You fidget too much. Unless you want me to sleep with Drew."

"No, that's okay. Sleep well, darling. Give me a kiss first."

She made big deal out of kissing her mother and telling her she loved her, before doing the same thing with Drew.

"I think I'm beginning to see another side of her that I didn't know existed before," Anna said before going to the bathroom herself.

Ten minutes later Anna stood at the bedroom door wearing a pair of short pajamas with string shoulder straps and rubbing her hair with a towel. You can use the bathroom now."

He turned to her and stared.

"What's wrong?"

"Nothing, I just thought…It doesn't matter. Thanks."

He waited for her to climb into bed before he used the bathroom himself. In a repeat of the previous night he slid in beside her.

Anna turned toward him, "Is it safe to touch you tonight?"

"Nature took its course last night."

"What…? Oh sorry."

"It happens." He lifted his arm to allow her to lay her head on his shoulder. She put her arm across his chest. "Is this a good idea?"

"I don't know, but at the moment I don't really care because it feels right, and it isn't doing anybody any harm."

Twenty-Six

Morning came and he woke to the smell of bacon cooking. Anna was in much the same position as the day before, as was his penis. He moved to get out of bed.

"Don't go yet. There's no hurry," Anna said.

"But…"

"That's okay, I'm not worried about it."

"Maybe not, but I am," he told her and pried himself from her arms.

"You got about five minutes," Cassie told them from the door, as Drew attempted to disguise his predicament.

He joined the young girl in the main room and picked up the coffee she'd poured him. "Did you have a nice night with Mummy?"

"Yes thank you."

"That's good. I'm making us all eggs and bacon this morning if we're travelling."

"You're very good."

"I listened to what you said last night about that charity thing. I thought that was a really lovely idea, and what you said about poor children. I agree with you, it's horrible. I've always been lucky, apart from what happened to Daddy and Izzy, and the Theo thing and what he's done to us all. I've always had everything I needed and lots of stuff I didn't really need, while lots of children don't have food, clothes, or even homes. That's not fair. If Mummy gets Theo's money and it went to help little kids who need it, that would be awesome."

"I think that for an eleven-year-old you say some very smart things."

"When I talked with Milly, I could see how different our lives had been. I really like Milly. I wish we lived closer. We could spend more time together. I don't have many friends at home."

"The best friends are the ones that if you see them after a long time apart you can pick up where you left off."

"Have you got friends like that?"

"Just Brady."

"Sit down. I'll serve your breakfast."

Anna was fully dressed when she joined them for breakfast.

"This is very nice darling, thank you."

"I liked doing it. I might do it at home sometimes. Drew said you had a nice night together, so I suppose you didn't fidget too much."

"I suppose not."

Three hours later, Brady's pickup drove into the yard, and the three temporary tenants came out to greet them.

Alice stepped down from the cab wearing a huge grin and opened the rear door to allow a huge husky-like dog to jump out. "I'm so pleased to meet you all. Brady's been telling me all about you, Drew, but he didn't know anything about you other two. Come inside and tell me all about yourselves. Don't worry about Buck; he's harmless."

The two men greeted each other with man hugs but stayed in the yard to catch up.

"You staying out of trouble these days?"

"The army kinda cured me of all that. It's what it does to guys like me, either makes 'em worse or straightens 'em out."

"So, bodyguard now eh?"

"Yeah kinda."

"How's that working out?"

"Great, but with complications."

"Wanna talk about it?"

"Probably not, I ain't big on sharing."

"I remember."

Drew turned to look at the cabin. "What you've done with this place is amazing."

"Yeah well, it weren't supposed to be this fancy, but then Alice came along and everything changed."

"I heard bits about that."

"I expect some of it might even be true."

"You kinda close then."

"You could say that, Drew. That girl is the air that I breath. There ain't anybody else I'd tell this too, but in three years or so we're going to be married." Drew raised his eyebrows, "I can guess what you're thinking. We ain't having sex or anything, and even if we never do I wouldn't care. I met her when I first came here. She was just eight, but she changed me. Very few people would accept that, but her mum and dad did. They saw it before I did. That's why they named me as guardian."

"I heard they got shot."

"That's a whole other story. Ellie had cancer and knew she was gonna die. Joe needed a heart transplant, and they didn't want Alice ending up in state foster care. They didn't trust anybody else except me, and they asked me to do it. When they got killed it was the worst thing ever. They were such good people. Then when Alice came to live with me it was the best thing ever for me. I would do anything for that girl, anything at all. Do you remember that grumpy bastard that fixed cabins with you? Well he don't exist anymore."

"Well me falling for a multi-millionaire and her kid that I'm guarding, seems kinda lame after that."

"Does the lady know how you feel?"

"Yeah, I think she does, and I think she feels the same."

"That's great, Parker. Guys like us don't often get to be this lucky."

"But she's a millionaire and I'm just an army grunt. Our backgrounds are so different. I don't see how it can work. It sounds like the plot of a Hallmark romcom. What worries me most is Cassie, she's had too much shit in her life already. If it were to go wrong, she would be the one to suffer most. I don't want to be responsible for that. I've never had kids, never believed I would have, but in little over a week that little girl has come to mean a lot to me."

"Sounds like you got a bad dose of what I got buddy. I'm guessing you'll find a way to work it out. Let's go join them."

An hour and a half later Drew and Brady were shaking hands while the girls were saying their goodbyes and vowing to stay in touch.

"Your friend is devoted to Alice isn't he?" Anna said, as they drove past the Ranger station.

"When I knew him before, he was a loner, grim, and introverted. If we went to a bar together, which weren't that often because neither of us drink, we'd sit together clutching a Bud Lite not saying much. What we did say was mostly about work. That guy you met today was a different guy, and it looked great on him."

"Alice told me they're going to get married as soon as she's sixteen," Cassie announced, to Anna's astonishment. "She said, that she'd never told anybody before."

"But..."

"Brady told me the same thing." Drew told them.

"She said they sleep together but they don't have sex. She really wants to, but Brady won't do it."

"I should hope not. She's twelve, just a child."

"She doesn't talk like a child."

"No, she doesn't..."

"And you can tell how much she loves him."

"Yes but…"

"And you can see how happy she is."

"I know but…"

"She said she fell in love with him when she was eight."

"It was just puppy love."

They were silent for a while until Drew said as they pulled onto the highway, "Four years is a pretty long puppy love."

"Yes, I suppose it is," she conceded.

They made really good time and were in Lexington earlier than they had expected.

"We could try and sell the car today, if you want," he said. "It would save time in the morning."

"Why not? It's worth a try."

The first dealer they found couldn't believe his luck when Drew accepted his first offer, on two conditions. First, that he drove them to somewhere to buy luggage to pack all the clothes they'd bought, which were still in the bags provided by the outfitters; and second that he drove them to the airport.

By 18:30 they were saying goodbye to the car dealer at Blue Grass International Airport. At the Delta Airlines desk they were lucky to get three economy seats on a 20:15 flight to Washington. They checked their bags including Drew's armory in a gun travel case he'd bought at the luggage store.

They hadn't eaten since lunch at the cabin, so the next thing they did was to get something to eat.

"We can't be sure of getting a room in Washington, can we?" she said.

"We'll get something. We might have to go a bit down market."

"I don't care. I'm exhausted, and I can tell Cassie is too. Aren't you?"

"Wouldn't say no to some shuteye. I've got a bit of a headache too."

"If I had a phone and a credit card I could book something from here. Would it be okay to ask Percy to try?"

"Great idea,' he said, handing her his phone.

It was noisy where they were sitting so she moved into a corner, when she returned fifteen minutes later, their food had arrived. "Double room at the Hyatt Regency. He did it while I was on the phone."

"I thought you took a long time."

"I asked him to book our flight home as well, and there was something else I wanted to speak to him while he was on the phone. It's half past midnight there. I woke him up. He'll send us our London flight details as soon as he's got them and he'll get Toby to pick us up again."

When they boarded the plane their seats weren't all together, and Cassie insisted on sitting next to Drew who was on the aisle. They hadn't been in the air long when she said, "I love you, Drew. Promise me not to leave us."

"I'll stay as long as your mom wants me to, I promise you that."

"Mummy won't want you to go. She loves you too."

"What makes you say that; has she told you?"

"No, she doesn't need to tell me. I can just tell. I can tell that you love her too."

"It's not that simple."

"Yes it is. You're the cleverest person I know. If you want it to happen then you can make it happen."

"We'll have to see."

"No we won't. It's going to work out just fine, I know it..."

The man in the window seat interrupted what she was about to say, "Excuse me, I'm an extremely busy person and I'm trying to sleep here."

"I'm sorry," she said.

"Yeah, sorry pal."

"For fucks sake! Fucking kid trying to arrange her mom's love life, what next?"

Drew leaned across Cassie with one of his huge hands and grabbed the man's leg just above the knee and squeezed.

"Listen pal, the young lady said sorry, so if the next words that come out of your mouth aren't, 'I'm really sorry for snapping but I'm a bit tired, please forgive me,' then it won't be your leg I squeeze next, and you won't be having any sort of love life. Go ahead, we're waiting."

Tears appeared in the man's eyes. "I'm v-very sorry for snapping b-but I'm tired. Please f-forgive me."

"That's better, now go to sleep like a good boy." Drew patted the man's leg and sat back.

"Is everything okay here?" A young cabin crew girl asked.

"Sure, thanks for asking. This extremely busy guy here had some leg cramps, but it's gone now. Ain't that right pal?"

"Y-yes."

"Perhaps it might be best if we try to get some rest ourselves."

On landing, *Busy Man* remained seated and allowed several people to join the queue to the exit before getting his bag from the overhead locker.

Anna caught up with them on the jetway and they made their way to baggage claim. On the short domestic flight at that time of the evening most other people were travelling with hand luggage only so the wait for their regular baggage wasn't long. However, they had to go to the desk to reclaim his gun case, and it was at least half an hour before that became available. While they waited Anna looked at Drew. "Are you okay? You look pale, and you're sweating."

"Maybe I got a cold coming."

At eleven-fifteen they finally checked in at the hotel and were in bed within the hour. Cassie insisted that her mother sleep with Drew because *she fidgets.*

"Drew doesn't complain about my fidgeting."

"That's because he likes sleeping with you."

Anna looked across at Drew, but he appeared to be asleep.

When morning came, Anna was first to wake. Drew had been the one to be restless during the night and he'd been sweating. She shook him awake, "Are you okay? You're sweating, and you're very pale."

"Getting a cold or flu or something."

"I'll order room service breakfast then. There's no hurry. Our flight's not until four p.m."

"Great,' he mumbled, and his eyes closed again.

She showered and dressed. Cassie did the same, and when their breakfast trolley arrived, she went to wake Drew.

"Mummy, quickly something's wrong with Drew!"

Anna rushed to the bedside and shook him several times but he wouldn't wake. He was shaking, his skin was blotchy, and his lips looked blue. She grabbed the phone from the beside the bed and called the switchboard. "Quick I need an ambulance now!...I don't know what's wrong, he's really ill, I can't wake him. He needs a doctor now....Make sure they hurry."

The two of them were left, each helplessly clutching a hand, pleading with him to wake up."

A first responder from the hotel staff was first to come. She confirmed that he was breathing, had a high temperature, an abnormally fast pulse, and was unconscious. She had a defibrillator and a respirator on the bed both ready to use.

"Can't you do anything?" Cassie pleaded.

"He's breathing and he has a heartbeat. I'm not qualified to do anything else. The paramedics will be here soon. Get me a cold washcloth, we might be able to cool him down."

Ten interminable minutes later a paramedic arrived at the door. She took less than a minute to assess the situation and radioed her partner, "Need a gurney up here right now, Room 304." Then she radioed the hospital and told them she had an incoming patient and rattled off a series of medical statistics. The other medic soon pushed the gurney into the room, they heaved him on to it and pressed an oxygen mask to his face.

"What's his name and date of birth?"

"Drew Parker. I don't know his date of birth."

"Has he got insurance?"

"I've no idea. It doesn't matter because I'll pay whatever it costs." She opened her purse, grabbed a $10,000 bundle of notes and told the woman, "There's four more in those bags, and plenty more available if necessary, but for God's sake get on with it."

The woman nodded and began pushing the trolley.

"Where are you taking him?"

"University Hospital, ma'am."

"Can we come?" Anna begged, grabbing her purse.

"No, ma'am. You'll need to grab a cab."

Cassie called after them as they raced toward the lift. "Is he going to be alright?"

"We don't know, miss. We'll do our best."

"What's wrong with Drew, Mummy?"

"I don't know sweetheart, we've got to go to join him, but I need to buy a phone first. Empty your purse will you and put some of this cash in it."

Between them they crammed as much of the cash as they could into the bags, grabbed Drew's wallet and all their passports.

"Right let's go."

Stopping at the desk only long enough to tell them they'd be needing the room for longer; they rushed outside and jumped the first cab. "University Hospital, emergency entrance please, but I need to stop somewhere to buy a phone on the way."

The cab stopped outside a gadget shop where she bought two prepaid smartphones and jumped back into the cab. Ten minutes more and she was in the hospital demanding to know what was happening with her *husband.*

"I'm scared, Mummy."

"Me too, darling."

Eventually a young doctor came out to see them.

"Mrs. Parker?"

"Yes, that's me. What's happening?"

"We've given him a high dose of antibiotics to fight the infection, and we think we've caught it in time."

"Caught what, and in time for what?"

"Mr. Parker has sepsis, ma'am, but we're hopeful we can avoid any further surgery or amputation."

"Surgery? Amputation?"

"His injury had become infected."

"On his head?"

"No, ma'am, the wound on his arm. We've had to do some minor surgery on the inside of his arm but if everything goes according to plan, he shouldn't suffer any major loss of function"

"That was me, I was the last person to stitch that. Did I cause it?"

"There's no way of knowing, ma'am. The infection may have begun before you treated it."

"Can we see him?"

"You can see him briefly before he's taken to a room in our surgical department, but it maybe an hour or two before he knows what's happening."

The doctor led them to one of the ER treatment areas. Drew was lying on his back and beside the bed there was a stand with blood and clear fluid drips as well as a monitor registering all his vital signs, and he had an oxygen mask over his face.

Anna said, "Why didn't you go to the hospital like I said? You'd better not fucking die, you stupid bastard. We need you."

They were soon chased out of the ER so they could move him to a room on an upper floor, and a woman with a clipboard approached them. "Mrs. Parker? I understand you want to pay for your husband's treatment with cash. Is that correct."

"If necessary yes, but I have his wallet here. He may have suitable insurance. Shall we look?"

"Let's go to my office."

"So you don't know if your husband has insurance. Is that right?"

"You can probably tell from my accent, I'm English. I'm not familiar with the things in the US, and technically he might not be regarded as my husband."

"In what way?"

"In the *I haven't married him yet* way, but I'm hoping it won't be long."

"I see, maybe now might be a good time to start looking to see if he has a medical insurance card then."

Anna looked through Drew's wallet, "Is this the sort of thing?"

"VA Tricare; yes that's exactly the sort of thing thank you." She typed some details from the card into her terminal.

"Just in case your *husband's* treatment becomes protracted, can I take your details so that we can forward any invoices for extended care."

"Certainly, you can send anything to Lady Annabelle Astley-West, Pangbourne Grange, Reading, Berkshire, United Kingdom."

"Thank you Lady Annabelle. I wish your future husband a speedy recovery."

They walked to the entrance. "We've got a long day ahead of us. We need to eat darling."

"I'm not hungry, Mummy."

"Listen it's bad enough that I have to worry about Drew. I want to worry about you too."

They found a diner not far from the hospital. It was still early and there were plenty of tables. Anna just ordered burger and fries with sparkling water for them both and began unwrapping one of the phones. After going through the set-up process, she called Percy and told him what was happening. He promised to put the tickets on hold for her but explained that the hotel had called him and said that they couldn't have the room for another night because they were fully booked.

"Okay I'll sort that out, but I need you to put some more credit on this phone, and Cassie's. Here's the number. Also, Drew has a sister. She lives in Wilmington, North Carolina; her Christian name is Carolina, but I don't know her married name. Could you try and find a phone number for her, tell her what's happening, and give her this number.

"Also can you let Judith and Jason know what's happening for me too. I'm so sorry to pile all this on you. I know you have so many other things that you have to do."

"I've seconded Sheila to work exclusively for you anyway for the time being. So most of the time it will be her doing all the practical side of things, so you can speak to either of us for that."

"Thanks Percy, you're a star."

"Give Drew my best wishes."

By the time she ended the call, the food had arrived. "Go ahead and eat, sweetie. I'm just going to call the hotel. "Reservations please....Mrs. Astley-West speaking, I understand you want me to move out of our room today...I understand it's inconvenient, but it also was inconvenient when my fiancé almost died in your hotel too. Mr. Parker is an American hero with two silver stars and the Medal of Honor, he's in hospital because he took a bullet that was intended for me. Are you saying you are going to throw me and my eleven-year-old daughter onto the street, for convenience? It's not a good look, is it?. How about you find the other couple a room in another hotel and you bill it to me. I'm too busy to be worrying about whether my daughter and I are going lose the one person in our lives we love, to think about searching for another room, and I don't have time to argue about it either...Good, I was sure you'd see sense. Thank you."

They made a good attempt at finishing the food, but neither did so with particular relish."

"Do you think Drew is going to lose an arm Mummy?"

"I don't know, darling; I do hope not."

"I'll still love him."

"So will I."

"Did you mean it when you said you were going to marry him?"

"I will if he asks me. I've moved on from pretending that I don't love him. I need him sweetheart almost as much as I need you."

"He loves you too. He told me on the plane."

"He told you?"

"I told him that I could tell he loved you. He wouldn't deny it. He just said it's difficult."

"It is difficult, but how can you tell that he loves me?"

"Because I've seen the way he looks at you, and because he gets a stiffy every time you're near him."

"Yes, well stiffies aren't the most reliable guide to a man's affection, and you shouldn't be looking at them anyway."

They gave it two hours, before returning to the hospital. When they got there, they were directed to his room, where once again Anna identified herself as his fiancée.

Drew still seemed unconscious but the blood had gone. So had the oxygen mask to be replaced by tubes to his nose. The drip of clear fluid was still connected along with the monitor, but his color had improved a little, and so had his skin tone.

"How is he?" Anna asked the nurse who was typing something into an electronic tablet.

"He's improved a little and woken up a few times although he's not really with it. The doctor says he was lucky. Another hour or two could have made a big difference, but he's not out of the woods yet. One of the doctors will be in to see him shortly. If you wait she'll be able to answer your questions more fully."

"Thank you."

She walked to stand beside the bed and stroked his face.

"Drew Parker, I love you more than I ever thought possible to love a man again. If you can hear me then try to remember those words, because Cassie and I need you to fight harder than you've ever fought before so you can be with us forever."

She leaned forward and kissed his lips.

Cassie stood the other side of the bed and held his hand. "You are the cleverest, bravest, and strongest person I will probably ever know. I want you to be in my life always. I want you to wake up and tell me that's what you want as well. I like when you tell stories. I like when you say naughty words. I like when you look at Mummy like she's the sexiest girl on the planet, and I like when you make bad and stupid people look silly. Mummy needs you a lot, and not just as a bodyguard. I would like for you to be my new daddy, that would be the best thing ever."

Anna's new phone vibrated.

"Anna, it's Lina. I'm just about to board a plane I'll be with you in less than two hours. How is he?"

"I just spoke to a nurse. She told me that he's improved a little, but not out of the woods yet. We think he looks a little better, but it's too soon to say."

"Did they say what it is?"

"Sepsis. From the wound on his arm."

"Fuck! Oh shit, they're calling my flight. I'll be with you as soon as I can."

They sat with him, mostly in silence, but occasionally speaking to him or to each other. From time to time he'd stir or mumble, but he didn't wake. When the doctor arrived, she looked at his readouts and felt his forehead.

"I understand we have an American hero in our care." She smiled, "Hi I'm Dr Morgan; you must be Mrs. West.

"He wouldn't thank me for mentioning that hero thing doctor. Wait a minute I don't think I did."

"You didn't. It was our Director of Administration who recognized the name. She's writing a book on recipients of the Medal of Honor because her father was one. She told us that nothing is to be spared to make sure he gets the best possible care. Redundant really because all our patients get that."

"What's happening doctor?"

"We've halted the spread as far as we're able to see, and we're optimistic we can limit the damage. We won't be certain about that for a day or two, although he seems to be responding well at the moment. He's under mild sedation for the time being because we don't want him getting excited. We'll gradually reduce that over the next twenty-four."

"When you say limit the damage, what do you mean?"

"He will almost certainly lose part or all of the third and fourth fingers of his left hand."

"Oh God."

"I know it sounds awful, but many people who have similar injuries function with little or no impact on their lives. He's young exceptionally fit and I'm confident that he'll do well. He was fortunate. If it had been allowed it to go on for longer he could have lost his arm or even died."

"When will you know for certain?"

"By the end of tomorrow, but we won't schedule surgery until the day after. He'll have to give his consent. He's in good hands here. Try not to worry too much Mrs. West."

"Thank you doctor."

Two hours later Lina arrived.

"Hi, you must be Drew's fiancée. Nice to meet you."

"Sorry about that Lina, but they won't take notice of you in these places unless you're a relative. I didn't want them to find a reason to delay treatment, so I told them that and waved bundles of cash under their nose."

Lina laughed. "You're my kinda lady. Tell me what's happening with my dumb brother."

Anna gave her a rundown of everything the doctor had said.

"He's not dumb," Cassie said. "He's the cleverest person in the world."

"I know but if he overhears me saying it he'd think he was on his death bed. How come I didn't know about a wound on his arm? When did that happen?"

"The day before we left England, when they sent those four men to my house to kill us, but he keeps refusing treatment every time he does something to open the wound."

"And you're trying to tell me he ain't dumb. Has he been conscious since you've been here?"

"He's stirred a few times, but not exactly come round. The doctor said he's mildly sedated, but they're reducing that over the next twenty-four hours."

"When did you last eat?"

"About five hours ago."

"You need to keep your strength up if you're going to get through this together."

"What do you mean?"

"Listen a minute. Tell me when I go wrong. You just spent a week trailing all over the Western world, living in close quarters with a man that keeps going out of his way to stick his body in front of bullets that were heading your way, a man who clearly worships you, then he ups and nearly dies. You blast into the hospital telling them you're his fiancée or wife or something, then sit by his bedside for hours clutching his hand with tears pouring down your face. Those aren't the actions of two people who don't need to be together."

Anna's shoulders slumped. "You're right; I love him; I really do. How can you be sure he feels the same way?"

"Because I ain't dumb. I could see that in Richmond from about ten feet away. He's smitten with you. I ain't never seen him like that before. What's more, I know I said he was dumb, but he ain't that dumb. He can see that you feel like too. It's like you got a big sign over your head saying, *I need to get laid, and you're the man to do it.* He'd follow you through the gates of hell if you asked. But getting back to the subject, I don't know how long it's gonna take to get him back where he should be but you're gonna be the girl to make him do it; you and this little thing here. So you're gonna need to keep your strength up."

"Will it take that long do you think?"

"Physically, I doubt it. He's strong as a bull elephant, but psychologically it might take a time. He'll be asking himself if he's still the man he was, is he still the man you thought he was. He'll be aware of his mortality in a way that never mattered before you came along. I only got a part-time degree in psychology, and I ain't qualified so I could be wrong."

"What can I do to help?" Cassie asked.

"You are helping. As far as he's concerned you come as a pair."

"We've barely met. How can you know all this?"

"I know my brother, and when we met in the motel room it was plain as day. The first words he said were, *Let me introduce you to Mrs. West and Cassandra, we're travelling together.* The look on his face was pure pride and pleasure. I'm not gonna pretend that you won't have a few hurdles to get over what with the differences in your backgrounds, but you don't strike me as the sort of girl who wants to put on airs and graces, and he ain't one to stand on ceremony either. Once you shake some of that military starch out of him you'll be fine."

When their food arrived she continued, "Are you allowed to tell me any of that secret shit yet?"

"Some of it I suppose…"

After swearing Lina to secrecy and ensuring that they couldn't be overheard, Anna filled Lina in with everything that had happened. "Drew thinks that Theo and his handler targeted Henry and I from the outset, and they may even have arranged Henry's death in order for Theo to court me while I was vulnerable."

"Jeez for a rich girl you sure manage to trawl up a shipload of trouble. Shall we go?"

They walked back to the hospital, and when they got there they found Drew awake, if not fully aware of what was going on.

Lina laid her hand on his forehead. "Hi bro, how's it going?"

"Lina?"

"How do you feel?"

"Like crap, what am I doin' in here?"

"You did another one of your dumb stunts again, but this time you got lucky. Some horny chick stepped in and saved your stupid skin."

"Hi, Drew."

"Anna, are you okay?"

"Am I okay? I'm not the one in hospital."

"What happened?"

"You let that wound on your arm get infected without getting treatment and it went septic."

"Is that all?"

"Is that all - what the , bro. You nearly died, you dumb asshole. You've got responsibilities; you can't go getting yourself killed."

"Responsibilities?"

"Me, and Ben, your last remaining blood relatives, and now there's Anna and Cassie."

"Anna and Cassie?"

"Stop repeating what I say or I'll just leave."

"Sorry, I'm tired."

"Okay, probably best if we let you have a few more hours. I'll go and have a word with the nurses. You chat with Anna and Cassie."

"We won't stay long; we want you to get your strength back."

"What's the time. We'll miss our flight."

"We missed that about an hour ago. It doesn't matter. There'll be plenty more."

"You could have gone ahead; I can follow when I feel better. You should be safe now,"

"I wonder if Lina is right, sometimes you can be so dense. If you haven't figured it out yet, I love you. Cassie loves you. You're stuck with us; we aren't going anywhere without you again, unless you tell us you don't want us."

His eyes filled, "I do want you."

Anna leaned down and kissed him soft and long. "I'm glad we got that sorted it out."

His eyes began to close so they left him and caught up with Lina at the nurses station.

"Have you got space for me in your room. I haven't booked anything," Lina asked.

"Of course. You can have Cassie's bed. She can share with me; I just hope I'm not too fidgety." She looked at her daughter.

"I just say that, so you'll sleep with Drew."

Lina laughed, "That's hilarious, the best thing I've heard this week."

"This is a step up from the motel the other day." Lina said, when they reached the hotel room.

"If Mummy and Drew get married, will you bring Ben to see us in England sometimes?"

"Wow, that's a pretty presumptive question, but let's just say I'd like that, but one step at a time eh? Anna, did you put a big bunch of cash in Drew's account? If you don't mind me asking?"

"Yes I did. How did you know?"

"Cos I've been managing his financials since he started doing all the covert stuff. Did you tell him you were gonna do that?"

"No."

"Well you'd better look out for a whole lotta grief about it. He's kinda touchy about money."

"Oh God, I didn't want to offend him. I just thought that if he was going to be living with us I didn't want him to feel as if he was an employee. I thought it would give him some independence."

"Yeah, that's one of them hurdles I was talking about. Good job I gave you a heads up about it then, so when the brown stuff hits the fan you can be up and running with a good excuse, cos that one needs some work."

Twenty-Seven

After breakfast the next morning they caught a cab and were at the hospital by ten. When they got to Drew's room they found him sitting up. Wasting no time for there to be any confusion about their status as a couple she went straight to the bed took his head in her hands and kissed him.

"I love you Drew Parker."

"I think I love you too Anna West, but it's gonna take some getting used to because I never expected to hear anybody say that, and I didn't expect anybody wanting to hear it from me."

"We'll work on it together."

"I found out we got engaged. I didn't remember any of that, did someone take pictures?"

"I kind of advance noticed it. How are you?"

"I'm okay I guess. Turns out I'm gonna be leaving here a couple of fingers light of a set."

"I heard; how do you feel about that?"

"I wasn't wild about the idea, but the alternative was less appealing."

"But how are you really?"

"Still a bit weak and muzzy headed to be honest, but I'm getting there. The doc says I'm doing better than expected."

He turned to see Cassie was crying,

"Hey, Cassie what's up?"

"I thought you were going to die. I'm just happy you're getting better."

"Come here and give me a hug."

She kneeled up on the bed and they hugged, and then she kissed him again.

"Hi sis how's it going?"

"Well I'm kinda suffering from shock. First I find out that my brother ain't Clark Kent after all, then I discover he's almost human and vulnerable to the wiles of womankind like most men, and then to cap it off I find myself relegated from first to third in the female echelons of his affections."

"Don't I get a kiss then?"

"Not until I get an apology for dragging me all the way up here thinking you're dying."

"I didn't expect sympathy, but maybe a little compassion."

She hugged him and looked him in the eye. "You frightened the freaking life outta , you asshole."

"Sorry about that Sis."

"Still could have been worse. At least it weren't the hand you jerk off with."

"Lina!" Anna exclaimed, unable to suppress a smile.

"What does that mean?" Cassie asked.

"Never you mind. You'll find out soon enough."

Dr Morgan and a nurse came in with a tray covered in a white cloth. "I'm going to have to ask you folks to step outside for a few minutes if that's okay."

"What's happening?" Anna asked.

"We're just doing a final check to clear Mr. Parker for Surgery."

"I thought it wasn't supposed to be until tomorrow."

"That was the original plan, but as he seems to have improved much quicker than expected Dr Havel, my attending surgeon, said to go ahead today after a theatre place unexpectedly became available for this morning."

"I thought you were the attending surgeon."

"Good God no. I'm only a second-year resident. I'll be doing the operation though; digital excision is well within my range of experience. There's nothing to worry about. In fact it's a good thing. With this type of problem, the earlier we remove the necrotic tissue the better."

"I see, thank you."

Ten minutes later Lina was back in the room.

"They want us to leave you alone in a minute. I'm going to fly back this afternoon so I won't see you after the op. I asked Anna to give us some time alone. I just wanted to tell you that, against all the odds and expectations you've somehow managed to hook a real classy broad there. You come from totally different backgrounds, but I think you can make it work - just don't expect it all to be plain sailing from day one. Anna and that kid have had a real shitty time of it and I think you're the right guy to help them out the other side. Same goes in reverse, so don't fuck it up. I love you bro."

"I ain't too good with words, Sis, as you know, but if it weren't for you, Grandma, and Grandpa, I'd probably have spent most my life doing time. I love you, and I'll never be able to repay you for that."

"You already did bro, you already did," she tearfully replied. "Listen to us, gettin' all sloppy. I'm goin' now, good luck with the op."

She said goodbye to Anna and Cassie before heading off. Then they said their own goodbyes to him and left him alone.

"What shall we do now, Mummy? Can we go sightseeing, see where the President lives and other places?"

"That's a good idea. It'll take our mind off things. We couldn't go far, and we wouldn't be able to go inside places where there's no phone signal."

"We could just get a cab to drive us around seeing places from the outside."

"If that's what you want to do, why not?"

The Ukrainian cab driver was delighted with the prospect of driving leisurely around the capital without having to tout for passengers. His knowledge of the landmark buildings was very good, but his accent often made his commentary unintelligible. He was happier still when they asked him to drop them at a restaurant and a pick them up after an hour.

They were at the Arlington Cemetery when the phone call from the hospital finally came at four-fifteen. The journey back to the hospital should have taken ten minutes at the most, but it took nearly forty-five minutes; a pile up on the Roosevelt Bridge had caused hundreds of vehicles to attempt to use the Arlington Memorial Bridge.

Anna hurriedly paid the driver, and they rushed inside.

When they arrived at the nurses' station they were told to wait - someone would be with them soon. Terrified that something had gone wrong, the next few minutes, felt like hours. Eventually Dr Morgan and two others in white coats emerged from Drew's room and approached the nervous pair.

"How is he, Dr Morgan?"

"The operation went well and we were able to restrict our excision to the distal, middle, and proximal phalanges of his third and fourth fingers. I was concerned that being too conservative I might leave the door open for reinfection, but Dr Havel was there to reassure me that he thought it unlikely. We will keep him in for another forty-eight hours just to be on the safe side."

"When will he be fit to fly?"

"I'd suggest at least seventy-two hours from now, barring any setbacks. Where will you be flying to?"

"England."

"Providing you can be sure that he has access to good wound management and pain management, there shouldn't be a problem."

"Thank you doctor, can we see him now?"

"A nurse is just redressing the wound. He won't be long but Mr. Parker may be quite groggy for another hour or two."

Drew was laying down but the bedhead was raised and he still had the nasal oxygen tubes on, the drip was still there, and he was still attached to a monitor. The only notable difference was his left hand encased in a massive bandage and his arm suspended from a hook attached to the bed.

The two visitors gingerly approached him.

He gave them a weak smile.

"How are you, darling, is it painful?"

"The pain's not too bad, but I'm a bit high with painkillers at the moment so if I say something stupid you'll have to be patient with me."

"Does it feel weird?"

"I don't really know yet Cassie, but it probably will once the bandages are off."

"How is your head now?"

"Actually I forget it's there most of the time. They changed the dressing on it again this morning and they said the paramedic had made a good job of stitching it, and it's closing up well."

"We need to talk about the future," she said."

"Yes, but not now eh?"

"Okay, but I've a confession to make, when you're a bit more with it. What are we going to do about your guns?"

"I guess the safest thing would be to sell them. There's bound to be a gun shop near here who will take them off your hands."

They talked for another hour before they were asked to let him rest.

On the way out Anna had a question for her daughter. "What did you say to him just before we left?"

"I told him I looked up *jerking off* on the Internet and told him he won't have to do it anymore because he's got you now."

"Cassie, that's terrible!"

"Well it's true isn't it?"

"Maybe, but even if it is it's not the sort of thing you talk about with a man."

The next two days they spent talking about their future. On the second day, Cassie volunteered to sit in the hospital restaurant for a couple of hours to give them some time on their own.

"Your Cassie is one smart little girl ain't she?"

"She's probably been the one person who's kept me afloat since Henry died, and I wasn't even aware of it. Izzy too of course. The tragedy is I don't think I fully appreciated the extent of her anguish for far too long. Cassie has been like a floating lifebelt that I unknowingly clung on to while my ship went down in a sea of grief."

"That's real expressive. I could never think of things like that to say."

"I doubt there's much call for it in special forces."

"That's true. What was that confession you were going to make?"

"I thought I was doing the right thing, but Lina told me off, so you'll have to try and forgive me."

"What did you do?"

"I didn't want you to feel like my employee anymore. So I cancelled your salary and paid a big sum into your account instead. You've paid out a lot of your own money on our account during the last week or two, and I felt so guilty."

"How much?"

She told him.

"Jesus! I'm glad you told me because I would have been real pissed. I understand why you did it though so don't worry. We're good, as long as you let me pay most of it back. You've got a lot of money but not everything needs to be rewarded with money. It makes it seem like a transaction. As for what I paid out, it's not that big a deal, I'm not rich by your standards, but for a soldier I don't do too bad, and I knew you'd pay me back if I wanted."

"You're right, I'm sorry. I'll try not to patronize you in the future. Cassie told me what she said to you the other day. She's growing up to be quite saucy sometimes, but just so we both know what we're talking about, making that facility available to you can't come soon enough in my book."

"Me neither," he said, standing from the chair where he'd been sitting, and pulling her one-handedly from her own. He nudged her chin up with his bandaged hand and pulled her toward him with the other. They kissed, his hand sliding down to her butt to press her against his growing erection.

"Those painkillers aren't quite as effective at sensation control as I thought it seems," she said.

"I've wanted to do this since that very first plane journey."

"I'm going to go now just in case Mother Nature takes her course again."

"I'll be ready for you to collect me tomorrow. Don't forget to bring me some clothes. But Anna, before we go rushing to announce anything to the world we need to be absolutely sure of what we're doing."

"Are you getting cold feet?"

"No, I don't think so, but I don't think either of us know what we want out of whatever comes next."

"I want you; I want us."

"That's what I want too, but I think that's too simplistic, and there's Cassie. What does she expect?"

"Does she frighten you?"

"No, what frightens me, is doing something to hurt her,"

"You would never do that."

"Not intentionally no, of course not. She's your daughter, you've known her all her life. I see how much you love her, and how much that's reciprocated. It frightens me that I could disrupt that. I need to get to know you both better, and you need to know me better. We can't let Cassie imagine that this would be some kind of fairy tale. There could be all sorts of road bumps."

"I understand. I think you're right, but I know I won't change my mind."

As it happened the hospital weren't ready to discharge him until after lunch. First the hard copy of his notes couldn't be printed until they'd been updated by the doctors. Then his painkillers hadn't been dispensed, and only after Drew flatly refused to be rolled to the entrance in a wheelchair did they finally allow him to leave.

As soon as the bedroom door closed behind them they grasped each other in a tight squeeze and kissed. Cassie put her arms around them both and announced, "This is the best day ever."

"What time is our flight tomorrow?" he asked.

"Ten a.m. I want to be at the airport by nine if that's alright."

"Isn't that cutting it a bit fine what with baggage check, security and passport control?"

"We're flying charter, so that won't be a problem."

"Jeez, how much was that?"

"You don't need to know. I couldn't get a direct scheduled flight for nearly three weeks, and in your condition I didn't want you having to traipse around half the airports in North America or Europe in some sort of Phileas Fogg reenactment, so that's that."

"Your mom don't mess around when she wants something does she?"

"I want you back in my den before you have second thoughts."

When the morning came he looked tired but cheerful and insisted that he was fine to travel. They packed the last of their belongings, and went down to checkout. A fellow guest saw them struggling with their bags and offered to help.

"Thanks buddy that was real kind," Drew told him at the checkout desk.

"No problem, sir. Hope those injuries clear up soon."

Anna settled their bill and they left their bags at the checkout desk while they ate breakfast in the hotel restaurant.

Twenty-Eight

The brief journey to the airport and the preliminary boarding checks had them sitting aboard their plane awaiting the tower giving clearance to taxi in less than an hour. The single cabin crew was a woman in her fifties, who made sure they were comfortable and read them the pre-flight safety information before the small but luxurious Cessna Citation jet began to move.

The six-and-a-half-hour journey had them touching down at Heathrow just after nine p.m. and the post-flight procedures were straightforward and quick. Toby and Percy were there to meet them again, and no time was wasted loading baggage and hustling everybody into the car.

"So what's new in Pangbourne, Toby?"

"Not very much Mrs. West. We've all been too worried about you and Miss Cassie, and Drew of course."

"There are going to be some small changes there soon; nothing for anyone to be too concerned about but sometime tomorrow morning I'm going to make a little announcement."

"We're all a bit in the dark, and there have been very strange and worrying rumors I'm afraid."

"I thought that would be the case, but rather than tell you one or two at a time I want to put it all to bed at once."

"Thank you, miss."

Percy called ahead and the gate opened as they approached.

"What's all that scaffolding?"

"They started upgrading the security system on Monday," Percy reminded her.

"I'd forgotten about that. It might be redundant now but never mind."

"Security is never redundant in today's world, especially in a house like this," Drew assured her.

The tearful reunions with Jason and Judith were soon over. Percy kissed Anna and then after making an appointment to meet the following Monday, he and Toby left for their homes. Surprisingly suddenly the three of them were on their own.

"You ought to go to bed now, sweetheart. No story time tonight," she said to Cassie.

Cassie giggled. "You and Drew have better things to do than tell stories."

"You're a saucy girl. See you in the morning." They all exchanged kisses and she went up the stairs dragging her bag with her."

"How are you, sweetheart?"

"Quite tired, and my hand is throbbing fit to bust, but pleased to be properly alone with you. But listen I have to say something. I want the three of us to be absolutely certain that what happens next is right. I think we need to spend time as lovers, not as a bodyguard and principal. I want to spend time with Cassie, just the two of us sometimes maybe, so that we really get to know each other. I love you. I never imagined saying that to anybody, and I love Cassie just as much, but this isn't the *Kevin Costner* movie.

"We come from completely different worlds, you're a polite, gentile, university-educated Englishwoman, born into wealth, used to socializing with people from similar backgrounds. I'm a Yank, an uncouth, poorly educated ex-con, the illegitimate child of a drug addict, a trained killer used to the company of similar people. Apart the fact that we've both been given the shitty end of the stick is on the face of things the only thing we have in common."

Anna's eyes showed her disappointment. "You're right; of course you are. Cassie will be upset."

"Will you let me explain it to her?"

"Yes, if that's what you want."

They went up the stairs together. Drew knocked on Cassie's door and she opened it in her pajamas.

"Can we talk?"

"Okay."

He took her hand and led her to the bed where they sat. She looked into his face and tears began to form in her eyes.

"You've changed your mind haven't you?"

"If you're asking do I still want to be with your mom, then no I haven't. If you're asking if I still want to be around for you, then the answer is yes. But I don't think that now is the right time to be talking about marriage, it's too soon. The world I come from is too removed from yours for us to make that decision so quickly. I think we need to see how well we fit first."

"Are you going to leave?"

"Cassie, I love your mom and I want this to work, I really do, so I'm not saying we won't ever marry. I want to always be part of your life, and you to be part of mine. Do you understand?"

"I think so."

She put her arms around his neck and kissed him.

"Will you still have sex with Mummy sometimes, because I think she wants to."

He laughed, "I hope so."

"And will you keep us safe?"

"I promise. Sleep well, sweetheart."

"How did she take it?" Anna asked. She'd nervously waited at her bedroom door.

"I think she understood."

"Tomorrow I'm going to tell the others that we're in a relationship though. Is that okay?"

"I'd like that. Could you help with my shower and toilet though?"

"Okay, but one day you're going to have to tell me about that ex-con thing."

The morning arrived and all three of the travelers slept until gone eight. Anna's door opened slowly and Cassie appeared, her facial expression of expectation changing to one of disappointment. "Where's Drew?"

"We decided to leave it one more night and make the great revelation that he and I are together before we make it obvious. I hope you don't mind."

"I suppose not, as long as you don't change your minds."

"I don't think that will happen; we're just going to let us all grow into the family we want to be before cementing it in place."

"Can I go and wake him up?"

"If you knock first and you wake him gently."

She knocked on the connecting door. There was no reply so she went in to find the bed empty.

"He's awake already."

"Go take your shower and dress for breakfast. I'll see if he needs a hand."

Cassie went out onto the landing just in time to catch Jason coming up the stairs with a tray containing cups and a teapot. "I'll take those Jason. Mummy's in the shower and Drew doesn't drink tea."

"Oh, okay thanks. How are you this morning? This must have all been so terrible for you."

"I'm okay now it's all over. I think everything will be okay from now on."

"Toby said that Anna is going to make an announcement this morning, and there are going to be some changes."

"Yes, that's what she said, but I don't think anybody needs to be worried. She just wants to everybody to find out at once."

"Okay."

"I'm just going to shower and I'll be down and we can talk better."

"Something's happened. You've changed."

"I think I've grown up a lot in the last few weeks that's all, and I'm twelve next week."

She took the tray into Anna's room, quickly showered in her own, dressed, and then joined Jason and Judith in the kitchen.

"I'm going to cook Drew's breakfast this morning. Does anybody else want egg and bacon?"

The siblings looked at each other in astonishment and shook their heads.

Cassie went about cooking the bacon, something in their experience, she'd never attempted before.

"So what have you been doing about schoolwork since I last saw you?" Judith asked.

"Nothing formal. I've read several books - some that you recommended and a couple of others. The one I've just finished was called *The Haunting of Sunshine Girl*. It was great."

Drew appeared in the kitchen doorway. "Morning folks. Everybody okay?"

"Good morning," they all chorused.

"I'm making you bacon and eggs, Drew, is that okay?"

"That's fantastic, I'd do it myself but…" he held up his bandaged hand.

She turned away from the cooker and gave him a hug. "I love you," she whispered.

"Oh God, Drew, we were all so upset when Percy told us about your hand, although we still don't know what happened. And you've got a head wound too, like me."

"How is that?"

"It's healing. It's ruined my hairline though."

"Are we ever going to be allowed to know what all this has been about?" Judith asked, "We've all heard bits and pieces and we've tried to piece them together, but it sounds more like something out *Alex Rider* than real life."

"I think Mrs. West is planning to tell everybody a lot more this morning."

"Sit down, Drew, it's almost ready," Cassie said, pouring him his coffee, and laying a plate in front of him. "Four eggs easy over two slices of bacon, and two toast. Is that okay. I cut up the bacon for you."

"Who are you, and what have you done with our Cassie," Jason asked.

"What do you mean?"

"Normally you come down in the morning, smile at everybody, grab a bowl of cereal, and a glass of juice and then not speak until you're spoken to."

"A lot has happened lately, and like I said, I think I've grown up a bit, that's all."

"I'm not criticizing. I think it looks good on you."

"Drew is a good influence."

Anna joined them a few minutes later with the tray.

Cassie put a plate on the table with two eggs and bacon, then the same for herself. "Blow it, I forgot to make some more tea."

"I'll make it. I seem to be the only one around here not doing anything," Judith offered. "So Anna, are you going to keep us on the edge of our seats until the very last minute."

"If Toby, Josh and Marilyn are here, we can begin as soon as we've finished eating."

Fifteen minutes later all the residents and staff were gathered in the drawing room.

"Right, I don't want this to be like an *Agatha Christie* denouement, but it may end up a bit like that. I'm going to tell you the whole thing warts and all, even though I'm not entirely certain I'm supposed to."

Anna ran off the tale of all that had happened since the day that Theo had come into their lives. She included Henry's death that they now regarded as suspicious, Theo's false claim to be gay, his marriage to or affair with Ariana and their children, the first hijack and all the subsequent attempts on her life up to the raid on the Pangbourne Grange. She explained the discovery of the forged will and the subterfuge of getting her to sign adoption papers for her daughters. She left nothing out. She also told them that Theo and Manos had been working as some kind of agents for the Russian government, and how Theo's marriage to her had been a ruse to gain control of Silico, even if that would require her and Cassie's murders.

She went on to describe the events of the previous week in America, and their stay in the forest cabin. She explained Drew's head injury during his intervention in the hostage incident in the store where Theo had died and how Drew's arm wound had developed into sepsis resulting in the amputation of two fingers.

"Any questions so far?"

"I was wrong, an *Alex Rider* couldn't do that justice, it's more like a *Tom Clancy*," Judith announced.

"You said there were going to be changes here at Pangbourne," Toby added.

"Ah yes, come here, Drew, would you?"

He moved to stand by her side. "While Drew was in hospital, I claimed that he was my husband in order to put the skids under the US healthcare system, and after the op we both said we quite liked the idea. Last night, after we'd had time to think about it, we decided that we still thought it would be something we might like, but that it was probably too soon to tie the knot. So we've agreed to wait a while and see how things pan out, but we both wanted you all to know that we are in a relationship. So you don't need to be surprised if you find one of our beds unslept in, or if you catch us in a clinch or two."

There was a stunned silence broken by Cassie hopping up and down clapping. One by one the others hesitantly joined in. Then, once they'd all calmed down, she added, "That's a bit of a surprise to you I know. It has been to me too. We both knew something was happening long before Drew's op but we hadn't really acknowledged it. In the end it was Cassie and Drew's sister who kicked our proverbial butts to accept that it was real. No doubt there will be gossip, although quite frankly I couldn't give a damn. Obviously I'd prefer you not talk about any of that outside these walls in too much detail, although I can't stop you if that's what you feel you have to do. Is there anything you'd like to add, Drew?"

"Only that, I expect you're all wondering what my status will be in the household. All I can say to that is, other than Anna's live-in significant other, at the moment I'm not sure. I won't be involved in running the house in any way, but I'll help if there is some way I can contribute. I'll be getting a job as soon as my wounds allow, and as soon as we're absolutely certain that she doesn't need a bodyguard 24/7. I'll continue to be in charge of security though and I should tell you that although the most recent threats appear to have passed, we shouldn't think that there can't be others. Anna is an extremely wealthy woman, and that will always make her vulnerable to some extent. When the new security system is complete we'll have a familiarization session so we all understand how it works. Anyway my name is Drew, not Sir, Mr. Parker or anything else, and most of the time I'm an easy-going guy until someone threatens the people close to me.

"One last thing, I know that most of you have been part of Anna's life in one way or another for many years, and it must seem strange to see her become so intimately involved with a guy who's only known her a matter of weeks. I imagine some of you may harbor doubts about the advisability of her decision, or even question my motives. I understand all that, but I promise you that I will do all I can to win your trust, and to prove to you and Anna every day that I love her. That was the longest speech I made in my life, so don't expect another one anytime soon."

Another muted round of applause followed before Anna said, "I don't need you to prove anything. You've already done that. But just to add that on Monday I'll be renouncing the title of Lady, dropping Astley and I'll go just by West until anything changes with Drew. I'll leave it up to Cassie to decide what she wishes to be called."

That evening, after Cassie had already retired, Anna said to Drew, "Is this it then. Is it time for us to do the deed?"

"We don't have to you know."

"I know we don't but I really want to. I'm shaking, I'm really horny. Isn't that what they say?"

"Yes, and you saying it is makes me hornier still. Feel." He took her hand and pressed it against his penis."

She reciprocated by placing his unbandaged hand on her breast. They kissed and climbed the stairs to what was now their shared bedroom.

"What about birth control?" he asked. "I don't have condoms."

"I just happen to have something in my purse that makes them redundant." She held up a small flat box, and he looked puzzled. "A morning after pill."

He smiled. "Where did you get that?"

She blushed, "From the that drug store in Lexington. I was sort of hoping you were going to make a move on me even then."

The following morning they came to breakfast smiling and holding hands. Judith and Jason looked up and smiled back, but Cassie paused her spoon halfway between bowl and mouth and grinned from ear to ear as if all her birthdays had come at once.

Twenty-Nine

The next three weeks were a frantic round of events. The most momentous of which was that Manos Stamelis was exposed as a Russian agent who'd been passing information to Moscow for years. However, the revelation only came after he'd slipped the F.B.I. net and reached Russia before they'd realized he was gone, leaving an enormous scandal behind him some of which, initially rubbed off on Anna.

On the same day that the news about Stamelis broke, a story appeared in the LA Times that a body found in the trunk of a burned-out car in Hollywood had been identified as Theo Lemonis, fueling speculation he'd been killed by his former handler. The dead hostage taker in the Pine Creek store had still had not been identified, and the second culprit remained unapprehended.

An investigative journalist exposed Ariana Georgiou as Stamelis' daughter, and Theo's mistress and a week later she and her children disappeared. They were eventually unearthed at her maternal grandmother's family home on Corfu where she steadfastly refused to comment about her father or her relationship with Lemonis.

Atticus had decided that life in the UK was far too tame and returned to his own country to take up an offer to join the close-body protection team for a tech billionaire.

Drew's wounds were healing well, both the side of his head and the gunshot wound in his arm were dressing free, and his new doctor was happy with the amputation sites. He'd been finding ways to adapt his fitness regime to accommodate his new circumstances and decided that when it was time, he'd get someone to design some sort of prosthesis to help him lift weights.

Thirty

A month after Atticus left for home, the new security system at Pangbourne Grange had been finished and apart from one or two teething problems it was working well. Drew was happy with it and monitored it closely.

One evening, while Anna was out at a Silico board meeting to discuss a potential merger with NorArm, and Cassie had been watching a movie with Judith and Jason, Drew found himself at a loose end, so, for the want of anything better to do, he went to the study to review footage from the hidden security cameras. He fast forwarded through much of it and was almost up to date when he noticed a momentary black spot on one camera. After rewinding to the place he replayed it at normal speed. The camera affected was the one he'd had installed in the big oak tree on the boundary where he'd rendezvoused with Sweeney, and that he'd used as the target when test firing the gun.

The blackout only lasted a very short time and had happened less than an hour earlier. Playing it again in slow motion he saw something fall across the lens and then lift again thirty seconds later. He speculated it might be a bird or leaves moving in the breeze, but running the sequence a third time, and only forwarding it a frame or two at a time he could clearly see the sharp rounded edge of an object like a lens cap close off the scene in view. He went to the drawer in the desk from which MI5 had removed the gun he'd retained until the second search of the premises. It still contained the knife he'd taken from Frenchie.

It was dusk now, and he expected to need a flashlight, but couldn't remember where one might be so he slipped the knife, blade first, up the sleeve of his injured hand, switched the light on his phone and headed out of the room. At that moment he heard a scream from the kitchen. Moving quickly to the open doorway he found Gates was there. He had hold of Cassie by the hair and was holding a knife to her throat.

"What no gun this time, Parker?"

"Why would I need a gun? I'm only facing up to a slimy asswipe who needs a defenseless child as a shield."

"I'm going to enjoy this."

"Yeah, but just what is *this*? Is it something you're getting paid for? I doubt it. You've fucked up everything you've touched since you got involved. Nobody is paying you for anything anymore. No, I think I know what this is, it's a pathetic little ego trip trying to convince yourself that your pitiful little pencil dick is as big as a real one."

"Shut the fuck up,' Gates snarled and pressed the knife closer to her neck prompting a high-pitched squeak. "You too bitch, or I'll cut your tits off."

"Okay Gates, okay," Drew said raising his arms in the air.

"Not such a smartass after…"

"What were those screams?" Toby said bursting in through the back door.

Taking advantage of the distraction and the slight loosening of Gates's grip, Cassie dropped to the floor. Gates spun toward the stable manager exposing the side of his head and Drew whipped the knife from his sleeve and threw it. The object took microseconds to cross the short space between them and imbed itself in the side of Gates' head. He was dead before he hit the floor.

"Fucking amateur," Drew said quietly and plucked Cassie away from the spreading pool of blood. "Toby, can you call the cops? Then find out if Jason and Judith are okay. If they are, tell them to stay in their rooms. They may not have heard anything. Tell them that the situation's under control and we're all okay. When you've done that, come down, let me know, and open the gate for the cops when they arrive."

Toby hurried away and Drew carried Cassie through to the family room and sat the weeping girl on his lap. She put her arms around his neck and began to sob.

"Why do they keep coming to hurt us Drew, we haven't done anything to them?"

"It's over now, sweetheart, he's the last of them."

He lifted his phone and dialed Firbank's number. It went to voicemail so he said, "Gates came after us again. He's dead now,' and ended the call, before texting Anna.

Toby came into the room a minute or two later. "Judith and Jason were gagged and tied up with cable ties. I cut them loose and told them to stay where they were. Is that alright?"

"Perfect; best wait outside for the cops now."

When the first patrol car arrived, Toby met them at the door, and gave them a brief account of what had happened.

In a very few minutes, and for the second time in little over a month, the drive and turning circle at Pangbourne Grange was filled with emergency vehicles.

Drew refused to leave Cassie until Anna returned but gave a brief account of the events to one of the first responders. He didn't have to wait long before he heard Anna's raised voice.

"Get out of my way you stupid oaf. This is my house, and my twelve-year-old daughter is in there, a five-time survivor of assassination attempts. Are you seriously trying to prevent her from being with her mother?"

Eventually the cop conceded and allowed her to enter. She came rushing inside as Drew kissed Cassie's head and lifted her off his lap.

"Drew saved me again, Mummy."

The following few hours were almost as chaotic as they had been after the previous raid, and it was beginning to look as if Drew would be arrested and taken to the police station for questioning but eventually Graves arrived, spoke to the detective in charge, and it was agreed he could go to the station the following day to make a voluntary statement under caution.

In the event Jason, Judith, and Toby all traveled with Drew, Anna, and Cassie to the station and made their statements one after the other. Inevitably there were no prosecutions but unsurprisingly the media made big play out of the series of events surrounding Pangbourne Grange and its residents. There were stories, editorials, and speculative articles for weeks; most were complete fiction, some almost libelous, only one actually alluded to parts of the truth, but Anna refused to confirm or deny any of them. That was until one tabloid newspaper inferred that she and Drew were in league with Lemonis and might in fact still be acting for Russian secret services. Anna demanded a complete withdrawal and front page apology within seven days, or she would sue both the paper and the journalist for defamation. No withdrawal was made, and the suit went ahead. In the end the paper agreed to settle out of court for an undisclosed sum and issued an unreserved apology stating their story to have been entirely without foundation. It had cost the paper over a million pounds plus costs and the journalist was forced into declaring bankruptcy. Anna used the money to kickstart the *Keep You Safe Foundation* for the protection from and prevention of child exploitation.

Needless to say the tabloids and gossip magazines went on to make great play of the now acknowledged romance between a millionairess and her bodyguard romance using all the obvious Hollywood references but steering clear of libelous inferences. In the end it became yesterday's news after all requests for interviews or photographs were refused.

No wills postdating the one that had been in the Pangbourne safe before being removed by Lemonis had been found, but the original had been discovered in an attaché case in the trunk of the rental car abandoned by Gates in Campton. Lawyers proceeded on the basis that it was legitimate and that Anna was his principal heir.

The settlement of Theodore's estate took over a year, and his properties in Seattle, Santa Monica, New York, and Greece were all sold. NorArm was taken over by Silico, leaving Anna as the majority shareholder of the merged companies. Neither she nor the governments of the UK and US were happy with that arrangement, so sixty percent of her shares were subsequently sold to arms companies in the two countries. Her remaining shares still gave her a powerful influence on the board, but she largely stayed out of company affairs.

Drew's Security Consultancy kept him relatively busy, but he limited his work to the UK, and by doing so kept travel to the minimum.

Two years later Anna and Drew went ahead and married. The following year later still, the couple announced the birth of Juno, Anna's third daughter. Cassie was understandably delighted.

Glossary

Inholding	Privately owned land inside the boundary of a national park
BFF	Best friend forever
Feds or Feebies	F.B.I. – The Federal Bureau of Investigation
FIFA	International Federation of Association Football
G22, G19, G17	Semi-automatic pistols
Glock G43	Small semi-automatic pistol
HK45	Heckler & Koch HK45 semi-automatic pistol (capable of use with suppressor/silencer)
LAPD	Los Angeles Police Dept
LAX	Los Angeles International Airport
M16	An automatic assault rifle
MLB	Major League Baseball
MMA	Mixed Martial Arts
NBA	National Basketball League
NFL	National Football League
PBS	Public Broadcasting Service
PTSD	Post-Traumatic Stress Disorder
RHD	Robbery/Homicide Division
SAS	Special Air Service
SIS	Secret Intelligence Service (formerly MI6)
SMPD	Santa Monica Police Dept
SNAFU	Situation Normal All Fucked Up
SO15	Special Operations Branch Scotland Yard (Formerly Special Branch)
Suppressor	Silencer
SUV	Sport Utility Vehicle
TARFU	Totally And Royally Fucked Up
UCLA	University College, Los Angeles
VPN	Virtual Private Network

FICTION FROM APS BOOKS
(www.andrewsparke.com)

Davey J Ashfield: *Footsteps On The Teign*
Davey J Ashfield *Contracting With The Devil*
Davey J Ashfield*: A Turkey And One More Easter Egg*
Davey J Ashfield*: Relentless Misery*
Fenella Bass: *Hornbeams*
Fenella Bass:: *Shadows*
Fenella Bass*: Darkness*
HR Beasley*: Nothing Left To Hide*
Lee Benson: *So You Want To Own An Art Gallery*
Lee Benson: *Where's Your Art gallery Now?*
Lee Benson*: Now You're The Artist...Deal With It*
Lee Benson: *No Naked Walls*
TF Byrne *Damage Limitation*
Nargis Darby: *A Different Shade Of Love*
J.W.Darcy *Looking For Luca*
J.W.Darcy: *Ladybird Ladybird*
J.W.Darcy: *Legacy Of Lies*
J.W.Darcy: *Love Lust & Needful Things*
Paul Dickinson: *Franzi The Hero*
Simon Falshaw: *The Stone*
Milton Godfrey: *The Danger Lies In Fear*
Chris Grayling: *A Week Is...A Long Time*
Jean Harvey: *Pandemic*
Michel Henri: *Mister Penny Whistle*
Michel Henri*: The Death Of The Duchess Of Grasmere*
Michel Henri: *Abducted By Faerie*
Laurie Hornsby: *Postcards From The Seaside*
Hugh Lupus *An Extra Knot (Parts I-VI)*
Alison Manning: *World Without Endless Sheep*
Ian Meacheam: *An Inspector Called*
Ian Meacheam: *Time And The Consequences*
Ian Meacheam*: Broad Lines Narrow Margins*
Alex O'Connor: *Time For The Polka Dot*
Mark Peckett: *Joffie's Mark*
Peter Raposo: *dUst*
Peter Raposo: *The Illusion Of Movement*

Peter Raposo: *Second Life*
Peter Raposo: *Pussy Foot*
Peter Raposo: *This Is Not The End*
Peter Raposo: *Talk About Proust*
Peter Raposo: *All Women Are Mortal*
Peter Raposo: *The Sinking City*
Tony Rowland: *Traitor Lodger German Spy*
Tony Saunders: *Publish and Be Dead*
Andrew Sparke: *Abuse Cocaine & Soft Furnishings*
Andrew Sparke: *Copper Trance & Motorways*
Phil Thompson: *Momentary Lapses In Concentration*
Paul C. Walsh: *A Place Between The Mountains*
Paul C. Walsh: *Hallowed Turf*
Martin White: *Life Unfinished*
AJ Woolfenden: *Mystique: A Bitten Past*
Various: *Unshriven*